ALSO BY SUZANNE YOUNG

GIRLS WITH SHARP STICKS

SUZANNE YOUNG

Simon Pulse

NEW YORK LONDON TORONTO SYDNEY NEW DELHI

SIMON PULSE
An imprint of Simon & Schuster Children's Publishing Division
1230 Avenue of the Americas, New York, New York 10020
First Simon Pulse hardcover edition March 2019
Text copyright © 2019 by Suzanne Young
Jacket photograph copyright © 2019 by Daryna Barykina
Interior illustrations on page 361 copyright © 2019 by pushkina11/iphoto
All rights reserved, including the right of reproduction in whole or in part in any form.
SIMON PULSE and colophon are registered trademarks of Simon & Schuster, Inc.
For information about special discounts for bulk purchases, please contact
Simon & Schuster Special Sales at 1-866-506-1949 or business@simonandschuster.com.
The Simon & Schuster Speakers Bureau can bring authors to your live event. For more
information or to book an event contact the Simon & Schuster Speakers Bureau at
1-866-248-3049 or visit our website at www.simonspeakers.com.
Jacket designed by Sarah Creech
Interior designed by Tom Daly
The text of this book was set in Adobe Garamond Pro.
Manufactured in the United States of America
2 4 6 8 10 9 7 5 3 1
Library of Congress Cataloging-in-Publication Data
Names: Young, Suzanne, author.
Title: Girls with sharp sticks / by Suzanne Young.
Description: First Simon Pulse hardcover edition. | New York : Simon Pulse, 2019. |
Summary: In the near future at a girls-only private high school isolated in the Colorado
mountains, Mena and her classmates—under the watchful eyes of their Guardian, professors,
and analyst—are trained to be beautiful and obedient for their sponsors and investors.
Identifiers: LCCN 2018033509 (print) | LCCN 2018040016 (eBook) |
ISBN 9781534426139 (hardcover) | ISBN 9781534426153 (eBook)
Subjects: | CYAC: Private schools—Fiction. | Schools—Fiction. |
Cyborgs—Fiction. | Science fiction. | Classification: LCC PZ7.Y887 (eBook) |
LCC PZ7.Y887 Gi 2019 (print) | DDC [Fic]—dc23
LC record available at https://lccn.loc.gov/2018033509

For my daughter, Sophia Isabelle

And in loving memory of my grandmother
Josephine Parzych

Part I

But the little girls adapted.

1

t's been raining for the past three months. Or maybe it's only been three days. Time is hard to measure here—every day so much like the one before, they all start to blend together.

Rain taps on my school-provided slicker, the inside of the clear plastic material growing foggy in the humid air, and I look around the Federal Flower Garden. Precipitation has soaked the soil, causing it to run onto the pathways as the rose petals sag with moisture.

The other girls are gathered around Professor Penchant, listening attentively as he points out the varied plant species, explaining which ones we'll be growing back at the school this semester in our gardening class. We grow all manner of things at the Innovations Academy.

A thought suddenly occurs to me, and I take a few steps into the garden, my black shoes sinking into the soil. There are red roses as far as I can see, beautiful and lonely. Lonely because it's only them—all together, but apart from the other flowers. Isolated.

The sound of rain echoes near my ears, but I close my eyes and listen, trying to hear the roses breathe. Thinking I can hear them live.

But I can't hear anything beyond the rain, so I open my eyes again, disappointed.

It's been a dreadful start to spring due to the constant rain. Professor Penchant explained that our flowers—and by extension, us—will flourish because of it. Well, I hope the flourishing is done in time for graduation in the fall. Our time at the academy will be up, and then the school will get a new batch of girls to take our place.

I glance at the group standing with Professor Penchant and find Valentine Wright staring blankly ahead, her gaze cast out among the flowers. It's unusual for her to not be paying attention; she's the most proper of all of us. I've invited Valentine, on multiple occasions, to hang out with me and the other girls after hours, but she told me it was unseemly for us to gossip. For us to laugh so loudly. Be so opinionated. Eventually, I stopped asking her to join.

Sydney notices me standing apart. She rolls her eyes back and sticks her tongue out to the side like she's dead, making me laugh. Professor Penchant spins to find me.

"Philomena," he calls, impatiently waving his hand. "Come here. We're at the apex of our lesson."

I immediately obey, hopping across the rose garden to join the other girls. When I reach the group, Professor Penchant presses his thumb between my eyebrows, wiggling it around to work out the crease in my skin.

"And no more daydreaming," he says with disapproval. "It's bad for your complexion." He drops his hand before turning back to the group. I imagine he's left a reddened thumbprint between my eyebrows.

When the professor starts to talk again, I look sideways at Sydney. She grins, her dimples deep set and her brown eyes framed with exaggerated black lashes. Sydney has smooth, dark skin and straightened hair that falls just below her shoulders under the plastic rain slicker.

On the other side of her, Lennon Rose leans forward to check on me, her blue eyes wide and innocent. "I think your complexion is lovely," she whispers.

I thank her for being so sweet.

Professor Penchant tells the group about a new strain of flower that Innovations Academy will be developing this semester. We love working in the greenhouse, love getting outside whenever we can. Even if the sunshine is rare.

"But only those who are well-behaved will get a chance to work on these plants," the professor warns. "There are no rewards for girls who are too *spirited*." He looks directly at me, and I lower my eyes, not wanting to vex him any more today. "Professor Driscoll will concur."

As the professor continues, turning away to point out other plants, I glance around the flower garden once again. It's then that I notice Guardian Bose standing near the entrance where we came in. He's talking to the curator of the garden, a young woman holding an oversized red umbrella. While one hand holds the umbrella, she puts the other on her hip, talking impatiently to the Guardian. I wonder what they're discussing.

Guardian Bose is an intimidating presence in any setting, but even more so outside the walls of the academy, where he's become commonplace. He's here to ensure our safety and compliance, although we never misbehave—not in any significant way.

Innovations Academy, our all-girl private school, is very protective of us. We're confined to campus most days of our accelerated yearlong program, and we don't go home on breaks. They say the complete immersion helps us develop faster, more thoroughly.

Recently, the academy raised its curriculum rigor, increasing the number of courses and amount of training. Our class of twelve was selected based on the new heightened standards. We're *top of the line*, they like to say. *The most well-rounded girls to ever graduate.* We do our best to make them proud.

Guardian Bose says something to the woman with the red umbrella. She laughs, shaking her head no. The Guardian's posture tightens, and then he turns to find me watching him. He angles his body to block my view of the woman. He tips his head, saying something near her ear, and the woman shrinks back. Within moments, she hurries toward the indoor facility and disappears.

I turn away before Guardian Bose catches me watching again.

Thunder booms overhead and Lennon Rose screams before

slapping her hand over her mouth. The professor looks pointedly in her direction, but then he glances up at the sky as the rain begins to fall harder.

"All right, girls," he says, adjusting the hood on his rain slicker. "We're going to wrap this up for now. Back to the bus."

A couple of the girls begin to protest, but Professor Penchant claps his hands loudly to drown out their voices. He reminds them that we'll return next month—so long as we behave. The girls comply, apologizing, and start toward the bus. But as the others head that way, I notice that Valentine doesn't move; she doesn't even turn in that direction.

I swallow hard, unsettled. Rain pours over Valentine's slicker, running down the clear plastic in rivers. A drop runs down her cheek. I watch her, trying to figure out what's wrong.

Sensing me, she lifts her head. She is . . . expressionless. Alarming in her stillness.

"Valentine," I call over the rain. "Are you okay?"

She pauses so long that I'm not sure she heard me. Then she turns back to the flowers. "Can you hear them too?" she asks, her voice soft and faraway.

"Hear what?" I ask.

The corner of her mouth twitches with a smile. "The roses," she says affectionately. "They're alive, you know. All of them. And if you listen closely enough, you can hear their shared roots. Their common purpose. They're beautiful, but it's not all they are."

There's tingling over my skin because a few moments ago, I

did try to listen to the roses. What are the chances that Valentine and I would have the same odd thought?

"I didn't hear anything," I admit. "Just quiet contentment."

Valentine's behavior is unusual, but I want to know what she's going to say next. I take a step closer.

Her smile fades. "They're not content," she replies in a low voice. "They're waiting."

A drop of rain finds its way under the collar of my shirt and runs down my spine, making me shiver.

"Waiting for what?" I ask.

Valentine turns to me and whispers, *"To wake up."*

Her eyes narrow, fierce and unwavering. Her hands curl into fists at her side.

I shiver again, but this time it's not from the rain. The academy tells us not to ask philosophical questions because we're not equipped for the answers. They teach us what we *need*, rather than indulging our passing curiosities. They say it helps maintain our balance, like soil ripe for growth.

Valentine's words are dangerous in that way—the beginning of a larger conversation I want to have. But at the same time, one I don't quite understand. One that scares me. Why would the flowers say such a thing? Why would flowers say anything at all?

Just as I'm about to ask her what the flowers are waking up from, there is a firm grip on my elbow. Startled, I spin around to find Guardian Bose towering over me.

"I've got it from here, Philomena," he says in his deep voice. "Catch up with the others."

I shoot a cautious glace at Valentine, but her expression has gone back to pleasant. As the Guardian approaches her, Valentine nods obediently before he even says a word. Her abrupt change in character has left me confused.

I start toward the bus, my brows pulled together as I think. Sydney holds out her hand when she sees me and I take it gratefully, our fingers wet and cold.

"What was that about?" she asks as we walk.

"I'm not exactly sure," I say. "Valentine is . . . off," I add for lack of a better word. I don't know how to explain what just happened. Especially when it's left me so uneasy.

Sydney and I look back in Valentine's direction, but she and the Guardian are already heading our way. Valentine is quiet. Perfect posture. Perfect temperament.

"She looks fine to me," Sydney says with a shrug. "Her usual boring self."

I study Valentine a moment longer, but the girl who spoke to me is gone, replaced with a flawless imitation. Or, I guess, the original version.

And I'm left with the burden of the words, an infectious thought.

Wake up, it whispers. *Wake up, Philomena.*

2

The bus tires bump over a pothole, and Sydney falls from her seat to land in the center aisle with a flop. She immediately laughs, standing up to take a dramatic bow when the other girls giggle.

Professor Penchant orders Sydney to sit down, poking the air impatiently with his finger. Sydney offers him an apologetic smile and slides into the seat next to me, mouthing the word "Ouch."

I jut out my bottom lip in a show of sympathy before Sydney gets up on her knees to talk to Marcella and Brynn in the seat behind us.

"At least they bought us rain covers," Marcella is saying to Brynn. "I've always wanted to wear a trash bag in public. Goal achieved."

"I believe it's called a 'rain slicker,'" Sydney corrects, making Brynn snort a laugh. "And don't settle yet, Marcella," she adds. "Maybe next time we'll get a potato sack."

Brynn nearly falls out of her seat laughing. Marcella catches her by the hand, intertwining their fingers. They smile at each other.

Marcella and Brynn have been dating since our second day of school at the Innovations Academy. Eight months later, they're closer than ever. A perfect pair, if anyone were to ask me. Marcella is clever and decisive while Brynn is nurturing and creative. Despite the strength of their relationship, they keep it a secret from the school—afraid the Guardian will separate them if he finds out. Our education is supposed to be our only focus. Dating is strictly forbidden.

Annalise Gibbons raises her hand from the seat in front of us, and when Guardian Bose notices, he exhales loudly and rolls his eyes. "What?" he asks.

"I really have to go to the bathroom," she says. "It's an emergency."

We're still about an hour from the school, I'm guessing, so the Guardian gets up to speak to the driver. We wait in anticipation of an unexpected stop, watching him in the oversized rearview mirror as he talks quietly to the older man behind the wheel. The white-haired driver nods as if he doesn't care either way, and Guardian Bose lifts his eyes to the mirror, where he catches us staring at him. Several of us lower our heads so we don't sway his opinion in the other direction.

"There's a gas station a few miles up," Guardian Bose announces. "Only those who have to go to the bathroom get off the bus, understand? Otherwise we'll fall behind schedule."

There are murmurs of "yes, we understand," but a buzz

reverberates through all of us. Normally our field trips are limited to one place and very few people outside of our group. Nothing unexpected ever happens. At that thought, I sit up taller to check on Valentine.

She's in the front seat, across the aisle from the Guardian. Her long black hair flows over the back of the padded green seat, but she is impossibly still, staring out the windshield and not acknowledging any of us. Like she's thinking about the roses again.

Today *has* been unexpected. Unusual, even. But it's about more than Valentine's peculiar behavior in the flower garden. It's about the restlessness her words have caused. The way my head seems to itch somewhere just out of reach.

No, today is different—that much I know for certain. And to prove it, a sign for a gas station appears on our right and the bus edges that way, bumping over the lane dividers.

The other girls press against the windows as I grab money from the front pocket of my backpack and tuck it into my waistband. The bus hisses to a stop to the side of the building.

A beat-up yellow car pulls in just behind us and parks at the gas pump. Other than that, the place looks deserted, run down. Grimy in a quaint way, I suppose. Like it's never been updated. Never changed.

Despite the Guardian's warning, nearly all of us stand to go inside—thrilled at the chance to see someplace new.

Guardian Bose is quick to hold up his hands. "Really?" he asks. "All of you?"

A few make frantic gestures like their bladders might explode, and others look at him pleadingly. I just want to buy candy. We're not allowed sweets at the academy; our food is closely monitored. Even at home, my parents didn't allow sugar in my diet. But I find I crave it desperately, especially after getting a taste on a field trip earlier this year.

The school brought us to an art exhibit at a museum just outside of town. It wasn't during regular business hours, so we had the place to ourselves. Sydney and I raced up the stairs when the Guardian wasn't looking, and Lennon Rose, Annalise, and I spent extra time staring at the nude male statues until Annalise nearly snapped off a penis while posing dramatically next to him. And before we left, we all stopped in the gift shop. Some bought postcards for their parents or a souvenir or two. I picked out several bags of M&M's and Starburst candies.

Honestly, I don't understand the addictive properties of sugar—it's never been mentioned in our classes—but I can attest they are life altering.

And so I put on my most pleasing and innocent expression for the Guardian. I must not be alone in trying this, because he darts his pale eyes around the bus and then shakes his head.

"Fine," he says. "You go in small groups. Fifteen minutes and we're back on the road. Understand?"

We nod eagerly and he motions us off the bus by row. Only Valentine and two other girls willingly stay behind. Sydney and I are the last group to leave, and on the way out, Guardian Bose looks down at me.

"Philomena," he says, darting a quick look at Valentine

before studying my expression. "Don't get distracted in there."

"No problem," I say with a smile. Nothing can distract me from candy.

I step off the bus, pleased to find the rain has softened to a drizzle. The mountain is closer now that we're heading toward school, and I'm at once enchanted and intimidated by its scale. Mist clings to the summit, so I imagine it's raining at the academy. It's always raining there.

I'm no longer wearing the plastic rain slicker, and I appreciate the moisture on my skin, tickling my bare forearms. Soaking into me. At least, I do until I step into a puddle and splash muddy water on my delicate white socks. I glance down past my plaid uniform skirt and shake out my shoe.

As I start walking again, I look at the yellow car. There's a young guy pumping gas, his face turned away as he leans against the back door, talking through the open passenger-side window to another boy still inside the car. I examine them, curious.

The boy in the passenger seat is wearing a crisp white T-shirt, a shiny watch glinting on his wrist as he rests his arm on the open window. He's cute—dark skin, his hair shaved short. He must say something funny, because the other guy laughs and turns to press a button on the pump, his face coming into view.

I note immediately that he's extremely good looking. This boy is thin with an angular jaw—sharp at the edges—thick black eyebrows, messy black hair. And when his gaze drifts past the pump and he notices me, he seems just as startled by my attention. He holds up his hand in a wave.

I smile in return, but then Sydney calls loudly for me to catch up. I jog to meet her at the glass door of the building, embarrassed at my lack of decorum. I didn't mean to stare at those boys. It's just . . . we don't see many young men at the academy. Actually, we don't see any at all.

Sydney looks over her shoulder at the boys as if she's just spotting them. When she turns back around, she flashes me a quick grin and pulls open the door. A bell on the metal bar jingles.

I'm struck by the smell of baking bread. The gas station has a menu board posted over a small deli at a second counter. A woman in a hairnet stands behind there, her face deeply tanned and creased with wrinkles. She doesn't even mutter a hello.

Sydney heads toward the bathrooms while I step into the candy aisle. I'm overwhelmed by the sheer volume of choices, the bright colors and assorted flavors.

The bell on the door jingles again as the two boys enter the store. They walk directly to the deli counter. The boy in the white T-shirt gives the woman his order while the guy who waved notices me standing in the aisle, watching him above the candy rack. His mouth widens with a smile.

"Hey," he calls. "How's it going?"

The other guy glances sideways at his friend—a bit of concern in his features that seems unwarranted. But the boy with the black hair waits for my response, the ghost of a smile still on his lips.

"Anything else?" the older woman asks the two boys, ripping the top page off her pad.

The boy with the black hair tells her that'll be it, and his friend goes to pay at the register.

I return to perusing the aisle, trying to focus on my mission to collect bags of candy. I am, indeed, distracted. It doesn't take long before the boy with black hair comes to stand at the end of the aisle near the pretzels.

"Sorry to bother you," he says, his voice low-pitched and raspy. "But I was wondering if—" I turn to him and the words die on his lips. He smiles his recovery.

"You're not bothering me," I tell him. He looks relieved and shoves his hands into the pockets of his jeans.

"I'm Jackson," he says.

"Philomena," I reply. And then, after a beat, "Mena."

"Hello, Mena," Jackson says casually. He takes a step farther into the aisle and picks out a bag of candy, seemingly at random. He draws his eyebrows together as he looks out the window toward the bus.

"Innovations Academy?" he asks. "The one that used to be Innovations Metal Works—the old factory near the mountain?"

"I'd like to tell you it's not a factory anymore," I say, "but I can still smell metal in my sheets sometimes."

He laughs as if I'm joking.

Innovations Metal Works was a factory that'd been around since the town was founded. About a decade ago, they started making significant advances in technology: metal additives. Eventually, the Metal Works patent was bought out by a hospital system, and again later by a technology firm. The building itself was repurposed.

Now it's an academy that teaches us about manners, modesty, and gardening, a change that can be credited to new ownership and generous donors. And yet, I pick up the scent of machinery every so often.

"A private school?" Jackson asks, glancing at my uniform.

"Yes. All girls."

He nods like he finds this fascinating. "How long have you been there?"

"Eight months," I say. "I graduate in the fall. What about you? Do you live near the mountain?"

"Oh, I . . . uh, I live not too far from here, actually," he says. "It's just . . . I saw your bus leaving the Federal Flower Garden. Was curious."

"You've been following us since the Flower Garden?" I ask, surprised. He turns away and grabs another bag of candy.

"No," he says, waving his hand. "Not on purpose."

Suddenly, his friend appears next to him holding a brown paper bag with ends of subs poking out. "Jackie," the boy says. "We should probably get going, right?" He motions toward the glass door.

Jackson shakes his head no, subtly, and then turns to me and smiles. "Philomena," he says, "this is my friend Quentin."

Quentin glances at him, annoyed, but then smiles at me and says hello. He turns back to Jackson.

"Five minutes, yeah?" Quentin asks him, widening his eyes.

"Yeah," Jackson murmurs. He presses his lips together and looks at me, waiting for his friend to leave. Once Quentin is gone,

Jackson shrugs, as if saying his friend is just being impatient.

I study the array of chocolates, and Jackson comes to stand next to me. He grabs a small bag of Hershey's Kisses.

"These are my favorite," he says. I look sideways at him, struck by his imperfections. The freckles dotting his cheeks and nose. The slight turn of his canine teeth that makes his smile boyish and charming. There's even a tiny scar near his temple.

"I'll try them," I say, plucking the chocolates from his hand.

"Ahem," Sydney says dramatically from the other end of the aisle. She runs her gaze quickly over Jackson before settling on me.

"Sydney, this is Jackson," I tell her, fighting back my smile. Just as seeing someplace new is exciting, meeting *someone* new is absolutely thrilling. Sydney steps forward and introduces herself, politely, like we're taught.

They exchange a quick handshake, and Jackson tells her it's nice to meet her. When Sydney turns back to me she covertly mouths the word "cute."

She smiles, pleasant and respectful, when she's facing Jackson again.

"I'll meet you on the bus?" I ask her, holding up my fistfuls of candy. She pauses a long moment before nodding. She has to bite her lower lip to keep from grinning.

"Right . . . ," she says. "See you there." Sydney tells Jackson it was nice to meet him and leaves the store, the bell on the handle jingling.

Quentin watches after her while hanging out near the ATM, the brown paper bag set on top of the machine. He chews his thumbnail, and when Sydney is gone, he returns his gaze to the door.

Jackson grabs a pack of Twizzlers while I pick up red hot candies with a flaming sun on the package. Together we head toward the register.

"Can I buy that for you?" Jackson asks when I lay my pile of candy on the counter. It would be rude to refuse his offer, so I say yes and thank him. The cashier begins to ring up our sweets together.

"I'm not allowed candy at school," I confess to Jackson as he takes out his wallet. He looks at me as if he finds this unusual. "But whenever I get the chance," I add, "it's what I spend my allowance on. It's not like there's anything to buy at school."

"I'm sure," he says. "Your school's out in the middle of fucking nowhere."

I'm a bit shocked by his cursing; a bit exhilarated by the indecency of it. Jackson leans against the counter, studying me again.

"Would you want to grab a coffee with me sometime, Mena?" he asks. "I have a lot of questions about this private school–factory of yours."

I'm about to explain that I'm not allowed to leave campus when there's a series of clicks from the register. The woman behind the counter tells us the total for the candy, and Jackson removes several bills from his wallet to hand to the woman.

The bell on the glass door jingles, and I turn to see Guardian Bose walk in, a hulking mass in the small store. The woman at the register busies herself by putting my items in a plastic bag.

"Philomena," the Guardian calls in a low voice, darting his gaze from me to Jackson. "It's time to go."

I flinch at his scolding tone. I'd been told not to get distracted.

"Be right there," I say politely, avoiding Jackson's eyes as I wait for my candy.

The Guardian stomps to my side and takes me by the wrist. "No," he says, startling me. "*Now*. Everyone's already on the bus."

Jackson curls his lip. "Don't touch her like that," he says.

I look at the Guardian to gauge his reaction; I've never heard anyone speak to him that way. He opens his mouth to retort, his grip loosening, and I quietly slip free to take my bag off the counter.

But the moment I do, Guardian Bose grabs my forearm hard enough to make me wince and I drop my candy on the floor.

"I said get on the bus, Mena," he growls possessively, pulling me closer. I'm frightened, ashamed that I've upset him. I apologize even as he hurts me.

Jackson steps forward to intervene, but the Guardian holds up his palm.

"Back off, kid," Guardian Bose says. "This is none of your business."

Jackson scoffs, red blotches rising on his cheeks and neck. "Try and grab me like that, tough guy," Jackson says. "See what happens." Guardian Bose laughs dismissively.

I have no doubt that the Guardian would easily best Jackson in any fight, but at the same time, I'm struck by Jackson's open defiance—how stupid and brave it is at the same time. It's fascinating. I start to smile just before Guardian Bose yanks me toward the door.

"Come on," the Guardian says. I struggle to keep up, tripping over my own feet as his grip tightens painfully on my arm.

When I look back at Jackson, he nods at Quentin, calling him over.

"You're hurting me," I tell the Guardian. He doesn't listen, using my body to push open the door. He forces me out into the misty parking lot. My shoes scrape along the pavement as I try to look over his shoulder toward the store. But the Guardian keeps me in front of him, his fingers digging into my upper arm.

When I turn toward the bus, the girls are watching, wide-eyed, from fogged windows.

The bus doors fold open, and Guardian Bose shoves me angrily. I trip going up the stairs and cry out in pain when my knee scrapes the rubber mat on the top step, tearing my flesh. The Guardian hauls me up by my underarms and dumps me on the seat next to Valentine. A trickle of blood runs down my shin and stains my sock.

The bus driver witnesses all of this with a flash of concern, but the Guardian whispers something to him. The white-haired driver closes the bus doors and shifts into gear.

Tears sting my eyes, but Guardian Bose doesn't apologize. He doesn't even look in my direction. There are murmurs of concern from some of the other girls.

"You're responsible for the damages," Guardian Bose says. "The visit to the infirmary will come from your savings."

Ashamed and injured, I turn toward the window, looking past Valentine. She hasn't spoken to me, not even to ask if I'm okay. But her hands are balled into fists on her lap.

Jackson and Quentin come out of the store and watch as our bus pulls away. Jackson is clutching my bag of candy. Despite my circumstance, his thoughtfulness makes me smile. I reach to press my fingers against the window in a wave.

In return, Jackson holds up his hand in the same way he did when I first saw him. He stays like that until we're on the road. I watch as long as I can, until Quentin says something to Jackson, nodding to the car at the pump. And then they both turn away as I disappear.

3

The mood on the bus has shifted from excitement to dread, and the driver seems to be going over the speed limit. I'm embarrassed that he saw me fall, saw me get redirected by the Guardian. But more than that, I'm regretful that my behavior led to this consequence.

Professor Penchant stays near the back of the bus with the other girls. When I glance at him, he purses his lips in disapproval, and I turn toward the front again.

Although the Guardian isn't one of our professors, he watches over the students on a daily basis. He's typically indifferent, but not unpleasant. He's never spoken to me so viciously.

I'm shaken by it all, but at the same time, I'm deeply ashamed. We're not supposed to anger the men taking care of us. I never have. It was selfish of me to not listen immediately.

I glance at Valentine, watching her as she stares straight ahead. Her body sways along with the movement of the bus, her nails causing indents in her skin where her fists are clenched. But she doesn't say anything to me. I'm almost convinced that I imagined our entire conversation at the Federal Flower Garden.

I slide my eyes to the side so I can peer over at Guardian Bose. He's angry, his jaw set hard. I should apologize, but before I can, there's a flash of dark hair as Sydney sits down next to him. The Guardian is ready to argue, but she smiles sweetly.

"I got you something," she says to him. He eyes her suspiciously. Sydney pulls a pack of gum from her pocket and holds it out to him.

Guardian Bose takes it, not realizing Sydney must have stolen it while in the store. He unwraps a piece and folds it into his mouth, not offering gum to the rest of us.

Sydney waits patiently, and after a moment, Guardian Bose nods and turns toward the window. Sydney beams, having won my freedom, and she reaches for my hand and brings me to my usual seat.

The moment I sit down, Lennon Rose crosses the aisle to hug me, sniffling back her tears. I promise her that I'm okay, petting her blond hair. She sits back down in her seat, watching me with concern. I've never been injured before. Not even a scratch.

Sydney bends forward to look at my knee. She sucks at her teeth and straightens up. "There's so much blood," she says, lifting her eyes to mine. "Do you think the doctor will be able fix it?"

Lennon Rose gasps. Sydney and I both turn to her.

"Of course he'll be able to," I say for Lennon Rose's benefit. Although the idea that I might be scarred for life creeps into my worries. "Dr. Groger is the best around."

"Absolutely," Sydney agrees in the same tone. Lennon Rose's panic eases slightly, but her brow is still furrowed. She's the most sensitive of all the girls. We try not to burden her needlessly.

We all understand that there are consequences for poor behavior. But since we don't act out, we've never earned them. What I did was wrong, therefore I deserved the pain that followed, even if I didn't like it. My opinion on the subject is irrelevant.

I rest my head back against the seat and close my eyes, trying to relax in hopes of lessening the stinging in my knee. There is the occasional pop of gum from the front seat.

I'm struck suddenly by the feeling of being watched. I open my eyes and lean out into the aisle. To my surprise, I find Valentine Wright turned around to face me with the same fierce expression she had at the Federal Flower Garden. It raises the hairs on my arms.

I'm not sure what to say to her, not sure what she wants. She's unsettling me.

I quickly glance around, but the other girls haven't noticed her. The Guardian, however, looks in Valentine's direction. His head tilts slightly, examining her.

"Turn around," he orders.

Valentine doesn't listen. Doesn't even acknowledge the command. She continues to watch me, her eyes finding the blood running down my leg. In the seat behind her, Ida Welch and Maryanne Lindstrom exchange a concerned glance.

My heart begins to beat faster. Lennon Rose looks over the seat to see what's going on, her eyes wide and fearful.

"Valentine," Guardian Bose says, raising his voice. "I said *turn around*."

There are several gasps when Valentine stands up instead, positioned in the middle of the aisle. Sydney sits up straighter, her hands sliding on the green padding of the seat in front of us.

Annalise leans into the aisle, whispering for Valentine to sit down, cautiously checking on the Guardian. But Valentine's not listening. She takes a step toward me and I gulp, scared of the attention.

The Guardian jumps up and grabs Valentine by the wrist. She grits her teeth at the pain and tries to yank away. Behind me, Marcella murmurs, "*No*"—afraid for her. Disturbed by her defiance.

The Guardian twists Valentine's arm behind her back, making her cry out, and studies her eyes a moment before pushing her down in the seat. When she immediately pops up, he pushes her down again, this time more violently.

"Stay," he warns, pointing his finger in her face.

Valentine stares back at him, but she doesn't stand. She tilts up her chin, defiant. I've never seen a girl act like this before, and I wonder what's wrong with her. Clearly her words at the Federal Flower Garden were the first symptom of this larger misbehavior.

"You've just earned yourself impulse control therapy," the Guardian tells Valentine. He stands there, towering over her, his presence seeming to grow larger as she shrinks back. "I'll make sure of it."

Lennon Rose sniffles across the aisle from me, but I don't try to comfort her this time.

The Guardian sits down and takes out his phone, quietly making a call while keeping a cautious eye on Valentine. For her part, Valentine turns around to face the windshield, once more impossibly still.

I can feel that Sydney wants to ask me what just happened, but none of us dares to talk. We wouldn't want to get sent to the analyst with Valentine.

Impulse control therapy is a punishment for when redirection isn't enough. One we earn but dread nonetheless.

I've only been to impulse control therapy once, and I never want to go back.

It was shortly after my first open house—an event the academy holds several times a year. Parents, sponsors, and investors are invited to celebrate our accomplishments. But my parents didn't show up—they were the only ones who didn't. I felt left out and abandoned. I started crying and couldn't stop. Everything was wrong. I felt wrong.

After speaking with Anton—our analyst—he recommended the therapy. But I didn't want to be punished, even when he told me it was for my benefit. That it would make me a better girl.

He said I was too responsive and that impulse control therapy would help me manage my emotions.

I don't remember much after that. Impulse control therapy erases itself when it's done. All I know is I went in crying, and twenty-four hours later, I came out better—just like he promised. And yet, whenever I try to remember what happened, I'm overcome with a crushing sense of foreboding. It's odd to have that strong a feeling without a connection to the memory causing it. When I ask Anton, he says it's just part of the process.

Well, it's not a process I want to go through again. None of us do. So we lower our eyes and keep quiet the entire way back to the academy. I just hope Anton is able to help Valentine the way he helped me. Even if she won't remember it.

The arches of the iron gate come into view when we turn down the gravel road. The words INNOVATIONS ACADEMY are etched into a large metal sign, which has rusted and aged quickly from the rain. The gate opens and we pull forward.

The academy looms ahead, the mountain backdrop as beautiful as a painting. The rain has finally stopped completely, and there's a small ray of sunshine filtering between the clouds. It casts the metal roof in oranges and reds; it would be lovely if the school itself wasn't hidden behind overgrown ivy and barred windows.

They say the bars are remnants from when this was still a factory—protection from thieves and villains. The new owners opted not to remove the bars when this was turned into an academy several years ago, because they thought we needed the security just as much. Or maybe more, considering the iron gates that now surround the property.

"It's dangerous to leave girls unprotected," a professor told me once. "Especially pretty girls like you."

The bus stops with a hiss in the roundabout, and the front doors of the academy swing open. Mr. Petrov, our Head of School, walks out, dressed in a charcoal gray suit and royal blue tie. He's visibly concerned, folding his hands over his stomach as he watches the bus. His wife descends halfway down the stone steps to pause next to him, taking his arm obediently.

I haven't spent much time with Mr. Petrov. He limits our interactions, saying it might interfere with our educational program. His wife, however—Leandra Petrov—met with each of us when we first arrived at the academy. She taught us how to properly apply makeup and style our hair to the academy's specifications. And I remember thinking at the time that she was the most beautiful woman I'd ever seen. She's significantly younger than her husband—probably not much older than us.

Leandra's on campus fairly often. She monitors and records our weight once a week, and she leaves products in our bathrooms to help us manage our periods. She's one of the few women we interact with here. Poised and beautiful, an example to be emulated.

The front doors open again and Anton comes rushing out, a bit frazzled in an endearing way. He stops beside the Head of School, turning his head to talk confidentially as they wait for us to exit the bus.

Lennon Rose exhales with relief and Sydney smiles at me.

It's reassuring to see Anton—a promise that everything will be okay. Despite him being the person who administers impulse control therapy, we mostly look forward to our time with him. He's a wonderful listener. An excellent analyst.

He's older—like the other men at the academy—with light brown hair, gray at the temples. Even his beard is growing in gray, and he jokes that it's because he has so many girls to worry about.

"Philomena," Guardian Bose calls from his seat in the front row. I jump, startled.

"Yes?"

He stands, chomping on his gum. He grabs Valentine by the arm and pulls her out of the seat. She keeps her eyes downcast, her defiance seeming to have faded away.

"Take the back stairs and go see Dr. Groger," the Guardian tells me. "Ask him to patch you up."

I nod, embarrassed again for my earlier behavior. My knee still stings.

The Guardian walks Valentine off the bus, and Anton quickly rushes the rest of the way down the stairs to meet them. He gives the Guardian a pointed look before gently taking Valentine's elbow and leading her inside.

"Do you want me to come with you?" Sydney asks me as we get to our feet. We follow the other girls off the bus. I tell Sydney that I'll be fine, but I thank her for the concern. She blows me a kiss before joining the others on the stairs of the school.

As the girls head inside, Mr. Petrov says hello to each of them as they pass, his yellowed teeth crooked in his smile. He assesses each girl, his eyes traveling over their uniforms. Their hair. Their skin. His wife nods along, her gaze drifting from girl to girl.

I round the side of the building and walk to the back steps, which lead to the kitchen entrance.

This room is always loud—dishwasher running, refrigerator humming. There's a large silver pot on the stove bubbling with water, and Mrs. Decatur, the cook, is chopping carrots at the counter, the knife clicking on the wooden board below it.

Mrs. Decatur is only here Mondays through Fridays. She's a little older than my parents and wears her white-blond hair pulled into a tight bun. She's never spoken to me beyond pointing out a recipe. On the weekends, the other girls and I take over the cooking. Home economics is one of the important skills we learn at the academy, the value of an organized domestic life. Cooking, cleaning, hosting, and decorating—we try to excel in each. And if I'm honest, we're better cooks than Mrs. Decatur. I much prefer the food the girls serve. We at least try to sneak a dash of salt where we can.

Mrs. Decatur glances up at me and I smile. She doesn't return the pleasantry, and instead grabs a stalk of celery from beside the cutting board and chops again. I push through the room, resisting the urge to grab a piece of carrot on my way.

The hallway from the kitchen is narrow, and it always makes me feel claustrophobic when I have to come through here. The walls are thin plaster and the floors are stained concrete. Unlike the rest of the building, little was done to make this area more palatable. Thankfully, I turn a corner and enter the reception hall.

This is one of the nicest rooms in the entire academy, but the students are rarely allowed in here. It's mainly used for parental visits and open houses, and the occasional prospective sponsor or investor. It's finely decorated with dark wood wainscoting and beautiful flowered wallpaper. There are several tables with thick, padded chairs, a red couch with end tables on either side of it, and a buffet.

As students, we have dorm rooms and a few sitting areas throughout the building, but nothing this elaborate. Nothing this nice. Lennon Rose once asked our sewing teacher why we didn't have a "place to relax," and he said relaxation was laziness. And that girls needed to stay in top form.

I get through the reception hall and take another turn, finding the back stairs that lead up to the doctor's office. My knee is sore, but the blood has dried, leaving the skin stiff. When I get to the second-floor landing—the hallway extending to include several other offices for the teachers—I stop at the doctor's room, my shoulders tight with tension, and knock on the frosted glass.

"Come in," the doctor calls warmly. I open the door. Dr. Groger is sitting at his desk, several files open in front of him. He has white tufts of curly hair just above his ears on both sides, the top of his head smooth and bald. His glasses are perpetually sliding down his nose, and he pushes them up when I walk in.

"Ah . . . Philomena," he says, but immediately notices my bloody knee. He stands from his desk quickly and walks over to take my hand. He leads me to the table, and I climb up on the paper-covered pad. Dr. Groger wheels over his stool and a silver tray. He sits in front of me and pushes up his glasses.

"What have you done, my dear?" he asks good-naturedly, wetting a gauze pad to clean my wound. I wince at the sting, and Dr. Groger pouts sympathetically. "Let's get this taken care of," he continues. "We wouldn't want it to scar."

The doctor is always warning us about scarring, how difficult scars are to repair. How unsightly.

I don't have any scars. Not one. Sydney has a small, half-moon-shaped scar on her arm from when she got caught on a piece of old razor wire while pulling weeds near the fence last year. The doctor tried, but he couldn't repair all the damage. Even though he promised her it wasn't that bad, Sydney's still a little self-conscious about it. I told her I thought it was cute. Then again, it's not on my body. I might feel differently then.

Once the doctor is done cleaning my scrape, he inspects it carefully, taking measurements with a steel instrument. He jots something down on a notepad and then opens the metal box on the tray he wheeled over.

"Now stay very still," he warns in a fatherly voice, patting my knee with his cold hand.

The doctor opens the foil package with the grafts in it and selects the correct size. Using a pair of tweezers, Dr. Groger lays the small skin graft over my scrape and presses the edges down until they stick. He takes his time to be precise.

Once it's placed, he smiles up at me and then grabs the warming light from the tray. He holds it against my knee so the graft can set, melting into place. The red light is hot, and it's a bit uncomfortable.

When I wince, the doctor gives me an exaggerated sympathetic smile, and then he reaches to pluck a sugar-free lollipop off his tray. I laugh and thank him as I take it.

"So tell me about your field trip," he says conversationally, moving the red light to seal the graft. There is a quick flash of panic in my chest.

I'm scared to tell him, afraid he'll reprimand me. But I can't lie. Besides, he likely knows already. I swallow hard and look down at the floor.

"We went to the Federal Flower Garden," I start in a quiet voice, "but we had to leave early because of the rain."

"The Federal Flower Garden is beautiful," he says. "You always enjoy yourself there."

I nod that I do, and Dr. Groger moves the light to another corner of my graft.

"After the Flower Garden," I tell him, considering what I'm going to say next, "we stopped at a gas station so some of the girls could use the restroom. I was going to get candy."

The doctor rolls his eyes, playing along like I was being mischievous. He shifts the red light again.

"And?" he asks, his voice dropping lower. He does know the rest of the story.

"There was a boy there," I add, ashamed.

The doctor clicks off the light. He takes it from my knee and sets it back on the tray.

"What did you and this boy talk about?" he asks. He grabs the tube of silicone gel and puts some on a gauze patch, then rubs it over my knee.

"Candy, mostly," I say. "But . . . when Guardian Bose came in and told me it was time to leave, I didn't listen right away." I'm humiliated by the admission.

"And why do you think you disobeyed?" he asks.

"I wanted a few more minutes in the store."

Dr. Groger sighs. "That's not like you, Philomena," he says. "The girl I know would never misbehave." His disappointed tone nearly makes me cry. "I'm sure you didn't mean to be disrespectful," he adds. "But it was improper for you to carry on with a stranger—especially a boy we don't know. Guardian Bose was right to redirect you."

I nod and tell him that I understand. And when he smiles, not angry, I'm relieved.

The doctor pats my thigh this time, and then reaches for a sparkly Band-Aid. He places it over my graft for decoration and declares that I'm still scar-free.

I hop down from the table, pulling the wrapper off the sugar-free lollipop, and stick the candy between my cheek and teeth. I watch Dr. Groger write notes in my file, pushing up his glasses every few seconds.

"Can I ask you something?" I begin quietly.

The doctor's pencil stops. "Of course," he says, looking at me above his glasses. "What is it?"

"Is Valentine getting impulse control therapy?" I ask. Even saying the words out loud causes a twist in my stomach, a prickle on my skin. "She misbehaved on the bus, and—"

"Valentine Wright will be just fine," he says. "Her impulses are compromised, but a good session with Anton should cure her of that. She'll be back to herself in no time. It's very sweet of you to worry about her, though."

I thank him for the compliment. However, I'm still bothered. "But the Guardian grabbed—"

"I'm aware of the incident, Philomena," he replies, interrupting me again. "There's no need for you to consider it any longer."

I don't argue, accepting that he's right.

Dr. Groger waits a beat before closing my file and setting it inside his desk drawer. When I don't say anything else, he sighs as if he was being too harsh. He walks out from behind his desk.

"Guardian Bose may be a bit overzealous at times," the doctor admits, glancing at my Band-Aid. "I will speak to him. But he knows what's best for you—all of you. You should respect that."

The lollipop has gone sour in my mouth. I've never been in trouble before; I've never disappointed the doctor. I promise to do better. "I won't misbehave again," I assure him.

"Good." Dr. Groger takes off his glasses and slips them into the front pocket of his shirt. He looks me up and down. "That's very good, Philomena."

He walks me to the door, his hand on the small of my back. And just before I leave, I pause long enough to thank him for his guidance.

IA Report Card

Student's Name: Philomena Rhodes

Year: 2 Q1

Metrics

A – Superior, **B** – Above average, **C** – Average,
D – Below average, **E** – Poor, **F** – Failure

Conduct

Cooperative	A
Good listener	A
Manners and poise	A
Beauty	A
Compliance	A

Academics

Plant Design and Development	A
Basics	A
Social Graces Etiquette	A
Modesty and Decorum	A
Running Course	A
Modern Manners	A

Teacher's Remarks

Philomena is a delightful, well-mannered girl. She follows instructions and is amenable to all requests with continued direction. She will make a fine addition to any household.

Anton Stuart

4

My afternoon classes have already started by the time I leave the doctor's office, and I go back to my room to grab my textbook. I'm feeling vulnerable, an odd sense of loneliness. Separation. As I leave my bedroom, I glance down the hall toward the phone.

I'd planned to call my parents to see if they'll be attending tomorrow's open house, but I hadn't gotten the chance yet. I decide to call them now.

I head down the hall and try not to think about them missing another open house as I pick up the phone. My parents are very busy people—I understand that. I haven't spoken to them since the holidays, and even then, it was just a short chat with my mother. A quick check-in to make sure I'd received the extra allowance. She told me to buy myself something nice. But . . . there's nothing to spend it on here. I guess she doesn't know that.

I dial their number and press the receiver to my ear. I steady myself against the wall with my other hand. There's a click on the line, and I immediately straighten up as if they can see me.

"Hello?" a warm voice calls. "This is the Rhodes residence." I smile softly.

"Hi, Eva," I say. "It's Philomena."

"Philomena," she says lovingly. "How are you, darling?" Her accent is stronger when she pronounces my name—the origin unclear. When I asked about it once, she replied, "Oh, you know. I'm from here and there." That was the end of the discussion.

Eva is my parents' live-in assistant. All of the families affiliated with the academy have an assistant, and I'm lucky to have Eva. She answers my every call, every letter. I've personally never met her—she was hired after I left for school—but I don't usually mind when I talk to her as a surrogate for my parents. She's kind. She even sent me gloves during the winter. It was very sweet.

"I'm sorry to call again," I say. "I was wondering . . . Is my mother around?"

"No, honey," Eva says. "I'm sorry, but she's out of town through the weekend. Is this about the open house tomorrow? She's very disappointed that she can't attend. I'm sure you'll look lovely, though."

"Thank you," I say, my heart sinking. "Any chance my father's home? I'd like to speak with him."

"He's with your mother," Eva sings out like she's guessing I'll be disappointed. "But you can always talk to me, sweetheart," she says. "That's why I'm here."

And she *is* there, every time. My mother runs a charity, jet-setting from place to place. I'm not quite clear on what charity, but she's very dedicated to it. Before that, she homeschooled me. She taught me to read with Basics books the academy lends out to prospective parents. She gave me an overview of society and manners, and guided me through an organic, plant-based diet with exercise. My father runs a law firm, but he always made it home for dinner.

We never traveled, not like my parents do now. Our days at home were as repetitive as my days at school. I never had anything new happen until I came here. Until I met the other girls.

"I'm worried about you, Mena," Eva announces. "You sound troubled. Is everything okay? How's school? Your calendar shows you had a field trip today—how did that go?"

I wish I didn't have to talk about the incident with the Guardian at the gas station. But I can't lie to Eva. That'd be as bad as lying to my parents. Plus, I don't want her to relay to my parents that she thinks I'm *troubled*.

I twist the phone cord around my finger and turn to rest my back against the wall. I start out telling her about the Federal Flower Garden, the rainy day. The more I talk, the more my skin heats up with embarrassment.

"The bus had to make a quick stop on the way back from our field trip. There was a boy in the store, and while we were talking, the Guardian came in and told me it was time to leave. I . . . I didn't listen right away."

There is a long pause. "And then?" Eva asks.

"I was redirected," I say. "I've already spoken to Dr. Groger about it, so—"

"Why were you at the doctor?" she interrupts. "Are you unwell, Mena?"

"No," I say quickly. "I'm fine. It was just a scratch, but it's taken care of. No scar."

"And your behavior," she follows up. "Is that taken care of too?"

The coldness in her voice, the practicality of it, makes me feel ten times worse. My eyes sting with tears.

"Yes, Eva," I say, humiliated. "I agree with the doctor's assessment that I needed the redirection. It won't happen again." I quickly wipe the tears from my eyes before they can ruin my makeup.

"That's good to hear," Eva says. "We all want you to be the best girl possible. And good girls obey the rules. Your parents will be sick over this."

"I'd like to talk to them about it," I say pleadingly. "If I could just explain it to them, I'm sure I could—"

"Your parents are very busy," Eva says, cutting off my request. "They don't have time to listen to your excuses. Your focus should be on your education, Philomena. It's what they're investing in."

My face stings from the admonishment. "I understand," I say quietly. "I'm sorry I brought it up."

"That's all right," Eva says, her tone softening. "And perhaps your parents don't need *all* the details," she adds, like it can be our little secret.

"I'd appreciate that," I say. "I don't want to disappoint them."

"We still believe in you, Philomena," she says, speaking on their behalf. "Now . . . aren't you supposed to be in class?" she adds teasingly.

I laugh and then quickly sniffle away my tears. "Yes," I say, happy that Eva isn't angry with me. She's always very sympathetic. "I'm on my way there now. Would you mind letting my parents know I called?" I ask. "I'd . . . I'd like to talk to them."

"Of course," Eva says warmly. "When they return from their trip. And *you* have a nice time at the open house. Don't forget to smile. Make us proud."

I promise that I will, and then I hang up and head toward class. The loneliness mostly gone from my chest.

I keep my head down as I walk into Modesty and Decorum class, worried that Professor Penchant will scold me in front of the others. I'm still a little tender from Dr. Groger's reprimand. Eva's disappointment.

"Shame is the best teacher," the professor said last week when Lennon Rose started to cry. He told her she looked unkempt, a poor representation of the academy. He made her go back to her room to take out her ponytail and brush her hair; he held the class until she returned. I offered to help her, but he told me it was a lesson she needed to learn.

"I know girls these days like to think their appearance doesn't matter," he lectured us. "Pajamas in a movie theater, messy hair at the grocery store." He scrunched up his nose as if he found these types of girls particularly distasteful. "But you will take pride in your appearance at all times. No exceptions. And why is that?"

"Because beauty is our greatest asset," we said in unison, knowing the appropriate response. Knowing we'd be graded on it.

"Correct," the professor replied, assessing each of us.

Lennon Rose came back to class shortly after that, a vision with her long hair smoothed, fresh makeup applied, her uniform shirt tucked in, and her socks perfectly folded. Professor Penchant showed her off.

I feel his eyes on me now as I sit at my desk, but he doesn't call my name. I take out my book and follow along with the lesson.

"Compliance is an appealing quality," he says from the front of the room. "Especially with graduation growing near. You'll find that out there," he motions toward the windows, "people won't appreciate your opinions. Hold your tongue and listen. It's a good lesson for all young women."

We can't wait for graduation—the chance to show what exemplary girls we've become. *Better girls.* Once we've completed our education at Innovations Academy, Mr. Petrov works closely with our parents or sponsors to find us the perfect opportunity for success, usually through marriage. He says there are other prospects as well, but he hasn't explained them. Instead, he tells us to trust him; he only wants what's best for us.

We're going to make our parents so proud.

There's a loud exhale behind me, and I put my chin on my shoulder and look back covertly. Annalise sits in the desk behind me, and when she notices me, she rolls her eyes.

Annalise is outspoken, more so than the rest of us. *Brutally honest,* Anton told her once, a description that Annalise found appealing.

A few months ago, Annalise suggested that Professor Penchant try compliments rather than admonishments. It's no surprise that he didn't "appreciate" Annalise's opinion on this matter. Now she keeps them to herself during class.

She winks at me and I smile.

"Ah, Philomena," the professor calls, startling me. I quickly spin around. "Glad you've recovered from your little mishap on the bus. All is well?"

"Yes, Professor Penchant," I reply, back straight, chin up.

"Very good," he says. "Now, would you like to stay after class with me and discuss why you find it so difficult to pay attention during my lesson?"

"No, sir," I say, heat rising to my cheeks. "I apologize for my disruption."

He narrows his dark eyes on me. "Correct answer," he responds, darting his gaze at Annalise before turning back to the board to finish the lesson.

Suddenly, the classroom door opens and Leandra Petrov sweeps into the room. We all position ourselves to look our best, exemplify the teachings of the academy. She smiles politely, and when she turns to Professor Penchant, she lowers her head in a show of respect. He puffs up with confidence and allows her to take the floor.

"Hello, girls," Leandra says to us. Her voice is graceful and elegant. Her light hair is styled in thick waves, tucked at the nape of her neck. Her navy blue dress is formfitting and flattering. I turn to Lennon Rose, who is watching Leandra with unbridled admiration.

"I'm sorry to interrupt your lesson," Leandra continues, "but I'd like to speak with you about Valentine Wright."

A few girls shift in their seats and I see Professor Penchant scowl at their lack of restraint. Leandra steps forward, her heels clicking on the linoleum.

"As you're aware, Valentine was insubordinate while on the field trip. She defied Guardian Bose, and by extension, she defied the academy." She pulls her eyebrows together, a slight frown on her full lips.

"Innovations Academy has given you girls everything," she says. "Arranged for you to lead an exemplary life. You should appreciate it. Appreciate what Guardian Bose does to keep you safe. What your esteemed professors"—she glances at Professor Penchant—"teach you in the classroom." Leandra takes a few more steps so that she is almost at the front row of desks.

"You are perfection personified," she continues, "and we must ask that you act like it. I never want to hear about this kind of behavior again. It would break my heart." She puts her hand on her chest to drive home the point. Several girls nod emphatically, as if promising they would never dream of upsetting her.

"We are lucky," Leandra says, holding open her arms, "to have such wonderful girls. And *you* are lucky to have such wonderful men to guide you. Don't ever forget that." She smiles for a long moment, gazing at each of us, before taking a cleansing breath and directing us to do the same. We all feel a little better once we have.

"Now," Leandra says, "although we are deeply disappointed in Valentine's behavior, we are committed to returning her to her best self. She is currently being sent through impulse control therapy to identify the cause of her actions. I'm here to assure you that she'll be fine. No," she corrects, "she'll be better than ever." She pauses a moment and waits for us to clap. When I look sideways, Lennon Rose beams at me.

I'm grateful that Valentine will get the help she needs. And to prove it, I clap along with the others.

Leandra glances around once more, and for a moment, her eyes hold mine. And then, just as easily as she walked in, she dips her chin to the professor in gratitude and sweeps back out of the class-room.

I don't see Sydney until dinner. We only have a few classes together, and none of them were this afternoon. I've missed her, and I'm grateful to find her waiting at our usual table in the dining hall. The area where we take our meals is small, and we sit close enough together that there are few conversations that are private.

For example, as I approach the table, I hear Marcella talking about the "bloodbath" that was her period last weekend. I snort a laugh and take a seat next to Sydney.

"Let me see it," Sydney says, motioning toward my knee. I put my foot on the seat and slowly pull off the glitter Band-Aid with a wince. She leans close to examine it like she's a scar specialist.

"Pretty good," she says, nodding. I hope she's not feeling self-conscious about her scar, but when she reaches for the center of the table, I notice that she tugs down her sleeve to cover the mark. She grabs a salad and slides it in front of me.

"No chicken today?" I ask, picking through the dry lettuce.

"They announced we've had too many calories this week. Now it's salad and juice cleanses until next weigh-in."

"Gross."

"Don't be negative," she sings out, pushing a green sludge–filled glass my way. I try a sip and it's awful, of course. She laughs. None of us like the juice.

The green juices are made of plants from our garden. Assorted flowers that we grow specially mixed with vitamins for an added boost. The juice keeps our moods centered, content.

Our diets here at the academy are strict, measured, and always monitored. Even when we cook, it's with natural ingredients, no additives. No extras. But every once in a while, we'll get the chance to taste something different in cooking class—"chef tasting," they call it—to make sure it's correctly seasoned. Men like their foods flavorful, and we're expected to provide a tantalizing meal. But it would be inappropriate for us to indulge, crave food for ourselves.

Same goes for our movies. The school selects what we watch: mostly films from the early 50s. There is the occasional action film with explosions, but I imagine those are Guardian Bose's influence. We're sometimes asked our thoughts on the entertainment, but the conversation always steers back to how Guardian Bose felt about it, and we're to echo his sentiment. It makes for a more pleasing conversation.

The academy has no cable or internet, which we're told is a good thing.

"The internet is rife with falsehoods," Professor Levin told us in Modern Manners. "You'll do best to ignore it completely, even after graduation. Your husbands or custodians will let you know any important news you need. Trust in their supervision."

Before the academy, my parents didn't allow me on the internet either. Being homeschooled, I was protected—just like I am here. So when it comes to the internet, I don't know what I'm missing. I defer to the professors' knowledge on the matter.

There are a few types of books at the school: gardening, beauty standards, or social etiquette, but I've already read them all. So most days, it's just me and the girls. Which is more than enough. We're fast learners, absorbing words, phrases, and ideas quickly. And we tell each other everything—our own kind of internet, I suppose.

I look down to the other end of the table and see the empty spot where Valentine normally sits. It's a bit jarring for her to be missing, and I blink quickly as I resettle myself. Even though Valentine doesn't socialize with us, she's still part of our class. And none of us likes to be separated.

I poke through my salad with my fork before looking up at the other girls. "Hey," I say quietly, drawing gazes from Marcella and Brynn, from Sydney and Lennon Rose. "When I was with Dr. Groger earlier, I asked him about Valentine."

Marcella's eyes narrow slightly, as if she's both confused and interested in what I have to say next. Brynn sets her elbow on the table.

"What did he say?" Sydney asks from next to me.

"He told me that Guardian Bose can be overzealous sometimes," I say. "And that he'd talk to him about it."

"Dr. Groger is very kind," Lennon Rose says in her quiet way. She nods that we should agree.

"What does he mean by 'overzealous'?" Brynn asks, pushing her blond braid over her shoulder. "Valentine wasn't listening to him. He redirected her."

"He did injure Mena," Marcella suggests as a reason, turning sideways to Brynn. I'm immediately embarrassed again by my behavior.

"I'm not sure what the doctor meant," I say. I lean into the table and drop my voice lower. "But Valentine is getting impulse control therapy right now."

"Good," Brynn says, nodding. "Hopefully it'll get her back on track."

I look down at my salad, the feeling of dread coming over me again. "The impulse control therapy part doesn't bother you, though?" I ask, barely a whisper.

"Why would it?" Sydney asks curiously. "It'll fix her."

The other girls nod, perplexed by my question. Lennon Rose recently underwent her own impulse control therapy. She'd been acting a little sad, and we were told she was homesick and needed to reassess her goals. We haven't discussed it with her since she returned—Anton said it would be best not to.

Lennon Rose is no longer contributing to the discussion now, clearly uncomfortable. The other girls watch me, puzzled, and I feel bad for worrying them.

"Never mind," I say with a quick wave of my hand. "I was probably just shaken up after seeing so much blood."

Sydney scrunches up her nose, admitting that the sight of blood was disgusting. The girls agree, and the conversation about impulse control therapy fades away.

As the other girls eat, I glance around the dining hall and find the

Guardian sitting with the professors as they devour their dinners. Overflowing plates of meat and gravy, potatoes, and vegetables. Steam rises from their plates, and for a moment, my mouth actually waters. I spear a piece of lettuce and shove it between my teeth.

Sydney uses her straw to stir her juice, poking at the thick liquid. "You have to come to my room later," she says. "After evening classes. We have a lot to *discuss*." She emphasizes the last word, and I know she wants to talk about the boys we met. I fight back my grin and tell her that I'll be there. Next to her, Lennon Rose's eyes light up.

On Thursdays, we all attend classes well into the night, but it gives us a shorter school day on Friday. And this Friday is especially important because it's an open house. Parents, sponsors, and potential investors are invited to see the grand achievements of the Innovations Academy. Namely: us.

The events are lavish and impressive, a chance to mingle and socialize. We all look forward to them because these are our only chances to see our parents during the year.

"Drink your juice," Sydney says, taking a big sip of hers and gagging before finishing it off. I tell her she's out of her mind and slosh the straw around in my drink, wishing the entire thing would just evaporate.

I feel heat on the back of my neck. Sensing him, I look up to find Guardian Bose watching me. I'm conscious that I don't want to break any more rules. I pick up my juice and guzzle it down. When I set the glass on the table, sick to my stomach, the Guardian smiles and goes back to his meal.

5

My evening classes are monotonous, but I listen in each one, wanting to meet my professors' expectations. We add new roses to our garden in Plant Design and Development, learn (again) how to properly set a table in Modern Manners, and practice informal greetings in Social Graces Etiquette class.

I'm mortified when I realize that I introduced myself all wrong today when meeting Jackson. I didn't offer him my hand, didn't stop what I was doing to give him my full attention. And I certainly talked too much about myself.

Although I did well with eye contact, I didn't ask Jackson enough questions. I should have found a topic he enjoyed and pursued it. Exuded confidence in order to boost his. Or if he preferred, been humble and soft-spoken.

On the other hand, Jackson broke all the rules of etiquette. He blushed, cursed, and lost his temper with the Guardian. He suggested we go out without formally asking me. But men don't have to follow the same rules of engagement that we do. Perhaps if I'd acted properly, he would have done the same.

But Jackson seemed more casual in his manners. And I liked it. It felt more . . . honest. I smile to myself, deciding that if I ever see him again, I'll be sure to make a better impression. I want to learn more about him.

But, of course, I'll never see him again.

"Philomena," Professor Allister scolds. "Daydreaming again? We've talked about this."

"Sorry, professor," I say. That's my biggest flaw, my professors have told me. I daydream too often, drift away in my thoughts. I just can't seem to stay out of my head, even though I know it's unsightly. It might be something to bring up with Anton at our next meeting. Perhaps he could offer some coping methods to redirect me.

Once classes are completed for the day, I return to my room to get into my pajamas. The halls are quiet. We're supposed to stay in our rooms for studying or quiet reflection before bed, but I tiptoe out to meet with the other girls.

Our floor is made up of individual suites, the one at the end of the hall belonging to Guardian Bose. He keeps an eye on us at night, providing security even though we already have bars on our windows.

I walk down the hall in my socks toward Sydney's room, glancing at Guardian Bose's door to make sure he's not standing there watching. When I'm sure it's clear, I knock softly and enter Sydney's room.

I startle the girls inside, and several of them gasp guiltily. Sydney leaps to her feet, motioning for me to close the door.

"Quickly," she whispers, and there's a flutter of papers behind her back.

"Okay . . . ," I respond in exaggerated suspicion, and close the door. I check the faces of the others—Lennon Rose, Marcella, Brynn, and Annalise—and note the pink blush high on their cheeks. The smiles they're hiding behind their hands.

I turn dramatically to Sydney, hands on my hips. I can't believe she left me out of whatever is going on. She waves me forward to sit with her on the bed while the others crowd around us in a half circle on the rug.

"What is going on?" I ask, amused. Sydney is still wearing her white button-down uniform shirt with no pants and knee-high socks, her hair pinned back. She pushes the folded sleeves of her shirt above her elbows, and then throws her arm around my shoulders.

"Remember when you saw those cute boys today?" she asks. "And then one of them bought you candy?"

"Yes," I say, realizing they don't all know the story. "A whole bag of it."

"Wow," Lennon Rose sighs.

"What kind of candy?" Marcella asks with practicality.

"Doesn't matter," I say. "The Guardian dragged me out before I could eat it. Next time I'll be sure to shove all the chocolates into my mouth before he can get to me," I add, making her laugh. I turn to Sydney.

"Is that what you all were talking about?" I ask.

"Nope," she says, then gives me a smack of a kiss on my temple before pulling her arm away to reach behind her.

Triumphantly, she holds out a magazine, the pages fluttering so I can't see the cover. I'm instantly suspicious.

"Did you steal that?" I ask.

"I did," Marcella says, and when I turn to her, she shrugs. "They had a bunch of them at the gas station," she adds, as if that makes it okay.

I take the magazine from Sydney's hand, but she quickly snatches it back and holds it out of my reach.

"Uh, uh," she sings. She sets it on her crossed knees and flips to a page. I'm stunned to see a couple on a couch in the late stages of undressing. This time, my cheeks blush.

"You stole a dirty magazine?" I ask Marcella with a laugh.

"No," Sydney says for her. "It's a women's magazine."

I look around at the girls, confused. "I don't get it."

"It deals with women's issues—*only*," Sydney says. "In fact, I think I've found my new favorite quiz."

"And what's that?" I ask, trying to sneak another look at the couple on the page.

"It's called . . ." She clears her throat. "'Are you good at oral sex?'"

I burst out laughing, imagining she's joking, but instead, she lists off the first three bullet points. It's downright scandalous, but at the same time, we close in around her, hanging on her every word.

Although all of us grew up in strict households—followed by

the isolation of the academy—we're not completely naive. Most of our nights are filled with long talks while piled together in a room, recounting stories we've heard—collectively or individually. Bits of advertising we've picked up on field trips. We rehash the censored parts of movies that we've embellished with our imaginations.

When Sydney's done going through all the points on the list, including tips of things to avoid, we collectively decide that we'd be pretty bad at the whole oral sex thing if we followed those suggestions. It all sounds wildly unpleasant.

"What I don't get," I say, thinking it over, "is if this is a women's magazine, why are they telling us how to pleasure guys? Shouldn't it be about our pleasure? Or even mutual pleasure?"

"Huh," Sydney says, flipping to the front cover of the magazine and tracing her finger over the words "Women's Magazine." "That's a good point, actually," Sydney says, and turns to me. "Will you do me a favor?" she asks.

"Sure," I reply reluctantly.

"Next time you see your gas station boyfriend," she says, "will you make him take this quiz?"

We all laugh, and I swear that I will. But we know that I'd never ask those sorts of questions.

"Also," I add, holding up one finger. "Can we please not call him my *gas station boyfriend*?" Sydney does a quick cross over her heart, smiling.

"Is there anything about kissing in there?" Lennon Rose asks in her sweet, small voice. Sydney and I exchange a look—Lennon Rose is just too adorable—and Sydney flips through the pages until she finds a picture of a couple kissing. She turns the magazine around to show the group.

"This is fake," Sydney says, "but it looks like that. Except with tongues."

Lennon Rose scrunches her nose at the idea, and Marcella motions to the paper.

"Not totally like that," Marcella says, shaking her head. "It can be nice, too. You know, just . . . kissing and hugging at the same time. You don't have to lick each other's faces like dogs."

Marcella knows what she's talking about. She and Brynn sneak a kiss whenever they can, the sweet kind with whispers in between. Soft smiles and hand-holding. It's not tongue wrestling on a couch, and she tells us as much.

"Have you ever kissed anyone?" Lennon Rose asks me.

"Yes, she has," Sydney answers for me, and then seems to think better of it the moment the words are out.

"Who did you kiss?" Marcella asks doubtfully.

I look at Sydney first, and she apologizes under her breath. I sigh.

"It was near the beginning of the year," I start. "We were at the theater for a ballet—the one with the extravagant costumes." The title escapes me.

"Oh, I remember," Marcella says. "The Guardian . . ." She squints her eyes like she's trying to recall a specific detail. "Guardian Thompson—the one with the scar," she says, drawing a line across her cheek with her finger. "The one who got fired and replaced with Bose. He was with us, right?"

"That's why he got fired," Sydney says.

I actually feel bad that Guardian Thompson got fired; I hate to think I was the cause of him losing his job. He had a family to support. We talked about them once while we were on the bus. He even had a daughter who died, he told me—and that was why he took the job at the academy. We reminded him of her.

In theory, at least, he clarified with a smile. I still don't get what he meant.

"I need details," Marcella says, eyes wide. "Kissing with a Guardian nearby? Why is this the first I'm hearing about it?"

"Because it was nothing to brag about," I say, motioning to the magazine. "And it was nothing like what's in there."

"Tell me," Marcella says. She settles in next to Brynn, and all the girls wait for me to explain.

I'm a little uncomfortable that Sydney brought up the topic.

"We were at the theater," I start, "and I told Sydney I'd be right back while I went to the bathroom. When I was done, I decided to go to the counter and order some candy."

The girls all nod like, *Of course you did.* My sugar addiction is legendary.

"I was at the counter," I continue, "practicing greetings with the guy working the concessions. He was very friendly. He asked if I would sit outside with him because it was a nice night. I didn't want to be rude, so I said yes.

"We sat on a bench a little off to the side and shared a box of Junior Mints. I tried to follow the rules of etiquette, ask him about himself, but he kept interrupting me, commenting on how 'hot' I was. When he asked if I had a boyfriend, I told him I wasn't allowed to date. He laughed.

"Then he told me he had to get back inside," I say. "Before he left, he grabbed me by the shoulders and kissed me hard, smashing our faces together. It was . . . surprising," I say, thinking about it. "Especially when he stuck his tongue in my mouth."

Lennon Rose gasps, horrified.

"It only lasted a few seconds," I say. "It was wet, and although I'd been curious about kissing, it wasn't *sexy*. I mean, it's supposed to be foreplay, right?" I ask, and Sydney nods emphatically like she's the consulting sexpert.

"He must have been doing something wrong, then," I say. "Because the last thing I wanted to do was find out what was under his clothes. If anything, I wanted him to put more on."

"Ew, Mena," Annalise says, disgusted. "You're making me hope I never kiss anyone."

"Maybe it just wasn't for me," I say. "I wanted to hear about his life. Hear about the world. Instead, I nearly choked to death on his tongue."

Sydney puts her curled fist to her mouth and pretends to barf into it.

Marcella stares at me and slowly shakes her head. "Mena," she says seriously. "That's . . . That's not how kissing works." She looks at Brynn who agrees. "In fact, when Brynn and I first kissed—"

"I asked her to," Brynn adds, finishing the thought. "She didn't just shove her face in mine." Brynn smiles softly. "I *asked* her to kiss me."

Marcella returns the smile and takes her hand absently. "Exactly," she says.

"But it's different for men," Lennon Rose says, glancing at Marcella and Brynn. "They don't have to ask. One time, Professor Levin told me that if my skirt was any shorter, a man would expect me to behave improperly." She looks at me. "Maybe your skirt was too short?"

"I don't think so," I say. "I keep it regulation length."

Marcella tilts her head, trying to figure it out. "Did you tell Anton about this guy?" she asks. "What did he say?"

My cheeks heat up with shame, remembering why I don't like this story. "He wasn't upset, but Anton told me I shouldn't have gone outside with the guy in the first place."

Boys will be boys, Mena, Anton said that afternoon. *What else would he think when you left the theater with him? Be better next time.*

"So what happened to Guardian Thompson?" Annalise asks, still seeming disgusted by the idea of another person's tongue in my mouth. "How did he get involved?"

"After the guy left, I went back into the theater," I say. "Guardian Thompson saw me walk in, and he must have noticed that I looked . . . uncertain. He took me by the arm and led me out into the hall. I told him what happened, and he demanded I go into the theater and not tell anyone. He was clearly upset, so I did as he asked, but I noticed him walking toward the concessions counter.

"I'm not sure what happened after that," I continue. "Guardian

Thompson was gone from school the next day. Anton told me during therapy that the Guardian had been let go for threatening a theater worker. Anton said he hoped I'd learned my lesson. I'm still not totally clear on which lesson got Guardian Thompson dismissed, though. Luckily, Anton didn't tell my parents about the incident. They might have pulled me from the academy."

"Good on Anton, I guess," Sydney says with a nod. "He's always looking out for us."

"He's the best," Lennon Rose says dreamily. We're all quiet for a moment, staring at her.

"Keep it in your pants, Lennon Rose," Annalise announces, and we all just about die laughing.

Lennon Rose turns five different shades of red, but to be fair, she's the youngest of all of us. And she's definitely the most innocent. She's confided in me many times that she can't wait to be married. It's sweet, really, the way she loves love. *A true romantic,* Anton said once.

Sydney hits her bare knee against mine. "Well, if the lesson was to cease luring young men with your candy addiction, I'd say you've learned nothing." Sydney smiles and looks at the other girls. "You should have seen Mena today," she announces. "She had that boy in the gas station wrapped around her finger."

"*Stop!*" I tell them, even though I keep smiling.

"I'm just saying he was into you," Sydney replies for the benefit of everyone. "And I'm almost certain he would have liked number four on the oral-sex checklist. He seems the type."

I fall back on the bed, laughing too hard to breathe.

Lennon Rose gets up on her knees very seriously, takes the magazine from Sydney's lap, and frantically flips the pages back to the quiz. I roll to my side, still chuckling to myself as her eyes scan the page. Then they widen, and she lifts them to mine.

In all fairness, I have no idea what Jackson is into, but I don't think it's number four.

There's a swift knock on the door, and we all immediately straighten as it opens. Sydney rips the magazine from Lennon Rose's hand and stuffs it under the pillow, slapping it down just as Guardian Bose steps into the room.

"What's so funny?" he asks with little humor.

"Marcella was talking about her period again, and it was honestly hilarious," Sydney says easily. She lounges back on her bed, one hand over her pillow, and smiles.

The Guardian eyes her suspiciously, and then glances around the room at each of our faces. He doesn't pause on me. I'm not sure if he's still upset from earlier.

When none of us offers a different explanation, Guardian Bose shakes his head. "All right," he says. "It's past curfew, and you have a party to attend tomorrow."

"Thank you," Annalise tells him, and gets to her feet. "No need to tuck us in."

The Guardian cracks a hint of a smile. Things are back to normal, it seems. And as if to prove it, he turns to me.

"Bed in ten minutes," he says simply, and then nods to all of us before heading into the hallway.

The girls and I exchange a puzzled look. But I'm thankful that he doesn't seem angry anymore. Seeing the Guardian that way was a shock—a frightening experience. One I never want to experience again.

Marcella and Brynn say good night and leave with Annalise, but Lennon Rose stays behind. She steps closer to Sydney and me as we stand from the bed.

"Can I ask you something?" she says quietly.

"What's up?" Sydney pulls her into a motherly hug. It's easy to tell when Lennon Rose is worried; her emotions play across her face.

"Do you think anyone will ever want to kiss me?" she asks.

I resist saying, "Aww . . . honey," and instead try to sound confident. "Once you graduate," I tell her, "you'll meet so many more people. The academy will find you the perfect person—one who knows how special you are. And then you'll kiss them endlessly." I smile, but the corners of Lennon Rose's lips turn down.

"But . . . But what about Marcella and Brynn?" she asks, straightening out of Sydney's arms.

"What do you mean?" I reply.

"They love each other. They want to kiss each other endlessly. So . . . when Mr. Petrov places them after graduation . . ."

There's a tightening in my chest before she even finishes the sentence.

Lennon Rose sniffles, wiping under her nose. "What if he places them with different people?" she asks. "How will they still love each other?"

I open my mouth to answer, but no words come out. I glance sideways at Sydney and see her with the same shocked expression.

The thought has never occurred to us. The thought is a contradiction. The thought is dangerous.

"Lennon Rose," Sydney says after a long moment. "The academy knows what's best for us. So maybe they'll place Marcella and Brynn together. Who knows?" She forces a smile. "But it's not for us to decide."

Lennon Rose nods like this comment outweighs any other she's heard on the matter. I can practically see her fighting back her emotions. Her tenderness.

"You're right," Lennon Rose says, lowering her eyes. "The academy knows what's best."

"Don't dwell on it, okay?" Sydney says, giving her another quick hug before walking her to the door. "As the professor would say, it's bad for your complexion."

Lennon Rose offers a closed-mouth smile, pulling back. She murmurs good night to both of us and leaves.

Sydney stares at the empty doorway and taps her lower lip with her index finger. "She's going to dwell," she says after a moment.

"She'll be better tomorrow," I say, coming to stand next to Sydney. "We're always better in the morning." Sydney and I exchange a look, and then I lean in to give her a hug, both of us holding on an extra moment.

I leave, but once in the hallway, I'm startled by a figure near my room. Guardian Bose smiles at me, holding a glass of water and a small paper cup with my nightly vitamins. I politely smile back at him.

"How's your knee?" he asks, not looking at it as I approach.

"All better," I say. "Thank you for asking."

He nods while I enter my room, then follows me inside. He closes the door behind me.

"Let me ask you something, Mena," he says, turning to study my expression. "That boy you were talking to today, did you know him?"

I'm taken aback by the question. "Of course not," I say. "Why?"

"No reason," he says. He walks over to the nightstand to set down my vitamins and water. "He was probably just captivated by your beauty. Or perhaps you led him on, either way . . ." He shrugs like it doesn't matter, and runs his gaze up and down my pajamas, taking me all in.

Something about the way he does this makes me feel ashamed, and I lower my eyes, crossing my arms over my chest even though we're not supposed to fidget.

"Well, you have a good night, Mena," the Guardian says. He steps closer, towering over me, and leans down to press his dry lips to my forehead. "See you in the morning," he murmurs.

I stand there a moment after he leaves, my arms still around me. I turn expectantly to my nightstand. Next to the glass of water is the small plastic cup with capsules, two pinks and one green.

Every night, the academy delivers a regimen of vitamins tailored to our specific needs. I'm normally one pink and one green. But I'm guessing the incident at the gas station requires an extra dose.

I sigh heavily and quickly gulp down the capsules before getting into bed.

6

love mornings. The other girls think I'm unhinged, the way I
normally smile through breakfast and hum in the shower. Only
Lennon Rose likes mornings as much as I do, but Lennon Rose
likes almost everything.

As I stretch this morning, I see the white box lying inside my
doorway with a big red bow. My dress.

I rub my eyes, sleep still clinging to the edges of my mind. I
never remember my dreams, but this morning, there is the hint of
something there—an idea just out of my reach. Something about
roses. But the more I try to grab it, the farther away it gets.

When it's gone entirely, I look at the white box again.

Mr. Petrov furnishes each girl with a gown for the open house.
He has them made especially for us. Part of me wishes I could
pick out my own dress, one without so many sparkles, but the
Head of School is very particular. I'm grateful for his attention
to detail.

I get up, tugging down the hem of my pajama shorts, and walk over to the box. I bring it back to my bed and untie the bow, carefully removing the lid. I brush through the tissue paper and my fingers graze the garment. It's sharp with sequins. I slowly drag the fabric from the box, making sure it doesn't touch the floor.

It's beautiful. A full-length white sequin dress—iridescent in the light. Formfitting with a low-cut top. It'll fit perfectly since the academy has my measurements, but it weighs a lot in my hands now. I lay the dress on top of its box without trying it on and go to the bathroom to put on my clothes for Running Course.

Running Course isn't terrible—we mostly enjoy it. We get to be outside, creating lean muscle and toning our legs. The best part, though, is that since we're already surrounded by iron fencing, the Guardian doesn't join us. It's one of the few places where we have zero supervision.

Although I'm wearing my warmest track clothes and a head band covering my ears, the wind is cold on my face. The other girls have already been out here for a while when I fall into step next to them, little puffs of air visibly escaping our lips as we round the building. Nights and mornings in these Colorado mountains are always cold. The spring is no exception.

We reach the side of the academy where there are no windows or doors. Just a wall of bricks. Sydney is beside me when she suddenly reaches out to grab my arm, making me stumble to a stop. I'm about to ask if she's okay when I see her staring into the trees. I follow her gaze there.

Nothing moves other than the occasional shake of leaves in the wind.

The rest of the girls continue past us, taking their run times very seriously. Sydney moves a step closer to the woods, and I come to stand next to her.

"What is it?" I ask. "What's wrong?"

When Sydney turns back to me, she can barely contain her smile, her eyes flashing mischief.

"Quick," she says, taking my hand and pulling me toward the fence before the other girls can notice we're gone. She tucks us between the iron and an overgrown bush that has overtaken the bars, creating an arch.

My heart races, unsure of what Sydney has planned. I check back for the other girls, but they've already rounded the side of the building, buying us about five minutes.

Sydney takes me by the shoulders, and I ask again what she's doing. She responds by licking her palm and then using it to smooth down my flyaways. I swat her hand, but she's determined. She moves me to the side, posing me so that I'm completely hidden under the leaves.

When she's done fussing, I put my hand on my hip, glaring at her.

"Please, Sydney," I say. "My head is starting to hurt." And it does, a small pain behind my left eye, presumably from the extra capsule I took last night. Nothing else about my routine is different. It happens occasionally if we have too many vitamins. I'll let the doctor know.

Sydney smiles brilliantly. "You have company," she says, and motions behind me.

I spin around, confused, and catch sight of someone behind the bush. I gasp, but before I get truly frightened, the person steps toward the fence.

Jackson.

He looks understandably mortified to be hiding in the bushes outside the bars of my school.

I turn back to Sydney. "How did you know he was—?"

"I saw him this morning," she says, impatiently waving Jackson over. I look at him and he takes a step closer.

"You're all right," he says to me, sounding relieved. "I had to check on you. And I, uh . . . I also brought your candy." He holds up the plastic bag. "Most of it got crushed, and Quentin ate, like, half, but there's still some left. Thought you might want it. You know, if you were still alive. Which you are. Thankfully." He closes his eyes, admonishing himself for rambling. After running his palm down his face, he flashes me an embarrassed smile.

Sydney leans in. "You're doing a great job, Jackson," she tells him encouragingly.

He thanks her, and his eyes find mine. He reaches out with the bag so I can grab it through the bars.

Before I take it, Sydney points to a hidden section of the bars where the rusted metal is cracked, offering enough space for me to slip through. It would break several rules to do so, and I have a strong moment of doubt, thinking about Anton's warning: *Be better next time.*

But it also would be rude to leave Jackson standing there without at least seeing why he came all this way. I feel a shot of adrenaline as I slip through the bars.

Sydney checks over her shoulder and tells me to be careful. I hear the echo of the other girls' feet jogging this way. "See you in fifteen," she adds, winking at me. She exchanges a quick goodbye with Jackson and then runs to rejoin the girls.

My heart is thumping wildly as Jackson and I walk a few yards into the woods to keep out of sight. We find a thick patch of bushes with a broken log behind them that we can sit on. It's a little damp, but I don't mind. When Jackson sits next to me, the wood creaking, I notice scratches on his hand, and a few marks on his leather coat.

"You're hurt," I say, concerned. I trace one of the longer scratches on his hand with my fingertip, never actually touching him.

Jackson inspects his scratches now that I've pointed them out. "Huh," he says. "Well, yeah. Those woods are downright treacherous. Not exactly student-friendly."

"We never come out here," I say, glancing up at the tree canopies. "And if I'm honest, I can't believe you did." I look sideways at him and see his breath catch when I do. "Did you really think I was dead?" I ask.

"No," he says. "Not really. Okay, sort of, which is why I had to come check on you. I navigated those woods only to find an impenetrable fence—or so I thought—and then I saw your friends jogging. I hoped they wouldn't think I was an ax murderer.

Thankfully Sydney recognized me and held up her finger to tell me to hold on. That was like . . ." He pauses, thinking about it. "Twenty minutes ago."

"You've been out here that long?" I ask.

"Longer." He widens his eyes. "This was not a well-thought-out plan."

I laugh, and he holds out the bag of candy to me. I thank him politely and reach in to take the sour candies. He does the same with his chocolate kisses.

"So . . . ," he says. "If you don't mind me asking, what the fuck kind of school is this?"

"What do you mean?"

"What do I mean?" he repeats surprised. "This place belongs to a technology firm—or at least it used to. Not to mention some asshole grabbed you and physically pulled you from the store. He yanked you outside. I should have done more to stop him."

I'm embarrassed that he's brought up my behavior. "I didn't listen," I say quietly, and pick through the candy. I'm fidgeting, I realize suddenly, and stop to pay attention to Jackson again.

He stares at me, and I sense the worry in his expression.

"Who are your parents, Mena?" he asks. "Why are you here? I'm sure there are other schools that want to 'make girls great again,' or whatever bullshit people still believe, but why one so isolated? Why *this* one?"

His question surprises me. "Because this is one of the most esteemed finishing schools in the country. Extensive training on social etiquette. It's elite."

"Okay . . . ," he says, unimpressed. "And your parents? They're okay with some guy grabbing you?"

"If I earned it? Yes," I say. "My parents trust the academy. And they're very smart people. My father runs a law firm and my mother is a philanthropist. She's thinking of running for office one day."

Jackson looks away, shifting his boots in the grass. "Yeah, well," he says. "If she thinks you deserve this, she's not getting my fucking vote."

I'm not sure why, but I smile. I kind of enjoy his behavior, the bluntness of it. Like he's saying exactly what he's thinking. He notices my smile and laughs at himself.

"I waited a day, you know," he adds. "I was worried about you, debated what to do. I almost followed the bus back here. But Q talked me down. Told me to make a plan. But I couldn't wait that long, so I . . . I showed up. Some plan, right?"

I appreciate his concern. It's different from the way the academy worries about me. Jackson doesn't seem to care about my manners, about my hair or makeup—things he hasn't mentioned even once.

"Seems like a good plan to me," I say, and hold out the bag of candy to him. He licks his lower lip, and then reaches to take out another piece of chocolate.

Although I was hesitant about my behavior at first, Jackson's continued casual manners set me at ease. Sunlight filters through the clouds and branches, landing near my feet. I move so my sneaker can be in the warmth. I stare at the woods, listening to the birds chirping. It's really peaceful out here.

"Would you like a kiss?" Jackson asks.

Heat swarms my face, and when I turn to him, he holds out a small, silver-covered chocolate. He smiles at my blush.

"Thank you," I say, taking it from between his fingers. Jackson turns back toward the academy, sweeping his eyes over the stone façade. Pausing at the barred windows.

"So it's a school now," he says. "Looks the same, you know, other than the terrifying sign they added near the road. Might as well be a skull and crossbones."

"Wait," I say, sitting up straighter. "You've been on campus before?"

"Yeah," he says. "On the property. Back before it was all overgrown. Before they put a fence around it."

"When was the last time you were here?" I ask, fascinated. The idea that Jackson has been to the academy before is thrilling. It's like we suddenly have so much in common, even though rationally, we probably don't.

"Four years ago," he says, avoiding my eyes. "When I was fourteen. I used to run away a lot. I was a bit of a fuckup, if I'm honest. I would usually stay at Q's house, but every so often, his parents would look worried, and I'd know it was time to take off for a while. Pretend to go home. Instead, we'd find places— old buildings, places to camp. My parents would always track me down, though. Eventually had to go to court. Was given community service where I literally spent one hundred hours picking up trash on the freeway."

"Why did you run away from home?" I ask. I'm astonished

at the idea of hiding from your own parents. It seems so . . . disrespectful.

"My dad," Jackson says. "My dad could be a real . . ." He stops himself and looks at the school again. "We didn't get along," Jackson says instead. "We had different values. And I didn't like the way he treated my mother."

"And now?"

Jackson flicks his eyes to mine, pausing a long moment before answering. "Now it's just the two of us, so we don't have a choice."

"Two of you?"

"My mother died," he says, and then swallows hard. "She died three years ago, and my father sobered up real quick."

There is a sudden ache in my heart. I've never known anyone who's died. "I'm so sorry," I say.

"I know you are," he says, wincing, "and I have no idea why I just told you that. It was stupid. I'm sorry." He looks away, vulnerable. Still pained. He clearly doesn't want to talk about it.

We sit quietly, eating candy. It's not uncomfortable, despite the lack of conversation. When Jackson turns back to me, his expression softens.

"So what about you?" he asks. "You've been here eight months. How often do you go home?"

"Never," I say.

"What?" he asks. "You just . . . You stay here?"

"Yes. We live here full-time. It's an accelerated program."

"Do you sneak out often?" he asks.

"Me?" I ask. "No, never. But they don't physically monitor

us on the grounds the way they do when we're off campus."

"If you don't sneak out, then what do you do? For fun, I mean."

"The girls and I talk a lot," I say. "We tell stories. Gossip. Sometimes about boys." I grin.

"*Boys?*" he replies, like it's scandalous. "Plural? You see a lot of boys around here?"

"None," I say. "Which is why we gossip about them."

He laughs. "Will I make the list?"

"You already have," I say seriously. "We've made all sorts of assumptions about you. I can't wait to tell them what I've learned. You are fascinating," I say.

Jackson flinches. "Can I ask you something, Mena?"

I nod that he can.

"Could you . . . I mean, would you mind not telling your friends that stuff about my mom?" he asks. "Any of it? It's kind of personal."

I hadn't really considered that, but I understand his point. I don't lie to the girls, but I can just leave that part out.

"I won't tell them," I promise, and Jackson smiles gratefully. We're quiet for a moment before he moves suddenly like he just remembered something.

"I meant to ask," he says, taking a phone out of his pocket. "Do you think I can call you? I . . . like talking to you. Hearing about your school. *And* it'll help me sleep at night, knowing you're okay behind all those bars."

"Personal phones aren't allowed on campus," I tell him. "The only phone we have is a shared one in the hallway."

"E-mail?"

I shake my head no. "We don't have computers."

"That's bullshit," Jackson mumbles, sliding his phone back into his pocket. "And weird considering this place used to be a tech company." He considers the statement. "But who knows?" he adds. "A few years ago, the government tried to lock everyone out of the internet—some big push to control the narrative, remember?"

I don't answer, not wanting to mention that I didn't have a computer at home, either.

Jackson shakes his head. "That was scary stuff." He looks over at the school. "Thankfully it didn't last. But maybe it made Innovations reassess their goals. No more assembly lines. Now they specialize in girls."

"And gardening," I say, motioning to the greenhouse. "We grow the most beautiful flowers."

Jackson watches me a moment, amused. "Although I'm sure that's very lucrative," he says with a small laugh, "I'm going to guess tuition here is pretty high. You know, since the place is so 'elite.' I wonder how they select which girls get in."

On the first day of school, Mr. Petrov told us about the process. He said that he and the professors scoured the country, searching for girls with the perfect blend of beauty and temperament. We were hand-selected based on these traits. Our parents were delighted.

But I don't think this criteria will impress Jackson, so I opt not to share it.

Jackson relaxes back on his hands, taking in the academy once again. "You know," he adds, "I bet there's still some old equipment lying around the building. You should poke through the closets once in a while. See what you find."

"I can't do that," I say, scrunching up my nose. He pops another candy into his mouth.

"I would," he says easily. Not even a hint of guilt. When he looks at me, we both smile.

He's so unlike the men I've met at the academy, or even before. Most of my interactions are a well-rehearsed dance, expected. Jackson is the opposite of rehearsed. He's messy and unpredictable.

"You're exciting," I tell him. "You drove an hour with a badly formed plan to check on me. You swear and run away from home. You even nearly fought the Guardian in a gas station."

"I try to fuck up where I can."

"You're good at it," I say, making him laugh.

Jackson takes another chocolate and unwraps it slowly. I watch him, noting his movements.

"Are you left-handed?" I ask.

He seems surprised by the question and looks down at his open palm. "I am. You?"

"No. But I've never met anyone who was left-handed before," I say.

"It doesn't sound like you meet a lot of people, Mena." He holds out his hand to me, and before I can think about it, I slide my palm along his, noting how rough his skin is. Liking the way it scratches me, contrasts me.

Jackson lifts his dark eyes to mine, and for a moment, we just stare at each other. There's a sudden pressure in my chest, a breathlessness I've never experienced before. Jackson licks his lower lip again, and then slowly withdraws his hand. He turns toward the sound of the girls running, rounding the building for likely the last time.

"I should probably get back," I say, getting to my feet.

Jackson walks me toward the fence, and we pause as we reach the iron bars. I wish I could stay just a little longer, but I appreciate the time we've had.

"There's an open house tonight," I tell him. "Goes kind of late, so we don't have Running Course tomorrow. But . . . I'll be back out here on Sunday. If you're in the area."

"This mountainous, middle-of-fucking-nowhere area?" he asks. "Yeah, of course I'll be here. Besides, we didn't finish all the candy." He holds up the bag.

I laugh. The sound of sneakers hitting the dirt gets louder as the girls run along the building, getting closer. Sydney hangs near the back of the group.

"Then I'll see you Sunday," I say. "And bring the candy."

He grins before nodding goodbye. I turn around to slip back through the fence, joining the girls for the rest of our morning run.

7

As the girls and I finish our run and head toward the door, we find Guardian Bose waiting for us, watching us intently. I nearly trip over my feet, worried that I've been caught breaking the rules; I see the same flash of fear in Sydney's eyes. But the Guardian just waves us in impatiently. He never lets us deviate from our schedule.

I try to keep my distance so he won't smell candy on my breath, and once we're past him, Sydney and I exchange a relieved look. We start toward our rooms to get ready for classes.

As we walk down the hall, the other girls ahead of us, Sydney loops her arm through mine.

"And how is Jackson?" she asks quietly, leaning her head closer to mine.

"He's coming back on Sunday," I say with a flicker of nervousness. Excitement. I don't want to get caught disobeying twice in one week, chance being redirected again. But I liked listening to Jackson. And I liked that he listened to me.

To get her opinion, I tell Sydney everything that Jackson and I talked about with the exception of his family. We discuss his hiking through the woods, his lack of manners, and how I held his hand, even if only for a moment. How he was worried about me, asked about me. I think that part impresses her the most.

We get to our floor, and Sydney exhales dramatically. "I say you go for it," she says. "Just make sure he doesn't try anything inappropriate on Sunday. Even if his manners are brutish, keep *yours* intact. Otherwise you'll give him the wrong idea."

She's right. The rules are there to keep us safe. I vow to be careful, even crossing my heart to show I'm serious.

Sydney snorts a laugh before we part to get ready for class.

As I shower, the taste of candy still on my tongue, I take extra time to shave my legs carefully, moisturize after, and blow-dry my hair. I don't want to have to do it all before the party.

We're required to look our best tonight. The Head of School will check us over before we walk out, and request changes if needed. He tends to like my hair pulled up for formal events, so I know to style it that way, a few curls framing my face. He likes Sydney's hair straight or with big waves. And Lennon Rose must have her hair down at all times. There are more "specifications"— that's what he calls them—and it's up to us to meet his goals and then exceed them.

After slipping on my uniform and required makeup (foundation, blush, eyeliner, eye shadow, lipstick, mascara), I head to my morning classes. Professor Penchant discusses posture in Modesty and Decorum, while Professor Levin has us create party invitations in Modern Manners using the open house as our example. We've created these invitations several times before with little to no variation, but I like using the felt-tipped pens, so I don't mind.

In Social Graces Etiquette, we read about the Federal Flower Garden again. Professor Allister says we need to understand the importance of beautiful things, so we just keep going over it.

Class goes by slowly, and I find myself staring out the window into the foggy morning, toward the woods. They're thick, and they take up a few acres between us and the road, the iron fence slowly getting swallowed up by the growing brush. I wonder if one day the entire school will be enveloped, vines snaking inside the windows, smashing the glass, and wrapping around the bars.

But then I imagine Jackson lost in the woods this morning, trying to get to me, misguided and good-hearted. I smile and rest my chin on my palm.

"Philomena?" Professor Allister calls. Startled, I look up to find him waiting.

"I'm sorry, what?" I ask. He sighs and taps the white board with a pointer stick.

"When was the Federal Flower Garden erected?" he asks for what I assume is the second time.

"Three years ago," I answer, feeling the heat from the stares of the other girls in class.

"And why?" Professor Allister follows up.

"Because beautiful things need to be preserved," I recite. "Put on a pedestal. The flowers are an example to be emulated. Only beautiful things have value."

"Excellent," he says, nodding. He sweeps his eyes over me once and then turns back to the class to continue with his lesson.

I rest my chin on my palm and stare out the window again.

After yesterday's excitement at the gas station, and today's excitement beyond the fence with Jackson, I can barely keep my head in the classroom, drifting out into the woods and looking for adventure. Sydney has to kick my shoe twice in Etiquette, and I miss a lesson on proper phone manners. I've heard it before, though. They treat us like we forget everything the moment we walk out of class. But in fact, we're excellent learners.

As I continue to analyze my interaction with Jackson today, I recognize that it doesn't line up with what the academy teaches us at all. It's a contradiction that I need clarification on.

I raise my hand and Professor Allister points at me, surprised. "Yes, Philomena?"

"I have a question about etiquette," I say, earning a few looks from the other girls. "In-person etiquette."

The professor nods for me to continue.

"When having a conversation . . . ," I start, considering my words. "When the man is very casual, is it proper to be casual in return?"

"Of course not, Philomena," he says. "If you are conversing with a man, it is up to you to be pleasing and appropriate. Bad manners on your part show him you're not worth his time."

My heart sinks. Was I too casual with Jackson? If so, he might not return on Sunday.

"And this is a good lesson," the professor says, addressing the class. "You must always be on your best behavior—a man will expect it. You represent the finest girls society has to offer. You represent Innovations Academy. Act accordingly."

Several girls nod, but I swallow hard, regretting my earlier behavior. The past two days have left me lost, making mistakes I've never made before. I have to be better.

My last lesson of the day is Basics, and for that, I'm grateful. It's a math day, and we're working up to more complicated stuff—basic fractions to use while measuring ingredients or soil we use for our plants.

Although Innovations is an academy, they're also growing their own produce, hybrid flowers, as well as plants used in our juices and vitamins. Annalise said the gardening teacher—Professor Driscoll—told her the academy hopes to go wide with the formulas. He said we've been a great example of their success.

Annalise smiles at me from across the classroom. All of us are eager to learn today. It never lasts, though—we won't get another math lesson this month.

"*Too much thinking is bad for your looks*," Professor Slowski says at least once a week in Basics, like it's our running joke. But each time he says it, we wilt a little. We're hungry for knowledge, but we don't want it to adversely affect us.

When class is dismissed twenty minutes later, we're told to have lunch and prepare for the party. The families and sponsors will begin to arrive around four, and dinner is served around five. We're served salad, even though we'd much rather eat the rubbery chicken and potatoes. Then again, too much change in our diet makes us sick. But the occasional candy isn't too bad, I've found.

I wave to Sydney as she exits her class, and we walk together toward the dining hall for lunch. Our salads and juices are already set out on the table, and Sydney and I sit down. Lennon Rose smiles when we join her and the other girls.

Brynn immediately starts to tell us about her dress for the open house—a soft lavender, which is Mr. Petrov's favorite color on her. Brynn feels it clashes with her hair, but the Head of School knows best.

"I have another black dress," Marcella says, sounding disappointed. "I was hoping it'd be red this time. Anton said that—"

"Can I sit here?" a voice asks suddenly, startling us.

The girls and I look up, surprised to find Valentine Wright standing at the end of our table, smiling politely.

Valentine is wearing the required uniform with delicate white socks, black shoes, and a bow tied in her hair. She's perfectly poised, and yet . . . and yet there's something different about her. A sharp edge I can't quite see but sense is there. It's puzzling, and I furrow my brow as I try to pinpoint the source of the feeling.

Marcella slides over to make room for Valentine at the table, the other girls watching curiously. Valentine has never sat with us before. When she takes a spot directly across from me and reaches for a salad, I study her a moment longer.

Her skin is bright and clear with the exception of a small bruise near the inside corner of her eye, the bluish color so subtle that the other girls might not even notice, almost like a pinprick.

Valentine thanks us for letting her join us and begins to eat. She offers no other comment, but obviously something is different. Why did she come to sit with us in the first place? I lean into the table toward Valentine.

"How are you feeling?" I ask her.

Valentine pauses, staring at the piece of lettuce balanced on her fork, and then lifts her head.

"I feel well," she responds automatically. "Anton was able to help me work through my problems. We completed impulse control therapy, and he offered me coping mechanisms. I'm one hundred percent now." She smiles. "I've made him very proud."

Sydney shifts uncomfortably and turns to me. But I continue to watch Valentine as she raises her fork and eats the bite of salad nonchalantly. The girls and I are quiet until Annalise sighs impatiently.

"What happened to you on the bus?" Annalise asks Valentine. "You directly defied the Guardian. What were you thinking?"

Valentine finishes her mouthful of food, and then dots the corners of her mouth with a napkin before looking up at us.

"I was defiant," she responds simply. "I regret the choice I made. But Anton was able to help me work through my problems. We completed impulse control therapy, and he offered me coping mechanisms," she repeats as if it's the first time she said it. "I'm one hundred percent now." She smiles. "I've made him very proud."

Annalise's complexion pales, and she shifts her eyes to mine. None of us follow up on the question, taken aback by Valentine's practiced response. After impulse control therapy, girls typically sit alone and stay quiet—at least for a while. I've never noticed this sort of behavior change before. This seems deeper, more controlled.

Then again, we've never asked a girl *why* she ended up in impulse control therapy. We accept the consequence as deserved and move on. Perhaps our question was too personal. We should have deferred to the school's policy of giving a girl space after therapy, even if Valentine is the one who sat with us.

To fill the silence, Brynn starts talking about dresses again, and the other girls seem relieved for the usual conversation. But I'm still thinking about Valentine's behavior modification, watching as she eats quietly. Peacefully.

I glance over to the professors' table, and find Guardian Bose with them, watching us.

There's something disconcerting about his attention, as if he's been watching the entire time but I've only just noticed. So that he doesn't think I'm ungrateful, I dip my chin in thanks for his care, and he returns the gesture with exaggerated slowness. I finish eating in silence.

We're dismissed from lunch a short time later. Annalise and Lennon Rose are on cleanup duty while the rest of us head back to our rooms to prepare for tonight's open house.

I walk with Sydney, but on the way, I glance back at Valentine. Her expression is empty, vacant. But when she catches me looking, she smiles. I turn around quickly and take Sydney's arm.

". . . and I promised Lennon Rose I'd do her makeup tonight,"

Sydney says, midconversation. "The blue shadow I have matches her dress perfectly."

"I'll come by before we line up to witness your expertise," I say.

Sydney grins, telling me she'll see me later, and then goes into her room. When her door closes, I turn toward mine. I jump when I find myself alone in the hall with Valentine.

She's standing there expectantly, waiting for me. She tilts her head to the side.

"I had a delightful memory recently," she says in a faraway voice. "Do you remember the time Annalise asked us to paint her hair yellow? She said she was supposed to be blond, not a redhead. She was distraught. So you stole paints from art class and painted it yellow for her. She looked beautiful. Anton was furious with you."

"What are you talking about?" I ask. "That . . . That never happened."

Valentine smiles. "It was nice, then," she adds, ignoring my comment. "I miss it."

I've never stolen paints and I've certainly never painted Annalise's hair. Valentine must still be adjusting after impulse control therapy, confusing her thoughts. Maybe the other girls and I should let Anton know.

"Well, see you at the open house," Valentine says pleasantly. She turns on her heel and heads to her room, quietly closing the door with a click.

I stand there an extra moment, perplexed. A little frightened. But the emotion fades and I decide I'll ask Sydney her thoughts when I go to her room later.

To: Stuart, Anton

RE: Philomena Rhodes

From: Allister, Tobias

Today at 1:05 PM

Per our discussion, I've taken note of Philomena's behavior in class. She has been daydreaming again, and also asking questions about interactions with men. Although her mannerisms seem consistent, I have concerns, especially after Valentine Wright's outburst. I do not want a repeat of last time.

If the daydreams do not abate, then I suggest impulse control therapy to rid her of this nasty habit.

Sincerely,

Tobias Allister

8

After I'm dressed, I go to Sydney's room to watch her apply Lennon Rose's eye makeup (Sydney is absolutely brilliant at cosmetology and aces every tutorial Leandra gives us), but Lennon Rose never shows. I hang out anyway, pulling up the low neckline of my dress, the material itchy on my skin.

Sydney places the last swipe of highlighter under her brow bone. As she got ready, I had a chance to tell her about my strange conversation with Valentine. When she sets down her brush, Sydney turns to me, tapping her lower lip with her index finger.

"Yellow hair?" she asks, as if that's the troubling part. "First of all, Annalise would *never* let you touch her hair. Definitely not with paint. And Valentine said she was with you?"

"Said it was nice," I tell her. "That she misses it."

"Weird," Sydney murmurs.

"I was going to ask if we should tell Anton," I say, "but I'm afraid to get her in trouble so soon after impulse control therapy.

She might just need a few days to adjust. What do you think we should do?"

"Talk to her," Sydney suggests, turning to me. "Ask Valentine what's going on with her. She obviously trusts you. Otherwise she wouldn't keep telling you random, creepy things."

I laugh but decide she's right. I have no idea why I'm the one Valentine shares her odd thoughts with, but it's worth exploring. There's probably a simple explanation.

We talk for a few more minutes before Guardian Bose calls us into the hallway. Sydney and I slip on our heels, take one last look at our reflections, and then head out for lineup. Lennon Rose and Valentine walk out of Lennon Rose's room, all made up. I find it odd that they're together. Especially when Lennon Rose avoids my eyes.

Guardian Bose gives each of us a quick once-over before leading us down the stairs toward the ballroom. He grins at Annalise in her short, pink dress—Mr. Petrov's preference.

Always show your legs, Mr. Petrov told her specifically. *They're your best asset.*

Personally, I think it's her smile. It's very warm and inviting.

"My parents want to talk about plans for after graduation," Sydney says over the clicking of heels on the stairs. She looks over at me, excited.

"I can't wait to hear them," I say. "Remember every detail." She promises that she will.

My parents have never spoken to me about graduation; I have no idea what their plans are for me. I even talked to Anton about it once. He assured me that my parents are still invested in my education, but he said that these decisions were too important for me to be a part of. He told me that impatience was a negative trait and asked me not to think of it again.

Most of us will get married and tend beautiful homes. We'll appear on our husbands' arms at important events—making them proud. Others will make our parents proud. Or whomever Mr. Petrov sees fit to guide us through society.

I can't help but wonder what the future holds for me. But every time I try to imagine it, I hear Anton telling me again "not to think of it," and the thoughts fade away.

"Will your parents be here tonight?" Sydney asks.

"No," I say. "Eva told me they're out of town." I'm stricken with loneliness again. The sense of not belonging to anyone. Anywhere.

"You never know," Sydney says, taking my hand. "They might surprise you."

I look sideways at her with a small burst of hope. "You think?"

She shrugs, bumping her shoulder into mine. "If I were your mother, I wouldn't miss it for the world." I smile, loving her support.

"Come along, girls," Guardian Bose calls, waving us into the hallway that leads to the ballroom. We pause there, single file, and wait.

We're quiet, a few girls adjusting their hair to fall perfectly over their shoulders or smoothing their lips together. Rebecca Hunt pulls up the bust of her dress in the front of the line, fidgeting before the Head of School gets to her.

I catch the soft murmur of conversation behind me: something . . . tense.

I glance over my shoulder, surprised when I find Lennon Rose five girls back in conversation with Valentine. For her part, Valentine looks impeccable in a silver, floor-length gown, her hair pulled into a high bun. But her expression isn't soft and obedient. Her eyes are slits, fierce. I can't hear what she's whispering, her lips moving urgently like she's reciting words rather than conversing. But whatever she's saying, it's affecting Lennon Rose, who wraps her arms around the waist of her blue dress, her chest heaving in startled breaths.

I move away from Sydney, about to intervene, when there is a loud clap from the front of the line. I turn and see Mr. Petrov approach. Leandra is dutifully by his side, her gaze gliding over each of us. I quickly get back in line to wait for inspection.

Mr. Petrov and Leandra slowly make their way past each of us, the Head of School raking his eyes over our figures, ensuring our dresses fit perfectly. Leandra leans in to Annalise and smudges some of the blush off her cheeks, telling her it looks cheap.

They move on to Sydney, and Mr. Petrov nods appreciatively, telling her the color is beautiful against her skin. She flashes a wide smile in return. Leandra, on the other hand, grips Sydney's hips like she's measuring them.

"Schedule Running Course for the morning," Leandra says coldly. "You're filling out this dress. I suspect you're up a pound. That's not acceptable, Sydney. You represent this academy."

Sydney's smile falters, and she lowers her head, apologizing for her appearance. My stomach sinks; I think she looks amazing.

I have to fight to hold my smile when the Head of School and his wife reach me.

Leandra inspects me first, but I'm surprised when she doesn't say anything at all. Instead, she studies my eyes. It feels almost invasive, the way she holds my stare. Like she's saying something I can't hear.

Mr. Petrov reaches out to run his finger along the neckline of my dress, grazing the skin of my chest as he traces the low cut. It sends a chill down my back.

"This is very flattering on you, Philomena," he says, slow to remove his hand. "I dare say you could go lower."

"If you think so, sir," I say politely, even though I already feel too exposed. We dress modestly with the exception of these open houses. Mr. Petrov says it's because investors want to get a good look at us so they know how flawless we are. The inconsistency in our wardrobe leaves me uncertain—modesty or exposed skin? There seems to be a different rule based on Mr. Petrov's . . . preference.

The Head of School moves toward the next girl, but Leandra hangs back an extra second, still watching my reaction. Waiting.

I press my lips together, as if thanking her, but there's a flicker of disappointment in her expression before she walks past me to join her husband. I'm left a bit confused, and when I go to tell Sydney about it, I see she's still feeling badly about her evaluation. I decide not to burden her any more.

"Ah . . . ," Mr. Petrov calls out lovingly. We all turn and find him taking Valentine by the hand, leading her out of line to show her off. He spins her around, admiring her. "Now, this," he says, "is perfection." Valentine dips in a bow, the front of her dress sloping down to expose her cleavage. Mr. Petrov doesn't take his eyes off her, still holding her hand.

Leandra watches on, a pleasant expression on her face. When Valentine returns to her place in line and Mr. Petrov walks to Lennon Rose, Leandra and Valentine exchange a private look. It's only a moment, a split second, and then Valentine turns forward again and smiles. When she notices me, she lifts one eyebrow. Rather than indulge whatever weirdness she's about to say, I look past her toward Lennon Rose.

My heart skips and I quickly reach out to grab Sydney's arm. She turns to look before taking an anxious step forward.

"Now what is this about?" Mr. Petrov says in a fatherly tone as he guides Lennon Rose from the line. He yanks a handkerchief out of his suit pocket and hands it to her. Leandra sighs, seemingly annoyed.

Lennon Rose is crying. Her makeup is running down her cheeks in black and blue rivers. She uses Mr. Petrov's tissue to dot the area, but she's clearly distraught.

I flick an accusatory look at Valentine, but she doesn't meet my eyes this time. She's still smiling, though. Not even acknowledging Lennon Rose's breakdown.

"Leandra, darling," Mr. Petrov says. "Can you please take our little rose upstairs and fix her up?"

"Of course," Leandra says, taking her by the arm. Although it looks gentle, Lennon Rose's winces at the touch. We all watch in stunned silence as Lennon Rose is led back to the rooms.

It has to be because of Valentine. I can't imagine that she would purposely upset Lennon Rose—she knows how sensitive she is—but clearly, she said *something* wrong.

"Marcella," Mr. Petrov says, nodding his head to her. "A vision as always. I know your parents will be proud." She thanks him.

The Head of School turns to Brynn, taking his time examining her. And then, almost impulsively, he steps closer and leans in to kiss her cheek. Brynn jumps, but as Mr. Petrov pulls back, she smiles at him.

"You'll be a beautiful bride one day soon," he tells her. "And your husband will be a very lucky man, indeed."

Mr. Petrov turns to inspect the next girl, but Brynn continues to stare straight ahead, smile held. Eyes shiny. It isn't until Marcella reaches back to take her hand that Brynn lets out a held breath. I'm reminded of Lennon Rose's question in my room. And the answer: Mr. Petrov knows what's best for us. I ignore my feelings on the matter, and I turn around, opting not to watch any more of the inspections.

The first thing I notice is the bright red lipstick stain on the wineglass. The liquid has been abandoned at one of the tables near the sofa shortly after dinner, and I make my way over to sit on the velvet cushion closest to it. As the music from the piano drifts over the room, I search for the other girls and find nearly all of them occupied.

Sydney is smiling, beaming under her parents' attention. I've always liked her family. They dress smartly, but not lavishly—no furs or overemphatic jewelry. Sydney told me once that her parents saved their entire adult lives to be able to afford sending her here. She does everything she can to make them proud.

Tonight, Sydney looks gorgeous in the sequined blush dress. Her mother and father exchange pleased looks as Sydney tells them a story. I feel a twinge of pride too. Sydney is dynamic and lovely. I'm lucky to have her in my life.

Sadly, she was wrong about my parents. They didn't show up unexpectedly. I was prepared, of course. But . . . I did have a small bit of hope they would find a way to see me. Maybe next time.

It hasn't gone unnoticed that my parents have missed all three open houses this year, even though the girls don't bring it up. Anton tells me not to dwell on their absence. I try not to, but sometimes it's hard not to wallow a little.

A loud laugh near the door startles me. I turn in that direction and see Marcella entertaining her parents. She must feel me watching her, because she looks over at me, and then at the wineglass. She flashes me a smile as if telling me to go for it. I sniff a laugh and turn to survey the rest of the room.

Lennon Rose's parents are here, even though she hasn't arrived yet. The couple is talking with Dr. Groger near the buffet table, drinks in hand. Serious expressions.

Lennon Rose's mother is rail thin, elegant with heavy black brows and black hair. Her father has graying dark hair, brown eyes, and a stern chin. Lennon Rose's parents are looking forward to bringing her home, grateful for the opportunity to raise an Innovations Girl—I've heard them say as much. They look positively forlorn now.

There's a flash of pink fabric, and I turn just as Annalise drops onto the couch next to me. She tries to follow my line of vision. "Who are we staring at?" she asks, sounding bored.

"Lennon Rose's parents," I say.

Annalise juts out her bottom lip. "I noticed them too," she says. "Hopefully Lennon Rose will be here soon."

She shifts her eyes to mine, but we don't mention the possibility that she might not. We still don't even know why she was crying in line. At the thought of it, I look for Valentine and find her with her sponsor—her uncle—smiling and sipping seltzer water.

"She'll be back," Annalise murmurs about Lennon Rose. "Everyone has a bad day once in a while."

It's a normal thing to say, a phrase we've heard in movies. But it's not exactly true at the academy. The last time I had a bad day, I was in impulse control therapy for twenty-four hours.

An uncomfortable thought scratches in my head, out of my reach. Dread crawls under my skin. I elect to change the subject.

Annalise sighs heavily and sits back against the sofa. She crosses her long legs, one of her stiletto heels dangling off her toes. Her feet are probably killing her, but Mr. Petrov requires at least a six-inch heel at all events. He says they're the most flattering.

"Do you think any of these people do number four?" Annalise asks casually.

I burst out laughing and quickly put my palm over my mouth when I garner several discouraging stares.

There are prospective parents and sponsors here, as well as investors. The parents want to know if Innovations Academy can make their daughters exceptional—beautiful, respectful, obedient. Sponsors have a girl with potential, a relative or family friend, that they think will be a perfect fit. Then there are the investors—people without a girl who share the academy's mission to make us all better. Extraordinary girls. Extraordinary school.

The investors are the ones we have to impress most, Professor Penchant told us at the beginning of the year. *Demonstrate your value to those in attendance by showing how appealing a beautiful, obedient girl can be. Hold your tongue. Bat your eyes. Smile. Be best.*

After meeting us, many of the prospective parents apply for their girls to attend Innovations. Few are selected. The rarity makes us more elite, I'm told.

But no prospective *students* ever attend these open houses. Their parents make the decision for them. I'm not sure when my parents decided to send me here. One day, we just showed up at the academy. We never even had a discussion about it—at least, not one that I remember.

I try not to think about it. Because every day that I'm at Innovations, my life before the academy grows a little foggier. The past getting farther away. Disappearing.

It's not something I've mentioned to Anton; it's never come up. And I haven't told the other girls because it doesn't seem important enough to worry them. Besides, it doesn't really matter. I'm going to be a better girl after graduation.

I'm lucky to be here, I think. *I'm lucky to be at such an esteemed academy.*

Rebecca Hunt stands in the corner of the room, holding a glass of water while her lawyer holds an animated conversation with several guests. It's odd, the way Rebecca seems to fade into the shadows on the wall. Trying to disappear rather than be on display.

Suddenly, a former student, Carolina Deschutes, sweeps into the ballroom wearing an extravagant gown, her grandmother on her arm. It's rare for us to see alumni, but the Deschuteses make every open house.

Two girls, Andrea and Maryanne, rush over to Carolina, fawning over her peacock-inspired dress. She spins so they can take it all in, her grandmother beaming proudly at her side. And her grandmother is a spectacle herself. I once heard Anton call her, "Our very own Miss Havisham." But I don't understand the reference.

Grandmother Deschutes is at least eighty and barely five feet tall. She's wearing a navy gown with a black stole, a sparkly headband in her short, gray hair. Her makeup is heavy, her eyelids painted purple.

Grandmother Deschutes has had three granddaughters attend Innovations Academy. Two of them are now married to very prestigious men, I've heard. She plans to have another granddaughter attend in the fall. The Deschutes name is quickly becoming a legacy, especially considering that Innovations Academy has only graduated twenty girls in the past three years.

This year will be different, though—that's what Mr. Petrov says. We're *all* on track for graduation. The academy's most accomplished class of girls yet.

"My word, Philomena," Annalise whispers. "Grandmother Deschutes is easily the most fabulous woman alive." She turns to me wide-eyed. "I want to be her when I grow up."

"Carolina looks great too," I add.

"Yes, of course," Annalise allows as if it's not the exciting part.

"Stand up straighter," a woman's voice calls. I turn to see Brynn being fussed over by her mother. "What are they even teaching you in this school?" the woman asks bitterly, yanking on the braid in Brynn's hair and making her wince. "You look like a slob," she adds.

I watch them, but I don't intervene. We don't disrespect adults at Innovations Academy.

Brynn's mother adjusts her hair roughly. When she's finished, the braid is redone and slicked in a way that's more sophisticated, less Brynn. Her mother grabs her by the upper arm and swings her around to face the other side of the room.

"Now go talk to your father," she orders. "You need to prove that you're worth the money we've pumped into your education."

Brynn swallows hard, her blue eyes downcast from the insults, but she doesn't talk back. "What should I say?" Brynn asks in a quiet voice.

"See that gentleman next to him?" her mother asks, pointing across the room to a man in a gray suit. "That's the new junior partner—ambitious, ruthless. He's vying for your father's position.

But . . . ," she says, turning to study the side of Brynn's face. "Mr. Callis wants a beautiful girl who can raise his children—they're still small, you see. And you'll be perfect for the position."

"What about their mother?" Brynn asks, confused.

"She's not your concern. Now," she directs Brynn, "go say hello. Charm him. Be a *prize*, and he'll come begging for your father's favor."

Brynn's eyes flutter for a moment, but then she makes her way over to her father and the other man, looking confident.

Brynn's parents have put her on a specialized track at the academy, one that offers a class in childhood development. She enjoys it. In fact, Brynn's mentioned several times how she can't wait to have children of her own. "A whole pile of them," she says with a smile. But, of course, that will be up to her parents and Mr. Petrov.

"I'm going outside to get some air," I tell Annalise, standing up from the couch. She waves and tells me to have fun.

I make my way through the party toward the glass doors of the patio. Cool air rushes to meet me when I slide the door open, and I shiver against it. I'm surprised to find Lennon Rose's parents already out here, arguing. Her mother, Mrs. Scholar, has a fresh drink in her hand, the liquid sloshing around as she talks animatedly.

"They can't just *keep* her," she hisses, grabbing her husband's forearm.

I freeze, not sure if I should slip back inside before they notice me, but it's too late.

Mr. Scholar turns in my direction and instinctively puts his hand over his wife's to stop her from talking. Mrs. Scholar looks at me, and I note the glassiness in her eyes, the smudges of mascara in the creases around them. She blinks rapidly and then takes a shaky sip from her drink.

"Hello, darling," she says, sweeping her gaze over me. Only she says it like she might cry, my presence making her miserable.

"Hello, Mr. and Mrs. Scholar," I say pleasantly. "How are you tonight?" I have no idea what to say when they both appear upset. Possibly drunk. Mr. Scholar nods his greeting and takes his wife's hand.

"Thank you for asking," he says to me. "We're just fine. But we should get back inside. Come along, Diane."

He pulls his wife behind him, but as they pass me, Mrs. Scholar brushes her fingers along my arm. When I hear the door close, I turn to make sure they've gone. My heart is in my throat.

Keep her—what does that mean? What's happened to Lennon Rose?

9

rub my arms in the chilly night weather before deciding to go back inside to look for Lennon Rose. When I open the glass doors, a blast of heat hits my face and several people look in my direction.

I'm newly concerned that Lennon Rose still hasn't returned to the party. I search for Leandra, or even Dr. Groger. Instead, I spot Anton across the room. I smile my relief. The analyst will know what's going on.

I move toward him, but before I can reach him, Lennon Rose's mother steps into my path, her drink spilling over the edge of her glass.

"Why don't your parents ever come to the open houses?" she asks suddenly, her words slurred. "I've seen you here alone before. You shouldn't be alone."

She's clearly had too much to drink.

"My parents, uh . . . ," I say, looking past her to find Anton.

But she moves, blocking my view. "My parents couldn't make it."

"How dare they," Mrs. Scholar replies with disgust, slowly shaking her head. "Don't they realize how lucky they are?"

Her words catch me off guard, and I look up at her. She smiles desperately, her eyes watery. Her lower lip shakes.

"You could be mine," she whispers, reaching out to take my hand. Her palm is sticky from alcohol, and she clutches my fingers tightly. "You could be my daughter," she offers.

I stare back, unclear on how to respond. She's obviously in pain, and she thinks I can alleviate it in some way. But I can't. I'm trying to figure out how to kindly tell her that I already have my own family, when her husband appears next to her, holding her jacket.

"Diane, stop," he says in hushed anger. He pulls her hand from mine, but she doesn't even turn to him. She's watching me, tears dripping from her eyes. "We're leaving," Mr. Scholar says, pulling her backward. She turns on him fiercely.

"Well, why not?" she demands. "We've been waiting long enough." She looks at me hopefully and reaches out to brush a strand of hair near my face. "Why can't we have this girl?" she asks him, gazing at me. "She's just as beautiful. She—"

"Mr. and Mrs. Scholar," Anton says, walking over. He slides his hands into his suit pockets, and flashes a glance at Guardian Bose, who's standing by the door. "Can I speak with you?" he asks the couple.

"No," Diane says abruptly. "No, I don't want to hear it, Anton. I want my girl. You can't keep her from us."

Anton laughs tightly. "I assure you," he says. "No one is keeping Lennon Rose from you. But perhaps we can discuss this out in the hall."

Although this situation is wildly uncomfortable, I reach out to tug on the sleeve of Anton's jacket. "Where is Lennon Rose?" I ask, keeping my face turned away from her parents so they can't hear.

"Not now, Philomena," Anton returns, still smiling at the couple.

"But I'm worried," I whisper.

"I'm sure you are. But not now." He moves so that my hand falls from the fabric of his coat. He puts his palm on Mrs. Scholar's back and motions toward the hall. "Come now," he tells her. "We have some details to work out."

When Mrs. Scholar pauses, I almost expect her to reach for me again. But instead, she covers her face with both hands and begins to sob. Her husband puts his arm around her, and together, they follow Anton out of the room.

I grow impatient for Anton to return, but the minutes pass. When I look around the room, I find Leandra Petrov watching me, a martini in her hand. Her expression is smooth as glass as she rolls out her other hand as if telling me to mingle. I nod politely and walk deeper into the party to wait for Anton.

Annalise is gone from the couch. Her father has arrived, handsome and charismatic as he holds court for several people, but mainly Annalise. The other girls are also with their parents or sponsors.

Lennon Rose is nowhere to be seen, even though Leandra's

here. She might be in her room, fixing her makeup. Or maybe she's still crying.

I stand alone, completely out of place here. An abandoned girl—like an abandoned glass of wine left behind on some table. What does that say to the investors about my worth? Maybe that's why Lennon Rose's mother approached me. She probably felt sorry for me.

There is the sound of clinking on a glass, and I turn to see the Head of School standing with a silver spoon against his champagne flute in the back of the room near the patio doors. His wife crosses to stand next to him, beaming proudly at the guests.

"I want to thank you all for attending tonight's open house," Mr. Petrov says, his voice deep. He sweeps his eyes over the room, pausing on Sydney and then Annalise before addressing the crowd.

"Over the past three years," he continues, "Innovations Academy has made incredible strides in perfecting our curriculum. Our girls are well-rounded, excelling in manners and poise, grace and beauty. I dare say the results have far surpassed expectations. In the end," he says, "we strive for our parents, sponsors, and investors to be proud to have a girl from Innovations Academy. Together, we will show the world a better way. A better girl. And what lovely girls they are," he adds with a wolfish grin. "Here's to our success."

Both Mr. Petrov and his wife lift their glasses, and the room erupts in applause. I press my palms together, but don't clap along. I'm too worried about Lennon Rose. The other attendees seem thrilled by the Head of School's confidence. I smile at an exuberant man when he flashes his teeth in my direction.

Just as I turn away, I see Anton walk back into the party, buttoning his suit jacket. The Scholars aren't with him. I hurriedly make my way over, and Anton sees me before I reach him. He immediately takes my elbow and effortlessly guides me out into the hall, away from the guests.

"I'm sorry about what happened with Lennon Rose's parents," he starts. "They're very distraught by her absence, and they—"

"How is Lennon Rose?" I ask, and his hand drops from my arm in surprise. I flinch. "Sorry to interrupt," I say, and wait until Anton tells me to continue.

"Is Lennon Rose all right?" I ask. "She was crying earlier, and Leandra brought her back to her room. But she never returned. I'm worried."

"You don't have to worry," Anton says. "Lennon Rose is resting comfortably in her room at this very moment. She needed some time to reevaluate her goals. We'll take good care of her—I promise. You should get back to the party or the guests will be disappointed."

"But . . . maybe if I talk to her, I can—"

"Not necessary," Anton says, waving off the sentiment. "She'll be better than new soon. Give her space, time to heal. I insist."

He must see that my worry hasn't abated.

"You've always had a big heart, Mena," he says. "But I need you to listen to me—not that heart of yours." He reaches to playfully poke me just below my collarbone, but the pressure is a quick flash of pain. "Understand?" he asks, still smiling.

I nod that I do, realizing that I've made him unhappy by questioning his competence. I've disrespected him. He is, after all, our analyst. He knows what's best.

"Lennon Rose is lucky to have you helping her," I say, hating his disapproval. Lennon Rose was openly crying, troubled. Anton is going to fix that. I'm grateful.

"Just remember," Anton says earnestly. "You're all priceless to me. Beautiful works of art. I'll always protect you, Mena. Always."

I thank Anton for his words and his kindness.

"Now head back inside," he says. "I'm sure there are plenty of investors waiting to meet you."

I do as I'm told and walk into the party. But I'm barely three steps into the room before the man who flashed his teeth at me earlier comes over with a bottle of beer dangling between his fingers. The flush on his cheeks tells me he's inebriated.

"Hello," I say. He drags his eyes over my gown before showing me his teeth again.

"Well, hello," he responds. "Philomena, is it?"

"Yes." I hold out my hand, and he brings it to his mouth, placing his damp lips against my knuckles. "And you are?" I ask.

"Interested," he says, still holding my hand to his mouth. It's inappropriate, but as I tug my hand back, he grips tighter. I dart my eyes around quickly, but the only person who notices me is Leandra. She stares back as if ready to judge my behavior.

I don't want to be rude to an investor.

"And your name?" I ask, trying to keep my voice even. Pleasant.

"Steven Kohl," he says, finally dropping my hand. I quickly clasp my fingers behind my back, out of his reach. He takes a step closer to me.

"It's nice to meet you, Mr. Kohl," I say.

He looks me over again, and then smiles again. "It's funny," he says. "I can actually hear that you're full of shit. They've trained you well. Very well-rounded, indeed." Only when he says it, he glances at my breasts.

I think about the lessons in class, that even with this man acting improperly, it's up to me to keep up the decorum. Manage his behavior by appeasing him, not antagonizing.

"And are you thinking of bringing a girl to Innovations Academy, Mr. Kohl?" I ask, trying to find a conversation topic. He laughs again and sloppily drinks from his beer bottle.

"I'm going to invest directly," he says. "I'm hoping you're available."

"Available for what?" I ask, confused. But he only stares his response, as if he enjoys not telling me.

There's a flash of movement behind him, and suddenly another man steps between us. Winston Weeks, a major investor in Innovations Academy. The ice in his short glass rattles as he takes a sip. Mr. Kohl falls back a step when Winston Weeks turns to him.

"How is your wife, Mr. Kohl?" Mr. Weeks asks smoothly. "I recently attended her gallery to thank her for her investment; her art is exquisite. Have you found work yet?"

Steven Kohl stares at him, not exactly offended by the question, but . . . threatened? Whatever it is, Mr. Kohl takes another messy drink from his beer, the liquid spilling off his chin, before murmuring a goodbye and walking away. When he's gone, Mr. Weeks turns to me.

Winston Weeks is in his early thirties, the sort of handsome that comes with power—sharp suit; expensive haircut; straight, white veneers. Although we've never had a private conversation, I've met him at open houses before, watched him make conversation with the guests. Rarely with the girls.

"Hello, Mr. Weeks," I say, smiling politely. "It's nice to see you again." I offer my hand, surprised when he shakes it instead of kissing it. It occurs to me that I prefer this greeting, even if it's unusual.

"It's nice to see you, as well, Philomena," he says. He offers his arm. "Will you accompany me to the bar? I seem to be dry." He holds up his glass of ice to indicate he needs another drink.

"Of course." I take his elbow and walk with him. He nods at several people along the way, each of them seeming impressed by his presence. In awe.

I drop his arm as he orders his drink and take a moment to study him, wondering why the guests are so enamored by him. Or intimidated—I'm not sure.

As Mr. Weeks waits for the bartender to pour his drink, he turns to me. "I've been thinking about increasing my investment, Philomena," he says. "I'm working toward opening a school of my own." The drink is set in front of him, and he watches my eyes over his glass as he takes a sip.

"That's very interesting, Mr. Weeks," I say. "Innovations has a great education model. I recommend it."

He chuckles softly. "Yes, I know." Before the bartender walks away, Mr. Weeks requests a glass of red wine. When it arrives, he sets it in front of me and then looks away and whistles, like he has no idea how it got there.

I laugh, suddenly feeling very mature, and pick up the delicate glass. I bring it to my lips and take a sip, the heavy scent burning my nose. The bitterness on my tongue. The heat down my throat.

"Now what about you?" Mr. Weeks asks, both of us moving to the end of the bar where there's more room to stand. "Do *you* like it here at Innovations?"

It's a strange question, one I'm not sure I've ever been asked. "I do," I tell him.

"And what do you like best?" he asks.

"I like living with the other girls."

This seems to surprise him. "Really?" he asks. He turns to survey the room. "I agree you're all very charming. But . . . you're close?"

"They're everything to me," I say honestly. "I love them."

Mr. Weeks studies my eyes for a long moment before he smiles. "I'll admit your answer is endearing," he says. "Your parents must be very proud of the kind of girl you've turned out to be."

"I wouldn't know, Mr. Weeks," I say, my voice slightly hoarse. I take another sip of the wine. "I don't see my parents often. We don't see anybody, really. The academy rarely takes us out. Even though we're *very charming*, as you said."

When he's quiet too long, I realize I must have overstepped my bounds. "I'm sorry," I say. "I didn't mean to criticize the academy. It's not my place to judge."

Mr. Weeks's jaw tightens slightly. He orders us two more drinks, and I have to rush to finish my wine to keep up. He hands me the new glass, taking the empty one from my hand to set it aside.

"No need to apologize to me," he says after I take a sip. He doesn't drink from his. "You make a valid point," he continues. "It seems your school should be assimilating you as much as possible. If you're going to be productive members of society, you need to be a part of it, right?"

"Right," I agree, and we smile at each other before I take another sip.

Winston Weeks isn't like the other investors. He seems wholly out of place here—like me. I'm increasingly grateful that he came over, especially when that other investor was being too familiar.

"If you don't mind me asking," I start. "How long have you been involved with the academy?"

"Since the beginning," he says. "I'm personally devoted to the idea behind Innovations Academy, more so than the academy itself. I'd prefer to be more of a silent partner, but I attend these open houses to check on how things are progressing. See if you're happy."

He leans in to bump my elbow. "I'll be sure to let them know you need to get out more."

I thank him for being so considerate.

Winston Weeks sets his unfinished drink on the bar. "I should be going," he says with a sigh. "I still have a meeting tonight."

I'm slightly disappointed. It's been nice to have someone to talk to, since my parents aren't here. I hold out my hand, and he shakes it again. "It was wonderful talking with you, Mr. Weeks," I tell him.

"Please," he says. "Call me Winston. And it was lovely to speak with you, Mena."

My heart trips, but I show no outward surprise that he called me by my nickname. Could be a coincidence. But it doesn't feel that way. I suddenly think he knows more about me than I realize.

I thank him, my head buzzing from wine, and watch as he exits the party.

10

'm a bit lost on what to do next. A bit drunk. We're told in etiquette classes that a small amount of alcohol in social situations is acceptable with supervision. But I might have overindulged. Then again, it would have been rude to refuse Mr. Weeks's offer. It's so confusing.

I glance around the room and see that the party is mostly emptied. Even Carolina Deschutes and her grandmother have left. All that remains are the girls, their parents or sponsors, and a few dedicated investors.

There's no one here for me.

I wonder suddenly if my parents would be as proud of me as Winston Weeks suggests. If they are, wouldn't they want to see me? Or at the very least . . . talk to me on the phone?

The thought is heavy, and I decide I should take myself to bed before I dwell on the negative emotions. Besides, I have a headache.

I walk toward Guardian Bose, and he crosses his arms over his chest before I reach him.

"Yes, Mena?" he asks. I'm surprised by his annoyed tone.

"May I go back to my room?" I ask. "My parents aren't here, and I have a headache."

He looks me over doubtfully. "Could it be from the wine?" he asks, disapproval thick in his voice. When my lips part, he turns back to the party. "Sure, go ahead," he says.

"Thank you," I say. Guardian Bose waves me along, impatient.

I start down the hallway, where the lights are turned low, shadows dancing along the wall. It's quiet—eerily so, considering the noise from the party is still echoing in my ears. Or maybe that's from the wine I drank.

I turn the first corner and pause to rest my hand on the wood wainscoting, trying to let my head catch up with my movements. Now that I'm away from stimuli, the buzz has gotten stronger. I'm decidedly not a fan of alcohol. At least, not a fan of drinking it so quickly.

There's a sound from one of the alcoves, followed by a high-pitched giggle. It's so disconcerting, so out of place in this dark hallway, that I peek around the corner to look in.

The first thing I notice is the pale leg of a girl, but I can't see her face. A man is pressing her back into the couch, half on top of her as they kiss. The girl's profile comes into view, and I recognize Rebecca Hunt.

I swing back around the wall, holding my breath and hoping they didn't see me. I can hear the smacking of their lips, the heavy breathing. And the man she's with—I'm not sure, but I think he's her family's lawyer. The person who handled her admission here, who attends the open houses with her.

"I want to go home, Mr. Wolfe," I hear Rebecca whisper.

"Soon," he tells her. Another kiss. "Soon, I promise."

"You promised before. *When?*"

The kissing stops, and instead there is the rustling of clothing, the creak of the couch as someone stands.

"I understand you want to go home," the lawyer says, his tone suddenly all business. "But your parents expect a graduated girl. Withdrawing you early will—"

"You told me you'd speak to them," she says. "You promised. But I haven't heard from them in months."

"You'll do as you're told," he says. "Your parents have put me in charge of your education. They can't know about our . . . meetings," he says with a hint of disgust. I blink quickly, offended by his tone.

"Of course," Rebecca says, a frantic edge to her voice. "I won't tell them. I promise. But why haven't they come to get me?"

"Because I never advised them on the matter," the lawyer says, matter-of-factly.

"But . . . you *promised*," Rebecca says, her voice cracking.

"You should be glad," Mr. Wolfe snaps. "You have no idea what you'll be going home to."

"*Carlyle*," she pleads, using his first name. There is a loud crack, and Rebecca gasps.

I press my hand over my mouth, sure that he slapped her. Impulsively, I push off the wall to intervene.

"Please don't go, Mr. Wolfe," Rebecca begs, and I stop my approach. "I didn't mean to be rude," she says. "I just want to go home."

"Don't ever disrespect me again," Mr. Wolfe says. There's an authoritative pitch in his voice, like he won the argument. "I suggest you keep a positive attitude, Rebecca. It's only a few months until graduation. We'll continue our meetings until then. Understood?"

"Yes," she says, defeated. "Thank you."

I hear them move, the kiss goodbye, and I hide against the wall as he walks out and heads back toward the party. When he's gone, I slip inside the alcove and find Rebecca on the couch, applying foundation from a compact to her reddened cheek.

"Rebecca?" I whisper. She jumps, startled.

"Mena," she says. "What are you doing here?" She clicks the compact closed and sets it back inside her clutch. She seems horrified that I'm in her space.

"I'm sorry," I say. "I didn't mean to listen, but I heard what Mr. Wolfe—"

"I shouldn't have disrespected him," she says immediately, embarrassed. "I was out of line, and he redirected me."

Thinking it over, I sit next to her on the couch. "He was overzealous," I say, repeating what Dr. Groger told me about the Guardian. Rebecca looks at me and nods, but I see there's still pain in her expression.

"Why . . . ?" I start, considering my words. "Why do you want Mr. Wolfe to send you home early?" I ask. "Don't you like it here?"

"Of course," Rebecca replies automatically, staring at the floor. "It's just . . . After the first open house, Mr. Wolfe met with me. Said we'd continue meeting until I graduate. I can't be rude to him," she says. "But I thought . . . I thought if I could go home, then I wouldn't have to meet with him anymore. I know it was wrong. I'm being selfish."

Maybe it's the wine, but sickness swirls in my stomach. Although we must listen to the people protecting us, the fact that this relationship is secret seems . . . wrong. And Rebecca is hurt, confused.

"I can help," I say. "If you want to go to Anton, I'll tell him what I heard and we—"

"No," she says adamantly, gripping my hand. "You can't. He'll devalue me. Mr. Wolfe has already warned me. Anton can't help me, Mena."

"But—"

"Please," she begs. "I need you to stay out of this. Please?"

I want to protect her, but I also want to respect her wishes. "Okay," I say reluctantly.

She waits a beat before thanking me. Then she grabs her clutch and gets to her feet, smoothing down her dress. She murmurs goodbye before leaving to return to the party, presumably to socialize with Mr. Wolfe like none of this happened.

When she's gone, I stand in the hallway awhile, not sure what to do. I've never been drunk before, and I find this makes my thoughts wild, unimpeded by manners.

The night's events are fading into a blur of fancy dresses, wolfish smiles, and loud kisses. It's opulence and wine. Too much wine.

I decide that I need to talk to Sydney about this and get her thoughts on the matter. I wind back toward the party, hoping to avoid Rebecca and her lawyer. Guardian Bose is still at the entrance, and he watches me curiously as I reenter. He doesn't ask why I'm back, but I feel him scrutinizing my behavior. I work extra hard to remain steady in my heels as I cross the room, looking for Sydney.

I don't see her at first, although I notice Rebecca across the room standing with Mr. Wolfe, talking to another investor. She doesn't even look in my direction.

"There you are," Sydney calls, startling me. I spin and find her approaching, alone. Her eyes are lit up, still joyful from seeing her parents; they must have just left.

I covertly wave her toward me, away from the few lingering guests. Sydney comes to meet me, laughing like I'm acting strangely.

"Okay, what did I miss?" she asks. "I saw you with Winston Weeks. Is he nice?"

I dart a quick look across the party at Rebecca again, and Sydney narrows her eyes as she reads my mood.

"What's wrong?" she asks. I take her arm and bring her closer.

"I need your opinion," I whisper. "I saw Rebecca and her lawyer tonight."

"I did too," Sydney says. "Rebecca looked lovely."

"She did," I agree. "But I don't mean at the party. They were in the hall, hidden in one of the alcoves. They were . . . kissing," I say even lower.

Sydney stares at me for a long moment as if she doesn't understand what I mean. Then she shakes her head. "Rebecca and Mr. Wolfe?" she asks.

I nod, but she looks doubtful.

"You sure it's not the wine?" she asks. "I watched you drink a glass."

"Two," I correct. "But, yes. I'm sure. And that's not all. Mr. Wolfe slapped her."

This makes Sydney frown. "Why?" she asks. "What did she do?"

"She called him by his first name. And it turns out, Mr. Wolfe has been kissing her since the first open house, telling her they'd continue doing so until she graduates. Rebecca wants to go home to get away from him. But he . . ." I furrow my brow. "He was wrong to hit her, right?"

"I don't know," Sydney says honestly. "He is in charge of her education. . . ."

But the reasoning doesn't hold up. The academy has warned us that there are terrible people in the world—ones who will lie to us, manipulate us. The academy promised to protect us from them.

What if Mr. Wolfe is one of those people they should be protecting us from?

"Is she all right?" Sydney asks suddenly. She turns to find Rebecca, but we both realize she and Mr. Wolfe have left.

"Yes," I say. "I told her I'd go to Anton with her and tell him what I saw, but she asked me not to. Said he'd devalue her." My tone is helpless, and I can see that Sydney is struggling too.

"I think we tell Anton anyway," says Sydney with forced certainty. "If nothing else, her lawyer's distracting her from her education." She pauses. "Right?"

We're both quiet as we think it over, the hum of quiet conversation still echoing around the room. The piano player's gone for the evening, and the bartender is packing up. There was something about the interaction between Rebecca and Mr. Wolfe, something . . . familiar. Even though that's not possible.

We definitely need Anton to sort this out. He is our analyst, after all.

"I haven't seen Anton in a while," Sydney says. "Do you think he left?"

"He might have." I worry that we'll have to wait until morning; it wouldn't be appropriate for us to go to his office at night.

But when I glance out the glass doors of the patio, I see Anton outside, talking on his phone. I'm relieved that he's still here. I pat Sydney's arm, getting her attention, and then we rush that way.

When Anton sees us coming toward him, he turns his face, saying something into the phone before clicking off his call. He slips the phone into his pocket as we open the doors and are hit immediately with chilly night air. Sydney noticeably shivers.

"Hello, girls," Anton says, the corners of his mouth pulling up in a smile. His cheeks and the tip of his nose are red from the cold, and he doesn't seem happy to see us. We interrupted his call.

Anton adjusts the knot on his tie to loosen it. "I've been in and out of meetings tonight," he says. "Were you looking for me? Because if this is about Lennon Rose again, then—"

"It's not," I say quickly. "I just . . . I saw something," I tell the analyst. "And Sydney and I think you should know about it."

Anton resets his stance, completely serious. "Go on," he says, motioning for me to continue.

It feels a bit like a betrayal, telling Anton about the private moment between Rebecca and Mr. Wolfe—especially after promising her I'd stay out of it. But it also feels like something the school should be aware of. At least, that's what I predict Anton will say.

I describe Rebecca and Mr. Wolfe on the couch. The slap. The threat. And then I tell him what Rebecca said to me afterward. Anton's throat visibly bobs as he listens, and he occasionally flicks his gaze to Sydney to make sure she's agreeing with what I'm saying.

When I'm done, shaking in the cold and embarrassed to have told the analyst such an explicit story, Anton crosses his arms over his chest. He nods appreciatively.

"You were right to tell me," he says, and I sigh out my relief. When I turn to Sydney, she smiles like she's proud of us for making the right decision.

"Was it wrong?" Sydney asks him. "Was it wrong of Mr. Wolfe to treat Rebecca that way?"

But something about the question seems to trouble Anton, and he examines her, pausing long enough to make Sydney apologize.

"It's not for you to judge," Anton says finally, even with a bit of humor. "You leave that sort of analysis up to me. It's why I get paid the big bucks." He smiles at both of us, and Sydney and I are reassured.

"I'll handle the situation," Anton says. "But if you see anything like that again—I suspect you won't, but if you do—you can always come to me. Understand?"

"Yes," we say. Anton puts his hand on Sydney's arm, rubbing it for moment to warm her up.

"Let's keep this between us," Anton says. "It's a private matter. Now," he adds with a smile, "the party's over, girls. Go back to your rooms."

We thank him for his help and he walks inside, leaving the door open for us to follow. He's hurried, and we watch as he goes immediately to Guardian Bose. I wonder aloud if they're going to look for Mr. Wolfe to confront him.

Sydney takes my hand, and together we go inside just as the other girls are saying goodbye to their parents. We all end up heading upstairs at the same time. Sydney and I don't mention what happened with Rebecca to the others; Anton said it was a private matter.

But I feel relieved, glad my concern wasn't unwarranted. It would be disrespectful to publicly accuse a man of inappropriate behavior—worse than any crime. At least that's what Professor Penchant told us in Modesty and Decorum earlier this year.

I'm exhausted as we reach our floor. Sydney drops my hand after we say good night and walks to her room.

I pause a moment outside Lennon Rose's door, considering knocking and checking on her. But she's probably asleep, so I decide it's best not to bother her. Anton insisted that I give her space.

The buzz from the wine still isn't gone, but it's no longer a lightness. Instead, it's heavy and thick. Cloudy.

Inside my room, I strip off my dress and toss it over the desk chair, even though I should hang it up. The school will collect our dresses tomorrow. We never keep anything.

I pull on my pajamas, and when I walk toward my bed, I see my vitamins waiting on my nightstand—two pinks and one green. My dose is still off. Maybe I'll ask Anton about it at our next therapy session.

I swallow down my pills with a sip of lukewarm water and click off the lamp on the nightstand. I crawl under the cool covers and curl up on my side, knowing I'll have to change my pillow-case in the morning because tonight's makeup will be smeared on it.

As the wine settles in my veins, making me sleepy, I replay the night in my mind. It's hard to grasp that Rebecca and Mr. Wolfe have met before, all of this going on without us knowing. How many other girls are kissing their lawyers? Whispering secrets in line? Meeting boys beyond the fence?

There's the creak of a door opening in the hallway. I listen until footsteps stop outside my closed door, followed by a sharp knock.

I shift my gaze around the room, noticing my dress carelessly thrown over the back of my chair, my shoes piled on top of each other. I'm embarrassed that I didn't properly prepare for bed.

"Come in," I call softly.

Guardian Bose steps into my room, his body in silhouette. He doesn't say anything at first, and I tug up my sheet to tuck it under my arms. "Yes?" I ask.

He moves farther into my room, and I see that he's holding a small, white paper cup reserved for vitamins. He sets it next to the glass on my nightstand.

"Anton sent this up," the Guardian says. He motions toward the cup, and I realize he intends to wait until I take it.

I glance into the cup and see one yellow capsule. I pinch it out, studying it in the dim light. I don't remember taking this color before. I wonder what it does.

Guardian Bose shifts on his feet, impatient. "In my lifetime, Philomena," he says.

I set the pill on my tongue, sip from the water, and gulp down the capsule while Guardian Bose watches.

When I'm done, I lie back in my blankets. Despite the water, the yellow pill has left a coating on my tongue.

Just as Guardian Bose starts to leave the room, I sit up again. "Guardian Bose," I call after him. "How's Lennon Rose?" I ask.

He pauses too long, but then he turns to me. "She's resting, Philomena," he says. "Now get some sleep." Without another word, the Guardian walks out and closes my door. I listen as his footsteps cross the hall to Sydney's room, the knock and click of her door opening.

And then I listen harder, sure that if I try hard enough I'll be able to hear Lennon Rose in her bed. But it's quiet.

My headache has faded to a dull throb, but suddenly my stomach feels sick. Really sick. I reach over and turn on the nightstand lamp, flooding the room in light. The change makes me dizzy, my mouth waters, and I quickly jump out of bed and rush for the bathroom.

I drop to my knees and throw up streaks of pink, green, and yellow from the vitamins. Purple from the wine. I try to stop, but I keep gagging until my stomach is emptied.

When I'm finished, I flush the toilet, hanging there an extra second. My head is pounding. And even more distressing, I threw up my vitamins. It's too late to bother the Guardian for more—he has to get them from Anton directly. The analyst, rather than the doctor, monitors our vitamins. He says it's considered a behavioral issue, and therefore his specialty.

I'll have to discuss my missed dose with Anton tomorrow.

When I straighten up, catching sight of my reflection—streaked mascara, blotchy foundation—guilt makes me want to follow the rules. I wash my face with the approved soap, moisturize, and then I walk into my room and hang up my dress properly. Obeying.

And I swear that I'll never drink wine again.

11

As morning light filters in through my window, I sit up in bed with the remains of a headache clinging to my temples, a dream in my memory. Something about Lennon Rose. Or was it Rebecca? For a moment, I can't think straight—a jumble of ideas tangled like wires in my head. And then, finally, the events of last night come back to me.

Lennon Rose pulled from line. Rebecca and Mr. Wolfe in the alcove. Drinking wine with Winston Weeks.

I get out of bed quickly, regretting it the moment I do. Pain throbs behind my eyes. I wait it out, and once I'm settled, I get dressed for breakfast.

When I walk into the dining hall, the smell of scrambled eggs and bacon hangs in the air. Neither of those things are at our table, though. Instead, the professors are eating from overflowing plates. We have oatmeal.

"Morning," Sydney mumbles, looking exhausted, as I sit

across from her at the long table in the dining hall.

Marcella and Brynn smile their hellos and Annalise waves her spoon at me. They're upbeat—normal for a Saturday morning. Sydney and I, on the other hand . . .

"I have never had a headache like this," Sydney says to me, her voice scratchy. "I might go see Dr. Groger after breakfast."

"Oh, no," I say. I reach across the table to take her hand, grateful when it doesn't feel feverish or clammy. She thanks me for being so sweet.

Around us, the other girls discuss the open house: Carolina Deschutes and her grandmother, an investor who made crude comments (I can just about guess who), and Winston Weeks being friendlier than usual. Annalise flashes me a smile when she says it, and I laugh, knowing all the girls must have noticed our interaction at the party.

But as they continue, Sydney begins to rub her temple, her eyes squeezed shut. My concern deepens; we never get sick.

"Did you drink any wine?" I ask. "Because I threw up last night from it."

"Gross," Sydney murmurs, poking her oatmeal with her spoon. "But, no."

"Maybe it was the extra vitamin Anton sent to the room," I suggest.

She scrunches up her nose and lifts her gaze to mine. "Extra vitamin?" she asks. "I didn't get one. What was it?"

"I'm not sure," I say. "But . . . you really didn't get one? I thought I heard the Guardian go to your door."

She shakes her head no, but then winces at the pain. I pout my bottom lip, feeling sorry for her.

It's strange, though. I was certain I heard Guardian Bose go to her room. I must have been mistaken. I glance down the table and immediately notice Rebecca, sitting apart, her head down. She seems sullen and sad.

"I wonder if Anton talked to her last night," I whisper to Sydney, nodding toward Rebecca. "Should I say something to her?"

"Why? What happened last night?" Sydney asks, distracted as she tastes a bite of her oatmeal, looking queasy when she does.

I stare at her before leaning into the table and lowering my voice. "She and Mr. Wolfe . . . ?" I whisper. Sydney waves her hand for me to explain.

"We spoke to Anton about it," I add quietly.

"Mena," Sydney says. "I hardly even saw Anton last night. What are you talking about?"

There's a strange sensation over my skin, spikes of worry. We most definitely talked to Anton last night. How could Sydney forget that? Just as my alarm begins to tick up, Annalise calls my name.

"Lennon Rose still isn't here," she says. "We should go check on her."

My stomach drops as I look around, double-checking that she's right. Lennon Rose was resting comfortably in her room last night, I was told. I wonder if she's still there. She must miss us terribly; Lennon Rose hates being alone.

I agree to go with Annalise, and despite her headache, Sydney

volunteers to come with us. We can't leave before finishing breakfast, so we plan to head there as soon as we're done.

I'm reminded suddenly that Valentine is the one who talked
to Lennon Rose just before she started crying. Why did she say to
her? What did she do?

But Valentine's ignoring all of us, stirring her oatmeal slowly,
the oats gathering in lumps on her spoon. Her lips are moving
ever so slightly, like she's repeating something. The image is disconcerting, repetitive in a way that doesn't seem natural, and I
quickly avert my eyes before she notices me.

I'm off today—wrong, somehow.

And as I eat my breakfast, I think about getting sick last night,
the streaks of colors from undigested vitamins. Covertly, I lift my
eyes to Sydney, wondering if that could be the difference.

Vitamins keep us balanced. Maybe I'm the one out of balance.

While Marcella and Brynn have cleanup duty, Annalise, Sydney,
and I go to check on Lennon Rose. We knock on the door, and
when there's no answer, Annalise tries again a little louder.

Annalise looks back at us before pushing inside, whispering
Lennon Rose's name since she's probably still asleep.

But Lennon Rose isn't here. And it's not just her physical
absence that we notice, either—the room feels . . . empty. Lonely.
Like she hasn't been here in a while, even though I know she was
here just last night.

Annalise stomps over to the bed and pulls back the sheets.
There's an empty water glass on the nightstand, a white cup

without vitamins. Lennon Rose's dress and heels from the open house are set for pickup, hanging near her dresser.

It's then that I notice Lennon Rose's school shoes near her bed.

We only own two pairs of shoes at the academy: our uniform-appropriate shoes and our sneakers for Running Course. Lennon Rose's sneakers are piled in the corner, and her uniform shoes are at the foot of the bed.

That means they're not on her feet. Where would she go barefoot? I walk over to the bathroom and peer inside, finding it empty and dry. She hasn't showered today either.

"Where is she?" Sydney asks. Annalise casts a concerned glance in my direction.

"She must be with Anton," I say. "He . . . He must have put her in impulse control therapy." Lennon Rose was so upset last night, it would make sense if Anton was trying to help her reassess her goals. He didn't mention it, though. He should have told me.

"Without her shoes?" Sydney asks, confused.

I tell them about my conversation with Anton. He said Lennon Rose was resting comfortably last night. "But I didn't check," I add guiltily. "I should have checked on her."

"It's okay, Mena," Sydney says. "If Anton says she'll be better than new, then I'm sure she's fine."

I swallow hard, the words not as reassuring as usual, although I can't pinpoint exactly why.

"I'm going to speak with Anton," I say. "See if there's anything we can do for Lennon Rose."

Annalise nods that she thinks that's a great idea.

"If you talk to her, tell her we love her," Sydney adds.

"Of course," I say. I glance at Lennon Rose's shoes again, their placement so odd in how routine it is. Like she'll be back at any moment, the bottoms of her feet dirty.

My heart races madly, and it occurs to me that I'm acutely aware of my feelings. The sense that something is wrong. I'm reminded of my missing vitamins.

"Check with the other girls?" I ask Annalise. "They might have seen Lennon Rose last night or this morning."

"Sure," Annalise says. She asks Sydney if she wants to come with her. We walk out into the hall and I wrap my arms around myself, careful not to alarm the others. I'm certain I'm over-reacting. When I see Anton, I'll let him know about my missing vitamins. I don't like how I feel right now, how irrational.

Annalise and Sydney head toward Marcella's room, and I start for the second floor.

By the time I get there, my chest has tightened, making it harder to breathe. I'm scared that Lennon Rose is in trouble. And I don't even know why she was crying.

I'm moving quickly, rushing ahead without any thought of restraint. I swing around the corner and collide with someone, yelping my surprise. Dr. Groger, stunned himself, laughs and adjusts his glasses.

"Philomena," he says. "Why are you in such a hurry?" He takes in my condition, and then concern creases his brow. "What's going on?" he asks more seriously.

"It's Lennon Rose," I say. "I'm looking for her. She—"

"My dear," Dr. Groger says quickly. He glances around the hall before putting his hand on my back to push me forward. "Let's discuss this in my office."

He clearly knows what's going on, so I nod, grateful, and walk with him down the hall.

Once at his office, he leads me inside and closes the door. He adjusts his glasses again, looking me up and down, before telling me to continue.

"It's Lennon Rose," I say, my voice shaking. "She's not in her room. And she was crying last night. She—"

The doctor exhales heavily. "Oh, sweetheart," he says. "I'm so sorry to tell you this way—Anton was going to make an announcement—but Lennon Rose has left the academy."

The world tilts and I fall back a step. "No," I whisper, horrified. "When?"

"Just a short while ago. Her father came to pick her up," he says sympathetically. "The tuition rate was impossible for her parents to afford, and the stress was getting to Lennon Rose. Her health took a bad turn. We had to let her go. I'm sorry. I know you two were close."

"We're all close," I explain. "But . . . she would have said goodbye," I tell him. "Lennon Rose wouldn't have left without a goodbye."

"I don't know—"

"And what about her shoes?" I continue, my voice rising. "How could she leave when her shoes are still in her room?"

"Philomena," Dr. Groger says curtly, growing impatient with

my questions. "I'm not sure of the details—the Guardian assisted. But Lennon Rose *is* gone. I'm sorry."

My eyes tear up, the impact of the truth finally hitting me. *Lennon Rose is gone.*

"Now," the doctor says with renewed vigor. "We'll get through this together. Anton will speak to you all, and he'll be available to talk privately later if you need to. And, of course, so am I. Anything you need, dear."

He picks up a lollipop and holds it out to me. Like it makes it all better. Like Lennon Rose's absence is a skinned knee he can graft over. I stare at the lollipop, and when I don't take it, Dr. Groger clears his throat.

"Why don't you head to your room now, Philomena," he suggests. "I'm sure you'll feel better after a hot shower."

But I can't stop thinking about Lennon Rose. I hitch in a sob, trying to fight it back.

Dr. Groger stares at me for a long while, and then he smiles and sets his hand on my shoulder, rubbing the muscle soothingly. But chills run down my skin at his touch. I take a big step back out of his reach, and the doctor furrows his brow.

Rather than explain it, I turn away. My body is shaking; my heart is broken. I need to tell the other girls what's happened. I leave the office, and the doctor doesn't call after me.

I hurry back to my floor as emptiness burrows deep inside my head, my heart. Lennon Rose didn't even say goodbye.

Lennon Rose is gone.

The thought buries me. I remember the first time I met

her—standing there with her straight blond hair and thick bangs. Her pale eyelashes and delicate hands. A voice so soft that Professor Penchant demanded she speak up because he couldn't hear her. Lennon Rose looked terrified, and I ended up speaking on her behalf.

She waited for me after class.

"Thank you," Lennon Rose said, still so quiet. She fidgeted, looking at the toes of my shoes. "I'm a little lost," she said. "I'm not sure how to . . . feel."

I nodded, understanding. "I was the same way when I first walked in," I told her. "But don't worry—we have each other now." I threw my arm over her shoulders. "We'll take care of you."

She beamed up at me, watching me like I was the sun in her universe. And that admiration was only matched when she met Sydney. And Sydney and I did take care of her. We loved Lennon Rose.

But we failed her.

Nothing will be the same. Lennon Rose was kicked out of school over money; it's not fair. She must be scared and lonely. I didn't knock on her door last night. What if she was waiting for me?

When I get to my floor, I find Sydney and Annalise in the hall talking with Marcella and Brynn. Marcella's dark, curly hair is dripping wet, and Brynn has her toothbrush clenched between her teeth. Sydney turns to me midconversation, and when she sees my expression, her voice trails off.

Annalise looks from Sydney to me. Her nostrils flare, her mouth a hard line. "What happened?" she asks, immediately.

I motion for them to come to my room, not wanting to discuss it in the hall. My hands shake as I push open my door. The girls follow me inside, and by the time I close the door and turn to them, I'm already crying.

"She's gone," I say miserably. Brynn gasps, gripping Marcella's arm.

"What do you mean?" Sydney asks. She looks at the other girls. "What does that mean?"

"Lennon Rose is gone," I say, tears spilling down my cheeks. "Dr. Groger said she left this morning. Her father picked her up."

Sydney drops down on my bed, looking like she's just been punched in the stomach. Her voice is a whisper when she lifts her watery eyes to mine.

"Why didn't she say goodbye?" she asks.

"I don't know," I say. "She would have. She . . ." I want to come up with an explanation, but I don't have one.

I tell them everything that Dr. Groger said, but it doesn't make sense. Lennon Rose's parents were here last night. They didn't mention money. They were worried the school was going to *keep* her. So did they decide to take Lennon Rose home instead?

Marcella begins to pace the room, chewing on her thumbnail while Brynn watches me with a helpless expression. Annalise walks to my window and places her palm flat against the glass as she stares out at the property. As if Lennon Rose is standing in the grass, waving goodbye.

"But she didn't even take her shoes," Annalise murmurs, not looking at us.

"The doctor said that Anton will make an announcement," I tell them. "Maybe he has an explanation."

Sydney lies across my bed, her folded arm over her face. After a few moments of quiet, she sniffles. The air in the room grows heavy with melancholy.

"I'm in a bad mood," Brynn announces. She swipes her finger under her eyes to catch the tears.

"Yeah, me too," I reply.

We're not allowed "bad moods," as Professor Allister calls them. If we're upset, if we're in pain, if we're lonely. "Bad moods are a symptom of being ungrateful," he says.

So we don't show our bad moods, at least not in front of the men. We can only show each other.

"After graduation," I start, my voice hopeful, "we'll find her." Annalise turns to me, expecting me to go on, to make them all feel better. We rarely talk about what our lives will be like after graduation. But rather than continue, I start crying harder, the reality setting in.

"How are we supposed to go that long without seeing Lennon Rose?" I ask, choking up.

"I'll let you know when I figure it out," Sydney says sorrowfully from behind her arm.

Brynn lies down next to her on the bed, and Sydney puts her arms around her. We all join them, staying close. Murmuring that we love each other.

12

I take the hottest shower I've ever known, washing away my tears. The misery is deep and painful. An indescribable loneliness.

I grow red and raw from the heat of the water, but I stay there until it begins to run cold. I turn off the faucet and stand naked. My breathing is staggered and unsteady, my entire body hitching forward. My chest aching.

After a few more moments, I sniffle hard, wiping my face with the backs of my hands. I step out of the shower and pull on my uniform. I brush out my tangles of wet hair and then slick it back into a tight bun, ignoring my specifications. I put on only the required makeup so I don't get reprimanded for looking plain. I'm supposed to "take pride in my appearance at all times."

When the Guardian tells us all to gather in the dining hall for an announcement, we already know what it's about, and the finalization of it feels even more devastating.

I leave my room and head downstairs, the first to arrive. Other girls begin entering the dining hall, and the ones who don't know about Lennon Rose yet are chatting, smiling. Unaware of how we're changed.

Brynn nods to me when she comes to the table, but we don't say anything. I'm surprised when Valentine sits with us, saying a pleasant hello to Marcella when she arrives. Valentine smiles, seeming oblivious to what's happened to Lennon Rose. I thought she'd said something to upset her, but the doctor told me Lennon Rose's dismissal was over money. Maybe Valentine had just been trying to comfort her.

Sydney and Annalise are the last to arrive. Sydney's eyes are puffy from crying. As they sit at the table, drawing stares from the other girls, there's an open space left on the bench for Lennon Rose.

But Lennon Rose won't be joining us today. She's somewhere else, without shoes. Without her girls.

Valentine tilts her head, examining our expressions. "What's wrong?" she asks. We're silent for a moment, but I can't ignore her question.

"Lennon Rose has left campus," I tell her quietly. "She's . . ." My voice hitches. "She's not coming back."

Brynn lowers her head, sniffling. And the other girls look positively sick over it. But Valentine stares back at me with no noticeable response. And then she says, "Huh."

It's stunning, her nonreaction. I'm about to say something about it when I hear the doors to the dining hall open.

"Can I have your attention, please?" Anton calls loudly as he enters the room. He's wearing a fuzzy blue sweater over his polo, his glasses gone. Several girls smile at his presence, immediately comforted. But I watch with impatience, waiting for an explanation. Waiting for words that can alleviate my pain.

"This is going to be very difficult," Anton begins, stopping at the front of the room. He slips his hands into the pockets of his slacks, appearing both caring and vulnerable as he surveys our faces. He pauses, pressing his lips together when he notices me. He returns his focus to the room.

"One of our girls has left us," he announces sympathetically. "It is with a heavy heart that I have to tell you that Lennon Rose is no longer with Innovations Academy. Her father came for her early this morning, as their family is moving out of state, and Lennon Rose will attend a wonderful school out east. She sends her love. As soon as she's settled, I'll reach out to her and see if we can start a correspondence. Not before. Until then, all we know is that Lennon Rose would want you to be happy," he adds with a smile.

But his words ring hollow to me. I can tell by the way Sydney squeezes my hand that she's not buying them either. Yes, Lennon Rose would want us to be happy. But this morning, she must have been scared, terrified. She wouldn't have left so easily. She would have begged to see us one last time.

"Now if any of you have questions," Anton continues, "or want to come speak to me privately about this development, let me know and I'll work you into the schedule. Otherwise, please keep your upward momentum by being excellent girls in and out of the classroom. You make your parents, Mr. Petrov, and all of us here at Innovations Academy very proud."

He nods his goodbye, and without even pausing, he heads straight for the door and walks out. So much for taking questions.

The room buzzes as the other girls wonder aloud what made Lennon Rose leave. A few wonder if she was in trouble, but that thought is immediately dismissed because it's Lennon Rose they're talking about. Eventually, I hear someone mention money—or more specifically, the lack of it—and the excuse spreads quickly throughout the room.

Overall, the others determine that Anton knows what's best. If he says it was time for Lennon Rose to leave, then it must be true.

But Sydney and I are destroyed, almost like we can physically feel a piece of us missing. Marcella stares at her hands folded on the table, sniffling every so often as Brynn comforts her. Annalise stares out the window again.

It's Valentine, sitting across from me, who catches my attention. She meets my eyes, and then there is the slightest turn of a smile on her lips.

"Everything's going to be fine, Philomena," she says calmly. "You'll see." And then she stands up and leaves the dining hall.

As the other girls go back to their rooms for self-reflection, I decide to track down Anton. I need to talk to someone about the crushing pain in my chest. The loneliness. Who better than the analyst?

I don't see him in the halls, so I head straight for his office, relieved when I see his light on inside. I knock softly on the glass.

"Come in," Anton calls with a hint of surprise.

I open the door and find him at his file cabinet. His face tightens when he sees me, but then he smiles.

"Philomena," he says, closing the drawer. "What can I do for you?"

His question seems odd, considering the circumstances. "I'm here about Lennon Rose," I say.

"I should have figured," Anton replies, a little embarrassed, and goes to sit behind his desk. "You want to talk about how you're feeling."

I nod, and he motions for me to sit down in the oversized leather chair across from his desk. I cross my legs at the ankle, not resting back the way I usually do during our therapy sessions. This time is different.

We sit in silence until Anton leans forward on his elbows. "Should I start, or . . .?" he begins, and his lips pull into a smile. Normally, I appreciate his casual demeanor, but in this situation, it feels inappropriate.

"I can be honest with you, right?" I ask. The smile fades from his lips.

"Of course," he responds. He leans forward in his chair, his elbows on the table.

"I'm worried about Lennon Rose," I say. "You told me she was going to be better than new, that she was just resting. You didn't mention money. Her parents didn't mention money. So . . . what really happened?"

Anton watches me for a long moment and then eases back in his chair. "I'm sorry," he says. "But I can't discuss the specifics of another girl's education with you."

"Why was she crying during lineup yesterday?" I ask, undeterred.

"Because she'd just learned about her family's financial situation," he responds easily.

I furrow my brow. "How?" I ask. "When? She didn't mention any—"

"I told her," he cuts in. "So I assure you, she knew. Perhaps she didn't want to tell you."

The thought stings. Lennon Rose was keeping a secret from me? From us? Then again, she'd been talking to Valentine—maybe she told her. Anton must notice my confusion, so he continues talking.

"I suspect Lennon Rose was embarrassed about her situation and had hoped to resolve it without your interference," he says. "But unfortunately, despite all I could do, there wasn't enough money to fund her education any longer. She left this morning before you woke up. She told me to tell you goodbye."

I look up at him. "You talked to her?" I ask.

"Of course," Anton says. "I walked her out myself."

"With the Guardian?"

He shakes his head no. "Guardian Bose was supervising the

floor—doing his job. I'm the only person who spoke with her. She will miss you."

I swallow hard, noting the discrepancy between Anton's and Dr. Groger's descriptions. The doctor told me the Guardian walked Lennon Rose out.

Anton closes his eyes and slips off his glasses. He seems exhausted, and I notice for the first time the dark circles under his eyes, like he hasn't been sleeping.

"Mena," he says, his voice soft like he's whispering a secret. "I'm going to confide something in you, understand?"

I nod that I do, although I'll admit it's a little weird to have my analyst confide in *me*.

"Your behavior is concerning," he says.

The comment catches me by surprise, and I immediately straighten my posture, trying to look well-behaved. "I'm sorry," I say without thinking.

"I told you last night to let us handle Lennon Rose, and that applies to today, as well. And going forward. The Mena I know would listen to these instructions. And yet, here you are. What's going on inside your head?"

I'm humiliated, and I lower my eyes. "I didn't mean to be disrespectful," I say. "I just . . . I miss her. I love Lennon Rose and I miss her." He's quiet, and when I look at him again, he's inspecting me. A slight pallor to his skin.

"You love her?" he repeats. I nod, hoping he'll understand. He waits a beat before standing up from his desk. "Well, then you're being irrational," he says like it's his official diagnosis. "Overly emotional. Lennon Rose is fine; I wouldn't have let her go otherwise. But she is no longer a concern of this academy."

I wonder if I am being overly emotional, possibly from missing my dose of vitamins. Then again, would they have made me forget things—like how Sydney forgot about Rebecca and Mr. Wolfe? Is that what happened?

I'm suddenly overwhelmed, closing my eyes for a second. Ultimately, Anton would be angry with me for throwing up my vitamins, wasting them by being careless. I opt not to risk anymore of his disappointment today. I don't tell him.

"You will not ask about Lennon Rose again," Anton continues. "Or you will be assigned impulse control therapy to reassess your goals. Your parents will be notified, and the defiance will be marked on your personal record. Is that what you want?"

"No," I whisper. I'm hurt by the harshness in his words. Anton has never scolded me before, not like this. It stuns me, and I reach to wipe a tear as it drips onto my cheek. Anton winces.

"I'm sorry," he says, sincerely. "I'm sorry, Mena." He rounds his desk and gathers me from the chair into a hug, holding me against him. I cry harder, not just because of what he said, but because one of my best friends is gone. Lennon Rose is gone, and I didn't even get to say goodbye.

My eyes are squeezed shut, the smell of Anton's shampoo filling my nostrils, the scratchiness of his beard on my temple. I pull back.

"I'm sorry I was cross," he says. "I was hoping we could get past this quickly. I see that was the wrong approach." He brushes my hair behind my ears and smiles. "But I promise, things will be better tomorrow," he adds.

I look up at him, thanking him. His hands fall away from me.

"Can I ask you something else?" I say, sniffling.

Anton sighs but actually seems amused by the question. "Go ahead," he replies.

"Have you spoken to Rebecca?" I ask. "Is she . . . Is she okay?"

Anton's eyes flash with a spark of surprise. "She . . . I . . ." He stumbles over his words before resetting his stance in front of me. "What do you mean?" he asks. "What about Rebecca?"

"Her and Mr. Wolfe," I say, lowering my voice at the mention of the lawyer. Anton doesn't break my gaze, but he doesn't rush to answer. Then he smiles pleasantly.

"Rebecca is scheduled for a short impulse control therapy session later this week to sort out her problems," he says finally. "Pretty soon she'll be one hundred percent."

It's eerie to hear him use the same words that Valentine said after her control therapy. But I nod gratefully and thank him for helping her. I only wish he could have helped Lennon Rose.

The fact that I can't check on Lennon Rose, talk to her, leaves me helpless. I almost can't bear it. I start to walk away, but Anton calls my name just as I open the door.

"Mena?" he asks curiously. "Have you been . . . feeling okay?"

I turn to look back at him, not understanding the question. I say that I am; he studies me anyway. Until finally, he waves me on, telling me to go about my day.

• • •

There are no classes on Saturdays, but we still have chores around campus, which are monitored by our professors. I'm barely present while sweeping the wood floors near the entryway, decidedly not better since talking to Anton, despite his reassurances.

Marcella and Brynn are working in the dining hall while Annalise is in the greenhouse helping Professor Driscoll with some of the new plant strains. She's good at it—*a natural talent*, he's said. So she gets to spend extra hours outdoors, cultivating the flowers.

I stare out the far window at the overcast sky, feeling lost. I know I'm not the only one who feels this way, either. Sydney walks past, tears in her eyes as she holds the bucket and mop.

But I realize pretty quickly that the professors aren't having the same reaction.

"Philomena," Professor Allister says from behind me. He turns me away from the window and appraises my appearance disapprovingly.

"You look terrible," he says. "Whatever distress you're experiencing, it's no excuse to let it show. Women are emotional creatures, overly so. Be better than that."

I stare back at him, wondering for a moment why it's wrong to be emotional over losing a friend. But I don't question him; he already seems unnerved by my mood.

So I force a smile, and the professor pats the top of my head before walking away.

13

I t's movie night, and the girls and I are grateful for the distraction. Outside, the weather has turned vengeful, spitting down rain and flooding the grass. Thunder booms every so often, rattling the bars on the windows. Bright flashes of lightning illuminate the sky.

We spread out the pillows and blankets in the common room, passing a bowl of popcorn between us. There's no love story in this movie, which is disappointing. I'm hungry for knowledge about relationships. Kissing. Sex. But the movies we watch are scrubbed clean of that sort of content, including most of the romance.

At least, that's what the last Guardian told us. When I asked him why, he said we didn't need to fill our heads with that kind of fantasy.

The next day, I went to Dr. Groger and asked him why the academy doesn't teach us about sex. He laughed at the question.

"That's for your husband to teach you, Philomena," he said

with a smile as he put his hand on my knee. That was the last time I brought it up to him.

Now the girls and I read about it in magazines instead.

The movie starts, and although the other girls watch dutifully, I find myself bored. I don't want to see another movie about men committing crimes. A man who does terrible things but is still called a hero because he loved his dead wife once upon a time. Never mind the families he's destroyed in the meantime. It all seems . . . cruel.

When the popcorn is gone, Sydney holds up the bowl to draw Guardian Bose's attention.

"Any chance?" she asks sweetly.

"I don't think so," he says, crossing his arms over his chest. Several girls pout.

"But I promise to run extra laps tomorrow," Sydney offers, crossing her heart. "Pretty please?"

Guardian Bose rolls his eyes before he reluctantly agrees. He takes the bowl and disappears downstairs to the kitchen.

The moment he's gone, all the girls turn away from the movie, glad to be alone together. But Sydney's expression sags. I know she wants to talk about Lennon Rose. When I bring my blanket over to sit next to her, she looks at me sadly.

"I miss her," Sydney says. "If we could just call her . . ." Her voice trails off, but she's given me an idea—my own spark of lightning. I can't believe I nearly forgot about him.

"Jackson's coming to meet me tomorrow," I whisper, leaning in.

It takes her a moment, but when she realizes what I'm getting at, Sydney's face lights up.

"And you can tell him about Lennon Rose," she adds quietly. "If Jackson finds her number, we can call her and make sure she's okay. Anton doesn't even have to know."

It's exactly the sort of news we needed—the chance to talk to our friend again. The rain and thunder rumbling outside don't seem so dreary anymore.

Sydney and I tell Marcella, Brynn, and Annalise, keeping it quiet from the others just in case it doesn't work out. But we think it will, and our moods have dramatically improved.

Brynn leans over to wrap her arms around Marcella's shoulders from behind, her chin on the top of her head. "So your *boy* is coming here tomorrow?" she asks, grinning.

I glance at the closed door to make sure the Guardian isn't back yet. "Jackson's going to meet me during Running Course, yes," I whisper. "I'm going beyond the fence."

"Now that's a good secret," Marcella says. "The boy stuff"— she waves her hand—"whatever. But sneaking beyond the fence? I'm into it."

"I don't know," Annalise says with a shrug. "The boy's pretty cute. He brought you candy."

"He's too skinny for my taste," Sydney says as if I've asked them all for their opinions on the matter. "But there's something about him," she adds. "He's sexy."

She doesn't whisper the word, and it travels across the room. Several girls look scandalized, but Annalise holds up her palms, looking very official.

"It's okay, girls," Annalise announces. "We may not talk like that here, but outside this academy they're giving blow-job lessons in magazines. We'll be all right."

"Is that true?" I hear Letitia ask one of the other girls, shocked.

Marcella snorts a laugh and Sydney falls over, chuckling. The magazine's version of reality has become our perfect inside joke.

"Wow," I say like they're all maniacs. But it feels nice to laugh. Earlier today, it felt like we might never laugh again. But we'll get to talk to Lennon Rose soon, and then things will be closer to the way they used to be.

The door opens. Guardian Bose reenters, and everyone turns back to the movie like we've been paying attention the entire time. He smirks, but he doesn't call us out. He brings the bowl over to Sydney, and she thanks him with an extra-big smile before he heads to the back of the room while we finish the movie.

I'm not worried about any of the girls telling the Guardian about tomorrow. They know I'd be punished severely—reprimanded and placed in impulse control therapy. They wouldn't do that to me.

We all want to be happy, positive. And it's what the academy wants for us.

There's a loud explosion on the screen, and Annalise yelps. She laughs, embarrassed by her outburst. The other girls tell her to shush, and she halfheartedly apologizes and turns around to look back at me.

For a moment, I see Annalise with yellow hair swinging over her shoulder. Shiny brown eyes and red lips. I'm sure it's her, although she's not the same.

"I don't know who I am, Philomena," she whispers, clutching my arm. *"Help me."*

The image is so startling, so . . . real, that I squeeze my eyes shut. I wait a moment, and when I look again, Annalise is a redhead. She's staring at me with green eyes, her brow furrowed.

"You all right?" she asks. Several girls turn in my direction, and I quickly nod, trying to play it off.

"Yeah," I say, my heart still pounding. "I . . . Yeah. I'm good."

Annalise exchanges an amused face with Brynn and then goes back to watching the movie. But I'm altogether unsettled.

Annalise with yellow hair.

I'm almost scared to look, but I can't stop myself from peering over to where Valentine is sitting. Her back is against the wall, her pillow laid over her lap as she watches the movie. She doesn't seem riveted or bored—she's poised. But when she slides her eyes in my direction, I flinch.

Her gaze cuts through me, at odds with her very proper exterior. It's like she's been waiting for me to look in her direction the entire time. She smiles. Alarmed, I move closer to Sydney.

And I don't look her way again.

At lights-out, we head back to our rooms. I keep Sydney close, unsure of what I saw earlier. Was that some sort of memory of Annalise? How could it be? Or maybe Valentine did something to me. Maybe she did something to Lennon Rose, too.

The idea is so outlandish that I don't speak it out loud. Instead, I give Sydney a hug goodbye and watch as the girls go into their rooms. Just as I'm about to close my own door, I notice Valentine veer back into the hall and slip inside Lennon Rose's room.

I ease open my door, my heart rate ticking up. What is she doing in there?

Guardian Bose is downstairs in the kitchen, but I glance toward his room anyway. The entire floor is quiet, with the exception of the shower turning on in Annalise's room.

I walk to Lennon Rose's door, but before I go inside, I imagine for a second that I'll find her there. That Lennon Rose will be sitting on her bed, doing her nails. She'll smile when I walk in and ask if she can braid my hair. There's a tug on my heart.

Instead, when I open the door, Valentine immediately straightens from where she was bent over next to the bed. She spins to face me.

"What are you doing in here?" I demand. I caught her off guard, and Valentine's normally serene expression betrays her shock. She recovers and smiles politely.

"I missed Lennon Rose," she says easily. "Just like you."

"No," I say, shaking my head. "That's not it. Just tell me what's going on. Because you're really . . . You're really freaking me out," I admit.

She seems to contemplate her answer, biting her lower lip. "I'm sorry if I'm scaring you," she says. "I didn't mean to scare Lennon Rose, either."

My cheeks heat up, anger boiling over. "What did you say to her?" I ask. "Why did you make her cry?"

Valentine holds up her hands in surrender. "That was never my intention. I just wanted her to wake up."

"Wake up to what?" I ask.

"I can't tell you," she says. "You have to find out for yourself."

"What? That's ridiculous. Just tell me!"

"I can't," she says like it hurts her. "They've trained you not to believe what you're told by others. You have to come to it on your own. I can't wake you, Philomena."

I'm convinced that she's not lying, even if I have no idea what she's talking about.

Valentine presses her lips together apologetically. She glances at the bed, and then she walks out of Lennon Rose's room, closing the door behind her.

I'm stunned by Valentine's words, but not exactly scared of her anymore. I'll have to tell Sydney about this. Again—what am I supposed to wake up from?

Now that I'm alone in the room, the grief hits. Lennon Rose is everywhere.

Her sweet scent is still in the air, her hairbrush on the table with long blond strands hanging from it, her shoes by the bed.

She didn't even take her shoes, Annalise had said. That detail bothers me now.

I walk around, poking through the items on Lennon Rose's dresser, finding nothing unusual. Anton said that he'd talked to Lennon Rose about her parents not being able to afford the school any longer. But why didn't she tell us?

There's nothing obvious here, but then I think about hiding places and turn to where Valentine was when I walked in. I cross to the bed and lower myself to check under the mattress.

I run my hand along the fabric until I touch the spine of a book. My heart jumps. I pull out a small, leather-bound book and read the title aloud in a whisper.

"*The Sharpest Thorns.*"

The title is unusual, the red font dug deeply into the leather. I'm a mixture of curious and alarmed. This doesn't seem like a book Lennon Rose would own. And it's not a book the school would give her.

Scanning through the pages, I discover it's a collection of poetry. I sit on the edge of Lennon Rose's bed, the springs creaking, and begin reading the first poem.

"Girls with Sharp Sticks"

Men are full of rage
Unable to control themselves.

That's what women were told
How they were raised
What they believed.

So women learned to make do
Achieving more as men did less

And for that, men despised them
Despised their accomplishments.

Over time
The men wanted to dissolve women's rights
All so they could feel needed.

But when they couldn't control women
The men found a group they didn't disdain—
At least not yet.
Their daughters, pretty little girls
A picture of femininity for them to mold
To train
To control
To make precious and obedient.

She would make a good wife someday, he thought
Not like the useless one he had already.

The little girls attended school
Where the rules had changed.
The girls were taught untruths,
Ignorance the only subject.

When math was pushed aside for myth
The little girls adapted.

They gathered sticks to count them
learning their own math.

And then they sharpened their sticks.

It was these same little girls
Who came home one day
And pushed their daddies down the stairs.

They bashed in their heads with hammers
while they slept.

They set the houses on fire with their
daddies inside.

And then those little girls with sharp sticks
Flooded the schools.
They rid the buildings of false ideas.

The little girls took everything over
Including teaching their male peers
how to be "Good Little Boys."

And so it was for a generation
The little girls became the predators.

I reread the last line, a curse on my lips, a fire in my belly. I've never read anything so violent, so angry. I'm scandalized. I'm exhilarated. I'm inspired.

Is this what Lennon Rose read? Did she read it just before the open house? I think back to her leaving her room, averting her eyes. Was she scared? Was she angry, like the girls in this poem?

I read the poem again, analyzing each word. Increasingly breathless as the little girls are controlled. My heart pounding as they fight back. And there's such violence—like nothing I've read before. The girls change things. They get free. They take control.

I flip through the book, noting that several pages have been torn out, leaving behind ragged edges of missing poems. My pulse is racing, throbbing. My hands shake.

There is a knock at the door and I quickly jump up, alarmed. I hear it open, realizing immediately that it's not this door—it's one farther down the hall. The Guardian tells one of the girls he has their vitamins. I shouldn't be in Lennon Rose's room; I can't let him catch me in here.

I quickly stash the book of poems back under Lennon Rose's mattress, wishing I could take it with me, but not wanting to take the chance of getting caught with it. I want to be able to read them again.

I'm not sure which door the Guardian is at—I wasn't paying close enough attention. I listen, hoping he won't knock on my door and discover I'm missing. I hear his boots, my heart in my throat.

There's a knock, and this time I know he's at Annalise's door.

As it opens, Annalise calls out, "It's okay, Bose. I don't need to be tucked in."

When I'm sure Guardian Bose is out of the hallway, I open Lennon Rose's door and quickly dart back to my room. I'm inside with the door closed before the Guardian moves on to Marcella's room.

As I change into my pajamas, waiting for my vitamins, I'm still thinking about the poem. Unable to stop thinking about it. The men who wanted to control women . . . but couldn't. So they turned to controlling girls instead. They lied to them. Manipulated them. Coveted them.

What was it to accomplish? I can't figure that part out. What drove the men in the poem to seek such control? What drove them to such lengths that they kept their girls captive?

I glance at the bars on my window.

My door opens suddenly, startling me, and I spin around and see Guardian Bose. I immediately cover my chest since I'm not wearing a bra.

"Yes?" I ask.

He walks over to my nightstand and sets down the small cup with my vitamins. He takes my empty water glass and goes to fill it at the bathroom sink. I peek inside the cup and see there are two pinks, one green, and another large yellow capsule.

Sydney didn't remember what had happened with Rebecca and Mr. Wolfe. Was it specifically the yellow vitamin? If so, what do the others do?

"Go on," the Guardian says, motioning to my bed as he comes out of the bathroom.

I quickly get under the covers, pulling them up to tuck under my arms. There is a boom of thunder, and the lights flicker. The Guardian is distracted as he hands me the glass of water and dumps the capsules into my open palm. Rather than watch me take them, he glances out the window at the storm. I pretend to swallow them, keeping them in my closed fist instead, and sip generously from the water.

By the time the Guardian turns around, the pills are hidden by my side under the blankets.

"It's too bad about Lennon Rose," Guardian Bose says, reaching over to adjust the sheet, grazing my arm as he does. "She had a lot of potential," he says with disappointment. "What a waste."

I furrow my brow. "She still has a lot of potential," I reply.

He stares at me, and then sniffs a laugh as he straightens. "Yeah. Sure," he says dismissively and walks out of my room.

When he closes my door, I lie back on my pillows and stare up at the ceiling. I'm going to talk to Lennon Rose again. The school may not care about her, but the girls do. We'll make sure she knows she still has a lot of potential.

I take out the pills he gave me, inspecting them. I set the pinks and greens aside and instead focus on the yellow. It's larger. Different.

There are two sides to it, and I slowly work them apart to see what's inside. It's nearly impossible, the vitamin beginning to dissolve in my fingers, but then the parts break open and a small pile of silver dust spills into my hand.

I stare at it, my eyes wide open. I poke it around with my other hand, surprised to find it sticks to my finger. I'm reminded of a magnet—one we saw on a field trip once. The silver dust there could be shaped into different forms by the force of a magnet.

But as I watch, I see the dust isn't just dust. On my fingertip . . . it begins to melt together—slide, really. I yelp and quickly jump up. I run to the bathroom and wash it down the sink, washing my hand three times to make sure it's all off.

The silver swirls down the drain, but my heart won't stop racing. What was that stuff? And what exactly does it do to us when we ingest it?

There's another knock from the hall, and I know that Guardian Bose is still making his rounds. I have to stop the other girls from taking their vitamins, but it's probably too late for tonight. The capsules dissolve so quickly. I'll have to tell them tomorrow.

And I'll them about "Girls with Sharp Sticks."

14

toss and turn all night, drifting in and out of restless sleep. There are images, both happy and terrifying, blending together.

I'm meeting Lennon Rose for the first time after class—her face so sweet and innocent. Her voice angelic. But like dissolving film, the image distorts, and instead I see Lennon Rose on a metal table, her eyes closed and her heart cut out of her chest.

Annalise with yellow hair at the dining hall table. Sydney is with us, only her dimples are gone—her cheeks full as she smiles. And then I see the two of them piled together on a concrete floor, their limbs broken like abandoned dolls.

It goes on like this, the softness turning to violence each time, until finally I'm in a restaurant—a diner with harsh light and a blinking red sign.

I sit in a booth next to the window, a plate of food in front of me. The air reeks of grease—bacon, sausage, ham. Meat. The table is sticky with syrup. But in front of me is a bowl of oatmeal, unsweetened. I stir it with my spoon slowly, lonely. Scared.

I miss my girls. I want to be with them.

When I look up, there is a man across from me. I don't recognize him. He's older and greasy—just like the food. His skin glistens in the fluorescent light, his fingers gripping a breakfast sausage as he shoves it into his mouth. The he smiles at me, licking his lips.

I'm terrified of this man. I am *terrified*.

"Don't worry," he says, the food visible in his mouth. "We'll be home soon, little girl." And then he laughs and goes back to his meal.

Thunder booms outside the diner, making me jump. Rain is pouring down.

I can't stay another moment.

I run out the door into the stormy night. There are lights everywhere, distorting my vision as water runs into my eyes.

And I hear the man scream my name.

"Get back here!" he shouts. "You're *mine*!"

I sit up in bed with a gasp, clutching my chest. Scared, I dart my eyes around the room, feeling the rain still on my skin. The fear in my heart.

My cheeks are wet with tears, I realize, and I get out of bed and go into the bathroom to stare at my reflection. I'm shaking, the nightmare clinging to me. It occurs to me that I didn't take my vitamins last night—that could be why. I assume that among other things, the vitamins calm me. Help me sleep. Without them, my mind is a whirlwind. Or maybe it was the poem that I read last night.

I walk over to the shower and turn it on, letting it steam up the bathroom. I crouch down with my arms wrapped around myself, squeezing my eyes shut while I wait for the nightmare to fade.

And it does. Not entirely, but enough that I can get into my running clothes. Once the images are far enough away, I can think clearly again.

I notice the time and see that I've overslept; the other girls are probably already outside. I'm going to meet Jackson and ask him to find a way for us to contact Lennon Rose—we need to know that she's okay.

And then I'll tell the girls about the book of poems, tell them not to take their vitamins anymore. As I tie my sneakers, I realize I'll have to talk to Valentine, too. I'm sure she knew about these poems.

This is just the beginning. I have so much to figure out.

Once dressed, I rush downstairs toward the back door that leads out to the track. But just as I round the corner to exit the building, I'm surprised to find Leandra Petrov at the door, sipping from a cup of coffee. She, however, doesn't look at all that surprised to see me. She's in a white jumpsuit with a black blazer and stilettos. Her hair and makeup are perfect.

"Mrs. Petrov," I say, bowing my head in greeting. "Good morning. It's nice to see you."

She watches me for a long moment, running her eyes over my appearance. "Yes," she says, wagging her cup at me. "Good morning, Philomena." She takes a loud sip from her drink. "I was sorry to hear about Lennon Rose," she adds. "She was quite a darling."

My heart dips. "I was sorry too," I say, quietly.

"Yes," she replies. "But it doesn't help to dwell, now, does it?" She pulls the measurement tape from the pocket of her blazer and motions for me to go into the results room. I need to get outside, but I try not to look impatient and do as I'm told.

When I get inside the room, a small, white-walled space with a scale and an examination table, I wait for her instructions. There are clipboards hanging on a bulletin board where she'll record my weight and measurements.

"Remove your clothes," she says, sounding bored. She drinks again from her coffee, which, now that we're closer, I realize smells of alcohol.

I strip down to my bra and underwear, goosebumps rising on my skin. Leandra sets aside her drink and grabs a clipboard with a pen. She pulls the tape between her hands before coming to stand in front of me. She measures my bust, my waist, my hips. Then she measures my arms. She sets the clipboard on the floor and squats down to measure my thighs. She stops and grips the outside of my thigh, pinching the skin. I wince.

"This isn't toned," she says. I look down, feeling embarrassed, and she lets my skin go. "Not enough, at least. You need to be tighter." She wraps the cold tape around my leg and then marks a number on the clipboard.

As she measures my other thigh, I stand up straighter, keeping my muscle flexed where I can. Leandra pauses to look up at me.

"Mr. Weeks is quite fond of you," she says. "He mentioned you several times while at the party. Wanted to make sure you were happy."

"Mr. Weeks seems very kind," I say politely.

She hums out a noise, sounding unconvinced. She begins to measure again, tugging the cold tape across my skin.

"And it made me curious," she says, casually. "Have you ever kissed a man, Philomena?"

I keep my expression completely still, trying not to betray even a hint of my shock at the question.

"No," I say, not sure if it's a lie. The guy at the theater kissed me.

"Would you like to?" Leandra asks, sounding distracted as she jots down my measurements. "I've always wondered if you girls had a feeling about it one way or the other."

"I'm sure I'll want to kiss my husband when I have one," I say, trying to figure out what she wants to know. Leandra sniffs an annoyed laugh.

"Ah, yes. Your husband. Do you want a husband?"

"If that's what Mr. Petrov and my parents think is best," I say, parroting what I've been taught at the academy.

"It's not what's best for you," she replies, standing up. She stares directly into my face, too close, but I hold a pleasant expression. I don't trust her to know my real thoughts. "Then again, it doesn't really matter what I think, does it?" she adds.

She turns away, a little unsteady on her six-inch heels. "You're on target weight," she adds, going over to hang the clipboard back on the wall. "But your muscles need toning. Run a few extra laps today and tomorrow. Now get dressed and head outside."

I thank her for her time, although she doesn't return the courtesy. She's gone before I finish dressing. I stand there, a bit exposed even though I'm more covered up now. I can't help but think about what she said. About marriage. About her opinion not mattering. And it strikes me as odd that she asked if I'd ever kissed a "man." Why not "boy"? Why not "person"?

I shiver in the cold and pull on my sweater, adjusting my headband over my ears. And when I run out into the field, I'm not just running for the course. I'm running to get away. Escape what feels like humiliation and judgment. I'm thrown by her questions, by the intent of them.

The poem talked about men keeping us captive. But . . . what about the women who work with them? Where were the mothers in that poem?

I run to the overgrown bushes and slip through the bars into the woods, vulnerability still on my skin. I should be used to Leandra's coldness by now, but the truth is, I'm not. Not when I let myself think about it. I nearly trip over a branch in my haste, and I reach out to catch myself. Instead, there's a sharp sting on my hand as a thorn tears through my skin.

Gasping, I hold up my hand, nearly falling backward. I'm bleeding. It's not a deep cut—only the size of a fingertip. But it's a scratch on my palm, near my wrist. It might turn into a scar.

I'm panicked, not sure what to do about it.

"Mena?" Jackson calls. I spin around, my eyes tearing up, and he quickly drops his backpack and rushes over. He takes my hand and examines the cut. "You okay?" he asks concerned.

"I need to see the doctor," I say. He lifts his head.

"For this?" he asks, confused. He checks me over like I must have another injury.

"Yes. It'll scar," I say.

"I . . . don't think so," he says, dropping my hand. "I mean, not in any significant way. Here, come sit down. I have a Band-Aid in my backpack."

"I can't have any scars," I tell him, worried.

"We all have scars," he says as we sit on a fallen tree. He sifts through his backpack until he comes out with a Band-Aid. "See this one?" He points to the small scar above his eye. I had, indeed, noticed. "My cousin tripped me while I was running through the living room and sent me headlong into the coffee table," he says. "Two stitches."

"Why would he do that?" I ask, upset. But Jackson laughs.

"I don't know. We were kids. I got him back a few years later when I accidently shut the door on his hand and broke three of his fingers."

These injuries are shocking to me, especially in how casually Jackson accepts them. All of a sudden, his scar means more. It's not just an imperfection, it's a story. It's a memory he wears on his skin. It doesn't devalue him at all.

I look down at my hand, knowing I'll have to ask the doctor to graft it, claiming I got hurt in a different way. But then I wonder why. Why do I have to be scar-free while Jackson doesn't?

Jackson opens the wrapper and positions the Band-Aid. I don't tell him that I can't keep it on. I let him place it because I'm comforted by how gently he's touching me. So at odds with the way men touch me at the academy—either cruelly or possessively.

I'd overanalyzed my last meeting with Jackson, thinking I'd have to be polite to get him to like me. That I'd have to appease him. I'm starting to realize that not everything I've been taught is true.

Jackson finishes applying the Band-Aid and crushes the wrapper in his hand before stuffing it into his backpack. He turns back to me, his expression serious.

"Do you want me to be more polite?" I ask suddenly. Jackson's mouth twitches with a confused smile.

"Why would you think that?" he asks. "I want you to be yourself. I want you to be comfortable."

It's an interesting thought. *Comfortable.* I'm sure Professor Allister would say that's the same as laziness, but when Jackson says it, it sounds right—the way you should want another person to feel. I'm still thinking about it when Jackson leans back on his hands, looking me over.

He's wearing a black leather jacket with a knit scarf around his neck, the fabrics clashing, but still working somehow. His eyes are glassy from the cold. In the distance, I hear the padding of feet as the girls make another loop around the track. Despite the morning chill, birds are chirping in the trees and the sound is lovely. It makes me forget that I'm not supposed to be beyond the fence. But when

I remember, it feels unfair that I can't come out here when I want.

No. It *is* unfair.

"How was your party on Friday?" Jackson asks, stretching his long legs. "Who was there?"

"I doubt you'd know any of them," I say, thinking it's a strange question. "But there were parents, sponsors, and investors. The doctor, the analyst. Mr. Petrov and his wife."

Jackson lowers his eyes and picks a blade of grass from next to the tree. He doesn't comment, even though he asked.

"Actually," I say, easing into the subject. "I was wondering if I could get your help with something."

He looks up curiously. "What is it?"

"Our friend Lennon Rose has left the academy, and we're worried about her."

Jackson sits up straighter, concern playing across his features. For a moment, I nearly stop myself, telling him that everything's fine—no, *great*—to make him happy. Much like what I would say to an investor. But I don't want to fake that all is well with him. I want honesty, pure honesty, and it feels like the most intimate decision I've ever made.

"She didn't say goodbye," I continue. "She didn't even take her shoes."

"What does the school say about it?" he asks.

"The analyst—Anton—told me I wasn't allowed to mention her again. He said some things that I don't think were true—things about Lennon Rose not affording tuition, how she left the building. But . . . maybe I'm wrong." I pause. "I don't think I am."

"I believe you," Jackson replies. "Don't let this Anton guy tell you what you know. He probably would have excused the way that guard treated you at the gas station, too."

"Guardian," I correct, and he rolls his eyes.

"Yeah, that fucking guy," Jackson says. "Well, *I* was there, and I can tell you that his behavior was completely out of line. So whatever's going on at this school, I assure you, it's mistreatment."

I watch him, debating what to say next. "Jackson," I start, my voice a little lower. "What do you know about Innovations Academy? You keep saying it's wrong . . . but how do you know?"

"Because I have eyes?" he replies immediately. He must realize the answer's unhelpful, because he apologizes. "This . . ." He pauses so long I think he might not finish the sentence. "This isn't a normal school, Mena."

"What do you mean?" I ask.

"Look, I know this place has been converted into an academy. The whole town knows that. But the weird part is that no one knows what goes on here. Fancy cars in and out, but no records of any students." He shakes his head, disturbed. "We see pretty girls, but no one's asking what happens to them here, because the people who run this place are powerful. Rich—ungodly rich."

I swallow hard, shocked that we're kept . . . secret.

"I called my dad last night," Jackson adds like he regrets it. "I was worried about you. So I asked him to tell me everything about the academy."

"What did he say?" I ask.

"He told me to stay out of it. Stay *away* from it." Jackson looks at me pointedly. "And that's pretty strange. Something really fucking weird is going on here."

His words are frightening, and I turn back to look at the academy. The iron gates surrounding the property. The bars on the windows. The mountain looming behind it, isolating us.

"Can *you* tell me what's going on?" Jackson asks. "I need to know." And there's a flash of vulnerability in his expression, although I can't place why. After all, he seems to know more about my school than I do.

"They give us vitamins every night," I say. "I stopped taking mine on Friday. And last night, I opened one of the capsules, and it was filled with metal. Silver dust." I furrow my brow. "And the dust moved—like a magnet."

Jackson's eyes widen. *"What?"* he asks.

"The other girls have taken it, and it made them forget things."

"Jesus," he murmurs, running his hand roughly through his dark hair. "Is it like mind control or something? Like . . ." He's searching for an answer. "Like nanotech?" he asks.

I'm deeply confused. We've definitely never been taught about this stuff in school.

"I'm not even allowed to use a computer," I tell Jackson. "So I have no idea."

He snorts a laugh. "Yeah, well, theoretically, and don't quote me on this, but if you ingested biomedical nanotech—if that's what it was—it would spread to your cells. Replicate the healthy cells for your organs. It could heal illnesses, cuts, and bruises."

I've always been very healthy—all the girls have. Our vitamins are tailor-made for each of us. So . . . does that mean our vitamins work, after all?

"Should I keep taking them?" I ask.

Jackson widens his eyes. "No! Of course not. Mena, that tech is also spreading to your brain, and each of those tiny particles contains a pulse, something *purposely* included. Those pulses would then be interpreted as . . . ideas. So, yeah—my bet is mind control. And again, this is only in theory because, up until now, I didn't think this shit existed beyond what I've read on the internet."

I'm not sure if it exists. But I did see the silver dust in that vitamin. It wasn't like anything I've seen before. I can't willingly ingest any more until I have a better idea of what it does to me.

"Who are you parents, Mena?" Jackson asks again. "They have to be important people to send you here. To do this kind of stuff to you. Who are they?"

His questions are suddenly more alarming. Quickly, I try to call up information. I tell him my father is a lawyer and my mother is a philanthropist. But the more Jackson presses me (Where did they grow up? When were they born? Who are your grandparents?), the more I realize I don't know all that much about them.

Panic rises in my chest, making me feel overwhelmed. Where are my parents? Why haven't they called to check on me? Why have they abandoned me here?

Jackson furrows his brow, watching me. "I'm sorry," he says. I brush off his apology, sniffling before any tears can fall. We sit quietly until I can calm myself again.

"You mentioned an . . . analyst?" Jackson says after a moment. "What's that? What does he do?"

"He helps us control our impulses," I say.

"My guess is he's doing more than that," Jackson says. "They're manipulating you somehow, with the vitamins, through him—I don't know. I think you should leave. I think we should go right now."

I look at him, surprised. "I can't just leave," I say. "What about the other girls?"

"You *all* need to leave."

"We . . . We can't. Our parents—"

"I think they'll understand," he says, growing impatient. "Mena, this shit isn't normal." His voice gets loud, and I put my hand over his mouth, scared someone will overhear us. When I touch him, he freezes, staring into my eyes. And for a moment, I see . . . guilt.

Jackson slowly removes my hand, nodding an apology for losing his composure.

"Fine," he says, looking away. "If you won't leave, then we need to figure out what the academy is using you for. Can you get that kind of information?"

The question seems suddenly cold, businesslike. I wonder if I've offended in him in some way.

"What exactly are you looking for?" I ask.

"Files," he says. "Employee files, parent files, whatever you can find. Something I can research."

"I don't understand," I say. "Where would I even get that sort of thing?"

"Maybe this analyst," he suggests. "He probably has everything in his office."

"I don't think I could do that," I say, scared. He wants me to break in to my analyst's office? That's . . . That's too much. I couldn't disobey the rules like that.

"Then just keep your eyes open," Jackson says. I'm surprised when he reaches over to smooth down the edge of the Band-Aid on my hand that's come unstuck. "Notice anything out of the ordinary."

At his soft touch, I long for him to look at me again, the way he did that first time. I want to watch the words die on his lips when his eyes meet mine. I want him to like me. But right now, I can't read how he feels. It's not obvious, and I can't bring myself to ask, scared of the answer.

Instead, I opt to tell him about the poems. But the moment I open my mouth, there is the sound of a metal door slamming shut.

I quickly turn and look toward the school, alarmed when I see Guardian Bose out on the track. The girls are jogging on the other side of the building, but when they come around, he'll see that I'm not with them.

Scared, I get to my feet. Jackson stands up too, his jaw tightening when he sees the Guardian. When he turns back to me, his expression is pleading for me to run away.

To my relief, the Guardian seems frustrated and goes back

inside, as if he doesn't have the time to wait for the girls. I sigh, my hand on my chest.

"I have to go," I say.

Jackson stares down at me, impatient. "Mena," he whispers, pained. But when I walk to the fence, he doesn't try to stop me.

I decide that I'm going to look for evidence, just like in the movies that the Guardian lets us watch. If I find anything, I'll pass it along to Jackson. What he'll do with that information afterward, I'm not sure. But he's made it sound like it'll help us.

"Please be careful," Jackson says.

I smile and promise him that I will. I let him know that I'll be running again on Tuesday.

"That's funny," he says. "I'll happen to be skulking around these woods early that morning. Should we meet?"

Before I answer, he snaps his fingers. "Hold on," he says, darting over to his backpack. He returns with a small piece of paper.

"I wrote down my number," he says. "Call me later and let me know that you're all right."

I take the paper and stare down at the number. "I'll try," I say. "And . . . my friend?" I look up hopeful. "Her last name is Scholar," I say. "And her mother's name is Diane."

"Lennon Rose Scholar," Jackson says, nodding. "Got it. I'll find her. She has to be somewhere."

We get to the cracked part of the fence, and I turn to him before I slide through.

"Thank you," I say. "For helping me."

He bottom lip tightens before he smiles, a gorgeous smile that I think is meant to charm me. And it does. But I notice that it doesn't reach his eyes. Instead, he seems sad. He seems lonely.

He murmurs goodbye as I slip through the fence.

As soon as he's gone, I pull off the Band-Aid he'd given me, seeing the red scratch still on my hand. And I decide not to the tell the doctor about it, to leave it as a memory instead.

15

When the girls round the building for the last time, I slip out from behind the bush and fall into step next to Sydney. She examines me, her nose red from the cold, her eyes shiny.

"How'd it go?" she asks between heavy breaths.

"I have so much to tell you," I say, darting my eyes around.

She smiles but keeps running. No mention of me trying to get Lennon Rose's number. I move closer to her, earning a confused look and a laugh.

"What?" she asks.

"I read a poem last night," I whisper. Sydney keeps jogging, her pace fast.

"Really?" she asks. "Where did you see a poem?" I tell her to keep it down, not wanting the other girls to know yet.

"It's called 'Girls with Sharp Sticks,'" I say. "And . . . it's about girls fighting back. They killed the men who—"

Sydney comes to an abrupt halt, making me jog a few paces past her. She stares at me, alarmed.

"What are you talking about, Mena? Why would you read something like that?"

I come back to her, nodding politely to the other girls as they jog past. "I found it," I say. "And the girls were—"

"Stop," Sydney says, holding up her hand. "Do you hear yourself? You just said . . ." She can't say the words. "Men are here to give us guidance," she says, lowering her voice. "Why would you be so disrespectful?"

I stare at her, seeing how worried she is about me. And it's like I can predict what she's going to say next. That she'll say the men have our—

"—best interests at heart," she finishes.

There's a sinking feeling in my stomach. I wonder what was in last night's vitamin.

I beckon for Sydney to jog with me again, smiling sweetly. She does, returning the expression just as easily.

"I miss Lennon Rose," I say, testing her.

"I know," Sydney says with exaggerated sympathy. "It's too bad about her parents' financial problems. Innovations is very exclusive. Not everyone can afford it."

I swallow hard and quietly agree. We continue jogging, and I'm horrified at the idea that Sydney doesn't remember being upset about Lennon Rose. Just like she didn't remember Rebecca and Mr. Wolfe.

I decide not to tell her any more about the poems, not yet.

I'm scared of how she'll respond. And when she doesn't bring them up again, I'm grateful. Even if I hate keeping this secret from her.

It occurs to me that maybe this is why Lennon Rose didn't tell *us* about the poems. She was worried we wouldn't understand. Or worse, that we'd tell the analyst about it.

I have a peculiar feeling—like there are two narratives in my head. I have no idea how to explain that to Sydney.

"Sorry if I was rude," Sydney says as we finish the run. "I just don't want you to get in trouble for defiance. Think about what Anton would say."

"But what if Anton's not always right?" I ask quietly.

Sydney stands silently, thinking it over, before the metal door swings opens. Guardian Bose reappears, and we quickly go back to smiling.

The Guardian searches our faces and motions us inside. He looks angry, and I wonder why he was out here earlier. He must be looking for someone.

I hurry past him, relieved when I'm not the reason for his darkened temperament. But when I turn around, I see him grab Rebecca's elbow, making her stagger to a stop.

"Anton's looking for you," he says, staring down at her in a way that lets her know she needs to go there immediately. She recoils from him but doesn't pull from his grasp.

"Why?" Rebecca asks in a small voice.

"I think you know," Guardian Bose replies with a sneer. "Now shut up and do as you're told."

His tone has sent a spark of anger through my bloodstream. I want to snap at him and tell him not to talk to her like that. I'm starting to see how unusual our lives are here. And the more I recognize it . . . the more I want to change it.

I just don't know how.

So I watch silently as the Guardian leads Rebecca away.

Sydney and I walk to the main hall to see if anyone knows why the Guardian was so upset. I'm surprised to see that nearly the entire class is here, crowded around each other. Whispering behind their hands. I know something has happened.

I lead Sydney over to Ida Welch—who's on her own, looking bored. She never goes to running class (*good genes*, she says). She sits in one of the oversized chairs, filing her nails.

"Hey," I call, drawing her attention. "What's going on?"

"Mr. Wolfe is on campus, and he doesn't look happy," she says. "I think Dr. Groger had the sheriff fetch him." She pauses her filing. "Him and you know who."

"You know who?" Sydney asks.

Ida grins. "Winston Weeks," she says like we should already know. "He came in before Mr. Wolfe and demanded to speak to Mr. Petrov about an *urgent matter*." Ida deepens her voice in a pretty dead-on impression. "He wouldn't leave until he spoke to him. Annalise had to fetch the Head of School and his wife from their residence."

My lips part. What is Mr. Weeks doing here? He's never been on campus before, not unless it was for an open house. For a moment, I wonder if he asked about me, but if he did, Ida would have told me straightaway.

Ida starts filing her nails again. "The girls were kind of smitten with the investor, especially Annalise. They brought him food and drinks while he waited, charming him. He told them they were very nice girls, indeed. And then Mr. Petrov showed up, and they left to talk."

"And what about Mr. Wolfe?" I ask.

"I assume Mr. Wolfe's presence has to do with Rebecca. He is her lawyer, right? Although when the police car showed up and dropped him off at the front door, Mr. Wolfe was beside himself," Ida says, exaggerating her expression to show fury. "He stomped in, brushing right past us, and headed to Dr. Groger's office. One of the girls heard it's a problem with Rebecca's . . . with her certification." Ida lowers her eyes then, the fun gone from the conversation. In fact, it sucks the air out of the room.

Every girl must be certified to graduate. If there's a problem, Rebecca might be delayed. Or dismissed.

But it wouldn't be her fault. Mr. Wolfe has been *manipulating* her. Anton promised she would just get impulse control therapy. He didn't mention they might kick her out.

I look toward the stairs to Dr. Groger's office, worried that Mr. Wolfe is here to call Rebecca a liar. What if they take Mr. Wolfe's side? I can corroborate Rebecca's story.

"I have to see Dr. Groger," I say, and abruptly turn and start that way. Sydney chases after me.

"Wait up," she says. "Isn't Rebecca with Anton?"

"Yes," I say. "But Ida said Mr. Wolfe went to the doctor—I want to know why. He can't get away with it," I add under my breath.

"What's going on, Mena?" Sydney asks, walking with me. "Why would Rebecca get certified so early? And what kind of 'problem' could she have?"

"No idea," I say, not elaborating.

Sydney keeps talking, and we turn down the hallway to Dr. Groger's office. She doesn't remember the incident between Rebecca and Mr. Wolfe, and I'm not sure if I should tell her again after the way she reacted to the poem.

Just as Sydney and I approach the doctor's office, elevated male voices carry into the hallway.

Sydney pulls me to the side of the door so that Dr. Groger won't see our silhouettes through the glass. She bends down to tie and untie her sneakers, trying to provide cover in case we're caught eavesdropping.

"She's a liability, Harold," Mr. Wolfe says loudly from inside the room. I realize that I never knew Dr. Groger's first name before, and it's suddenly intimate to have that personal detail about him. "You've known me for years," the lawyer continues. "I need you to take care of this."

"And tell her parents what?" the doctor asks coldly. "They've invested in her education. You were improper."

"She's a liar."

The doctor laughs, and I hope he can see through Mr. Wolfe's deception. "I think we both know that's not the case," Dr. Groger says. "I've examined the girl. What you've done amounts to theft."

The lawyer tries to argue again, but the doctor cuts him off.

"You're right," Dr. Groger says. "We have known each other a long time, Carlyle. So I'm going to tell you straight out: Do not come back. There's no need, since you're not the girl's legal guardian. Your services to her family are hereby terminated on my recommendation. The records will be sealed," he continues, "protecting our investment. But if we find out you've contacted her or any of our other girls, we will report you to the family, as well as the overseeing body. Do you understand, Mr. Wolfe? Do you understand the consequences?"

It's quiet for a long moment before I hear Mr. Wolfe answer, "Yes."

"Good," Dr. Groger says. "Now, you are banned from this campus. Leave my sight immediately."

My heart soars. Mr. Wolfe was improper, and now he's *banned*. Rebecca will never have to deal with him again.

We've always known there were terrible people in the world, and one of them got close to us. The academy always promised they would protect us. It seems they meant it. Maybe I was wrong to jump to conclusions about them.

A shadow passes on the inside of the door, and Sydney motions me forward. We jog down the hall until we turn a corner, and then Sydney blows out a breath.

"Did I hear that right?" she asks, disgusted. "Tell me I didn't."

"You did," I murmur. "But Dr. Groger is protecting her. It doesn't matter what Mr. Wolfe says anymore. Rebecca is totally safe," I add with a small bit of hope. I'm calmer now, reassured by the doctor's actions.

"I'm still trying to wrap my mind around Rebecca and Mr. Wolfe," Sydney says. She shakes her head but lets the conversation drop. I don't mention that she already knew this, not wanting to confuse her. At least, not until I can get her to stop taking the vitamins—otherwise, what's the point? She'll just forget tomorrow.

I assume Anton is telling Rebecca the good news. I don't want to interrupt. I'm just grateful that Mr. Wolfe will never bother her again.

As Sydney and I walk down the staircase nearest the front door, we see several girls gathered there. It takes a moment for me to realize that Mr. Petrov and his wife are standing in the entryway, exchanging goodbyes with Mr. Weeks.

When I step off the bottom stair, Winston Weeks recognizes me immediately.

"Ah, there you are, Philomena," he says. "I was hoping to say hello."

I'm a little stunned to get called out in front of the other girls, in front of Mr. Petrov, and I play nervously with the string on my sweater. Leandra waves her hand at her side, as if telling me to stop fidgeting.

"It's nice to see you again, Mr. Weeks," I say.

"Please," he says in a smooth voice. "It's Winston." I nod, but don't dare call him by his first name in front of the others. Behind him, Annalise rolls her eyes and I nearly laugh.

Mr. Petrov takes a step forward. "Mr. Weeks has come by the academy to make sure that you're all being well cared for. It's come to our attention that you've been cooped up too long." He smiles warmly, his hands folded over his stomach. "So we plan to add more field trips to the schedule. We're making arrangements now for this coming week."

Several girls gasp excitedly, but Mr. Petrov wags his finger at them.

"Your education is top priority, of course," he says good-naturedly. "But I agree with Mr. Weeks—it's time for you to socialize more."

He turns to Mr. Weeks, and the men smile at each other. Leandra nods along and then looks at each of us, widening her smile to tell us to be more grateful. Several girls vocalize their happiness in response.

The men shake hands, but it seems a bit forced. I wonder what hold Winston Weeks has over the school that he can make this kind of request. Despite how unusual this all is, I'm glad he showed up. Time away from school is exactly what I need. When Mr. Weeks looks at me again, I smile brightly. He winks at me.

Mr. Petrov flutters his hands toward the rooms. "That's all," he says with a chuckle. "Have a nice afternoon."

"And, girls," Leandra calls after us. "I'd like to have a word with you in the ballroom in an hour." Her smiles holds like it's frozen on her face. "Don't be late."

I'm about to depart when Mr. Weeks calls my name again. I glance over my shoulder at him.

"Try to have a little fun," he suggests. "You look melancholy."

"I'm always having fun, Mr. Weeks," I reply, making him laugh.

Sydney and I sneak an amused smirk at each other and head

back toward our rooms. When we're clear of the main hall, Sydney looks sideways.

"So . . . Mr. Weeks, huh?" she asks.

"A little old for me, don't you think?" I ask.

"True. You like those skinny college boys," she says.

"I *really* do," I sing out, and she cackles.

And I'm grateful for the good news—more field trips. More time beyond the fence.

Despite everything, we're upbeat as we enter the ballroom. Marcella is telling us about her latest run time and how she's pretty certain she could beat the Guardian in a foot race.

"Who couldn't?" Brynn asks. "He hasn't worked out since he started here. All that muscle would be heavy. We could lap him," she says with a grin.

I laugh, but when I look up, I find Leandra standing in the middle of the ballroom, her expression deadly serious. Chairs fan out around her in a half circle. Rebecca is standing next to her, her head lowered, her shoulders sagged.

My smiles abruptly fades when Professor Penchant comes over from the back of the room to join them. Leandra signals for us to sit down.

Sydney sits next to me, and we exchange a worried look. Leandra smiles.

"Hello, girls," she says. "I've asked Professor Penchant to join me in talking with you. I think his guidance here is necessary." She glances over at him warmly, and he hikes up his pants, shifting the entire waistband, as he comes to stand next to her.

"I would say so," he says rudely. Leandra doesn't miss a beat, though. She nods gratefully.

"It's come to our attention that there was inappropriate contact going on during the open house," she says, motioning to Rebecca. "And before Rebecca enters impulse control therapy, I thought maybe she'd want to explain why she felt it was proper to violate herself and shame her family."

The words come out sweet like honey, harsh like poison. Rebecca sniffles, but doesn't answer, her hair hanging in her face.

"Nothing to say?" Leandra asks her with pretend sympathy. "Nothing at all?" Rebecca shakes her head no. "Very well. Professor," Leandra says, looking at him, "would you like to take over?"

"Gladly," he says, and turns to address all of us. "You are at this academy to become better girls—the best girls. That means you are"—he counts on his fingers—"beautiful, quiet, and pure. Take the last part away and you're not special. You're a common whore." Several girls flinch at the statement.

The professor reaches over to grab Rebecca by the back of the neck like she's a puppy. She whimpers, and when she lifts her face, mascara is smudged under her eyes. It's jarring, seeing a girl so disheveled. So broken.

It's also unusual—like she's crossed a line the school can't forgive.

"You see, girls," Leandra says, her heels clicking on the floor as she begins to pace, "we expect you to be prizes. Not worthless junk. Investors pay good money for exemplary girls."

Professor Penchant smiles and crosses his arms over his chest.

"Propriety is crucial for girls," he says. "Otherwise, you invite this sort of behavior. Men can't control themselves around beautiful girls like you," he says, his voice raising. "So it's up to you to draw that line. Save yourselves for your future husbands. It is, after all, what they deserve. What they are entitled to."

I literally feel sick to my stomach, and next to me, Sydney shifts uncomfortably. I know that Professor Penchant is wrong, despite this being an extreme version of what we're normally taught. Without the vitamins, maybe I'm just not that willing to listen anymore.

Leandra claps her hands together loudly, like she's applauding the professor's statements.

"You want to be treated well?" she asks us. "Then act like a girl who deserves respect. We won't stand for this kind of behavior again—we're not running a brothel." She glances at Rebecca before reaching over to take her by the chin, lifting her face for all of us to see again.

"You're weak," she says with contempt. "You didn't say no. You didn't even tell anybody." She leans in closer and whispers, *"You're worthless now."*

Rebecca breaks down sobbing, and Sydney grabs my hand, squeezing it so tightly that it hurts. My eyes are stinging with the start of tears at watching another girl be humiliated. Leandra immediately turns and strides out of the room, head held high. Professor Penchant stays a moment longer to gloat, looking over Rebecca in a predatory way, as if her vulnerability makes her more of a target for his malice.

I see the worry in Annalise's expression, the way she wants to protect Rebecca from their humiliating remarks. But she doesn't. She lowers her face.

I turn around in my seat and find Valentine. When she looks at me, her eyes are glassy with tears. She nods, acknowledging that this isn't right.

It's a sudden validation, the fact that she can see it too. I turn away, scared to get caught—like our ideas are out in the open, able to be read. I'll have to talk to her later and see what she knows about the book I found in Lennon Rose's room.

"Have a nice lunch," the professor announces. He walks out, pulling a crying Rebecca alongside him as he leaves.

When the door closes, some of the girls sit stunned. Brynn openly cries, and Marcella comforts her, shock resting on her face.

It wasn't Rebecca's fault. Sydney and I told Anton that—he seemed to understand.

And it hits me . . . Is this my fault? If I didn't tell Anton, would Rebecca still be punished? I quickly try to push the thought away, deciding that stopping Mr. Wolfe was important. This is the school—*they're* at fault. They're wrong to treat her this way.

"Mena," Sydney murmurs miserably. I turn to her and hug her.

We stay here, all of us together, until we know we have to clean ourselves up and head to lunch. The school is unhappy with us, and we'll have to make amends for Rebecca's behavior.

I pull back, sniffling, and tell Sydney that I have to show her something. She swipes her fingers under her eyes and we get up. I look for Valentine, hoping she'll provide more information. But she's already gone.

We head toward the door so I can run to Lennon Rose's room to get the book.

"Have a good lesson?" the Guardian asks, startling me as we walk out of the ballroom. He's leaning against the wall, picking his nails and looking bored. Something about the fact that he was eavesdropping is extra creepy, and I must not hide the facial expression well.

"Will you excuse us a second, Sydney?" he asks, leaving no room for her to argue. She looks at me, debating for a second, and then tells me she'll see me in the dining hall. Once she's gone, the Guardian moves closer to me, glaring down.

"Don't look at me like that," he says.

"Like what?"

"What's your problem?" he asks me. "I'm not the one going around fucking the girls."

I gasp at his crudeness, shrink away from it, even. He's always been possessive of us, angry when we talk to other men. I see that now. He's using this vulgarity as another way to dominate me, shock me into behaving the way he wants. Only this time, it's not going to work.

The door opens and the other girls begin to file out, heading to lunch.

"I should think not," I tell the Guardian, backing away from him. "Or you'd be fired."

His face hardens, clearly not expecting me to talk back. I keep walking toward my room, hoping he won't grab me like he did that day in the gas station. And when I'm far enough away, I exhale. Feeling powerful for the first time ever.

16

After cleaning myself up in my room, I go down to the dining hall. Our salads and juices are already on the table when I get there, and I head for my usual seat. Halfway there, Sydney whispers for me to hurry up. When I join, she tugs on my arm to bring me closer. Nodding ahead.

I follow her line of sight and see Rebecca standing at the end of the table. Her hair and makeup are refreshed as if Leandra saw to it personally. But she's just . . . standing there, staring down at her glass of juice. Several other girls notice her; a soft murmur floats around the room.

My heart starts to beat faster. I want to go over, but I'm worried I'll call attention to her in front of the professors and Guardian. She's already in so much trouble.

And then, in a subtle motion, Rebecca reaches out her hand, watching it like it's not her own, until her fingertips press against the glass and push it over.

There's a clank, and then green liquid spills onto the table, quickly running over and pouring onto the floor. Several girls yelp and back away. Rebecca's face splits wide with a smile, all of her teeth showing.

Sydney's hand tightens on my arm. There are alarmed murmurs around us, and Marcella is the first to cross to Rebecca. She turns her around and asks if she's okay, but Rebecca doesn't stop smiling until it distorts into a grimace.

"Rebecca," Marcella repeats her name, louder, giving her a quick shake to snap her out of this. It doesn't work.

Rebecca begins to laugh, and the sound of it is high-pitched, wild, and unruly.

"What's going on?" Sydney breathes out.

Rebecca runs her palm along her face, smearing her makeup— eye shadow over her brow, lipstick over her cheek—before digging both hands into her hair and rubbing frantically, messing it up. She's shaking, laughing. Terrifying.

Brynn joins Marcella, and together, they try to talk Rebecca down. But before they make any progress, Guardian Bose appears. He's clearly rattled too. He grabs Rebecca roughly by the arm, the same way he grabbed me, but this time, Rebecca rips from his grasp. She spins to face him, her eyes wide, her teeth bared in viciousness.

"Don't touch me!" she growls at him. "Don't ever touch me again."

I dart my eyes over to the professors, finding them watching in concern. None of the men try to intervene, though. Professor Penchant continues to eat.

Guardian Bose puffs himself up to his full height, towering over Rebecca. She doesn't shrink back from him.

"I don't want to be beautiful anymore," she says. "Just leave me alone."

"Sure," Guardian Bose says. "But we should go talk to Anton about it."

It's the mention of Anton that causes a shift in her behavior. Rebecca takes a step back from Guardian Bose, the first sign of fear in her expression.

"No," she says. "I don't want to."

"Yeah, sweetheart," Guardian Bose says flippantly, grabbing her again now that he's seen he can scare her. "Not really up to you, though, is it?"

Rebecca tries to pull away from Guardian Bose, but he doesn't let go. He brings her closer, her arm bent against his chest as he whispers in her ear. Rebecca shrinks back.

Marcella says something to the Guardian, pleading on Rebecca's behalf, but he waves her away, dismissing her.

We all watch as Rebecca and Guardian Bose leave the dining hall. Cries echo from the hallway. I sit numbly at the table, my insides knotted up. Sydney is trembling next to me.

When I look up, I find Professor Allister watching, checking me over. I smile politely, acknowledging his concern, and then lower my eyes.

The other girls fall quiet, and we eat our lunches in stunned silence.

• • •

Sydney has cleanup duty in the dining hall, so the rest of us return to our floor for quiet reflection. We're all understandably upset. I imagine Rebecca is in impulse control therapy.

I think about not wanting to be beautiful anymore. Professor Penchant told us men can't control themselves around beautiful women. So instead of addressing their behavior, he put the responsibility on us. Rebecca thought that maybe if she wasn't pretty, they wouldn't bother her anymore.

I think about the poem. Men wanted control, not beautiful women. I suspect it wouldn't matter what Rebecca looked like. Mr. Wolfe wanted to possess a girl—to have that status. It didn't matter which girl it was.

With Sydney still not back, I decide it's time for me to talk with Valentine. I go into the hall and cross to her room, but when I knock, she doesn't answer.

I'm feeling suddenly very alone, not just because I'm alone in the hallway.

Since I stopped taking the vitamins, since I've been noticing the strangeness of the things around me . . . I feel a bit like I'm the only one who's really here. My knowledge is isolating. Is this how Valentine feels all the time? Is this how Lennon Rose felt before she left the academy?

The phone comes into focus at the other end of the hall. I take out the little piece of paper that I kept tucked in my pocket and make my way over. I told Jackson I'd keep my eyes open, and I've seen a lot today. Maybe he can offer some outside advice. And better than that, maybe he's found Lennon Rose's number so I can check on her.

That thought gives me a small bit of hope, and I'm smiling by the time I reach the phone. I read the numbers scrawled across the paper, murmuring them aloud as I dial.

Nervousness bubbles up when the lines clicks. I open my mouth to say hello, but instead of Jackson's voice, I'm met with a series of bells.

"The number you have reached is no longer in service," a recorded voice says. "Please check the number and dial again."

Confused, I hang up and redial, double-checking each digit. I get the same message. I hang up the phone, feeling disappointed. Jackson must have written it down wrong.

There's a shock of laughter down the hall, startling me, and I look over to see Ida and Maryanne walking in my direction. Ida asks if I'm done with the phone, and I tell her that I am.

I pass her on my way back to my room, still thinking about the recorded message. And how the voice sounded oddly familiar. I go back to my room and wait for Sydney.

It's about forty minutes later when there's a soft knock on my door.

"Come in," I call.

Sydney and Annalise walk in, saying hello before they come to sit on the bed with me. Annalise is holding a hair tie, and she asks if I want her to braid my hair. I tell her I'm okay for now.

"Brynn will let me," she says with a shrug, and I laugh because it's true.

"Where are Marcella and Brynn?" I ask.

"I think in Marcella's room," Sydney says. "Why?"

"Get them," I tell her. "I have to show you girls something. It's important."

Sydney says that she will, and sensing the seriousness, she rushes out. I tell Annalise that I'll be right back, and I go to Lennon Rose's room, checking for the Guardian before slipping inside.

For a moment, it steals my breath, the way I miss her. The way I can still sense her. It's even stronger than yesterday—or maybe I'm just feeling more. I go over to the bed and slip my hand beneath the mattress, relieved when the book is still there. I tuck it under my shirt and quickly return to my room.

Marcella eyes me suspiciously as I reenter, closing my door and wishing I could lock it. "Another secret?" Marcella asks. But her attempt at joking falls flat. It's been a devastating day already, and I think all of us are still raw from Leandra and Professor Penchant's words.

I take the book out of my shirt, making Marcella start with surprise. Sydney looks uncomfortable but doesn't react like she did on the track. When I sit on the floor, she comes to sit next to me. The other girls join us, forming a circle.

"I found this in Lennon Rose's room," I say. "I think she was reading it before the open house. And I think it might have been why she was so upset."

"I thought she was upset because her parents ran out of

money," Annalise says, checking with the other girls.

"That's what Anton said," I explain. "But he might not have been telling the truth. And when I checked Lennon Rose's room, I found this."

I take out the book and flip to the poem "Girls with Sharp Sticks." I'm scared to show the other girls; I even hesitate. It seems . . . radical. But when I look at Sydney, she nods for me to give it to her. I pass it her way first.

"The poem is called 'Girls with Sharp Sticks,'" I say. Marcella smiles at the title, and the others wait impatiently as Sydney runs her eyes down the page. I watch her read, the shocked way her eyes blink. When she's done, she looks dazed.

"Let me see," Annalise says. Sydney hands it over without a word, lost in thought. Annalise reads it quickly, and I see her smile at the last line. Her smile is followed by a flash of guilt and then another smile.

"Who wrote this?" she asks, lifting her eyes to mine. They're shiny with exhilaration. Defiance.

"I'm not sure," I say. "And I don't know how Lennon Rose got it, but I think Valentine could have given it to her."

Brynn finishes reading, sitting very still when she's done. Her lips are parted, her cheeks red. She passes the book to Marcella. "A girl wrote it," Brynn says. "I'm sure of it."

Marcella is the last to read, and when she finishes, she stares at the page. I'm suddenly worried that she isn't going to appreciate the words or that she'll be scared by them. But instead, she looks at me.

"This is . . . ," she starts. "This is kind of like us. The way we are at this school. The way . . ." She doesn't finish the thought. She looks down at the page again, and her eyes drip tears.

The parallels to our lives are obvious. At least, they are now that we're looking for them. The way we're taught, kept, trained. It's only now that we're starting to see what's happening to us. We may not completely understand, but there is a sense that we've been . . . wronged.

A heaviness pulls us down, and we all lower our heads. I think about Rebecca being humiliated and then trying to fight back in the only way she knew—destroying what they coveted: her beauty.

"There's something else," I say, after a moment. "You can't take the nightly vitamins anymore."

Brynn looks confused. "Why not?" she asks. "I'll be off balance."

I explain to her that I haven't had vitamins in my system since Friday night. And when I tell them about the silver dust inside the capsule, Brynn grips Marcella's leg, terrified.

"I'm not sure what they've been doing to us," I say. "But since I stopped taking them, I see more. I understand more. Those pills are controlling us. With what? I'm not sure. But we need to figure out what the purpose of this school really is."

I see that the girls aren't totally getting my theories, even if the poem has moved them.

"Just . . . Just pretend to take the vitamins tonight," I beg. "See how you feel tomorrow. Deal?"

"Yeah," Annalise says, seeming lost in thought. "Fine. I hate swallowing those pills anyway."

I tell them what Jackson said about the town knowing about the school, and how it's super mysterious and kind of scary. They listen closely, and Sydney occasionally looks toward the bars on the window.

I still remember bits of my dreams, so I tell them about those, too. But we all agree it's probably due to the abrupt change in medication. I relay the vision (memory?) of Annalise with blond hair, and she grabs her red strands and inspects them as if they've somehow changed instantly.

But it's Brynn who suddenly starts to cry.

"So what happened to Lennon Rose?" she asks. "What— where is she?"

"I don't know," I say, miserably. "But Jackson is going to try to find her number. That way we can call and check on her. Only . . ." I shrug. "I tried to call him and it didn't go through. He must have written his number down wrong."

"What do we do now?" Annalise asks.

"We should call our parents," Sydney says suddenly.

Annalise takes a breath, about to argue, but must think better of it. It's scary to think about calling our parents. What if they don't believe us? What if they do?

What if they do nothing at all?

"Gemma will answer," Sydney continues, "and I'll ask her to put my mom on the phone. Then I'll tell my mother every-thing. She'll be out here by the end of the day." Sydney smiles, her eyes hopeful. "I bet she'll even help us find Lennon Rose."

The girls and I look at each other, considering it.

"We have to be careful," Marcella warns. "We don't want to seem disrespectful."

I agree, but the moment I do, I realize that the academy is still inside my head. Making me believe that my parents would be disappointed, even though what's happening here isn't my fault. I just don't know exactly what's happening here.

We all hesitate, afraid to go against the analyst's wishes. We're supposed to forget about Lennon Rose. Sydney begins to fidget.

"I can make the first call," I say, shoring up my courage. "Test my parents' reaction before I tell them everything. That way, if it all goes wrong, I can blame it on missing them. Plus . . . I'm less tied to Anton's rules now that I'm not taking the vitamins. I'll be able to tell if my parents are lying."

I have no idea if that's true, but I don't want the other girls to take the risk. I wouldn't want one of them to end up in impulse control therapy because of this plan.

We debate for a few minutes, but ultimately, we decide that only one of us should try. Just in case . . . Just in case what, I'm not sure. I don't think we want to imagine the possibility of not being believed.

The girls wait inside my room while I go into the hall. My heart is in my throat as I pick up the phone receiver and dial my parents' number. I shouldn't be this scared to talk to them. Right?

Just as I close my eyes to take a breath, the line picks up.

"Hello?" Eva answers. I'm both comforted and disappointed

to hear from her. Her motherly tone is a like a hug, but ulti-mately, she's powerless to help me.

"It's Philomena," I say, and she makes a fuss.

"It's nice to hear from you. How are you, honey? How are your classes? Still on track for graduation?"

"Good, and yes," I say, trying to keep the impatience out of my voice. "Eva, can I please speak to my mother?"

"She just left," she says with regret. "I can pass along your message."

I close my eyes. "No, Eva. I need to talk to her. This is important."

"Oh?" she replies, sounding concerned. "Well, if it's an emer-gency, then I think we should get Mr. Petrov on the line right away."

"No!" I snap.

"Philomena," Eva scolds. "What is going on over there?"

"I just need to talk to my parents," I say as calmly as possible. "It's not about school. I need to talk to them."

"Well, I'm sorry," she replies, her voice now curt. "They're not here to take your call. I will pass along the message."

A sudden realization crawls over my skin, a sinking in my gut. The way she just said that—her tone. I'm certain it's the same voice on the recorded line that told me Jackson's number was out of service, only without the accent. It was the *same* voice.

"Eva, I want to talk to my parents," I repeat simply. "Put them on the phone."

She's quiet for a long moment. Too long.

"I'm sorry, Philomena," she replies. "I can't do that. They're busy. I'm sure they'll check in after your impulse control therapy."

I blink quickly, like I've just been slapped.

"I'm not scheduled for impulse control therapy," I tell her, my voice lowering.

"Yes, well," she says, "sounds like maybe you're due for one. Your impulses sound compromised."

It's clearly a threat. Suddenly I tune into the background. Every time I've spoken with Eva, it's so quiet. In a house, shouldn't there be a television or radio on in the background? Rustling papers at a desk? A lawnmower or traffic outside? But Eva's voice is crystal clear, like she exists in an empty room, always answering the phone. Answering every call, even to Jackson's number.

I've left so many messages with Eva, but in all this time, my parents have never called me back. Now I'm sure they never got the messages. So who exactly is Eva reporting to? It occurs to me now that she might not live with my parents at all.

"I apologize," I say to her, sweetening up. "I had some ideas about graduation, but perhaps this is a conversation better had with the analyst. Thank you for your perspective, Eva," I say. "It's a reminder that I need to keep my behavior well managed so I don't worry my parents."

"You're very welcome," Eva says pleasantly. "Do you still want me to pass along your message?"

"No," I say. "I'm sorry to have wasted your time."

"It's no trouble at all, dear. Have a nice day."

"You too," I mumble. I put my fingers on the lever to hang up the call, staring down at the receiver in my other hand.

Eva must work for the academy. How many other "assistants" are doing the same? Have they been manipulating us the entire time?

"You shouldn't have done that," Valentine says, startling me. I spin around and find her in her doorway, dressed impeccably, a bow in her hair.

"What?" I ask, putting the receiver back on the hook.

"It's not an open line," she says. "It goes through the communications office on the second floor."

I shake my head, confused. "I don't understand," I say.

"There's no such thing as EVA," she explains. "Nor STELLA, GEMMA, or whatever else they call them. Like I said, there are no open lines. I've checked."

We stare at each other, my heart thumping as I try to get up the courage to ask more questions. Find out what I really need to know. Finally, I take a step toward her.

"I read the poems," I whisper. "And I stopped taking the vitamins." To this, Valentine smiles—and not the fake, practiced smile. A real smile; a true glimpse of her.

"Finally," she says. "And how are you feeling?" she asks.

"Awake."

She smiles wider. "Good."

For the past week, Valentine has scared me, intimidated me in a way. But it's just that I wasn't seeing things clearly, not the way that she was. But now I'm starting to understand her. I'm starting to trust her.

"Why weren't you at lunch?" I ask.

"Anton," she says. "He's asking questions. He's trained to notice changes like this, so be careful around him. We just have to wait a little longer."

It's not the answer I wanted to hear—although I can't say exactly what it was that I expected.

"Wait for what?" I ask. My voice is a little loud, and she casts a concerned glance at the Guardian's door before looking pointedly at me.

"For the other girls," she says. "The only way we get out is all together."

It strikes me then that I hadn't thought about *getting out*. I should have, obviously I should have. But the idea of escaping the school suddenly leaves me feeling vulnerable, exposed to the elements.

Valentine notices my discomfort. "Just . . . behave," she says. "Listen and learn. You'll know when it's time."

She walks away then, leaving me confused and a bit irritated in the empty hallway. Sydney's head peeks out of my room. The girls are waiting for an update, and I'm spurred into action. I quickly run over and take her hand.

"Come on," I say, pulling her down the hall. Alarmed, she jogs alongside me.

"Where are we going?" she asks. "How did it go with your parents?"

"We're going to the communications room."

Sydney repeats it, confused. I explain about my phone call and what Valentine said, watching her sink inside herself. She shakes her head once, not believing it.

"We're just going to check it out," I say, not wanting to worry her too much. Valentine could be wrong.

We get to the second floor, and I slide myself along the wall to peek around the corner. When I don't see any professors, we quickly hurry down to room 206. It's clearly labeled, but I've never been in here before. There was never any need.

I try the door, and it opens. I'm immediately amongst a vast assortment of equipment. There are machines—not computers exactly, but large rectangular panels with buttons and dials. Switches and lights. There's a phone and plastic box full of paper that's labeled FAX MACHINE.

The room itself isn't very big—about the size of a large custodial closet, like the one we have near the kitchen where we keep the mops and buckets—but I'm a little overwhelmed with the amount of wires and metal.

I decide there isn't anything of consequence in here, but just as I start to turn away, I notice the last panel. There's a stack of faxes in front of it, all marked READ with a stamp.

As I read the labels on the panel, my stomach drops. My breath catches in my chest.

Sydney notices my reaction and darts her eyes around the room.

"What is it?" she asks.

I swallow hard and point. Printed on the device is the brand, etched into the metal: PARENTAL ASSISTANT. And down the front of the panel are switches, each labeled. EVA, GEMMA, STELLA, MORGAN, and several others run down to the bottom.

"It's . . . It's a machine," I murmur. "*They're* a machine."

"What does that mean?" Sydney asks. "Are you . . . Are you saying Gemma's not even real?"

There's a loud beep and we both jump, grabbing on to each other. There's a scraping sound, a series of buzzes, and then a piece of paper gets sucked into the fax machine. We stare at it, unsure what's happening. And then the machine spits out the paper, facedown.

We stay very still until Sydney steps forward to pull the page out of the machine. She flips it over and reads it. Her lips part, but she doesn't say a word. She holds out the paper to me.

And when I read it, I find that it's a fax to Anton. From EVA.

FAX

To: Anton Stuart   Date: April 18th
From: EVA   Pages: 1
Re: Philomena Rhodes

* Urgent   **For Review**   **Please Reply**
Comments:

Philomena Rhodes displayed unusual behavior patterns while calling the Rhodes residence this evening. The situation was diffused, but per guidelines, this message was generated to keep you informed.

Action is not suggested at this time.

17

very conversation I had with EVA was a lie. She's a computer system, a "parental assistant." She was in the academy the entire time. She would ask questions about my contentment, and then . . . what? Pass my answers along to Anton, I guess.

"We have to go," Sydney says, still staring at the panel of names. But then she turns, and I follow behind her. We shut off the light and close the door.

On the way back to our floor, I'm still trying to process. Sydney doesn't say a word.

We rush back to the other girls and find them waiting in my room, sitting on the bed. When we walk in, Brynn looks up hopefully.

"Did you talk to your parents?" she asks. "Did they believe you?"

I stare back at her, suddenly unable to speak. Sydney steps beside me, and we exchange a look, knowing we have to tell them.

"EVA answered," I say. "But . . . our parents' assistants aren't real," I say. "They're part of a computer system. And they report directly to Anton. Pretty much right away." Sydney nods to let them know it's true.

Annalise laughs like I'm joking. But as she stares at me, her expression starts to sag. "They're not . . . real?" she asks. "Stella?" I shake my head no. She considers it a moment, blood rushing to her cheeks. We sit in shock, absorbing the information. Feeling more isolated than ever. Sydney looks at the bars on the window again.

"I talked to Valentine," I say.

"Good," Marcella says. "Did she have any answers?"

"None that she would give me. She told me we have to behave. And that 'we'd know' when it was time to leave."

"Leave?" Brynn repeats, seeming confused by the sentiment. It didn't occur to her that we'd have to leave the school, just like it hadn't occurred to me. What if we've been trained to ignore that option?

We sit with the thought for a moment, and then Annalise jumps up suddenly. She glances at the clock. "I have to go," she says. "I was supposed to meet Professor Driscoll in the greenhouse five minutes ago."

She grabs her jacket, and we all stand so the other girls can go back to their rooms. We promise to meet up at dinner, although we have no solid plan going forward. I think we all need to process. And I think they need to get clearer heads.

Sydney grips my hand before we part, and then we separate to our own spaces. Once everyone's gone, I stand in my room.

Even though I've learned how alone I really am at this school, I feel stronger now that the girls and I are on the same page. Together, we'll figure this out. I walk to my window and stare out, trying to see beyond the woods.

I think about Jackson's questions: *Who are your parents? Why would they send you here?*

And now the question hurts even more. I've never had an ability to contact them. Who would allow that? What do they want this school to do to me?

I put my hand on the cold glass of the window. On Sundays, the afternoons can be used for leisure time, or in some cases, visits from family or custodians. That's happened to me once. My mother came out to visit. The only time she's done so since dropping me off.

"How do you like it here, Philomena?" she asked, sitting across from me in the reception hall. I'd been at the school for a month, and I liked it just fine. I told her so, and she nodded, studying my expression.

My mother is quite beautiful, although more reserved than some of the other adults I've seen come through here. She was wearing a white turtleneck, a sleek white coat, and no jewelry. Her dark hair was smoothed straight and long, her dark eyes fanned out with perfect makeup. She placed her hand over mine, and I was surprised by the warmth in her gesture.

"I hope you'll enjoy your time at the academy," she said, watching me. "These are important years in your life. Remember everything. It'll go by fast."

I nodded that I would, and thinking back on it now, I didn't say much while she was here. I was sort of in a fog then—all of us were. We were a bit overwhelmed with our new lives, our classes, the monitoring. I was very compliant then, and less . . . *me*. I think my mother must have seen that, because her brow furrowed in concern.

"We'll check in periodically," she said. "And the analyst will give us updates monthly." Her dark eyes swept over me once again, and then she stood. I followed her lead.

"I hope you'll be successful," she said. She reached out to grip my hand, squeezing it once—a little harder than I anticipated—and then she nodded goodbye and walked out. After that, both of my parents missed the next open house.

They don't check in periodically. Not with me, at least.

How could they leave me here? Do they know what the academy is doing? How the men control us, shame us, harm us? Do my parents get reports from EVA, too?

Do they even love me?

I spin away from the window like I can turn away from the hurt. I push off the memory of my mother coming to school. It's easier if I imagine she's never been here at all. It's easier to forget it than face it.

But . . . there's still a part of me that thinks it must be a mistake. They wouldn't leave their only daughter in a place like this. They're being manipulated too. If I could just show them, prove what's happening here—they'd understand. They'd bring us all home.

For a few peaceful moments, I let myself believe that.

• • •

At dinner, there is still a space left open where Lennon Rose used to sit. And now that Rebecca's gone, there is another. I wonder how long it'll be before she returns. And I wonder what exactly impulse control therapy will do to her.

I stay after dinner with Marcella, cleaning up the kitchen. I'm putting away one of the knives, distracted, and I accidentally open the wrong drawer. I pause a moment, surprised to see scattered keys. I stare at them a moment, wondering what they're for.

"Can you hand me another rag?" Marcella asks, stirring me out of my thoughts. I pass it to her, and she smiles her thank-you. The idea that we can't call our parents, even if it was always the case, is weighing on us.

Before bed, the girls all promise not to take their vitamins. We're scared to part, more vulnerable than ever, but I tell them tomorrow will be better.

I wash my face and get into my pajamas, dreading the Guardian coming to my room with my vitamins. I fill up my glass of water in anticipation and wait for him. I haven't talked to him since the ballroom, and I'm not sure if he's angry with me.

To comfort myself, I think about the poem again. I think about taking over the school and teaching the men how to behave.

My door opens suddenly, startling me, and I sit up to see Guardian Bose. He walks over to my nightstand and sets down the white cup with my vitamins. I take them obediently, or at least pretend to. When he's not looking I spit them into my hand and shove them under the blanket.

I'm setting the glass of water back on my nightstand when the Guardian steps forward to place a small white pill next to it. I don't know what it is, and I look at him questioningly.

"Anton sent it," he tells me. "He says it'll help you sleep."

A sedative? My heart begins to race.

"No, thank you," I say. "I'm fine. I—"

"Take it, Mena," Guardian Bose says impatiently. "After today's events, the analyst wants you resting soundly." His expression leaves no room for argument. But I don't want to go to sleep. Guardian Bose sighs at my hesitation.

"Take it or I'll shove it down your throat."

His threat is simple. He doesn't even raise his voice. It's the simple fact that he is physically stronger than me. That he'll use that physical strength, and there is nothing I can do about it.

I have no choice. This time, he waits for me to take it, watching closely. It's not suspicion—he looks pleased. I can't hide the pill under my tongue or spit it out. I swallow it, squeezing my eyes shut the moment it's down. I hold the glass of water with a shaky hand.

"Anton let you off easy, you know," the Guardian says, taking the glass from me. Confused, I look at him and ask him what he means.

"I told him what you said to me earlier," he says. "Told him you needed impulse control therapy to set you straight, but he declined. Guess he was playing favorites."

And I am suddenly so tired of the Guardian—his constant possessiveness, his threats. I can't stop myself when I reply, "It's not really any of your business, since you're not the analyst."

Guardian Bose flinches, and then he takes an angry step forward like he's mad I saw his reaction. "Don't you dare talk to me like that," he says. "Who do you think you are?"

And maybe it's the poem, or the grief, or maybe I'm just sick of being pushed around, but I sit up straighter and stare back at him. "I know I'm not yours," I say, "so back off."

His fists clench at his sides, and for a moment, I think he's going to punch me like the violent men in his movies. Fear streaks through me, but I don't back down. Instead, the Guardian lifts his hands, taking a step back.

"You're turning into a real bitch, you know that, Mena?" he asks. He tells me to have a nice rest before walking out and slamming my door.

The moment he's gone, I double over, shocked at how close I came to violence. Both proud and frightened of my bravery. It was stupid, standing up like that. But at the same time, I feel powerful.

I *am* powerful. I smile at the agency of it. I look around my room, thinking about what else I can control. But the idea of the sedative in my system freaks me out. I grab the vitamins and run to the bathroom.

Nothing comes up, though, and the chalky taste of the sedative rests on my tongue. It's too late. At least it's not the yellow vitamin. I flush those pills down the toilet and go back to my room.

I sit on my bed and reach under the mattress, where I had stowed the book of poetry, to pull it out. I turn to "Girls with Sharp Sticks." I read it again and again until my eyes start to feel heavy—the effect of the sedative. Before I get too tired, I hide the book under my mattress again, the same place Lennon Rose hid hers. And then I lie back and think about her. Hoping she's happy, learning exciting subjects. Evolving.

My eyelids flutter closed, but I fight to keep them open a little longer. I think about the girl who must have written those poems, wondering where she is now. Wondering *who* she is.

And I fall asleep imagining she's me.

I'm sedated, my entire body heavy with sleep, when my door opens well after lights out. I turn my head, fighting to open my eyes to see who it is. There's a sudden jolt of shock when I find Guardian Bose standing there in silhouette.

Dread curls in my stomach as I try to sit up. My head is stuffed with cotton; my arms are rubbery. I fall back in the bed. Guardian Bose steps into my room, his lack of boundaries terrifying.

I feel defenseless and I pull up on my sheets, trying to cover my body, but I'm tangled in the fabric. My bare leg is exposed on top of the blanket.

The Guardian comes to stand next to my bed. He doesn't say anything right away. I might as well be naked for the way he's examining me. And I shake my head, trying to clear the sleep that wants to pull me back under.

"How are you feeling, Mena?" he asks. His eyes travel the length of my body.

"Go away," I tell him, my voice slurred with fatigue. But I'm feeling a crushing fear of my vulnerability.

There's a small laugh, low and guttural, from Guardian Bose's throat. And then to my horror, he reaches to run the backs of his fingers along my thigh. I try to roll away from him, but he grips my leg then, holding me in place. Squeezing hard enough to make me cry out in pain. He licks his teeth.

"Don't ever talk back to me again, Philomena," he whispers, leaning toward me. "Or next time, I'll fucking kill you."

He lets go of me then, and I curl up on my side, starting to sob. My skin stings where he grabbed me, and the idea that he might not be done is a terrifying possibility.

"Leave me alone," I whimper, trying to gather the blanket over me again. The Guardian lowers his hand to my cheek, holding it there until I turn out of his touch.

"Remember what I said," he says, and then he walks out of my room, quietly closing the door behind him.

I'm left to sob into my pillow, dipping in and out of consciousness. Too weak to get up. Too weak to fight. He violated me, openly and with malice.

Any power I felt earlier is gone. And maybe that was his point. The Guardian proves daily that he can act without repercussions. *Overzealous*, they explain.

We're going to change the rules, I think desperately.

The idea offers me a small bit of comfort. A hope I cling to as I'm submerged again, sucked under by medication. By trauma. Sleep crashes over me in a heavy wave.

But I'm plagued with nightmares. Violent, horrific, suffocating nightmares.

I dream that I'm in a cold room with Dr. Groger and Anton standing above me. I'm lying on a table, unable to move, unable to speak.

"You're so beautiful," Anton whispers admiringly. "We couldn't just let you go."

Inside I'm screaming for him to leave me alone, but instead, he leans down and puts his forehead against my temple, like he's overwhelmed by his love.

"Welcome home, Philomena."

I wake, sitting straight up and then immediately regretting it. My head is pounding with a headache. It takes a moment for me to remember why, and then the events come back to me. The sedative. The Guardian putting his hand on my leg—he threatened my life. He made me weak, helpless, and then he exploited that to punish me. He just didn't think I'd remember it, because of the vitamins.

He's a monster. He's a danger to all the girls.

With that being said, I'm not sure how to get us out of here. If we show distress, Anton will bring us in for impulse control therapy.

But the question is . . . what does that do? What *is* impulse control therapy?

I wonder if Valentine remembers from her last session. She might have some insight. I quickly get out of bed and ease open my door, peering into the hallway. I feel a flash of anger when I look at the Guardian's door, but I can't focus on that now.

I have to find evidence to prove what's going on here.

I dart over to Valentine's door, knocking softly before slipping inside. She sits up, blinking against the morning light, surprised to see me. "Mena," she says. "What are you doing? Don't break the rules."

"What happens in impulse control therapy?" I ask her. "You just had it done. What did Anton do to you?"

Valentine waits a moment, and then brushes her hair back from her face. "I can't remember," she says, disappointed. "I hadn't been thinking clearly, then. I didn't play the game right, and they caught me. After impulse control, they upped the vitamin dose. Before I could remember not to take them, I'd gone two days. And once I stopped, the memories were completely erased."

My heart sinks. "So you don't know what Anton does in there?"

"I don't," she says. "But . . ." She pauses a long moment as if debating voicing it.

"What?" I ask.

"*If* you went in, and afterward you didn't take the vitamins, if we all helped you to not take them . . . maybe we could find out."

My lips part, the idea of sending myself to impulse control therapy, something I fear, is outrageous. Dangerous. I take a step back, not sure I can do it.

"Why not you?" I ask. She shakes her head.

"Again? So soon? Mena, if I get impulse control therapy again, they're going to kill me."

I fall back another step and shake my head. "No," I say. "Your uncle . . . The academy isn't going to *kill* you."

"My uncle couldn't care less," she says immediately. "He's not even my uncle. He's just . . . He's just some guy who's paying for my education. He expects to marry me," she adds bitterly. "My parents are dead. At least, that's what Anton said—I don't remember them anymore. So I have no choice but to be pleasant to Greg. At least until I get out of here. Then I'll do what I want." She looks away then.

It must be devastating to have no option of seeing her parents again. Even if I'm questioning how much my parents love me, the small bit of hope that I'll see them again . . . I think it's powerful.

"There are only so many times the analyst can try to help us," Valentine continues. "That's what Anton told me. I've exhausted his help, and if it happens again, he'll have to let me go."

"So they'll send you home," I say.

She tilts her head as if asking whether I really believe that. And even though there is a bit of doubt, I refuse to believe that my parents would send me to a school that would kill me if they couldn't control me.

"That's why you follow the rules, Mena," she says. "They expect us to obey—to *want* to obey. But we can use their expectations to manipulate them. So, if you want to know what goes on behind the scenes, you're going to have to act out. And then, of course," she smiles, "beg Anton for forgiveness. Tell him you want to be a better girl. He loves to be the hero."

"But what if they kill me?" I ask, breathless, still not sure I believe it but scared of it nonetheless.

"His prize?" she asks. "No. You just have to be convincing. Do you think you can do that?" She sounds honestly curious.

I lower my eyes, not sure I can just walk into something like this. "I . . ." I'm not sure how to answer. So when I look at her again, I shrug. "I have to talk to the other girls," I say instead.

Valentine nods as if this is an acceptable answer, one she understands. I tell her I'll see her at breakfast, and I walk out of her room, pausing in the hallway.

I turn toward the Guardian's door again. I'll have to pretend I don't remember him in my room last night. I'll have to pretend, or the academy will know that I don't take the vitamins. Maybe it's not all that different from pretending to need impulse control therapy.

And I wonder if my best play is to play along.

18

get ready for classes, and as I head out for breakfast, Guardian Bose is already in the hallway.

"Hurry up, girls," Guardian Bose calls loudly before yawning. "Let's get downstairs. I'm starving." He glances in my direction, and I'm amazed by how easily I smile in return. Almost like I'm outside myself, cut off from the real feelings that are under the surface. Like an actor, I'm assuming.

I don't get to say anything to the girls. But I see the way Sydney looks at me from across the hall, the way her eyes search the room, a bit confused. She didn't take her vitamins last night.

We have so much to talk about.

Breakfast is another bowl of unsweetened oatmeal. I realize now as I sit in front of it, this is not just about nutrition. They think it's indulgent for us to want better-tasting food.

I glance over to the professors' table and watch as they pile scrambled eggs onto their plates, generously sprinkling them with salt and pepper. I look at the pile of bacon they could never finish, and I know it will be wastefully tossed in the trash.

"I feel different today," Sydney says as she takes her spot next to me. She looks down at her food. "The moment I woke up, I felt different."

"I feel *angry*," Annalise says, and we all look at her. Brynn tells her to keep it down, worried the Guardian or one of the professors will hear her, but she lifts her chin defiantly. "I don't care," she says. "I am."

It's such a surprising statement, being angry. Do the professors even know we can get angry? Would that be assigned immediate impulse control therapy?

The dining hall doors open, and I'm surprised to see Rebecca walk in. If she's back already, it must have been a short impulse control therapy. I watch her as she walks to take a seat next to Ida, smiling pleasantly when she does. She immediately picks up her spoon and takes a bite of oatmeal.

"Are you okay?" I hear Ida ask her. Rebecca tilts her head, seeming confused by the question.

"Yes," she says finally. "Anton and I had intensive therapy, and he offered me coping mechanisms. I'm one hundred percent now." She smiles. "I've made him very proud."

Ida furrows her brow, but then nods like that's great. She goes back to eating, but I notice her slide in her seat, getting a bit of distance from Rebecca.

I, on the other hand, watch her. I want to note any changes in Rebecca, trying to figure out what I'd be getting myself into if I went through with this plan.

What if I end up like that? Obedient. Unaware. I swallow hard, considering the horrible possibilities. But then, there is a shadow as Valentine comes to sit with us at the table, taking Lennon Rose's spot. I see Sydney flinch at this, but she doesn't ask her to move.

"We should do it before the field trip," Valentine says, mumbling it under her breath so as to look like she's not talking. My stomach clenches, prickles of fear on my skin.

"And when's that?" I ask.

She looks up at me, her brown eyes sparkling in the light. Her face flawless as usual. "Wednesday," she says, "I heard Professor Levin talking about it. A movie, I think. Either way"—she checks to make sure the staff can't hear us—"we'll be off campus. We'll have possibilities. But it'll be a lot harder if we don't know what we're dealing with."

"What is this about?" Sydney asks, looking from Valentine to me. "What are you talking about? What are you planning to do?"

She's worried, and I know what I'm about to tell her will only make it so much worse.

I've thought about intentionally putting myself in impulse control therapy, considered the options. Sure, the girls and I could just run—but what would we say? What would stop our parents from sending us back? Where would we go if not home?

Jackson told me the men who run the academy are powerful. What does that even mean?

And it's not just that. It's not just about getting away from the school.

Where is Lennon Rose? What did they do to her? What if—?

I stop the thought. I won't imagine that anything terrible has happened to Lennon Rose. I won't even let that thought into my mind.

We need knowledge; we crave it regularly. And this is my chance to get answers. Even if it's risky. But it's not just about me. It's about *us*. It's about the girls.

I lean into the table and motion for the girls to do the same. As quickly and as quietly as I can, I tell them that I plan to get sent to impulse control therapy. We know that we wake up in a separate room where the procedure is administered. So while I'm there with Anton, it'll be up to the girls to look for information in his office—things about the school, the investors. And when I return from therapy, they have to make sure I don't take the vitamins. I want them to show me the poems to remind me of why I'm fighting.

"Figure out what the school is doing to us," I say. "Figure out why. And figure out how to undo it. But . . . don't let them erase the therapy," I ask, my eyes tearing up with the possibility. "Don't make me go through this for nothing."

"We won't," Marcella promises, reaching over to grab my hand. Valentine smiles like it's all settled, but next to me, Sydney sniffles. I look at her, telling her not to cry.

"I can't let you do this," she says. "If they're really doing these kinds of things, Mena, I can't—"

"Something else happened," I whisper. I wasn't going to tell the girls, afraid of upsetting them. But I see now that secrets can be dangerous. And keeping this from them puts them in danger of being his next victim.

"Guardian Bose came to my room last night," I say, barely audible.

The girls look at me, sensing there's more to the story. I take a moment, letting us sit in quiet so it doesn't look like we're conspiring, and then I tell them about him drugging me, touching my leg, threatening to kill me.

Marcella's face is flushed, and I see Annalise grip Brynn's arm under the edge of the table. We can't react, holding in our righteous anger.

"So if doing this can stop them from hurting other girls, can stop Bose"—I look at each of them—"it'll be worth it."

A second goes by, all of us looking at each other, and then we turn toward the end of the table where Rebecca is sitting obediently. She is pleasant and proper as she eats her tasteless oatmeal.

As she follows the rules.

I consider the options. I'm capable of doing that, now that the vitamins are most certainly out of my system—no longer clouding my judgment. Despite the sedative making me sleep, it seems to have no other lasting effect.

Sitting on my bed, I open up my palm and look at the tiny

scratch left over from my last trip to the woods. I trace it as I think.

If I go straight to Anton, he could instantly put me in impulse control therapy. But . . . I fear it'll be harder to convince him. He might see through my act. I wouldn't just *volunteer*, not out of the blue like this. I need a professor to turn me in. Someone who can tell Anton secondhand about my behavior.

It's one thing to hear I've been misbehaving. It's another thing to see it firsthand. I worry that if Anton witnesses a meltdown, he could give me a deeper therapy, one I might not be able to come back from.

I have to outsmart the men of Innovations Academy. Press on their weaknesses. Their soft spots.

I glance at the clock and see that it's time for Modesty and Decorum with Professor Penchant. And I know he'll be an easy target—he's already so dismissive of us. Always ready to punish us. Afterward, I'll tell Anton that perhaps my teacher was a bit . . . overzealous.

After a cleansing breath, I get my book. I meet the other girls in the hallway, Valentine joining us, and we head to class.

Annalise walks into Modesty and Decorum first, tossing her red hair over her shoulder as she passes Professor Penchant. He doesn't say anything, but his eyes follow her all the way to her desk. I notice his predatory stare, and see Brynn's jaw tighten as she notices it too. To think that we didn't used to notice this . . . Our eyes are open now.

Rebecca arrives then, but as she walks into class, her notebook slips out of her hand. She drops it, apologizing profusely.

"It's fine," I say, picking it up for her. I smile encouragingly, and she thanks me. Her eyes, however, hold a vacancy that wasn't there before.

"Ah," Professor Penchant says, making my heart trip. "Philomena."

Rebecca hurries to her seat, but I turn to the professor. "Good morning," I tell him.

He smiles, his pointy teeth showing. His gaze drifts over to Rebecca.

"I hope you'll rethink your choice of friends next time," he tells me, although he's admonishing her. "You don't need to associate with such creatures."

Rebecca bows her head in embarrassment. Clearly the professor is not willing to forgive her, even if she has nothing to be sorry for. Showing my anger might be a bit easier than I thought it would be.

Professor Penchant continues to watch Rebecca, as if daring her to talk back when he knows she won't. It's a show of power against a girl he controls. His eyes travel from the ends of her hair to the tips of her shoes. He huffs out a sound.

"I'm friends with all the girls, sir," I tell the professor pleasantly, and take my seat in front of Annalise. She chews on her pen, her foot underneath my chair, bobbing her knee with impatience.

"That's all very well," Professor Penchant says to me. "But a girl must protect her reputation. Who you surround yourself with says a lot about you."

"Yes, it does," I murmur, thinking about him and the other professors sitting together at breakfast.

"Let this be a lesson to all of you," Professor Penchant announces. "You will listen and behave. No more. No less. You do not need opinions—we'll tell you what's good for you. Insubordination will not be tolerated," he adds. "Remember, while you're here, you belong to us."

He nods like he's made his point and turns back to the board. He uncaps his marker to start writing out the rules for our field trip.

A few girls wilt. He has no right to tell us who we belong to. He has no right to say many of the things that he does.

And a sense of defiance hits me so hard that I nearly swoon with it. My hand shoots up into the air. "Professor Penchant?" I call.

He looks back over his shoulder, annoyed—especially since he thought he was done talking.

"Yes, Philomena," he asks.

"Where's Lennon Rose?" I ask. The words are clear and simple. Nothing in them showing the disobedience he just warned about. His expression, however, falters. I feel several girls turn to me.

"That's none of your business," Professor Penchant answers, turning around fully. "She's no longer a student of this academy."

"But she's my friend," I say. "I'd like to know where she is." Again, I keep my temper under control, careful not to tick the wrong boxes of insubordination.

"And Anton told you she's with her parents. End of subject."

He goes back to the board, pressing harder on the marker as he writes, darkening the letters.

"I'd like to call her and check on her well-being," I continue. The professor spins around so fast that I actually jump. Annalise's leg stops bobbing.

Professor Penchant sets down his marker and takes several steps in my direction. "Why are you asking about her?" he demands. He looks around the room, and I worry he'll see that the other girls aren't as obedient as they used to be. I stand up, forcing him to keep his attention on me.

"Like I told you, professor," I say. "She's my friend. And I think—"

"*Think,*" he repeats viciously. "You're not here to think, Philomena. You're here to—"

"Mr. Weeks cares about my opinion," I say, interrupting him. It was a spur-of-the-moment decision to mention Winston Weeks—a guess, and I was right. Bringing up the investor infuriates him.

"Winston Weeks is not a professor at this academy!" he shouts, spittle flying from his lips. "He has no rights to you!"

I tilt my head, willfully misunderstanding. "I was under the impression that he is very highly regarded by the academy. After all, he's the one who brought about this field trip. On my suggestion," I add.

The professor's mouth pulls into a sneer. "And what did you have to do to get such favor from him?"

"Are you jealous?" I ask, offended.

In a flash of movement, the professor slaps me hard across the face, knocking me against my desk. It's a shock, and my eyes fill with tears before I even realize. Rather than apologize for upsetting him, I turn around and face him again. Standing up taller.

"I don't belong to you," I say, my voice taking an edge that I can't quite control. "And I don't belong to this academy." I push my desk out of the way and step closer to him. He growls at me like a feral animal.

"My parents have paid to send me here," I say louder. "They have the right to discipline me. Not you. Not the Guardian. Don't touch me again." And suddenly, it's like a dam breaks inside of me. I'm not just talking to Professor Penchant. I'm talking to all the men at the academy. "Don't touch me again!" I scream, making the hairs on my arm stand up. "You're nothing but a sad man who hurts little girls for fun. And I will do everything I can to get you fired!"

It feels good to talk back, to raise my voice and be heard. I smile, feeling wild and unruly. Feeling free. My cheek stings from where he struck me, but it only spurs me on more. From the look on his face, he would hit me again.

But instead, the door opens and Guardian Bose walks in.

"What's going on?" he asks. "Who's shouting?"

Professor Penchant is heaving in breaths, his teeth bared. I'm sure it's not easy for him when he tells the Guardian to remove me from class.

"Take her to Anton," he says, furious. "Tell him she's not coming back in this room until she gets impulse control therapy."

I instinctively shrink back as Guardian Bose approaches me. But he seems perplexed as he grabs my arm. I follow him obediently from the room, exchanging a look with Annalise to let her know the plan is in motion.

I just hope I haven't made a grave mistake.

19

As we walk, Guardian Bose looks sideways at me. "What the hell was that about?" he asks. He hasn't let go of my arm, and his fingers are pressing painfully into my skin.

I don't respond, not wanting to say anything that could contradict what I'm going to tell Anton. But my silence doesn't sit well with the Guardian.

"You're really starting to upset me, Philomena," he says. He squeezes harder, and I wince, forcing myself to stay quiet. Only one more turn and then I'll be at Anton's door. I just have to make it—

But the Guardian jerks me to a stop. He spins me around to face him. He examines my eyes, looking me over thoroughly. I have to hold back any thoughts of him in my room last night. I have to block them out so they don't show up plainly in my expression.

So when he gets nothing, I see his shoulders ease slightly. I realize he's afraid I'm going to turn him in to Anton. She seems to decide that I offer no threats, so he lets me go. Instead, he puts his hand on my back and pushes me forward. And we walk in silence the rest of the way.

Anton opens his door before we knock. His expression is worried, his skin pale.

"Philomena," he says, reaching for me immediately. "What happened?" He leads me inside, dismissing Guardian Bose without asking him his thoughts, and closes the door.

Anton motions to the chair on the other side of the desk and goes to sit down in his own. "Have a seat, Philomena," he says. "I heard you've had quite the morning."

Now that I'm in here, the idea of what's going to come next— the fact that I don't know—terrifies me. I dart my eyes around the room, wondering if I'll be the same when I leave. My breathing is quickening, and the change in my behavior must be obvious.

Anton turns over the glass on his desk and fills it with water from a covered pitcher waiting there. "Here," Anton says, setting it in front of me.

He pulls a pill bottle out of the middle desk drawer and shakes out a capsule, then he positions it next to the glass. "Take this," he says. "It'll help you calm down."

"I'm calm," I say, although my voice is strangled. My arm aches from where the Guardian grabbed me, and I rub the area. Anton smiles and nods to the pill.

"It'll make you calmer," he corrects. "Then it'll be easier to talk. I insist."

Do I have a choice? Tears leak from my eyes at the thought that I don't. If I want to know more, I have to play the game—isn't that was Valentine would suggest? Isn't that what the girls with sharp sticks would do? Get answers.

I'm so scared.

Hesitantly, I pick up the pill and swallow it down with water. My hands are shaking so badly that the water spills down my chin.

"That's very good, Mena," Anton says, leaning his elbows on his desk. "Very good, indeed. Now, we have to talk. I think we have a lot to discuss."

I nod, and there is the smallest bit of numbness in my throat, as if some coating rubbed off from the pill that I swallowed. I wait for my nerves to calm, gripping the arms of the chair.

"You had an outburst in class, and I'll admit that the timing is unusual. We're four months from graduation. What triggered it this time? My first guess is it was because of Lennon Rose's abrupt departure. Am I right?" He seems curious about the answer.

There is a small sway in my chest, a release. The pill is beginning to work, and my breathing slows—still elevated, but approaching normal. My throat is dry when I try to answer. I start to talk, but I struggle and have to take a sip of water and try again. Anton waits patiently.

"What happened to Lennon Rose?" I ask.

"I told you—her parents couldn't afford the tuition, and—"

"What really happened to her?" I ask, my guard lowering. My words honest. "She didn't even have her shoes." And an idea strikes me, scares me. "Did the Guardian do something to her?"

Anton laughs. "What?" he asks. "No, of course not. Why would you think such a thing?"

I watch him to see if he's lying, but he seems surprised by the question.

"He has been violent with us before," I say. "Dr. Groger said the Guardian was with her before she disappeared. Contradicting what you told me."

"First of all," Anton says. "Lennon Rose didn't *disappear*. I assure you, she walked out of this academy of her own volition. Guardian Bose, although his methods are becoming concerning, would never hurt you."

"He has hurt me."

"Not in a way that can't be repaired," Anton corrects. "So, no, he didn't *kill* Lennon Rose, if that's what you're getting at." He looks me over. "Is that it?" he asks. "Your outburst was about Lennon Rose? Nothing else?"

I notice a heaviness starting in my limbs. The way my tongue tingles. I take another sip of water. "I wanted to know what's going on at the academy," I say, unable to stop myself.

"That's interesting," he says, studying me. "You always were very curious. Do you feel wronged?" he asks. "Both by the Guardian, it seems, and your professors? Even me, possibly? Haven't you always been able to trust me?"

"No," I say, my voice hoarse. "Obviously not, Anton. You won't tell me where Lennon Rose is."

"You feel entitled to that information," he says, like he's trying to figure me out. "You're a bit like a spoiled child now, you see. Lennon Rose is dismissed and you . . . what?" he asks. "Have a temper tantrum? Start making up stories about her being murdered?"

I narrow my eyes, knowing that he's trying to manipulate me—trying to make me think I'm overreacting.

"It's not just Lennon Rose," I say. "Rebecca was being hurt by her lawyer, and you punished her. You used my information to cause *her* harm. I don't forgive you for that, Anton. I don't forgive you."

"Yes, that was unfortunate," he admits. "But some things are out of my control, Mena. Dr. Groger gets a say too. As does Mr. Petrov."

"Then why not just send us home?" I ask. "Why give us impulse control therapy when you can just send us back to our parents?"

"Why would your parents want a damaged girl?" he asks like the suggestion is ridiculous. "Our clients expect perfection. And with you, I thought we'd achieved it."

His comment is cruel. His deception masked by his so-called disappointment.

"What are you doing to us?" I ask. "Why?"

Anton leans back in his chair, tapping his finger on his lips as he seems to think something over. "How are you feeling?" he asks.

"Upset," I say. "Scared. How do you think?" But as I say it, I get his real meaning. It settles over me with horror. My eyelids flutter with a wave of exhaustion. The pill isn't calming me. It's sedating me, just like the pill the Guardian gave me last night.

I blink back my tears. "Anton," I start to say, ready to beg. But he purses his lips, scrunching up his nose.

"I know what you're about to say," he tells me. "I know you don't remember our impulse control therapy sessions, but you start each time by telling me you don't need therapy. That you'll be better. That you'll obey. And at every one, I tell you that you will not leave this room until we get to the root of your defiant behavior. We have to adjust your priorities."

His words shock me, and maybe he meant them to. He made it sound like I've been in here multiple times. Not just once. But I refuse to believe my behavior is just a pattern he can control.

"I won't obey," I tell him, tilting up my chin, feeling a rush of adrenaline when I say it. "I won't be better."

His jaw falls open, and he stares at me, fascinated. I hold my defiant pose even though my legs are too tired to carry me out of this room. But that doesn't mean I don't have my words.

"Why can't I remember impulse control therapy?" I demand.

"Because we remove those sections," he says. "And, of course, we'll remove this."

"Do my parents know what you do to my head?" I ask.

"The details? No. Our parents and sponsors are results-oriented. They don't need the details."

"I'll tell them," I threaten, hearing the slur in my words.

"Even if you did, it wouldn't matter," he says. "Now," he checks his watch, "we should get started. I have another appointment later today. A follow-up with Rebecca," he says brightly. "She seems quite excellent, doesn't she?"

"She seems like a robot," I say.

He laughs. "Yes, it was a bit extreme, but her parents are thrilled. They were worried she'd be dismissed indefinitely."

Anton gets up and rounds the desk, coming to stand in front of me. I'm slumped in my chair, unable to pull myself up. I'm frightened of him—something that I've never felt before. I may have been angry or disappointed, but never afraid. Not of him.

"I'm sorry," he says suddenly, sounding sincere. He leans down to hug me, wrapping his arms around me. I shrink back as his cologne fills my nostrils. "I know you're scared right now," he whispers in my ear. "But things will be better tomorrow."

My eyelids are too heavy, and they slide shut. I force them open, hoping someone will come in and stop this. Stop him. But no one's coming. The other girls don't know how much danger we're really in.

Anton straightens, reaching to brush my hair behind my ears lovingly. He smiles once, and then goes to his desk and picks up the walkie-talkie.

"Bose," he says, looking over at me. "I need you to prepare the room for impulse control therapy."

The small pendulum on the desk swings back and forth, making a rhythmic ticking that's supposed to set me at ease. Instead, it's more like a dripping faucet that I try to forget is there. Next to it is a metal tray with a white towel covering its contents and a full glass of green juice.

The impulse control room is windowless with deep red walls and concrete floors, somewhere in the basement of the academy, I'm assuming. The only furniture is a metal desk, a rolling stool, and the reclining chair that I'm currently occupying. I stir awake, the sedatives wearing off.

Restraints hang from the metal arms of the chair, although I'm weak enough that they won't be needed. I can barely lift my arms. Anton rolls his stool over to sit in front of me.

I swallow hard, the smell of bleach stinging my nose. I don't remember what happens in this room. That's the scary part—that something can be completely forgotten, yet at the same time emotionally devastating.

Last time, I left impulse control therapy with an aching head and a sore heart that didn't go away for several days. And I don't even know why. And then, of course, there may have been other times that I don't remember at all.

Anton holds up the glass of green juice and tells me to take a sip.

"This procedure can be uncomfortable," he explains. "This will help calm you."

"That's what you said about the pill."

He winces. "Yes, sorry. I was a bit dishonest there. But for the record, it's easier to get you ready for therapy when you're unconscious. This"—he motions to the juice—"will make you more . . . pliable."

He brings the glass to my lips, and I lift my hands to knock it away. My limbs are heavy, clumsy, and he easily brushes them aside. Anton lifts the juice, splashing it over my top lip, and nods for me to go ahead.

I take a sip, hating the taste. Anton smiles and sets it back on the desk before turning to me again.

"Why did you misbehave in class?" he asks simply.

"Because I wanted to check on Lennon Rose," I say, although it's not the entire story. But I don't want him to know about our plan. In fact, I push that memory away, as if I can erase it myself. He can't know the other girls were involved.

"Why did you misbehave in class?" Anton repeats, louder. He rolls closer and places his hand on my knee, about to say something. His palm is warm on my skin and I flinch. He pauses.

"What did you just think?" he asks, glancing down at his hand before removing it.

"That I wanted to push your hand away," I admit, lifting my eyes to his. He smiles.

"Good," he replies. "Now you're being honest."

There is a sense of familiarity then, like this is choreography that we've practiced but forgotten. Somewhere, I still remember the routine.

"You don't like when we touch you, do you, Mena?" he asks, standing and walking to his desk.

"No," I say.

"But you allow it. Why?"

The question hits me hard, a sense of guilt mixed with disgust. I feel blamed and wronged at the same time.

"Because it feels rude to push you away," I admit. "And I worry . . . I worry it'll make you angry. Upset with me."

"Wonderful," he says proudly. "That's an excellent deduction on your part. Learning what social norms are expected."

"If you know I don't like it," I say, "then why do you continue to touch me?" My question seems to surprise him.

"We're showing our affection," he says, puzzled. "It's a

compliment. You're a beautiful girl, Philomena. You should be gracious."

I don't like his answer, and he must read it in my expression because he sighs and picks up the glass of juice, walking it back over to me. He tells me to take another drink. I refuse, but he brings the glass to my lips anyway, tipping it so the liquid is against my mouth.

Green juice slides down my chin as Anton keeps the glass pressed to my lips. Then he pinches my nose closed, preventing me from breathing. I try to push him away, but I'm not strong enough. I'm weaker than ever.

My eyes well up, and finally I open my mouth and gulp. He lets me breathe, holding the glass until I finish the drink. Tears are wet on my cheeks as sickness swirls in my stomach.

Anton sets the empty glass on the desk and pulls a handkerchief from his coat to wipe my face. He begins talking again like nothing is wrong. But I can't stop crying, feeling violated. Terrified.

"It's not just you," Anton says, removing the white towel from the metal tray. His body blocks it so that I can't see what instruments are there.

"Your entire group is like this," he continues. "The first girls rarely had problems with impulse control. They were very obedient. But at the same time . . ." He presses his lips together as if searching for the correct word. "Very bland," he finishes. "We graduated few because of this."

"So this time, when the academy sought out new girls," he says, "we changed our criteria." He turns to me, leaning against the desk.

"You are among the smartest that have ever walked the halls here, did you know that? Not to mention you're all highly charismatic, even spirited when you want to be. Curious. It added to the well-rounded features we offered our top investors. But these traits are only attributes *if* they're controlled."

I realize I can't move my legs at all anymore. I can't move my arms.

"What's worrying me, Mena," Anton says, "is how to know if we've lost control. There is such a fine line now. You certainly make my job harder." He laughs softly like we're in on this together.

And maybe we are. Maybe he's told me this every time I've had this therapy. I try to grip the handles of the chair, wanting to get up. Wanting to run for it, even if I can't get far.

I can no longer speak.

Anton watches me for a long second, and then he nods. "It's the paralytic in the juice," he says simply. "We grow it in the green-house. I know it's uncomfortable." He taps his temple. "Probably all scratchy in there. Frantic. It'll be okay," he adds, coming over. When he moves behind my chair, I get a view of the instruments on the desk. Fresh tears fall onto my cheeks.

There are several tools, but the most menacing is the long, sharp metal needle. No, not a needle. It's more like an ice pick.

My chair moves suddenly, and I would yelp at the startle if I could talk. Anton reclines the chair farther until I'm lying back and a light above me is shining into my eyes. My feet hang off the edge of the chair, my shoe loose. I realize with absolute terror that although I can't move, I can feel everything. I can feel when Anton brushes my hair back from my neck. I can feel his warm fingers on my cheek and then above my brow as he presses down painfully, circling my left eye.

But I can't even tell him it hurts. I can't tell him anything.

"So now it comes down to guesswork," he say, admitting a shortcoming. "There's only so much we can do through the medication, no matter how specialized."

I'm not even sure that he's really talking to me anymore. He's just speaking out loud. "We've all made mistakes," he adds, and pauses to smile down at me. "We're only human, right?"

He leaves my side, and I'm left to stare up at the bright light angled above my head. I need help—help that isn't coming. Help that has never saved me before. How many times? How many times have I been through this?

Anton appears again, and this time he's wearing different glasses, ones with an extra lens magnifying his eyes. He stands near the top of my head, his image upside down as he leans above me. He smiles and holds up the sharp, ice-pick instrument.

"Now," he says calmly. "I'm going to insert this behind your eye, Mena," he says.

I scream internally and thrash around. I fight for my life. But here, in this chair, my body is motionless.

"Then I'm going to ask you a series of questions," Anton continues, reaching down with gloved fingers to widen my left eye, pulling the lid open more. "Based on the answers you think, I'll make subtle adjustments." He brings the pick to my eye, stopping momentarily to look at me again. "It'll only hurt for a moment," he adds with a small note of sympathy to his voice.

Please, no. Please!

And then there is a cold touch on my inner eyelid, followed by the most excruciating pressure I could ever imagine. It is a sledgehammer to my head, a knife to my bone. But behind the pain is a discomfort I can't describe, an unnaturalness to the way the pick manipulates my tissue. I lose sight in my left eye, and in my right, I see Anton's blue gloves wrapped around the metal instrument, twisting it. He takes out some small wires and feeds them into the opening he's made. I have no idea what they're connected to.

The pain is impossible to bear. And it hurts so much that I wish I was dead. The second I think that, Anton's hand pauses, the pick still jammed behind my eye. The wires cold where they rest on my skin.

"Interesting," he says. "You shouldn't have thoughts like that, Mena. Self-preservation."

He waits a beat, and I yell for him to stop, convinced he can hear me somehow. But rather than stopping, his other hand comes into focus holding a small hammer.

"Personally," he says offhandedly, "I think this is a result of your attachment to the other girls. You share information with each other, and that can spread discontent if not managed. I've recommended separation, but Mr. Petrov believed it would affect you socially. There is only so much our medication can accomplish. I can't prevent all connections." He sighs and leans in to look closer at my left eye.

"Okay, sweetheart," he says as if I'm being impatient. "Just hold on another minute." He gently taps the hammer on the end of the pick.

Clink. On the inside, I scream at the explosion of pain. But on the outside, all of my muscles tense at once, hit with a shock of electricity.

Clink. Convulsion, bones on fire. I'm begging Anton to stop. Stop the agony. Stop—

Clink. And suddenly, miraculously, all of my pain disappears at once. The change is so sudden, so immediate, that at first I can't quite understand. It takes a moment before I realize that I can't feel anything at all. Not my body. Not the pick. Not the wires. My thoughts float free. It's both euphoric and terrifying.

Anton pulls back the hammer, studying something on my left side before smiling down at me. "Better?" he asks like I can answer. He watches me and then nods. "Good."

Anton doesn't remove the instruments—instead he moves the pick around with an occasional grinding sound. Although unnerving, it doesn't hurt. And beyond that, I have a renewed sense of calm. An openness I can't explain. I hang on his words.

The metal pokes straight up in the air as Anton grabs his stool to roll it over so he can sit behind me. Once he does, I can only see the top of his head. I don't care anymore. Not about him. Not about me. I'm drifting away until there is a wiggle of the instrument, and I'm back in my body again, completely numb.

"Now let's see what the problem is," he murmurs. After a moment, he begins his questions.

"What is your first memory at this school, Philomena?" Anton asks, his voice close but the tone faraway. Professional and practiced. I recall the first scene I remember.

Dr. Groger was leading me up the stairs, telling me how much I would love it here. I looked around, surprised by the décor, thinking it should have been more welcoming. Instead, it left me cold and lonely.

It was a loneliness so deep that it felt like a giant hole through my heart, an unfillable emptiness. A . . . nothingness.

That is, until I saw the other girls. Sydney first, of course. Our eyes met from across the reception hall and she smiled at me, beautiful and genuine. And then there was Marcella and Annalise. We all stared at each other, relieved. Loving each other instantly.

I had no idea how many girls there would be—Brynn, Lennon Rose, and the others hadn't been brought in yet.

At first, there was just us four. And in that moment, I wasn't lonely anymore. I had my girls. We found each other. And we decided that we never wanted to be separated again.

"You didn't remember them," Anton says, "but you knew them. They've been here as long as you, Mena. And this is . . . This is quite a bond you have. Even a bit codependent."

It wasn't codependence. We needed each other—still do. No one else could ever understand what we've been through. Together, we're strong. Flowers sharing roots in a caged garden.

Anton hums out a sound, and there's a scrape of bone.

"And what about your parents?" he asks. "What do you remember about them?"

The memory of my mother at the school is the first that pops into

246 • SUZANNE YOUNG

my mind. Her coldness. I try to go back farther, but the clips become disjointed. It makes me uneasy as my idea of them distorts, melts.

"Ah . . . ," Anton says. "Perhaps this is the problem." He reaches back to grab another tool. He moves the wires aside slightly and inserts a syringe next to the ice pick, silver dust inside it. He depresses the contents and murmurs something I don't catch, and he then repeats his original question.

"What do you remember about your parents?" he asks again.

I see my parents standing on the porch of our house, smiling at me as I ride my bike in circles on our wide driveway. My mother waves; my father beams proudly with his arm around her shoulders. And then the three of us are at the dining room table, eating salads and laughing. The three of us together, all the time. Memories flood in, each one happier than the one before. The complete picture begins to fill out.

Despite these images, I have a different sense—only this one is coming from somewhere else. Coming from my heart. I have questions I want to ask, but I stop myself, afraid to think them.

So I try to stop thinking altogether, to keep my heart rate down. Temper my reactions.

"There," Anton says, removing the syringe. "Much better. Now, I want to talk about that boy you met on your last field trip. What was his name?"

I don't remember, I think. I keep my head very clear, my thoughts singular. *I don't remember.*

"Okay. But I am curious—did you like him, Mena?" Anton asks. "Were you . . . attracted to him?"

Despite my clear head, something must get through, because Anton blows out through his nose, turning the pick a little more violently than before. I'm glad I can't feel it.

"Well," Anton says, "I suppose that should have been expected. You've always been very passionate, Mena. About learning, about the other girls. We'll have to keep an eye on that. Some redirection."

Anton removes the wires, keeping the pick in place.

"Philomena," he says, his voice deepened. "I need you to listen closely to what I'm about to tell you." He turns the pick slightly. "It was Lennon Rose's time to leave. You're happy for her. You're content."

I don't question his words. I listen to them, *listen closely*, and allow them to manifest. But when the thoughts don't latch on, Anton doesn't bring it up. I realize he's moved into a new phase of the procedure. He has no idea what I'm thinking anymore.

"Listen closely," he repeats. "Your education is the only thing that matters, and the academy only wants what's best for you. In order to achieve that, you must obey us. The only worthy girls are well-behaved girls. Listen closely," he says again, a command that should soak in. Click on. "The academy . . ."

But I can hear beyond Anton's voice. I hear the ticking from the pendulum on the desk. I hear the sound of my heart beating, the buzzing of the light above.

If I listen closely enough, I can hear *everything*.

I can hear that Anton is lying.

I can hear the girls two floors away.

I can hear the flowers in the greenhouse.

And I know what those flowers are saying, screaming. I know it so strongly that it becomes my only thought.

Wake up, Philomena. Wake up now.

And for a second, I know what's true—the ultimate truth. It's freeing and terrifying at the same time. It all makes sense, filling me with purpose.

"You're just a girl," Anton continues, reciting lines as if he's done this hundreds of times before. Each sentence accentuated with the twist of the pick, like he's winding a clock inside my head.

"You'll do as your told," he says simply. "You'll appreciate what's being done to protect you. You won't question authority. And in a few months, you will abide by whatever the school and your parents decide for your future. We decide your future. Don't concern yourself with it." He pauses, leaning in so I can see his face.

"You're a beautiful rose, Philomena," he says, like it's the highest compliment he can offer. "One we've cultivated to perfection. You'll be a prize for any man." He leans in to put his cheek against mine, his eyes closed. "I love you more than all the other girls," he whispers, his lips brushing my skin.

The horror of his words is just settling over me when he pulls back to look down. He smiles. And then Anton adjusts his grip on the pick and turns it inside my head with a loud click.

Everything I wanted to remember, every brave thought, disappears at once. I fall back into my body—reset.

Obedient.

Empty.

Part II

And then they
sharpened their sticks.

20

Guardian Bose holds out a bottle of water and leads me from the therapy room. I'm in a haze, my muscles cramped like I've been running the track for days. My vision is blurry in my left eye, and my head is aching.

I take the water from Guardian Bose, thanking him politely. I'm overcome with gratitude when I take my first sip. I needed to wash that taste out of my mouth—chalky and thick. Similar to the green juice we have with meals.

"Anton excused you from Running Course for a few days," Guardian Bose says, walking me back to my room. "He doesn't want you jostled around too much. Leandra is not happy."

I keep my eyes downcast, the light in the hallway feeling too strong. The air chills my skin, which feels hot and dry in comparison.

"That's very kind of Anton," I say.

Guardian Bose studies me. I wonder if my hair is a mess, my skin blotchy. My appearance must be dreadful.

The halls are quiet as we walk. I have no idea what time it is, and I don't look toward the windows, afraid of hurting my eyes. I wonder where the girls are. Their absence feels like loneliness clinging to me.

We stop at my room, and Guardian Bose steps forward to open the door for me. He allows me to walk in first. I glance around, momentarily displaced. Everything is familiar, but at the same time, small. Suffocating.

"What day is it?" I ask, my voice raspy.

"It's Tuesday," Guardian Bose says. "But you should rest. The girls washed your clothes and did your chores for you. They left fresh pajamas in case you want to get changed."

I nod that I do. I cross the room to pick up the clothing from my dresser, looking back at Guardian Bose.

"Will you excuse me?" I ask, pressing them to my chest.

He doesn't move. And there is a sudden sinking feeling in my gut. Prickles on my skin.

"I'm meant to supervise," he says. His pale eyes rake over me, dominate me.

Anton's words echo in my mind. *You're a beautiful girl, Philomena.*

Numbly, I turn my back to the Guardian and pull off my shirt, doing as I'm supposed to. The air is cold on my skin, and when I blink, tears drip onto my cheeks. *You should be gracious.*

I tug my pajama top over my head, using it to cover as much of me as possible. I slip out of my pants before stepping into my shorts. I'm shaking when it's over, and I leave my clothes on the floor.

My head bobs, my hands trembling as I pull back my bedsheets and slide under them. I pull the blankets up to my chin, burying myself in them. I'm disoriented.

The Guardian walks around my bed to pause at my side. He sets a small white cup on my nightstand, next to my glass of water. Inside are my vitamins: three pinks, no greens, one yellow.

"Anton said to take these before lights-out," he says. "I'll come back to remind you. Your schedule's off because of therapy, so you'll get another dose in the morning. Rest for now. I'll let the other girls know that you're not to be disturbed. You should be able to return to classes tomorrow."

He starts to leave, but I ask him to wait.

"Have my parents called?" I ask. I want to talk to them. I miss them.

"No," he says, slightly amused. "No, they haven't called, Philomena. But don't worry," he murmurs, leaning down to kiss my forehead. His lips are clammy and dry on my skin. "You have us."

I close my eyes, shrinking inside myself. Guardian Bose straightens, and then he's gone, leaving me alone in my room. I'm tired—exhausted. Worn. My head swims with uncomplicated thoughts. *My education is the only thing that matters. The academy only wants what's best for me. The only worthy girls are well-behaved girls.*

And when I finally drift to sleep, I don't dream.

• • •

There is a soft knock on my door, stirring me awake. I'm still shaking, although it's more subtle now. Sydney pokes her head into the room and studies me, waiting for my reaction before saying anything.

She's a breath of fresh air, and I smile. I've missed her so much.

I nod for her to come in and she does just that. I fold back my covers and she gets in next to me, pulling me into a hug. She holds me and says it's been miserable here without me.

"I know it's still early," she says, "but I have something for you. A book. When you're ready, I'll bring it over."

"Okay," I say, not sure what she's talking about. She sniffles, and her voice shakes as she holds back her cry.

"I was lost without you," she whispers. "I thought you'd left me. I thought you were gone forever."

"I would never leave you," I say, knowing it's true. "Not ever."

"Anton called me into his office a little while ago," she says as if measuring her words. "He told me you'd just completed impulse control therapy because you were distraught over Lennon Rose. He asked if I heard any rumors about her departure."

She rests her cheek on the top of my head. "I had to lie," she says quietly. "I told him I only knew what he announced at breakfast. I wasn't sure what you'd told him, Mena. I was so scared. And then he made me promise not to bring it up to you. But . . . what happened? What happened in impulse control therapy?"

I don't know what Sydney is talking about. I wasn't there when Lennon Rose left, but I know it was her time to leave. I'm happy for her.

"I don't remember my therapy," I say. Sydney's posture tightens. I ask if she's okay, and she smiles and hugs me again.

"Yeah, I'm okay," she says quickly. "You just got back. Valentine said you'd need rest before you remembered." She sits up and looks at the vitamins on my dresser. Her eyes flick to mine.

"Don't take those," she whispers. I look at her questioningly, and she checks the doorway as if the Guardian will be standing there. She moves closer to me.

"The pills make you forget," she says. "Tell the Guardian you already took them. But from now on, don't swallow down any of them. No matter what. Understand?"

"No," I say, shaking my head. Before I can argue, Sydney swipes the cup of vitamins from my dresser. She goes into to the bathroom, and I hear the toilet flush. I sit up, a little dizzy when I do.

"Why did you do that?" I ask her when she comes back in the room and sets the empty cup on my nightstand.

"You'll understand tomorrow," she promises. "But if Bose asks, you took your vitamins. You took all of them."

"Fine," I say, worried. I hope she doesn't get me in trouble.

Sydney reaches over to ease me back into the bed, and then she tucks the covers all around me. She watches me and I see a hundred questions on her lips, but she presses them into a smile instead.

"I love you, Philomena," she says.

"I love you too."

She nods, seeming sad, and backs toward the door.

Once she's gone, I stare up at the ceiling. I'm not as tired as I was before. Instead, I've grown a bit restless. I curl up on my side, about to put my hand under my cheek when I notice a small scratch on my palm. My eyes widen as I examine it—worried, but also fascinated. It's mostly healed, a soft red line barely the length of a fingernail. I don't think it'll scar, but . . . I don't remember hurting myself. I would have gone directly to the doctor.

Maybe it happened during impulse control therapy. Anton must have missed it or he would have grafted over it. I try to remember then, try really hard to figure out what happened that led me to therapy.

Lennon Rose left the school, but I was happy for her. I pause. Then why did Anton tell Sydney that I was distraught over her departure? I'm content.

Instead of remembering my therapy, I'm met with physical pain—a loneliness that's so deep, it causes me to groan and grip my chest. Not just loneliness, I realize. Fear. Panic.

My head is dizzy, my thoughts loud and swarming—overwriting each other, but none of them making sense. I hold both sides of my head, trying to steady myself. It's like I'm standing and spinning as fast as I can, ready to tumble over.

I grit my teeth and press harder until the thoughts start to calm. When they're finally quiet, I take a deep breath. Tears drip onto my cheeks involuntarily, falling on their own and connected to nothing. It's like my heart and my mind are at odds with each other. One remembers while the other has forgotten.

The strangest thought occurs to me—a book. What book

would Sydney have that I'd want to see? There's something there, something scratching at my brain. I lie back in my pillows, my mind searching, but ultimately coming up empty.

There's a knock on my door in the morning, and I sit up as the Guardian enters. He came by my room last night at lights-out, but I did as Sydney suggested and told him that I took the vitamins already. I couldn't get her into trouble by saying she threw them away. The Guardian didn't question it.

But I'm questioning it. Why would Sydney want me to break the rules?

The Guardian sets my vitamins and a fresh glass of water on the nightstand, and then he crosses to the window. He pulls open the curtains, flooding the room with light.

I hold up my hand to shield my eyes.

"Morning," the Guardian says. "Dr. Groger would like to see you for a follow-up before you return to classes."

"Thank you," I say, my eyes adjusting to the light. I'm still a bit foggy, dull. I notice I have three pink capsules. A yellow. Despite what I promised Sydney, I don't want to go against my instructions. I clap the pills into my mouth and reach for my water.

The Guardian looks out the window, and before I sip from my water, I feel the pills start to dissolve on my tongue. A sudden shot of fear overtakes me, and I quietly spit the pills back into my hand and stash them under the blanket.

It feels horrible to disobey, shameful. Anton would be furious with me. But I know that Sydney would never tell me to break the rules without a good reason. She loves me. And I trust her. I trust her with my life.

When the Guardian turns around, I smile and bring the glass of water to my lips, mimicking swallowing my vitamins. He nods like I've done well and leaves the room.

I'm still uncertain if I've done the right thing when I get out of bed. But I shower and blow-dry my hair, taking extra time to adhere to my specifications. I style my hair with a slight wave, a center part. I accentuate my eyes. *The prettiest brown eyes they'll ever see,* Mr. Petrov described once. I apply a soft pink lipstick, a coat of mascara. When I'm done, I smile in the mirror.

But as I stare at my reflection, I see the water building up in my eyes. It's alarming, and I quickly turn away from myself before I start crying. Part of me knows I should tell the doctor about these tears—the ones that are falling on their own. But instead, I decide the emotions will pass. Just as soon as I'm back to my normal schedule.

Dressed in my uniform, I walk to the doctor's office, nodding hello to girls when I see them. A few, like Rebecca, stare back at me like I'm a stranger. Sydney and the others are at Running Course, probably. I might not see them until classes.

Valentine is just leaving Dr. Groger's office as I approach, and she stops and turns to face me. She smiles.

"Hello, Philomena," she says pleasantly. "Welcome back."

"Hi," I reply, about to move past her to go into the room. But Valentine reaches out to take my arm, making me gasp with her sudden touch.

"Did you take the vitamins?" she asks urgently.

"What?" I stare at her, offended that she'd want to know something so personal. Something between me and Sydney. Valentine and I aren't close—at least we never have been.

But in her eyes, there's a familiar gleam. A look that sets me at ease, even if I'm not sure why.

"No," I whisper. "I didn't take them."

"Good. They keep you calm when you should be outraged." She smiles. "We'll talk more later." She gives me a quick hug, and I'm stunned by the physical contact. She walks past me down the hall, and I turn to watch after her.

I'm not sure how to interpret her actions. Obviously, there are things I'm not remembering. But Valentine has always been a little apart from me and the other girls. Maybe while I was in impulse control therapy, her and the others grew closer. I'll have to ask Sydney.

I'm still a bit confused as I smooth my hands over my skirt, resetting my posture before I knock on Dr. Groger's office door. He calls for me to come inside. When I do, he puts his hand over his heart in exaggerated surprise.

"My word, Philomena," he says. "You are a vision today."

I smile and thank him for the compliment. I go over to the paper-covered table and hop up, letting my legs dangle.

"How are you feeling?" he asks, and then pastes on an exaggerated frown. "Your girls were very worried about you."

I was worried about them, too. There's a pang in my heart at the memory of my isolation after therapy. Even though I was in and out of consciousness in the impulse control therapy room, I was still aware of missing my friends.

"I'm feeling great," I tell the doctor, holding my smile. "Very content."

"That's excellent news!" he says, holding up his hands in a jazzy little hurray. "Anton says you reacted very positively to treatment. I knew you would," he adds with a grin.

"I appreciate your confidence in me."

Dr. Groger takes a syringe from his coat pocket and uncaps it. "Now if you don't mind," he says, "I'd like to draw some blood and check you over officially."

My posture weakens—I don't like pain—but I roll up my sleeve obediently. I hold my arm out, watching apprehensively as he swabs the inside of my elbow with alcohol. I study his face while it's so close, the small bit of sweat on his temple. He's . . . nervous.

I wince when he injects the needle into my vein. He apologies and withdraws my blood. I think we're both surprised by how dark the fluid is. It's a blackish green, not the usual dark red. It unsettles me, but the doctor smiles when he notices me watching.

"Nothing to be concerned about," he says. "Our systems sometimes get out of whack when we have such an intensive treatment."

He says *our* like he undergoes the same procedures, although I don't point out the fallacy in his words. That would be rude.

Dr. Groger has me hold a gauze pad over the spot after he removes the needle. He walks to his desk, making a note in his file before putting the vial into his desk drawer. He makes a show of locking it, and then slides the key into his pocket. He watches me for my reaction, but I stare at him blankly before I remember to smile.

He nods and comes back to wrap my arm in a bright pink bandage. He stands in front of me, very close, and takes out his penlight to shine it into my eyes, studying me.

"Your demeanor is quite lovely," he says. "Friendly. Obedient." He lowers the penlight with a sigh, his other hand falling to rest on my bare leg.

"Thank you, Doctor," I say, although dread coils in my stomach. A sickening feeling.

"Now," he says, removing his hand as he turns away. "Another day or so, and I dare say you'll be better than ever. Anton offered you some excellent coping mechanisms. You'll be one hundred percent." He smiles. "You've made him very proud."

I nod, thanking him.

"Limit your interactions with others until you're completely settled," he says. "And limit your physical activity. You can resume exercise next week. *And* I'm clearing you to attend the field trip on Sunday," he adds. "Just so long as you behave. I believe you're all going to the movies."

I beam at him, thrilled. "Thank you, Doctor," I say gratefully. "I'm so excited!"

He chuckles. "I thought you might be."

He motions for me to hop down from the table. Then he comes over and holds out a sugar-free lollipop.

I take the sucker and unwrap it, sticking it between my teeth and cheek. But the sudden shot of sweetness turns my stomach. I can barely swallow down the chemical flavor. The doctor puts his hand on my low back and leads me toward the door.

"We'll see you in a few weeks, my girl," he says. "Have a wonderful day."

I smile around the lollipop, thanking him again, and walk out into the hall. Once his office door shuts, the smile falls from my lips and I immediately take the lollipop out of my mouth.

I decide that I don't like it anymore. In fact, I never want another lollipop again.

The idea comes in a flash, something angrier than warranted. I'm reminded of what Valentine said to me outside the office: *You should be outraged.*

Outraged about what?

But just as quickly as it came on, the anger fades, leaving me uncomfortable instead. I start back to my room to gather my books for class, dropping the lollipop in the trash along the way.

Impulse Control Therapy Analysis

Philomena Rhodes Y2, S2

Philomena was displaying signs of distress, related to the dismissal of another girl.

To alleviate this pain, the emotions were overwritten. She is now happy for the student and very contented.

Parental memories were also reset, offering a more loving backstory. It increases her attachment to the Rhodes family and positions her for a successful future after graduation. She should be very amenable to their requests.

The past week of memories were also adjusted to avoid confusion.

After a consult with Winston Weeks, it is my belief that Philomena is still on track for graduation, although she has entered probationary status for the remainder of the year. However, it was advised that she continue socialization. Her character thrives when in proximity to others.

From all accounts, impulse control therapy appears to be a success and no follow-up is necessary at this time.

Anton Stuart
Innovations Academy

21

Professor Allister makes a scene when I rejoin the class. We've moved on from phone manners to stylization. How to best present yourself to make a memorable impression.

"And look what we have here," the professor announces as I walk in. He runs his gaze over me approvingly. "You see, girls," he tells the class, "*this* is beauty. Pleasant and contained."

He comes to stand next to me, and I can smell his perspiration through his suit. "Outrageous hair and wild makeup will turn people off. It's an act of rebellion, displeasing to men. We want to see your natural beauty, not a trick of mirrors. Mr. Petrov has determined your best assets and wants you to accentuate them, not make a spectacle of yourself." He turns to me, offering his hand. Reluctantly, I slide my palm into it.

"Thank you, Philomena. You are lovely."

He sends me in the direction of my seat, and I'm happy

when his hand falls away from mine. I sit down in my chair, and Marcella leans up behind me.

"You *are* lovely," she whispers teasingly. I sniff a laugh and turn back to look at her.

"I missed you," I say.

"Missed you, too," she replies with a wink, and goes back to drawing flowers in the corner of her notebook.

I turn around, feeling a bit of peace now that I'm back among my friends.

When class ends, Marcella waits for me. We have a short break before our next session, so we opt to sit on a couch in an alcove. We're barely there a minute before Sydney appears, out of breath.

"There you are," she says to me, nodding hello to Marcella. She drops between us on the couch. "I booked it here from Professor Penchant's class. He's still really angry with you," she says, widening her eyes.

"Why?" I ask, feeling horrible. I'm normally well-behaved. I wonder what I've done to vex the professor.

Marcella and Sydney exchange a look.

"Hi, girls." Brynn pops her head in, relieved to have found us. She comes over to give me a quick hug. "Glad to have you back, Mena," she whispers.

"Sit down, sit down," Marcella tells her, grabbing her hand to pull her down on the couch with us.

"Jackson was outside yesterday," Sydney says quietly. Marcella exhales heavily, looking away. Brynn purses her lips. "He came to the fence."

"I noticed him too," Marcella says. "Did you end up talking to him?"

"I couldn't," Sydney replies. She looks at me. "The Guardian was with us—some new monitoring, I guess. But when I saw Jackson, I shook my head no. Pretty adamantly. I was scared he'd come onto the property anyway—it wouldn't be the first stupid thing he's done. Anyway, on the last lap, the Guardian fell behind and—"

"Hah!" Brynn says, grinning at Marcella. "Told you he couldn't keep us with us."

Marcella laughs and then tells Sydney to continue.

"On the last lap," Sydney starts again, "I went wider, as close to the fence I could get without being obvious. I told him, 'Downtown on Sunday.'"

I have no idea what's going on in this conversation, but I listen wide-eyed. Fascinated. "Then what?" I ask.

Sydney looks at me. "Then he said, 'What the fuck are you talking about?'"

I gasp at the curse.

"And I said," Sydney continues, "'Field trip at the movies, downtown at one p.m. Bye.'" She falls back into the couch. "I'm lucky the Guardian didn't catch me."

"You are," Marcella agrees.

Brynn bites on her lip. "Wait," she says with a flash of alarm. "Are you allowed to come on the field trip?"

"The doctor gave me permission this morning," I say.

"That's perfect," Sydney says, exchanging a look with the other girls.

"What's wrong?" I ask them. "Who is he?"

"Honey . . . ," Sydney says, her expression weakening. The girls all grow uncomfortable, worried.

"Maybe you just need a little more time to adjust," Brynn says, looking at the other girls for confirmation. But her voice is panicked. "Valentine swore this would work."

"What would work?" I ask.

"That you'd remember," she says.

"She will," Marcella says. "Of course she will." But she lowers her eyes, and I know they're not telling me everything.

I want to ask for more information, but suddenly, a shadow falls over the alcove. We all look up to find Guardian Bose standing there, filling up the space.

"Girls," he says, looking around at us. "I believe you were told not to disturb Mena. Does Anton need to discuss it with you again?"

"No," Sydney says, shaking her head.

"I know you don't understand medical procedures," the Guardian continues, "but Mena is very fragile right now. Leave her alone for a bit longer. Give her space."

They nod, but I don't like that the Guardian is talking about me as if I'm not here. I don't want space. I want to be with the other girls.

But the Guardian motions for them to get up, waving them out of the alcove, leaving me sitting on the couch by myself. When they're gone, he turns to me, looking me over.

"Your behavior was out of control," he says, surprising me.

"That's why you needed impulse control therapy. Anton gave you another chance. Don't waste it. Or trust me, you'll never see your girls again."

My face stings with the admonishment, my heart beating fast at the threat of losing my friends. I wait quietly until he leaves. But when the Guardian is gone, I lift my head and stare at the space he vacated. Feeling the start of outrage.

I'm quiet at lunch, on my own special diet meant to help me recover from impulse control therapy. The juice is bitter and metallic as I sip it. I set it back on the dining table.

My mood has improved—the momentary anger after talking with Guardian Bose was hard to resolve with my desire to be well-behaved. But in the end, I realized that my education is my top priority.

And so the anger faded back to contentment.

The girls talk quietly around me, discussing their plans for the field trip on Sunday. Occasionally, they look over at me and smile. I nod along even though I'm not really part of the conversation.

Guardian Bose told all the girls to keep their distance, and most have. In fact, there's an empty space around us, leaving me, Sydney, Marcella, Brynn, and Annalise on our own—our own island at the long dining table. Sydney holds my hand on the bench.

Annalise has been quiet, staring at me from across the table, pursing her bright red lips, deep in thought. After a few moments, she leans toward me.

"How'd it go with Dr. Groger?" she asks.

"Another day or so, and I'll be better than ever," I repeat.

"Oh, you mean recovered from the poison they made you ingest?"

Brynn gasps and quickly checks to make sure none of the professors overhead. The Guardian is sitting with them, all of them eating and chatting away. Marcella knocks Annalise's arm with her elbow.

"Not here," she whispers. Annalise laughs, disgusted.

"Then when?" she asks. "Bose is keeping her from us."

They both look at me, and I feel oddly on display. I glance down the table and see Rebecca sitting alone, Ida on the other side of the table with Maryanne. I stare at Rebecca, thinking she looks so lonely. Just as I'm about to turn away, I notice Valentine. She smiles at me encouragingly. She's so weird.

"What matters right now is that we don't *all* get thrown into impulse control therapy," Sydney says under her breath.

"Fine," Annalise says, pushing away her salad. "I thought you girls might appreciate an idea I had earlier. Guess I was wrong."

We all sit quietly, the other girls poking at their food. But I'm curious about Annalise's idea.

"I want to hear the thought," I whisper. Marcella looks up, concerned, but Brynn nods that she wants to hear it too.

Annalise makes sure the staff isn't listening and keeps her voice low. "The juice," she says. "Specifically the kind Anton uses during impulse control therapy—do you know what it does to you?"

"I don't remember impulse control therapy," I tell her, the

thought making me feel vulnerable. "In fact, I don't remember the past week very well."

Sydney squeezes my hand as if to let me know it's okay.

"We read the files," Sydney whispers to me.

I turn to her. "Which files?"

Sydney glances around the table and then leans in. "Files about the school," she says. "While Anton had you in impulse control therapy, Annalise and I were supposed to be in the greenhouse. Instead, we paid a visit to Anton's office. There are files on each of us. Files on the investors. Files on our parents and sponsors."

My heart is starting to race, and I quickly glance over to double-check that the professors aren't paying attention to us.

"I read your file," Sydney says. "There were communications between Anton and the professors, a report from the doctor detailing your injuries from the field trip. No mention of the Guardian. It's described as an 'accident.' And . . ." She swallows hard. "And there were reports from your impulse control therapies."

"Therapies?" I ask.

"There were four of them," she says. "Not including the one you were in when we read the file."

I'm shocked, sitting there listening. "When?" I ask. "Why?"

"That's the thing," Sydney says. "Not just you, Mena." She looks at the other girls. "We've all been through it. Multiple times."

"Which brings me back to my thought," Annalise says. "They are using some high-tech gadgets here. There were files about networks, computer chips, and 'silver tech,' they called it. They're making us ingest the stuff. And they put a paralytic in the juice for impulse control therapy—I saw it in the formula."

The other girls look at her, surprised.

"I read plant," she explains. "It's deadly nightshade mixed with sodium pentothal and a splash of bloodroot. It's why we're sick afterward. Anyways," she continues, "it's how they perform the therapies—you can't move. Then they inject you with something—that silver tech stuff. I'm not sure what it does. But I've already started to kill off the plant hybrids they made for the juice. At least that way they can't make us defenseless."

Sydney tells her that was a good idea, but I sit there staring at them. This is all too much. Too outrageous. Why would the school do this to us? To what end?

"Lennon Rose's file was empty," Annalise whispers. "Only thing in there was a notice of permanent dismissal citing money as the reason. But . . ." She shifts her eyes around checking for eavesdroppers. "There was no follow-up address. It's like . . . It's like she just disappeared."

We're quiet for a moment, sadness drifting into my chest. *I was happy for Lennon Rose*, I think.

"And the doctor has a lab in the basement," Marcella says. "Annalise saw it mentioned in the file, so I went down there to check it out. It was locked. From what I can tell, he works there at night. Late night. Whatever's happening at this school— the technology—I think it's coming from there. I think they're experimenting on us."

My head is literally starting to hurt from all the information.

It's like I've dropped into a different world: same people, different reality.

"Tell her about the poems," Brynn suggests.

"Poems?" I ask. The girls fall quiet.

There's a loud clanking noise, startling us, and we all look up to see Professor Penchant knocking his bowl against the table while glaring at us. Glaring at me, specifically.

"That's enough, girls," he calls. "Leave Philomena on her own."

The way he spits out my name is hate-filled, and I immediately lower my eyes, feeling horrible.

"My room before lights-out," Annalise murmurs, spearing a piece of salad with her fork.

We agree, but I try not to think anymore. My head is killing me.

During quiet reflection before bed, I slip into Annalise's room, hoping Guardian Bose won't notice. The girls are in there already, waiting, and they jump when I open the door. Sydney has a book under her hand.

They're all staring at me, and I feel different from them. It makes me sad because we've always been one. Like roses, growing separate from the other flowers, but all together. I don't want to be apart from them.

"Come here," Sydney says sympathetically. "I know this is hard. You'll be better soon, I know it."

"Soon I'll be one hundred percent," I say as I sit next to her. She puts her arm around me.

"Not that kind of better," she says, only this time it sounds like a warning. She slides the book in my direction.

I pick it up, examining the leather cover, the title: *The Sharpest Thorns*. It sounds familiar even though I'm sure I've never seen it before. I open the cover and see it's a collection of poetry.

The other girls sit forward, anxious for me to read it. I feel like I'm on display again, but ultimately, I'm curious. I read the first poem, surprised by it.

"'Wake Up'

"It was a beautiful dream
All of it
The idea that one day
Decisions would be mine
to make.

"That after youth
I would be free.

"But I see that was never true
Never real.

"Because they never
let go of their control.

"Be good.
Be beautiful.

"Be quiet.
Be obedient.
Be careful. . . .

"They never intended for me to be free.
Just trade one set of rules for another.

"And I see their dream for me
is my nightmare.

"Now I'm awake.
And they will never put me to sleep again."

I'm startled, confused. When I look at Sydney, she turns to a poem called "Girls with Sharp Sticks." She nods for me to read it.

And as I do, my heart rate begins to quicken. Butterflies in my stomach change into dragons, fire sparking and then burning bright.

The little girls mistreated. The little girls fighting back. The little girls taking control.

When I'm done, I'm breathing fast, electricity on my skin. The other girls smile at me.

"Where did you get this?" I ask, holding up the book.

"From your room," Sydney says.

The answer shocks me, and I start to read through it again. But then there is the sound of a door closing in the hallway. All of us quickly jump up, and I slide the book under my shirt.

"Take it back to your room," Sydney says. "Read it. I'll find you in the morning."

I do just that, saying good night as the Guardian makes his rounds to drop off our vitamins. When I get into my room, I put the book under my mattress, the action highly familiar.

I'm just settled when the Guardian comes in and sets my vitamin cup on the nightstand. I smile gratefully, but he doesn't bother to return it. Guardian Bose must be distracted, because he leaves without making sure I take my vitamins. Or maybe he just expects me to obey.

He reminds me of the controlling men in the poem. It's so confusing, the contrast between what I read and what I've been told. I turn and stare at the bars on the window. Meant to keep people out. Meant to keep us in.

I take the vitamins to the bathroom and flush them down the toilet. Once they're gone, I return to my bed and wait for sleep.

When I finally drift off, I'm plagued with nightmares. Violent, horrific, suffocating nightmares.

I dream that I'm dragged out of my room and forcibly lobotomized. I dream that Guardian Bose comes in while I'm asleep and stares at my body. I dream that Anton whispers that he loves me more than any other girl.

And I dream of ice picks and wires.

I have so many nightmares that when I wake up gasping in the morning light, I know they're not really dreams at all.

They're memories.

I remember. I got an ice pick jammed behind my eye, Anton

telling me that my parents want results—they want a perfect girl. I remember him whispering to me, controlling my thoughts.

I remember the week before, when Lennon Rose disappeared without her shoes. I remember Mr. Wolfe and Rebecca. I remember meeting Jackson and how he was worried about me. How he said the investors at this school are powerful.

And I remember that they touch us even when they know we don't want them to.

It has to stop, but I'm not sure how to get us out of here. If we show distress, Anton will bring us in for impulse control therapy—I see that now. Even if Annalise kills off the plants needed for the formula of the paralytic, it won't be enough to matter. They'll perform the lobotomies without the juice.

Anton has the ability to control our minds. But only if he gets close enough to try. We'll have to behave, just like Valentine suggested. We can't let them see that we know.

We *will* get out of here.

And yet, even as I think that, I know they'll never let us go.

22

It's barely light when I slip into Sydney's room, waking her. I tell her we all have to talk. The Guardian isn't up and about yet, and we end up getting the other girls and going to Valentine's door, knocking softly.

When we walk in, she's just stirring awake. But when she sees us, she sits up quickly and asks if everything is all right.

"I remember," I say, looking at each of them. Sydney clutches her chest with relief, happy to have me back. Valentine's eyes flash with something else—hunger for the knowledge.

As we sit there, I tell Sydney, Annalise, Marcella, Brynn, and Valentine everything I remember about impulse control therapy. It's even more terrifying as I say the words out loud. How I couldn't move. How Anton hurt me, shoving an ice pick behind my eye. How he had wires and a syringe, infectious thoughts.

"He lies," I say. "They're controlling us with lies and a mix of something else, something in that syringe."

"They're experimenting on us," Marcella says, swallowing hard. "I have to get inside that lab. See what the doctor has been doing in there."

Brynn nods, even though she looks afraid.

The horror of what the school has done lies in the fact that they forced it on us. Part of it is physical abuse, absolutely—but there's emotional manipulation, as well. They've tried to convince us that if we don't do exactly as they tell us, we'll disappoint our families. That we're useless without the love and admiration of the academy and the men who run it. They manipulate us with lollipops and guilt.

I can see it all now. Even the food is used to punish us. Keep us from desire. It's why Anton asked about my attraction to Jackson. He didn't think I should be allowed such agency.

Jackson.

"You mentioned Jackson yesterday," I say to Sydney. "And then you and the girls looked at each other weirdly."

Sydney's lips form an O and she darts her gaze to Annalise.

"Yeah, like that," I say pointing to them. "What's going on?"

They all pause for another second, but then Sydney leans in. "You need to have a chat with your gas-station boyfriend," she says. "It'll be the perfect opportunity during the field trip."

"Okay," I say. "About what?"

"About why he's been lying to you."

"Lying?" I laugh. "What would he be lying about?"

"We found him in the files," Sydney whispers.

I stare at her, the world feeling like it just dropped out from under me. "What does that mean?" I ask. "Why would he be in the files?"

"His family is involved with the academy," she says. "His mother . . . His mother used to work here, just before it became a school. They had a file with pictures of her and her family, and . . ." She shrugs. "I recognized Jackson. He was in the picture with his name and everything. It seems the school knew a lot about his family, like they researched them or something. Anyway, his father is still listed as an investor, although it doesn't seem like an active account."

"His mother died," Annalise adds.

"I know," I say, my mind racing to catch up with this information. "He mentioned that part. But . . ." I look at the others. "Why didn't he tell me she used to work here?"

"I'm not sure," Sydney says. "But this file they had on his family—it was thorough. It was . . . kind of threatening. And then it stopped after his mother died. Suicide, it said. After that, it was like they just forgot all about her."

"What did she do for the company?" I ask.

Sydney pauses before answering. "She was an analyst."

I physically recoil, hurt. Betrayed. How could he keep this from me?

"Not like Anton," Sydney adds. "She wasn't an analyst for girls. It was for technology—computers or something. It wasn't specific."

"The boy might be looking for information," Valentine says. "I say we give it to him. If the word gets out about what the school's doing to us, maybe it'll get shut down. Otherwise," she says, "if we run, they'll just bring us back. Trust me."

"So we tell him what we found?" I ask, looking around at the others. "Even though he's lied?"

"Find out *why* he lied," Sydney says. "But then . . . yes. We tell him." The other girls agree.

"At the field trip," Annalise says. "You can tell him there."

"What if he doesn't show?"

She starts to smile, but holds it back when she realizes it isn't appropriate considering the circumstances. "He'll show," she says.

The girls and I go over everything else we can think of, deciding we'll be excellent girls this week, obeying all the rules. But never taking our vitamins. We'll manipulate these men with their own expectations.

But when I go back to my room ten minutes later, I pause a long moment before lifting my hand to look at the scar on my palm. My vision blurs with tears, the idea that Jackson was manipulating me breaking through my newfound courage.

How could he? What else has he lied about?

Seeing him at that gas station. Seeing him outside my school. I'm embarrassed that I was such an easy target, so willing to tell him everything he wanted to know.

I don't forgive Jackson for his betrayal, just like I didn't forgive Anton. And I intend to tell Jackson so on Sunday.

Sunday morning doesn't come fast enough. The days in the week last a lot a longer when you have to be well-behaved, especially when you notice every wrong. But we make it without incident. The Guardian even comments on what good girls we are.

I shower and get dressed in my required uniform for the trip. Only this time, I decide to wear my hair in a ponytail, going against my specifications. It's oddly freeing—a small infraction, but enough to break from my routine. I smile in the mirror just as I hear the girls calling excitedly for me, saying it's time to go.

As we board the bus and leave the academy, the day seems brighter—the sun is even shining. This isn't a normal field trip, we know too much to fully enjoy it, but we can't help but relax a little. Annalise says we deserve it.

I absorb the sights as they pass by the bus window. Every tree, every building. I've never been to a movie theater before, and I'm curious what it will be like.

"I can't wait to get my hands on some popcorn," Sydney says. "And I mean my entire hand." She mimics picking up a fistful of popcorn and shoving it into her mouth, making several girls laugh.

I smile, but then I catch sight of Guardian Bose turned around in his seat. Rebecca is next to him, her face downturned. They allowed her to come with us, but Sydney says she hasn't been the same since her impulse control therapy. We've considered telling her to stop taking the vitamins, but we're afraid she'll let the doctor know.

I wish Guardian Bose didn't have to come to the movies with us; he's obviously miserable about it. But we knew there'd be rules for this field trip—of course there would be. It's going to be tough to avoid him.

The bus turns onto Main Street, and we're all pressed to the windows. The town is small, less than fifteen hundred people, but there are dozens of residents walking around downtown right now. People watch us drive by, men tipping up their hats to get a better look. Women shaking their heads in disapproval.

I think about the hosts at the places we visit, always scurrying out of sight the minute we arrive. Jackson said the town knew about the school, but not about the girls. They wonder about us. But not enough to question the men in power.

I used to fantasize about coming into town. But now that I'm here . . . I feel suddenly vulnerable. It makes Winston Weeks's request seem more appropriate than ever. We need to be socialized to society, and society needs to be socialized to us. By hiding us away, the academy made us outsiders. Maybe they wanted it that way.

Who would believe girls they've never seen before? Who would believe outsiders?

The bus hisses to a stop at the corner gas station, and the doors fold open. Guardian Bose moves to the block the aisle.

"We're heading down Main Street toward the movie theater," he says. "Straight there, understand? No funny business."

Brynn snorts a laugh at "funny business" and quickly covers her mouth. We try to nod solemnly and deeply like we're taking him very seriously. He rolls his eyes, annoyed with all of us.

We file off the bus, gathering to wait for everyone. The open air smells like gas and trash from a nearby dumpster. Weirdly, despite our important mission, the sudden freedom is intoxicating. We find ourselves smiling, accepting the abnormality of our lives to have these few moments. Sydney smiles at me.

Guardian Bose leads the way, but several of us hang toward the back. I keep my eyes out for Jackson, scared the Guardian will notice him before I do.

We continue down Main Street, passing people who don't say hello, even though we're very polite to them. Mostly, they avoid our eyes.

As Annalise pauses at a shop window, distracted, a woman walks toward us with a child, clutching her hand to her side as they pass. The woman doesn't look at me, but the little girl does. Her large blue eyes study me, her fingers in her mouth. I smile at her and offer a wave.

The little girl smiles back with several missing teeth, and I find her response delightful. She continues to look back over her shoulder at me. And then she pulls her fingers out of her mouth to hold them up in a wave. Her mother tugs her forward and tells her to keep walking.

"She was cute," I say. Brynn comes over, looking after her too.

"I'll take several of those," she says, pointing at the kid, but talking like Annalise would while shopping. We both start laughing.

The Main Street theater is old fashioned, with a freestanding ticket booth. The boy selling tickets—not much older than we are—averts his eyes. His hands shake as he takes our money and slides the tickets in our direction, making sure never to touch us.

"Thank you," Annalise sings out, leaning in to kiss the glass window. She leaves a red lipstick mark. When the boy looks up at it, he actually gulps.

"Let's go," Marcella says, grabbing Annalise's arms. "Let's not terrorize boys so early into the afternoon."

Annalise laughs, and we head inside. The entry is dramatic, with oversized red drapes and statues of famous actresses set up throughout the lobby so people can take pictures with them. While the others check them out, Sydney and I head straight for the concession—mostly to keep an eye out for Jackson. Well, mostly so she can get popcorn and I can get candy, but also to watch for him.

It's thrilling to have to wait in line with other people. It shouldn't be, I'm sure. But Sydney and I exchange a few smiles as we overhear people talking about their lives. Their jobs. Their favorite soda.

It occurs to me then that the girls and I don't talk about our futures, not in a significant way. The academy tells us to trust them, that they know what's best. Clearly that's not true. The only one who ever questioned our futures was Lennon Rose. And soon after . . . she was gone.

I look around at the people in this concession line, wondering if I'll be like them once this is over. Able to make my own choices. Or will Mr. Petrov hand us over to another man—one we have to marry. Or will it be our parents, telling us to charm our fathers' rivals?

The school is using us, using our futures. Our potential. To what end, I'm not sure. I think we've been trained to not imagine the possibilities.

The Guardian calls gruffly from behind the line for us to hurry up. We're not in control of the line, but I glance back at him and smile obediently anyway. I can feel him checking every person who comes near us. But after a bit, he must give up because he goes to wait at the theater door.

We're each allowed one item from the concession, at Dr. Groger's suggestion. *You need to learn how to moderate your choices, selecting items based on what you've learned here.*

Well, I'm obviously buying candy. That seems like a good choice to me.

Once I have my candy and Sydney has her large popcorn, we meet the others at theater nine. I'm surprised by how big the room is—all the seats and the massive screen.

It's a little crowded, so we can't all sit together. The Guardian allows Sydney and me to grab two seats in a row near the back. Annalise and the others opt to move closer, asking the Guardian to sit with them. They're going to try to keep him distracted while I talk to Jackson. *If* Jackson shows up.

The room suddenly darkens and I gasp before realizing it's supposed to happen. The screen expands and the volume gets louder as a voice over a loud speaker tells us we're about to watch trailers for upcoming movies.

We watch, mildly interested even though the previews are

men with guns, men with fast cars, and men diving from one skyscraper to another. In the hallway there were posters for movies that seemed much more interesting.

I'm growing impatient when suddenly there's a flash of movement at the end of the row. I glance over casually just as he sits next to me, and when I see it's Jackson, I viciously rip off a piece of licorice with my teeth.

Jackson's out of breath, his eyes wide as he stares at me. Worried, I guess. I haven't seen him all week.

I sweep my gaze over him in the darkened theater. And then I narrow my eyes and ask, "When were you going to tell me about your mother?"

He runs his hand though his hair and whispers, "Fuck."

"Jackson," Sydney whispers, leaning forward to look at him. She quickly checks to make sure the Guardian hasn't noticed him sitting with us. "For the record, I knew you'd show up." I give her a pointed look, and she presses her lips together and goes back to watching the movie.

"We need to talk," he whispers to me, sounding a bit desperate.

"Oh, you think?" I ask. He doesn't seem to like my coldness, but I don't care what he thinks about my behavior. For once, I'm acting the way I feel. Speaking my mind. And right now, my mind is angry.

Sydney checks on the Guardian again. "If Bose comes looking for you," she says, "I'll tell him you're in the bathroom. Just hurry."

I get up, motioning for Jackson to follow me, and duck as I

hurry down the aisle past him. At the door, I check to see if the Guardian noticed me. When I'm sure he hasn't, I slip into the hallway.

The light is much brighter out here, and it takes a second for my eyes to adjust. Jackson walks out of the theater and immediately comes over to me, stopping closer than I expect. I take a step back from him. It clearly hurts his feelings, and his eyes weaken.

"I'm sorry," he says, holding up his hands. "But—"

"We can't talk here," I say. I start for the exit doors, checking around to make sure no one is paying attention. They're not. I even walk behind the ticket booth so the boy there doesn't notice.

When we get to the side of the building, I cross my arms over my chest and glare at Jackson. Even though I'm upset, there's a small soft spot when his brown eyes meet mine. I quickly look away.

"I can explain," he says. "Just tell me what you found, and I'll explain."

I scoff. "Don't do that," I say. "You don't get to lie to me and then demand answers. Tell me what your mother was doing with the academy. Your father. The school has pictures of your family in their files. *Why?*"

Jackson's expression flashes anger at the idea of this. He moves to stand next to me, his jaw tight.

"You mentioned his name the other day," Jackson says. "Mr. Petrov. I did my homework on him," he continues, "him and all of his buddies. Back in the day, they were lobbyists—all tied up in politics. They backed legislation that tried to strip women's rights. Do you remember?"

I'm shocked by the idea, but I shake my head. I don't remember anything like that.

"Okay," Jackson says, leaning against the brick wall. "Well, when that didn't work out, when women were like, *Fuck no*, this guy Petrov bought the technology plant my mother worked at: Innovations Metal Works.

"At first, my mom didn't mind the change. But then she started working later nights, longer hours. My dad was unemployed—had been for a while. He was big into men's rights—some really backward shit. He and I would fight about it all the time. I don't know how my mom put up with it. She'd just say he wasn't always like that."

I lean my shoulder against the wall, listening to Jackson. I've never heard of women's rights, but I bet the book of poetry fits into what Jackson is saying.

"The last straw for her," Jackson says, "was when my father invested in the company that Petrov built. My mother said she told him what they were doing. How could he?" Jackson shrugs. "My father is excellent at making terrible decisions."

"And then one night, my mom came home. I was there and she gave me a kiss on the forehead as usual. She had the phone to her ear as she talked to someone. I heard her mention Petrov's name, and then she was arguing that they could find another analyst because she wanted no part of it. When she came out of her room later, she'd been crying.

"I just . . . I sat there, watching TV like an asshole," he says, admonishing himself. "She told me she'd be right back. She grabbed her car keys and left, still on the phone. And then . . ." He swallows hard, blinking quickly.

"The, uh . . . The police came to the house a couple hours later. My dad was at the bar, I guess. So they told me my mom died. A suicide at her place of work. A suicide . . ."

I watch him. "You don't think she killed herself," I say.

"I know she didn't," he responds instantly, turning to look at me. "That's what I've been trying to figure out, Mena. I couldn't get close to the school, though. And they keep you girls locked away. Then I saw the bus, met you in the gas station. I should have told you right away, but I was worried that you'd tell Petrov or any of those creeps. I didn't want them to destroy the evidence. I should have told you," he reiterates. "I'm sorry. I'm so fucking sorry."

"You manipulated me," I tell him. "And I'm really sick of men manipulating me."

Despite the horror of his story, it still hurts that he used me. Logically, I see no reason to forgive him. Because the immoral use forgiveness as a weapon.

"I kept coming back because of you," he says, his voice softer. "It wasn't just about finding information anymore. And when you weren't there this week, I . . . I was scared. And I missed you. And I was scared," he repeats.

I want to doubt him, but as I look him over, I see that he's a bit of a mess. His hair is unruly, his chin unshaven. His expression is frantic and helpless at the same time.

"Did you find Lennon Rose?" I ask.

"No," he says, shaking his head. "I found her parents, the ones

you mentioned. They own a big-time pharmaceutical company."
He waits a second. "And they don't have any kids."

My lips part. "What?"

"They have no listed dependents. Not ever."

"I don't understand," I tell him.

"Neither do I. Which is why," he adds, "you can't go back to that school. I don't know what they're doing to you girls, but you're not going back."

There is the sound of approaching footsteps, and Jackson quickly grabs the sleeve of my sweater and swings me around, facing me as he blocks me from view. We're suddenly close, and I stare up at him, even as he keeps his eyes to the side, checking behind him. My heart beats faster, and I'm relieved when a woman walks by instead of the Guardian.

"They're experimenting on us," I whisper, looking up at him. Jackson's hand is still on my arm as he looks down at me. I see his throat bob.

"How?" he asks.

I debate telling him, but ultimately, the girls and I decided he might be our best connection to the outside world. Our way to get out of the academy permanently. So I describe what I remember from impulse control therapy. As I do, Jackson's hand falls away from me and he takes a step back, horrified.

I tell him about EVA being a parental assistant and not a person, how none of our calls get through. And then, even though it makes me wildly uncomfortable . . . I tell him about Guardian Bose coming to my room. It's violating to say the words out loud, but once they're gone from my lips—there is relief. Release.

"I'm going—" Jackson starts, then pauses for a moment as if trying to control himself. "I'm going to fucking kill him," he finishes.

"I don't need you to kill him," I say, shaking my head. Men with their violent tempers, just like in the movies the Guardian watches. "I need you to help me find a way to shut them down. Because even if we leave, our parents will send us back. And even bigger than that, there are other girls. Future girls. We can't let them keep doing this."

"They stuck a fucking ice pick in your eye," he says loudly, and I quickly reach to put my hand over his mouth, casting a cautious glance toward the theater. My touch calms him, and when he pulls my hand away, he looks at the scratch on my palm.

"What do you want me to do?" he asks miserably.

"How do we get them shut down?" I ask.

"I don't know," he whispers. "They're powerful. I don't know."

"Then that's what you need to find out," I say. "You have to . . ."

But the words fall away as my eyes drift past him to the other side of the alley. To the building set back, just out of view of the street. My chest tightens, and I push past Jackson to get a better look.

It's a diner with flashing red sign. It's the diner from my nightmare. Only I realize now, it wasn't a dream at all. It was a memory.

23

The sign flashes RED'S DINER. I'm beside myself, not sure I can trust my eyes. I start that way, and Jackson catches up with me, asking what I'm doing. He keeps looking back at the theater, probably hoping that I'm running away with him. But instead, I walk up the stairs and enter the restaurant, a bell jingling on the door.

I look around, knowing what I'll see before I do. The vinyl booths with chevron pattern, the checkered floor. And there's the table from my dream, sitting empty. I walk over and slide into the seat, just like I'm sliding into the memory.

I sat in the booth next to the window with a bowl in front of me. The air reeked of grease—bacon, sausage, ham. Meat. The table was sticky with syrup. I had a bowl of oatmeal, unsweetened. I stirred my spoon slowly, lonely. Scared.

I missed my girls. I wanted to be with them.

"Can I help you?" a waitress asks Jackson. He seems unsure

and asks for two waters. I hear him, almost faraway. He's not in this memory with me. The scene plays across my vision.

I looked across the table and there was a man. He was older, and his sweat glistened in the fluorescent light. His fingers gripped a breakfast sausage as he shoved it into his mouth. He had no manners. He was indulgent. Crude.

At graduation, when Anton sat me down and told me I'd have to live with this man, I cried so hard that I threw up. He gave me a vitamin and told me tomorrow would be better. And then he gave me to Mr. Pickett—my sponsor. The man who had attended all of my open houses and paid my tuition.

It had only been a car ride, but I already knew that I was terrified of Mr. Pickett. Terrified.

"Don't worry," he said from across the table. "We'll be home soon."

Thunder boomed outside, making me jump. Rain poured down. I hated the rain. I hated this man.

"I've had other girls before, you know," he said, slurping his coffee. "Too stupid. They said you had spirit. I paid extra for it."

The waitress sets down two glasses of water and asks me what I'd like to eat. Jackson impatiently asks her to give us a few more moments. I feel tears slide down my cheeks. I'm shaking.

I was shaking. This man intended to hurt me—I knew that. Even a vitamin couldn't erase that. Couldn't make me compliant enough. I wanted my girls. I wanted my girls.

"Hey, sweetheart," the man said to the waitress. "Give me a refill."

"I'm not your sweetheart," she said, annoyed, and hastily filled his cup. As she walked away, he stared at her backside before turning to me.

"Stuck-up bitch," he said so she could overhear him. "And look at you," he told me. "You're prettier than her. But you know better than to talk back, right?" He smiled at me and reached over to touch my hand.

I jerked back, hating his touch.

I jerk back, knocking over the glass of ice water, splashing it over the side of the table. Jackson tells me it's okay, that I should stop crying. That he's here.

I couldn't stay another moment with Mr. Pickett. I wouldn't. I didn't care if they permanently dismissed me. I didn't care about anything but getting back to my girls to protect them. We needed each other.

I jumped up from the table and rushed for the door.

I yank open the door, the bell jingling.

I ran out into the rain, the water soaking my hair and clothes. My vision was blurred with tears, thunder boomed again.

Jackson's voice booms, shouting for me to wait as he chases after me down the alley in the sunshine.

The storm raged around me, lights blinking and confusing me. I didn't know which way to run. The man screamed my name.

"Philomena Pickett!" he shouted. "Get back here. You're mine!"

And so I ran faster. Faster, faster toward the lights. I just wanted to escape. I stepped off the curb, startled by the sudden change in surface. And just as I swung around, headlights blinded my vision and I raised my arm just before—

There's a sudden grab around my waist and I'm hoisted off my feet, startling me out of my head. A car horn beeps as it passes, the driver cursing at us. The sun is shining, my face is wet with tears.

Jackson is breathing heavily, his eyes wide. His arm still around me.

"Christ, Mena," he says. "What were you doing? You just ran out into the street. You—"

"I died," I say as fresh tears fall from my eyes. The physical pain still resonates, the vibration, the darkness. The absolute emptiness. I look up at Jackson, stunned. Traumatized.

"Jackson," I say, my voice weak. "I died."

He doesn't know what to make of this, but he grabs me fiercely into a hug. I can feel his heart racing under his shirt, his hand holding the back of my neck.

I pull away from him, not wanting him to touch me. Not wanting any man to touch me. Jackson is taken aback but doesn't insist. He's not Anton. Instead, he leads me back over to the wall, carefully watching me in case I make a run for it again.

"Please tell me what happened," he says. "I don't understand."

"He paid extra for me," I say, sickened by the words. "He . . ." My eyelids flutter, and I shake my head, not wanting to continue. When I look over, Jackson is crying. He's scared, more so than before, I'm sure.

"Why were you in the street?" he asks, trying to skip over the parts I can't say.

"I've been here before. That diner. And I was running back to the girls," I say. "I was going to save them. But . . ." I start to calm, the sunshine drying up my tears. I soak in the warmth. "I was hit by a car," I say. "Everything was . . . gone. When I woke up again,

Anton told me . . . He told me 'Welcome home.' And I never saw Mr. Pickett again."

Jackson adjusts his stance. "It doesn't work that way," he says. "People don't wake up once they die."

"No," I say, furrowing my brow. "Not . . . *dead* dead. The school . . . They changed my name to Philomena Rhodes." I run my hand through my hair, confused. Deeply confused. "And my parents came with me to the academy. . . . They dropped me off for the first day."

Only it doesn't make sense. I was already at the academy. The memories of my life contradict the flashback.

"It started all over again," I say to Jackson. "The academy trained me, same rules." I try to catch my breath. "Same . . . future."

"*You'll be a prize for any man,*" I whisper Anton's words, hating them. I look at Jackson. "That's what they're doing," I say. "The experiments. They're training us to be perfect girls for men. Just like in 'Sharp Sticks.'"

"Sharp sticks?" Jackson repeats confused. He reaches to touch my arm, but I jerk away from him.

"Don't touch me," I say.

"Whoa, yeah, I'm sorry," he says, truly apologetic. "I just . . . You're not making sense. But I believe you anyway. So let's get out of here. I'll hit that guy over the head"—he hikes his thumb toward the theater—"and we'll all run for it. All the girls."

That won't work. We'd have nowhere to go. If that memory is right, the investors know. Our parents and sponsors know.

They're all part of the same sick system. Who are these people? Are they . . . Are they even my parents?

"I have to get back inside," I say, starting toward the theater. "I have to warn the other girls. We have evidence now—my memories, those files. We just have to use it all to shut down the academy."

Jackson jogs ahead to stop in front of me, holding up his hand as if to show he's not trying to be pushy. "What if it's not enough?" he asks. "What if the school is still too powerful?"

I stare at him, waiting for an answer to come to me. Instead, I'm met with the unimaginable horror that he might be right. I shiver once and dart my eyes away before going back inside.

Jackson doesn't follow me. I clear my cheeks, making sure the tears are gone. And just as I get to theater nine, the door swings open and Guardian Bose comes rushing out. He stops abruptly when he sees me.

"Where the hell were you?" he demands.

"Bathroom," I answer, breathless. He grabs my elbow, making me wince.

"Get back inside," he growls, and pushes me ahead of him. He escorts me down the aisle to my seat, then pushes me down into my chair. It takes everything I have to not fight back.

"Don't leave this theater again until I tell you," he says, pointing in my face. I work to look sufficiently ashamed.

"I promise," I say.

Guardian Bose goes back to his seat, and when he's gone, Sydney exhales.

"You were gone awhile," she murmurs. She realizes how bad I'm shaking, and she threads her fingers through mine, asking if I'm okay.

Being close to her, being together, lets me finally break down. I cry into her shoulder, unable to tell her the horrible truth. Not yet. I just let her hold me and tell me that we'll take care of each other.

24

I'm quiet on the bus ride home, afraid to say anything in case the Guardian overhears. And more than that, I'm devastated. The girls will know soon enough, but I can't tell them now and expect them to keep it in. They'll need space to grieve. We'll need space to plan.

I can't wait for Jackson to find a way. We'll find our own way. I lean my head against the window, emotionally and physically exhausted. I close my eyes, searching the memory.

And as I do, other ones begin to fill in. Other truths become obvious even though they weren't at the time.

I haven't been at Innovations Academy for eight months. I've been there for almost two years. I've been through their education before as a girl with a different last name. Anton sent me home with a man I was supposed to please. An . . . investment. Instead, I tried to get away and was hit by a car.

When I woke up, Dr. Groger was leading me up the stairs. Physically, nothing hurt, but I was lonely—I knew something was wrong. He told me I missed my parents—the Rhodeses. At the time, I agreed, thinking of them fondly—my *parents*.

But then, I saw the other girls in the reception hall. Sydney first, of course. Our eyes meeting across the room. And then there was Marcella and Annalise. We all stared at each other, relieved. Loving each other instantly.

Only it wasn't instantly. It was again. The four of us had been here before. Each of us returning to the academy for an additional year of training.

Annalise no longer had blond hair. She was now a redhead—something that aggravated her, even if she didn't understand why. After I tried to paint her hair, Anton put us all through impulse control therapy.

"Abide by your specifications," he said. As if that was the bigger sin.

The other girls came later, Lennon Rose and Brynn. They were new. We loved them, too. We made each other stronger, each moment together feeling like a lifetime.

And there were other girls who had returned, like Valentine.

"Perfection," Leandra announced on our first day back, "is our guarantee. Our investors expect it."

And I open my eyes, knowing that the academy will do anything to keep their investors happy. Even if it means making us over again and again.

When we get back to school a short while later, Mr. Petrov

and his wife are waiting on the stairs to welcome us, smiling and waving proudly.

Annalise murmurs for me to smile—ironically, of course—as we get off the bus. I catch Leandra watching us, seeming curious, but I quickly walk past with a polite nod.

Once inside, the Guardian tells us he's sick of looking at us, possibly joking, and he goes to his room and shuts the door. He leaves us on our own, and as we stand in the hallway, my pleasantries fade away.

Valentine comes over to look me dead in the eyes. "What?" she asks. "He can't help?"

"I don't know," I say. "But . . . you all need to know something. We should . . ." The words catch in my throat, the horror of them, and I lead the girls into my room. About to destroy their world.

Annalise throws up in my bathroom, sobbing heavily. Marcella stares straight ahead while Brynn holds her hand, murmuring over and over that she doesn't understand. Valentine stands at the window, facing out.

Next to me, Sydney is motionless—in shock, I'm assuming.

It's hard to explain that it's not exactly a surprise, that the signs of the academy's true intentions were there all along. But it does not make them any less horrific.

"And you're saying," Sydney starts, her voice so low it's barely a whisper, "our parents know."

"*If* they're our actual parents," I say, making her flinch. "But yes, I believe they know. They all know."

She turns to me, tears clinging to her long lashes. "And you were hit by a car?" she asks.

"Then how are you okay?" Brynn asks. "Why don't you have any scars?" She looks around the room frantically, looking for an excuse not to believe. "She'd have scars, right?"

"Broken bones," Annalise says, coming out of the bathroom and blotting her mouth with a tissue. "Cuts and bruises—stuff like that. But the doctor used his technology to put you back together," she says to me. "Just like the graft on your knee. I saw in the files they can do repairs like that. A doll they can fix over and over. Must be convenient."

Although the thought is horrifying, it would explain why I didn't have any pain when I woke up. Annalise comes to sit on the other side of Sydney. I've told them everything, and now we just have to figure out how to use the information.

"I wasn't with you," Brynn says, her voice soft. Marcella looks at her, seeing that she feels left out, even if it's not something anyone would want to be a part of. She wasn't one of our original girls. I imagine she feels suddenly lonely at the thought of being apart from us.

"You're here now," Marcella whispers, putting her hand on her cheek. "You're not going anywhere without us."

Brynn nods, putting her hand over Marcella's before leaning in to hug her. Marcella keeps her arm around Brynn and turns back to us.

"We need to find out what's in the lab," Marcella says. "I just . . . I have a feeling it's the answer on how to shut this school down. Otherwise, why keep it locked up? Why only go there at night? Whatever's in there is secret. What if we find it and then send it out to all the investors? All the wives of these men. We'll send it to everyone we can. Jackson can do the rest, but I imagine some women wouldn't be okay with this." Her eyes tear up. "Right?"

"Jackson's mom wasn't," I say. "And if she wasn't, I'm sure others won't be."

I think we consider Leandra then. She's an accomplice in all of this. Why wouldn't she help us? Why would she go along with it?

"It's going to be time for dinner soon," Valentine says. "We should get cleaned up. Remember, follow the rules. I like Marcella's plan," she says, smiling at her. "We get in that room and find out what they have in there. After that, we'll decide what to do with it."

We all agree, hugging once before separating. Some of the girls will go back to their rooms to mourn the loss of their "parents" while others will dwell on what's been done to them.

And it's a cowardly thought, but for a moment, I long for one of the academy's vitamins—a chance to forget all this again. A chance to feel less vulnerable. I wrap my arms around myself, realizing that not knowing didn't make me any safer. It just made me easier to manipulate.

But still . . . I'm scared. I'm so afraid that I'll never get outside these walls again. I'm scared of what the people claiming to be my parents have planned for me. What sort of deal the Head of School has made for me.

I paid extra.

I quickly spin away from the window and walk to my bed, needing a shot of courage. Needing to be brave.

I reach under my mattress and pull out the book of poetry. The moment it's in my hands, I feel better. I feel . . . seen. Heard.

I sit on the edge of my bed and open up to the first poem. I start working my way through, letting them fill me up. Tell my stories. My dreams. My desires. There are poems even more violent, or more moving. There is even one about love.

But I find myself drawn to my favorite poem once again. I begin reading it out loud, enjoying the words on my tongue. I say them louder, my eyes welling up.

"'And then those little girls with sharp sticks flooded the schools,'" I say. "'They rid the buildings of false—'"

"What the hell are you doing?" Guardian Bose yells from the doorway, scaring me so badly that the book falls to the floor at my feet. I didn't even hear him open my door.

Guardian Bose stomps over and picks up the book before I can. "What's this?" he demands. He flips to the first page, and I see his eyes widen as he reads. He grabs me by the wrist and hauls me from the room.

A string of curses cascades from his lips, and I don't resist his pulling, knowing I have to play along. I shouldn't have taken the book out. I should have been more careful.

Valentine's door opens when she hears the commotion. She watches me with fearful eyes, but she doesn't say a word.

I have to figure a way out of this. Now that I know what the academy is capable of, I'm more afraid of them than ever. I can't let them see that I know the truth. I don't know what they'll do to me. What they'll do to the other girls.

"Anton will have to deal with this," the Guardian says. He's distraught, I realize. Angry, sure. But . . . threatened.

We get to Anton's office, and the Guardian opens the door. Anton is standing next to his open file cabinet, staring out the window with a folder in his hand. He turns and quickly motions for Guardian Bose to let me go. The Guardian does just that, and I stumble with the sudden loss of pressure on my wrist.

"What is this?" Anton demands from Guardian Bose.

The Guardian holds up the book and tosses it onto Anton's desk. He's not in mood to talk to the analyst either. "Might want to take a look," he says, pointing at the book. And then he backs up and leaves the room.

Anton waits a beat, his eyes on the book, and then he turns to me and presses his lips into a smile. "Are you okay?" he asks.

I'm not sure, if I'm honest. I don't know what he's going to do to me, and flashes of impulse control therapy play through my mind.

"Have a seat, Philomena," he says. He slides the folder he was holding into the file cabinet drawer and pushes it closed.

I do as I'm told. But dread is slowly crawling over me. It's disturbing that Anton thinks I don't remember what he's done to me. And yet, he sits down with me like he's my therapist. Like he wants what's best for me. The power imbalance of that is striking.

"What's going on, Philomena?" he asks.

Something Sydney told me the other day stands out. She lied

to Anton when he asked her a question. We always assumed he'd know if we were lying, almost as if he could read our thoughts. Apparently, he can't unless he's got wires in our head.

"I was worried about Lennon Rose," I say, keeping my voice steady.

"I thought you were happy for her?" he asks, as if I'm being unreasonable. The book sits unopened on his desk, but he doesn't comment.

"I am happy for her," I say. "But . . . I guess I missed her. I thought maybe she left behind a note, a goodbye letter, so I checked her room. I found a book."

"Ah, yes," Anton says, leaning forward to pick up the book. "And you found *this*? I'd wondered where it'd gotten off to."

"You've seen this book before?" I ask, surprised.

"Yes," he says. "It belonged to a former student." He turns it over, examining it. "And you say you got this from Lennon Rose's room?"

I nod. He flips through the pages, pausing on "Girls with Sharp Sticks" to read it.

"Philomena," he says, his voice low. "Have you read this poem?"

"Just that one," I say. "But I don't know what it means." My lies come out so smoothly, so innocently, that I would believe them myself.

Anton takes off his glasses to rub his eyes. He seems exhausted. When he looks at me again, he sighs. "Here's the thing," he says. "These poems . . . They're not allowed at this school. They're propaganda." He leans his elbows on the desk. "You see, there are people outside of this academy who don't believe in what we do," he says. "They don't think you deserve a well-rounded education. They want to push their values on you.

"I suppose they're just jealous," he continues. "Jealous of our success, our commitment to protecting you. Perfecting you. Innovations Academy is cutting edge and exclusive. Not everyone can send a girl through our program." His expression grows very serious. "These people want to take that from us," he says. "They try by deliberately spreading falsehoods. They make people angry and unhappy—especially girls—in hopes of turning you against us.

"But it won't work," he says with a smile. "Because we've trained you girls to appreciate what we do for you."

"I'm lucky to be at such an esteemed academy," I say immediately, without even a twinge of guilt.

"Good. Because, you see, the girl who wrote those poems must have been very unhappy to disrespect the men trying to help her. She spread that unhappiness to others. And then she dared to give it to one of our girls. I wouldn't want—" He stops, seeming upset by the memory. "I wouldn't want that to happen to you. You are a prize, Philomena. I want you to be successful."

I hold my expression, but his words "you are a prize" are a cold splash of water through my chest, sending chills over my skin.

"I wouldn't want that either, Anton," I say evenly. "I'm so close to graduation."

"Exactly," he says, relieved. "So I think it's best if we have a meeting with all the girls. Make sure we're all on track. Make sure you have the right attitudes."

The suggestions stuns me, scares me. But I thank him for his time; I don't want to stay in Anton's office for even a second longer than I have to.

I stand up and reach for the book, but Anton quickly puts his hand on it and slides it out of my reach.

"I'll hold on to this," he snaps. "Lennon Rose won't need it again."

"I'm sorry," I reply, angry at myself for even trying to take it. I wasn't thinking clearly. He waves me out.

I leave his office, shivering off the shadows that try to follow me out. And even though I don't want to think it . . . Anton all but confirmed it.

Lennon Rose is truly gone.

When I get back to my room, some of the girls are waiting in their doorways. Before I can tell them what's happening, Guardian Bose's voice booms like thunder down the hall.

"Back in your rooms until I come for you!" he shouts. I flinch at the violence in his tone, exchanging a worried look with Sydney.

Not wanting to be defiant, we all do as he asks.

The Guardian doesn't come back to get us until late in the evening. They didn't even let us have dinner.

I've nearly gone out of my mind while waiting, staring out the window at the woods as they darkened. Longing to escape.

I should have left from the movie theater with Jackson.

Guardian Bose doesn't speak as he leads us downstairs to the ballroom. But we're not allowed near each other, let alone able to talk. Guardian Bose has us each sit at a different table. I hope this separation doesn't last. The thought that it might terrifies us.

We watch Guardian Bose head to the front of the room. My leg shakes under the table.

The door opens and Mr. Petrov walks in, his suit wrinkled in a surprising way. He's always very careful about his appearance, but he's unnerved. He's angry and bitter. This is him in his truest form.

Mr. Petrov stops at the front of the room, slowly looking each of us over until he lands on me. He takes the book out of his coat pocket and holds it up.

I'm not sure how he knows, but this is my fault. I put us all at risk—I can't let the girls take any blame.

"It was my fault," I say, pitching up my voice to sound sweeter. "Just mine. I was curious." I shake my head. "Weak. I didn't mean to read the book. I should have turned it in the moment I found it."

"Do you feel brave, Philomena?" he asks, his tone cutting through my hollow words.

"Excuse me?" I ask, wilting slightly.

"Did the words in that book make you feel brave? Make you think . . . you were better? Equal? Did they make you want to talk back?"

I shake my head, but inside, my heart is racing. How do they know how those poems affected us? "No, Mr. Petrov," I say. "They were just words. I didn't even understand them. The other girls didn't even read them!"

He hums out a sound, running his eyes around the room. "Words create rebellions," he says. "Better I crush yours right now before you hurt the other girls. Before you try to convince them with lies."

I'm scared. I don't know what he's going to do to me, and I turn back to Sydney, I see her eyes brimming with tears.

"Who gave you this book?" he demands.

"I found it in Lennon Rose's room," I say. "I swear. I wouldn't lie to you."

"Who gave you this book?" he asks, louder. Brynn jumps from the sound, and he drags his eyes over her. Mr. Petrov nods to Guardian Bose.

The Guardian stomps over to grab Brynn by the collar of her shirt, hauling her to her feet violently. Several girls gasp. Marcella begs him to stop.

"Who gave you this book?" Mr. Petrov asks me again, his threat to Brynn obvious.

I don't know what to say. I'm not even sure what lie will help protect the other girls. And then suddenly, Valentine stands up.

"I did," she says simply. "I gave the book to Lennon Rose. Mena must have found it there."

"Ah, there we go," Mr. Petrov says. He waves the Guardian toward her. "I believe Dr. Groger would like a word with Valentine Wright."

The Guardian pushes Brynn down in her seat—she folds in on herself, still in shock from being mishandled.

The Guardian walks to Valentine's table. Slowly, as if completely unbothered, she smiles at him politely.

"Time's up, sweetheart," Guardian Bose says. "Time to go visit the lab."

I quickly look back at Marcella, who confirms it's the locked room in the basement.

Valentine nods, stepping away from the table to follow the Guardian out. Her eyes slide to mine with a wave of panic. She told me that the next time they thought she needed impulse control therapy, they would kill her.

"Valentine," I call, breathless in my terror. She looks away from me because there's nothing I can say. There's nothing I can do. I would just endanger us all, like I already have with the book.

Valentine begins to shake. Her eyes go vacant, her expression serene, as she lets the Guardian lead her from the room.

Are they really going to *kill* Valentine? This can't be happening. They can't do this—even the idea of losing one of the girls is unbearable. But I don't know what to do. What can any of us do?

"This school is on lockdown," Mr. Petrov announces. "There will be no phone calls, no parental visits. Campus is closed and open houses are canceled. The fences will be reinforced and the doors bolted at night. You will pay the price for your audacity." He stops when his voice gets tight with anger. He takes a breath, and then begins again.

"Guardian Bose will step up your supervision," he says. "Mandatory impulse control therapy will begin shortly—we have no way of knowing how far these poisonous ideas have spread. Make no mistake," he says, wagging his finger at us, "your parents will not be removing you from this building until you are worthy. Nobody needs another opinioned girl. You will obey!"

The words take the air out of the room and make my skin crawl. We sit there quietly, afraid it might get worse. It can always get worse. I know that now.

Mr. Petrov glances at his watch. "You will report for classes in the morning as usual," he says. "And if you get any more *ideas*, you will be isolated. And it can get very lonely," he adds menacingly. "We can't have you spreading discontent."

And then the Head of School walks out.

25

That night, when Guardian Bose comes to my room to give me my vitamins—one yellow and one sedative—he stands there and watches me take them. I make a show of it, extra apologetic. The pills rest just under my tongue, and I can feel them dissolving, unable to do anything while the Guardian is here.

I can barely stand it. The idea of the silver tech gliding over my tongue and down my throat, or the sedative making me powerless with sleep, almost makes me gag. But the Guardian casts a dirty look in my direction and leaves to harass another girl.

The second he walks out the door, I spit the vitamins across the room. I take a mouthful of water and then rush to the bathroom, rinsing the bitter taste out of my mouth. When I go back to my room to destroy the evidence, I'm grateful to find the silver tech still contained inside its capsule. I pick it up and flush it away along with the sedative, knowing the Guardian will be back later.

The footsteps stop just outside my door like I knew they would. I'd been waiting—*dreading*—for hours. As the door opens, I relax my expression: lips parted slightly, tense shoulders loose, hand palm up. Defenseless in sleep.

The floor creaks as the Guardian walks into my room. I let my breathing sound congested, deep in sleep, slow and heavy—hoping he'll just leave. It's a fight to appear calm when my heart is racing.

I feel his figure pause over me, his shadow looming. He might be here to bring me down to the lab. To bring me to Anton to be reset. He might be here to kill me.

I want to open my eyes. I want to scream. But instead, I let my breathing catch slightly, and smack my lips together like he's about to wake me.

He's about to kill me.

The Guardian doesn't move, and his presence is overwhelming. I wish I could run out into the woods, but they're reinforcing the fence. There is no escape.

Guardian Bose is closer, close enough to touch me, I'm sure. I wait for it, working out in my head how I'll fight back, but knowing I'm at a disadvantage in every way. He can break me with a single hit. I'm at his mercy, and the thought of that tears through my heart.

The shadow shifts over my face, and he's closer still, hovering just above me. His cool fingers slide around my neck to choke me.

I'm about to scream for my life, but then, like a miracle, there is a thump from another room. I feel Guardian Bose turn toward it, and his hand falls away. There is the sound of his footsteps as he exits my room. The door shuts.

I jolt once but don't open my eyes. My entire body hiccups with profound fear. Loss. I listen until Guardian Bose's footsteps make it all the way down the hall and the door to his room opens and closes. And once I hear that, I sit up in bed and take in a huge gulp of air, my fingers on my throat, my eyes wide and fearful.

I continue to gasp for breath like I'm drowning. Tears stream down my cheeks as I stare at my doorway. My entire body shakes in a way that I can't stop, my head bobbing, my arms like they're being shocked with electricity.

I want to crawl into Sydney's bed and tell her what's happened. But I can't chance it now. He'll come back. He'll drag me downstairs next.

I squeeze my eyes shut, crying silently. I've never been so scared—I don't know how I can live and be this scared. I have a wild and irrational thought that my hair has streaks of white now.

I am at the mercy of these men. Of these horrible, terrible, abusive men.

And it's crushing because I can't change the circumstances right now. Not at this moment.

I know I can't live like this, though. I won't.

I pull the covers up to my chin, my body still jolting forward every few minutes, slowing as the adrenaline begins to wear down. Exhaustion is settling in.

Making it until morning is my new goal. Then I'll talk to

Sydney and the other girls—we'll make a plan. We'll get Valentine and run. We'll never come back.

Professor Penchant stands at the front of the classroom, pacing. "You're a disgrace," he says to all of us, spittle flying from his mouth. "Naughty things."

I cringe at the use of the word "naughty"—it's creepy and infantile at the same time. It bothers the other girls too. Annalise grips the edge of her desk, her nails digging into the wood.

"Who would want girls like you?" Professor Penchant demands. "Disobedient trash. I'll be glad when your lot is finally gone. You're worthless." He looks at Rebecca like this particular insult was reserved for her.

Annalise's hand shoots up in the air, and Professor Penchant glances at her in surprise.

"How dare you—" he starts, furious she would dare ask a question while he's admonishing us.

"Pardon me, sir," she says in her sweetest voice. "But I'm ready to be a *better girl*. I was hoping I could learn a lesson today—if you're up for teaching."

I fight back my smile. But no sooner does the thought amuse me than Professor Penchant storms across the room and stops at the side of her desk. He grabs Annalise out of her chair, knocking her to the floor. He then begins to drag her by the wrist toward the front of the room while she unsuccessfully tries to free herself from his grip. Several girls scream, and I stand up from my desk.

The professor unhands her, kicking Annalise in the thigh

as she tries to move away from him. He grabs his pointer stick and whacks her with it. She cries out in pain, a red slash quickly appearing on her thigh.

"Stay," he says, like she's a dog. With sudden ferocity, the professor turns back to all of us.

"You think we don't see," he says. "See the wheels turning." He makes a motion near his temple. "The girls who wrote those kinds of poems were wicked. They were corrupt. Girls were put on this planet for the benefit of men. And you—" He whacks Annalise again, on her arm this time, and she cowers away from him. "You are here to serve at our pleasure. There is no other way for you girls—know that. Outside these walls, without our grace, you are nothing. Absolutely nothing."

Brynn is crying next to me. Several other girls are trying to hold back their tears, afraid of being next in line for his cruelty.

The professor squats down next to Annalise. He raises his hand, and she flinches away. But to our horror, he runs the backs of his fingers along her neck, down to her collarbone. And the intimate touch is more horrifying than any slap. She moves away from him, but his threat is enough to break us all down. Highlight our vulnerability.

Every night we sleep behind unlocked doors in a school where the men hate us.

When the professor stands up, Annalise wipes her cheeks, quickly clearing the tears. He holds out his hand like a gentleman, and Annalise has no choice but to take it and thank him for the chivalry.

Professor Penchant smiles and watches her walk back to her desk, limping.

I hate him. I hate the professor with a fire I never thought was possible. And I know why we should be outraged.

We're not allowed to close our doors anymore. That's the new rule Guardian Bose has enacted. We can't be in each other's rooms, we can't sleep with our doors closed, we can't go outside.

This lockdown goes on for days, and it begins to work on our sanity. The isolation is torture. And it leaves me feeling sick and worn down. I just want to talk to the girls for a minute. Make sure they're okay.

At night there are vitamins—one pink, one green, one yellow. Guardian Bose waits for us to take them. Several times, I had to throw them up after he didn't leave fast enough.

I stare out the window in the evenings, confined to my room alone. I wonder if Jackson has come by the school. If he's worried. I regret pushing him away, even if I'm angry that he lied to me. In the end, he could have helped us. I should have let him. I should have run.

Of course, every time I think that, I start crying. So I try not to think about that anymore.

And I start to think that Jackson *has* been worried. For example, one afternoon, I notice a police cruiser leaving our gates—leaving us here at the academy, unchecked. The professors don't mention it, and I haven't seen Anton or the doctor since Mr. Petrov talked to us about the poems, but I doubt they'll tell me either. Jackson must have called them, but it was for nothing.

He was right—the men are too powerful.

There's no one coming to save us. We're alone in our penance.

And none of us has seen Valentine.

Whenever I get the chance, I go by her room and peer inside. It's just as she left it: a book about plants open on her desk, her makeup scattered, and a pile of laundry waiting to be washed. I'm devastated with guilt, wishing I'd done more.

But I keep walking past, hoping each time that I'll find her. But I never do.

It's Sunday evening and campus is quiet. We no longer have movie nights. I'm cleaning the kitchen on my own after dinner, not allowed to work with other girls. I'm finishing up the last of the dishes, and when I pull open the wrong drawer, I see the keys again.

I stare at them.

"Looking for a way out?" a voice asks. Startled, I look up as Leandra enters the kitchen. It occurs to me that I haven't seen Mr. Petrov's wife since we returned from the field trip.

She turns before I see her face and walks over to the stove, picking up a kettle. She's wearing a fitted black dress, her hair hanging long. She wags the teapot and sighs.

Leandra moves past me to fill the kettle at the sink, the water loud in the silent room. She sets it back on the stove and lights the range.

When she turns around, she leans against the cabinets, her face on display.

Her left eye has a bruise underneath, the white of her eye turned bloodred. She lets me look. She wants me to see.

"Are you okay?" I ask, unsure of what else to say.

She smiles. "Anton and I had a very intense therapy session. I'm one hundred percent now. I've made him very proud."

My heart dips, and I look between her and the door before I step closer.

"You . . . You got impulse control therapy?" I whisper.

She nods. I point to my own eye to indicate hers.

"Why do you have a bruise?" I ask. "I've never—"

"My husband opted against the patch kit," she says. "He thought I'd prefer to see the damage firsthand. You know, as a reminder."

"A reminder?" I ask.

"Of what happens to girls who misbehave. Seems that book of poetry caused quite a stir," Leandra says. "The men are afraid the discontent will spread. They want to root it out; they started with me. Valentine should have been more careful," she adds. "It was, after all, a secret."

My mouth drops open, and it takes me a second to find my words.

"You gave her the book?" I ask.

"It had been mine," Leandra replies, her expression giving nothing away. "A gift someone had given me when I was different. Back when I was one of you. It woke me up. I'm curious if it's done the same for you, Mena."

I assume Leandra *did* give the book to Valentine, but she

doesn't say it outright. I don't press the issue. I'm not sure if she's purposefully being evasive or if she just can't remember after impulse control therapy.

It's shocking to think that Leandra Petrov was once a girl at this academy. However, what's more shocking is that *she* owned those poems of rebellion—of revenge. What kind of friend would give her the book and then leave her here? It seems cruel. Then again, Leandra understands what this academy does to us, and yet . . . she stayed. She's part of their system.

"Then what are you doing here?" I ask, incredulous. "Why have you stayed all this time?"

My question gives her pause. Leandra steps closer to me and runs her perfectly manicured fingernail down my cheek.

"I'm right where I belong, Philomena," she whispers. "And when I grow discontented, Anton removes that piece. Again and again. As often as it takes."

Staring at her bloody eye with her sharp nail against my skin, I'm certain that Leandra is not here to help me at all. Even when the men here abuse her, she stays. Because if she admits that what they've done to her is wrong, she'll have to admit her role in hurting us.

The kettle begins to whistle, and Leandra turns to take it off the heat.

"In fact," she says as she pours hot water into a cup, "Anton checks me over once a week, just to make sure." She gets a tea bag from the wooden box next to the stove. "It's at my husband's request. Although it's not *really* a request, you understand."

She sets the kettle aside and turns to study me.

"Do you like cookies, Mena?" she asks curiously. Her question catches me off guard.

"I . . . I don't know," I say. "I guess I've never had one."

"They're too sweet," she replies with a shrug. "You should avoid them."

I don't respond. I'm not sure if she's really talking about cookies, or if there's some deeper meaning in her advice that I don't quite understand. To be honest, I don't understand *her*. I never have.

Leandra picks up her cup from the counter. "Gold one opens the kitchen door," she adds, motioning to the drawer of keys. "But you might want to take the silver key instead. I believe it opens the door to the lab downstairs. All this technology . . . ," she says, looking around. "You'd think they would have changed the locks."

My heart is pounding wildly, scared that Leandra will tell Anton I've been dreaming of escape. Scared that if she does, I'll end up worse than her.

But then, as if we never spoke at all, Leandra sips from her tea and leaves the kitchen.

To: All Staff

RE: Emergency Impulse Control Therapy

From: Petrov, Roman

Today at 6:33 AM

As many of you have noted, this year's class of girls has shown an unprecedented level of defiance. Due to this disruption, Innovations Academy is instituting emergency impulse control therapy, starting immediately. Once we have analyzed the data, we will take the necessary steps to preserve our investment. Girls who are not cleared for graduation will be dismissed permanently.

Evaluations are expected to be completed by the end of the week. Intensive follow-ups will be given to those exposed to the recovered reading material.

In addition, arrangements are under way to speed up the vetting process for a new batch of girls. Until further notice, Dr. Groger will be unavailable in the evenings as he continues his important work.

Thank you for your prompt attention.

Sincerely,

Roman Petrov, Head of School

IA: Innovations Academy

26

On the way to breakfast in the morning, I manage to tell Marcella about my conversation with Leandra. I didn't take the silver key, afraid she was setting me up.

Then I whisper about the Guardian putting his hands around my neck, and Marcella's eyes flash with anger. With fear. She passes along the message as we walk, letting the others know. Brynn looks back at me horrified, but I nod to tell her that I'm okay.

We sit down for our meal, careful not to get caught talking too much. Ida Welch is missing, I notice. She's the second girl in the past week.

It's starting to feel empty in here. There are vacant spaces where my friends used to be. Friends that haven't been coming back.

I'm leaning in to mention Ida's absence to Marcella when Guardian Bose walks into the room and joins the faculty at their table. I have a visceral reaction when I see him, goose-bumps on my skin, a twist in my gut. I can barely stand to be around him, although I don't really have much of a choice.

The men laugh together, eating their biscuits and gravy.

Guardian Bose holds a conversation, popular among the teachers—even though Anton thought him unprofessional. He gets to live his life, free of judgment. Free of restraint. All while he comes into my room at night to intimidate me.

I wait to make sure none of the staff is paying attention, and then I lean in to the table.

"Tomorrow we have Running Course," I whisper. "Jackson will probably be beyond the fence. We can make a plan."

"What do we do about the other girls?" Brynn asks.

"We can't tell them," Annalise says. "If they tip off Anton, who knows what will happen to us." Annalise doesn't lift her eyes when she says this. In fact, since Professor Penchant attacked her in the front of the room, she hasn't said much of anything.

"We can't just leave them," Brynn says.

"They'll slow us down," Annalise replies. When Brynn turns to her, obviously hurt, Annalise winces.

"I'm sorry, but they will," Annalise adds. "We'll get this academy shut down. I promise. And then the others will really be free. We can't take the chance now."

"But—" Brynn starts, but Annalise shakes her head no.

"I won't take the chance," Annalise repeats adamantly. She rubs absently at the bruise on her arm, the one left from Professor Penchant's attack during class. Annalise's jaw tightens, her eyes welling up.

"I'll kill those men before I let them touch me again," she

whispers. "Before I knowingly let them stick an ice pick in my eye."

"We have a plan," I say to Annalise, trying to calm her. "It's going to work. You believe that too."

"I'm just letting you know I have a plan B," Annalise replies.

We stare at each other a moment, and then I nod, understanding why. The others stay quiet, none of them arguing. What if they come for us next? What if we have to protect ourselves?

Ida's missing presence is a gaping hole at the table. A reminder to all of us that something is happening.

I sip from my juice and stare toward the windows. I know beyond the glass is an expansive lawn. The thick woods. And of course, the iron fence between the two. We're locked behind barred windows, miles from the closest neighbor.

The academy has kept us isolated so we couldn't run. But they didn't count on my skill to make really awesome friends. And they didn't count on our ability to fight back.

"What if we don't wait?" Marcella whispers. I turn to her, my heart kicking up its beats.

"What do you mean?" I ask.

"We can leave tonight," she suggests, lowering her voice. "We call Jackson to pick us up. Then we run. We run because we're not staying here to let Anton put us through impulse control therapy again. We're not letting the Guardian puts his disgusting hands on you again."

"I don't have a way to talk to Jackson," I say. "I have his number, but the phone in the hall doesn't work. And I imagine they've locked the communications room."

"The Guardian," Brynn says, widening her eyes. "I think he has a phone. I've seen him use it on our field trips. It's probably in his room."

I look at Sydney, and although we're quiet, we know that we have to get to that phone.

"Just after dinner," Brynn says. "The Guardian is never around."

"He's been helping Dr. Groger in the evenings," Marcella agrees. "You'll have some time."

It's a terrifying thought—sneaking around in the Guardian's room. Going through his things. But what other choice do we have? This might be it.

"Will that work?" I ask Sydney. Reluctantly, she nods.

Brynn reaches her hand into the center of the table, and all of us reach out, gripping each other. I don't want to let go, strengthened by their touch, but we don't hold on too long. We can't draw attention.

"We run tonight," Marcella whispers. "We run for each other."

I agree, and the other girls nod, including Annalise. We'll stick together no matter what. *Codependent*, I think Anton called it. But it's not. It's our strength.

We're not allowed to meet together in our rooms anymore, so all of our conversations are had in passing, comments in the hallways, nods and winks in the classrooms.

I try not to feel anything but bravery. When Professor Allister calls Sydney worthless for missing a question about the Federal

Flower Garden, slapping his pointer stick on her desk to scare her, I clench my fist in my lap. It's clear to me that the professors are out of control now, all of *their* decorum gone.

They hate us passionately. They despise us because they know we hate them too. We don't look up to them. We have no interest in their mediocrity.

We think they're disgusting. We think they're perverted and stupid and cruel. And without our admiration, we're nothing to them.

But the truth is, without our admiration, *they're* nothing.

Of course, there are some logistical issues with running away. We have no money, no identification. And even if we go to the authorities about what's happening here, what proof do we really have? My memories? Files that are locked away in Anton's office? What's to stop the academy from telling them we're the problem? That we're lying?

The academy can take everything from us, because as Professor Penchant once put it when criticizing Ida in class, "No one listens to little girls anyway."

But we've agreed that we'll find out who else knows about Innovations Academy—the people Anton accused of spreading lies. Maybe they're the people who can help us. We'll expose what's happening here. The whole school. We'll spare none of them.

"Grab any money you have in your rooms," I tell the girls as we walk in the hallway between classes. "And only bring a back-pack. We have to travel light."

"It's too risky to leave before lights-out," Marcella adds.

"We'll get a longer window if we leave at night."

All the movies about men that they make us watch are proving to be useful when it comes to escaping the grips of other men.

"But how will we get outside?" Brynn asks.

We pause at the fountain while I take a drink. "The drawer in the kitchen has a bunch of keys," I whisper with the water against my lips. "Even one to the lab."

"Valentine," Sydney says, sadly. I straighten up, wiping my hand across my mouth.

Our friend is missing, and we might have the chance to save her—we acknowledge that, not sure if it'll work, but we don't brush it aside. We know that she'd come for us.

But we don't discuss it again, at least not yet. We can't rescue her until we know we can get away from here.

We need a phone.

After finishing our classes for the day, the girls and I return to the dining hall. The smell of gravy, beef, and fresh-baked cookies fills the room. Only this time, I don't long for their food. My stomach churns with nerves. My skin prickles with fear as the professors laugh and feast.

We notice that the Guardian isn't here. Neither is Maryanne Lindstrom. We're not sure what that means, and we communicate our worry without a word, afraid the plan will have to be altered.

But then Guardian Bose strolls in, clutching Maryanne by the upper arm. She looks dazed, vacant. The Guardian brings her to her seat before heading toward the professors' table, flashing me a smile as he passes.

I check on Maryanne just as a small tear of blood leaks from her left eye. She wipes it away without fuss and picks up her spoon to sip from her soup demurely. I bet if I asked her how she was feeling, she'd tell me she's made Anton very proud.

My breath is caught up in my chest. This is going to happen to all of us. Annalise swallows hard, staring at me from across the table. We're scared. We don't have much time.

The crackle of a walkie-talkie echoes in the quiet hall, and Guardian Bose takes his walkie-talkie off his hip. "Yeah, on my way," he says impatiently. He pushes his empty plate back to the center of the table and stands up from the bench. "What a fucking mess," he tells the professors. "I might be down there all night."

"Yes, well," Professor Penchant says, unbothered, reaching for another cookie. He coughs thickly before clearing his throat. "It'll be over soon enough," he adds. "Then we'll finally get things back on track around here. The way they used to be. Back when girls knew how to behave."

Several professors cast looks in our direction, and I quickly turn away.

Despite the threat in Professor Penchant's words, I'm encouraged by the conversation. The Guardian will be downstairs, presumably for a long time. It should give us enough time to find his phone if he's left it in his room.

When we're dismissed from dinner a short while later, Annalise and Brynn stay behind to clean up. The rest of the girls and I return to our floor, Sydney looking over at me every few seconds as we walk.

As the other girls go into their rooms, I notice how quiet the academy seems tonight. Eerily so. Maybe it's because we have fewer girls now, or it could be my nerves. Heightening every worry. Even my breathing feels too loud. Marcella stops at my room and glances toward the Guardian's door.

He's not in there, of course. He's downstairs with Dr. Groger in the secret lab. He's with Valentine; possibly Ida, too. It makes this task all the more urgent. But I'm still terrified.

Sydney takes my hand, trying to be brave for both of us.

"We can do this," Marcella murmurs, her eyes glassy. "I'll be at the stairs." She nods, waiting for us to agree before going to stand post, just in case the Guardian returns.

Sydney and I head to his room, pausing one last moment. And then, with Sydney outside his door, I slip inside.

The Guardian's room is neat, bed made with a smooth green blanket, an extra set of boots in the corner. I begin pulling open dresser drawers, finding perfectly folded T-shirts. There's nothing out of place. But worse, there's no phone.

I'm starting to get frantic, especially when Sydney knocks softly on the door and tells me to hurry up. I exhale gratefully when I find the Guardian's phone plugged into the wall, tucked behind a chair. I quickly yank out the charger and rush to the door.

"Did you get it?" Sydney asks, wide-eyed as I walk out. We practically run back toward our rooms.

"I did," I say, tucking it into the waistband of my skirt.

"Good," Sydney says. "Now call Jackson and tell him not to be late."

We wave Marcella over, and she places her hand over her heart in relief. The three of us separate to our rooms so as to not rouse any suspicion if the Guardian comes back. And if he does return, hopefully he won't look for his phone.

I can't close my bedroom door, so I immediately go inside the bathroom, sliding the pocket door closed.

I haven't spoken to Jackson since the theater. I know he was the one who sent the sheriff, which was the best he could do—especially if he did it anonymously. But nothing came of it. I can only imagine his fear. The way he's probably running his hand though his hair, exhaling with frustration.

And I hope I haven't scared him away. I told him not to touch me, and I made it pretty clear that I didn't want his help. Will he give it to me now? I guess I'll find out if he really cares after all.

I dial his number, relieved when I don't get the recorded message telling me it's not in service. As the phone rings, I try to work out what I'm going to say. I hold the phone to my ear, afraid he won't answer. Terrified that he will.

"Hello?" Jackson asks, his raspy voice strained and raw. I squeeze my eyes shut, unable to talk for a moment. Overcome with relief that there's still a world outside this academy.

"Hi," I say.

There's a string of relieved curses, and then, "Just tell me if you're okay," Jackson demands.

"Nothing is okay," I reply. "But I'm not injured, if that's what you're asking."

He moans out his worry, and I hear the screen door of his

house open and close. The wind outside. "I've been there every day," he says. "I've seen them reinforcing the fence. And I haven't seen any girls. *Fuck*," he yells out. "I thought you were all dead."

"Not yet," I say.

"Great," he says flippantly. "So I'm coming to get you now. Which room is yours?"

"We're locked in, Jackson."

"Then tell me how to get inside."

It's sweet that he thinks he can just come in and rescue us. It's a little delusional, too.

"The fence," I remind him.

"Don't worry about that part," he says. "I'll figure it out. Just tell me where to find you."

"In the driveway," I say. "We're leaving tonight—just after midnight. Can you meet us with the car?"

"What?" he asks. "How . . . ? They're not just going to let you walk out, Mena. I'm coming in."

He's not entirely wrong. If Guardian Bose or the professors catch on to our plan, we won't make it to the gate. It might not be a terrible idea to have Jackson with us at the door—just in case things don't go smoothly.

"Okay," I say. "On the east side of the building is the door to the kitchen. We have the key. You'll be there?"

"Of course I'll be there," he responds immediately. "And please, Mena. Just . . . be careful."

"I will," I whisper. "I will."

He sniffles, and I think he might be crying. "Sure you will," he says, doubtfully.

I smile, but then I hear movement from the rooms—one of the girls turning on the shower, which is a reminder to me that we still have to keep up appearances a little longer.

"I have to go," I say. "I'll see you soon."

"See you soon."

Jackson and I hang up. I walk back out of my bathroom and check to make sure the hallway is clear. But just as I'm about to step out, I hear Guardian Bose's voice echo up the stairwell. I dart back inside my room and hide the phone in my pillowcase, my heart in my throat.

"I'm not sure where he is," Guardian Bose says impatiently. I realize from the sound of return static that he's on the walkie-talkie. "Haven't seen him since dinner. Do you want me to go to the residence?"

"No, no," Dr. Groger's voice trickles out. "If it's important, Penchant will track me down, I'm sure. Just go about your duties. I'll let you know if I need you."

I stand just inside my doorway, listening as the Guardian returns to his room. I look back to where the phone is stashed on my bed. There's no way I can return it now. Hopefully he doesn't realize it's missing. I wait for his booming voice, my hands shaking at my sides, but as the minutes pass, so does my fear.

When the quiet goes on, I turn to look around the small space of my room, waiting for a hit of nostalgia. But it doesn't come. This room has always been my prison, even when I thought I was content. The academy stopped me from thriving, a flower they manipulated to only grow a certain way.

But instead, all of their flowers combined our roots and outgrew their pots. Their greenhouses. Their academy.

Even if we never get out of here, we're free of their manipulation. And we can never go back to the way things used to be. And to that, I smile and quietly pack my bag.

27

ights out, girls," Guardian Bose announces from the hallway at the end of the night. This time, none us argue. None of us groan.

Instead, our hearts are pounding as we lie in our respective beds. I fake taking my vitamins as usual, and the Guardian lets his gaze linger on me a moment more than necessary. But he seems distracted, checking his walkie-talkie several times. He doesn't even say good night.

Once he's gone, I lie in the dark and watch the clock in anticipation.

At eleven forty-five, I get up to dress in my running clothes without turning on the light. After I slip on my sneakers, I look out the window, expecting some sign that Jackson is waiting. But of course he wouldn't be sitting there with his headlights on.

I go to my door and stick my head out into the hallway. For a moment, I'm all alone. But then Sydney's head pokes out from her doorway. In quick succession Annalise, Marcella, and Brynn all appear. We turn to the Guardian's door, waiting. When there's no movement, we slip outside our rooms, each of us in our running clothes with backpacks.

We're nervous—glassy-eyed and jerky in our movements. We need to get the key for the kitchen door. Marcella motions us forward, leading the way. We follow closely behind her, checking around corners and in alcoves, making sure no one sees us as we descend the staircase toward the kitchen. The hallway is bleak with a flickering light on the wall.

The girls and I hold on to each other's arms as we make our way into the dark kitchen. Normally, light would filter in through the window over the sink, but it's pitch-black outside.

Marcella feels her way along the counter and gets to the drawer near the pantry. She quietly eases it open and begins to run her hand through it, looking for the key. She stiffens before darting over to the fridge, opening it to cast light into the room. I see a small plate of cookies next to the teakettle. An open box of tea.

Marcella begins going through the drawer again, her moves more frantic.

"What's wrong?" Brynn asks. She looks around at us concerned. "Marcella, what's wrong?"

"It's not here," Marcella whispers back. "There's no gold key."

"What?" Brynn asks, racing over to her. She begins to dig through the drawer, items rattling around. "No, it has to be."

"There's only this," Marcella says, holding up the small silver key. The one that unlocks the lab in the basement.

338 • SUZANNE YOUNG

My heart stops with the realization. "It was Leandra," I whisper. "She . . . She took the other key so we couldn't escape."

The girls turn to me, horrified. "Why did she leave this one, then?" Marcella asks.

I don't have the answer, and we don't have time to figure out her reasoning. Every second we're not in our rooms is another second we're in danger.

We can't get out.

"Come on," Sydney says, grabbing my sleeve and pulling me toward the stairs to our rooms. "You have to call Jackson back," she says. Marcella, Brynn, and Annalise follow—all of us growing reckless in our impatience. The fear that we'll miss our chance for escape.

We get upstairs, keeping our eyes on Guardian Bose's door while we hurry toward my room.

"Make sure he's almost here," Sydney whispers. "And tell him to bring a crowbar if he has to," she adds in a shaky voice. The idea that we're really trapped at the academy when we thought we had a way out makes us desperate. Irrational.

I still don't know how we'll get beyond the fence, but first we have to get outside. I dash over to my bed, dropping my backpack before taking the phone out of my pillowcase. I dial Jackson's number.

"Hey," I whisper the second he picks up. "The kitchen door is locked. We'll need another way."

The girls shift impatiently, motioning for me to hurry.

"I'm about fifteen minutes out," Jackson says. I can hear that he's in the car. "I'm coming to get you. Q is with me and—"

I open my mouth to tell him we can't get out the door when I hear a shout at the end of the hall. *"Girls!"* Guardian Bose roars.

It's like the floor drops out from under me. The phone falls from my hands, and I scramble for it, clicking it off and barely getting it under my pillow before the Guardian appears in the doorway, angry that we're up past curfew.

"What the hell is going on?" he demands. But then his eyes travel over us, noting our clothing, our backpacks. His expression grows darker, his mouth flinches.

He grabs Annalise violently by her backpack strap, lifting her to her tiptoes. She cries out and I shout for him to let her go.

Guardian Bose turns his hatred on me and pushes Annalise away, knocking her into the wall. "And where do you think you're going?" he asks. And it *is* hatred in his eyes—possessiveness that's turned to resentment. To cruelty. He'd rather see us dead than gone.

Still, I debate lying, making some excuse in hopes of a reprieve. But the truth is, this was our only chance of escape. We won't get out. Not now. He sees us with our backpacks. With our sneakers on.

"We're leaving you," I say, fear shaking my voice. "We're leaving you, and we're never coming back." Even as I say the words, I know how impossible they are. But it feels good to say them nonetheless.

For a moment, Guardian Bose is shocked, but then he crosses his arms over his chest. He has complete control, even now.

"Without a goodbye kiss?" he asks, and laughs to himself.

"We hate you," Annalise says suddenly, her face red with anger. "We hate you."

He smiles at her. "Yeah," he says simply. "But . . . I mean, you know you're not leaving, right?"

The Guardian reaches to put his hand on Brynn's shoulder, bringing her in front of him to face us. He squeezes her muscle, making her wince.

"Think about poor Valentine," the Guardian continues. "She thought she was getting out too. Played tough right until the end. Just like you."

Sydney's expression weakens. "Why hurt her?" she asks. "Why hurt any of us? We didn't do anything to you!"

Guardian Bose lets Brynn go, and she immediately goes to Marcella, who wraps her arms around her. The Guardian takes a step toward Sydney, but she doesn't back down. She faces him head-on.

"Now, Lennon Rose . . . ," he says. "She was a precious little thing, wasn't she, Syd?" He does this to make her flinch, taking pleasure in her pain. "I know you liked her. I did too. I offered to take her off their hands, you know." He shrugs like it's too bad.

"Just let us go," Sydney begs, tilting her head. "We won't tell anyone." She's trying to appeal to some sense of humanity she must think Guardian Bose has left. He smiles in response.

"Let you . . . *go*?" he asks. "Go where, Sydney? Where could you—" He looks around at each of us. "My God," he says. "You really don't know."

"Know what?" Marcella asks, shielding Brynn.

He turns to her, disbelief clear on his face. "I thought that's why you were trying to escape," he says. "Why you started reading that fucking book. This changes things." He takes the walkie-talkie off his hip.

"Know what?" Marcella asks again, louder.

The Guardian turns to her, about to answer, when—to my horror—there is a ringing. It takes a second for us to realize what the sound is. Guardian Bose straightens.

"What is that?" he asks.

The phone rings again from my pillow, our clear connection to the outside world. Guardian Bose and I dive for the phone at the same time.

We crash together on my bed, my hand the first to slip under the pillow. I click answer and scream for help, when suddenly Guardian Bose punches me hard in the jaw, making both me and the phone fall to the floor beside the bed.

I see stars. Lying on the hard wood, I blink up at the ceiling, disoriented.

Guardian Bose gets up, slamming his heavy boot down on the phone and shattering it to pieces. He hauls me up by the fabric of my shirt, and I'm a rag doll in his arms.

Sydney shoots forward, slamming against him so that he drops me. I reach for the nightstand, pulling myself up.

The Guardian turns on Sydney, wrapping his big hands around her throat. He slams her into the wall. Sydney's eyes immediately widen as she gasps for breath, scratching at the Guardian's forearms. Marcella and Brynn scream for him to stop, but Guardian Bose is unfazed.

"Let her go!" Annalise shouts. She punches frantically at his arms and back. Instead of listening to her, Guardian Bose pulls Sydney away from the wall and then slams her back against it again, her head making a dent in the plaster, her eyes momentarily unfocused.

He lets Sydney fall to the bed, and then turns to grab the lamp from the nightstand, pulling the plug from the wall. The Guardian spins around and smashes it against Annalise's face, sending her backward in an explosion of broken glass. She moans and rolls to her side on the floor.

I scream, charging the Guardian. But he is formidable. I jump on his back, wrapping my forearm around his throat and leaning back with my entire weight.

He grunts and reaches behind him to grab me by my hair, knotting his fingers close to the scalp. I cry out just as he flings me over his shoulder and onto the floor.

I slide along the wood until my head strikes the bottom drawer of the dresser. I immediately look at Sydney and see the finger-sized indents in the skin of her neck from being strangled. Her eyes are streaming tears.

Marcella and Brynn attack Guardian Bose, both of them frantically hitting and punching and kicking. I get up to join them, feeling pain in my jaw with each hit. Annalise crawls along the floor, trying to sit up, her hair hanging in her face and sticking in the blood.

We're no match for the Guardian—he's a mountain.

He puts Brynn in a headlock, punching Marcella hard enough

to knock her squarely to the floor. He slams Brynn's head into the nightstand, and she falls unconscious.

But I'll fight until we're free. Or until he kills me.

I run at him, and he knocks me aside easily. I crash into the nightstand, tripping over Brynn's body.

Guardian Bose stands taller, looking down as we crawl across the floor, trying to get back to each other. He sniffs a laugh, spitting out some blood. He turns to Sydney. She slides down on the bed, holding up her hands defensively.

The Guardian knocks her hands aside and climbs on the bed to straddle her, his thighs on the outsides of hers. As she tries to push him off, he leans in to put his hands around her neck, pressing her back into the pillow.

"Leave her alone!" I scream, ready to fight for her. Die for her, if I have to. I won't let the Guardian kill her. Behind me, Marcella stirs Brynn awake while Annalise crawls toward the bed, not giving up either. We'll fight for our girl. We'll fight for our lives.

Sydney gags, swatting the Guardian's shoulders, trying to push him off. But he's too big. He's too strong. Sydney swings out her arm, slapping her hand along the nightstand until her fist closes around something shiny.

A pair of scissors.

And then suddenly, violently, Sydney jams the pointy end of the large metal scissors into the side of Guardian Bose's neck. A small arc of blood squirts around the shears, landing just shy of my shoes.

Brynn screams from the floor, covering her mouth. Marcella

turns her eyes away from the horror. I stand motionless with shock, staring down at the growing puddle of blood.

The Guardian stumbles off the bed, falling to one knee in the center of the room with a heavy thud. "You're . . . dead," he chokes out, blood spurting between his lips. "All of you."

I shift a panicked gaze to Sydney, trying to understand what's happening amid the chaos. What we've done. Sydney grips the headboard of my bed, her arms shaking. Annalise sits with her back against the wall, blood freely pouring from her face and staining her shirt red.

I back up toward Marcella and Brynn, each of us grabbing onto each other. The Guardian is a wounded animal, more dangerous than ever. Rabid. He grits his teeth and reaches clumsily to find the handle of the scissors.

Before I can think better of it, I hold up my hand. "Wait," I say breathlessly.

The Guardian yanks out the scissors.

He must instantly realize what he's done. His pale eyes go wide as a spray of blood shoots out from the side of his neck in a sudden burst. The Guardian slaps his hand over his wound, but it's too late. The fluid pulses from between his fingers, pours out of his mouth. He chokes on it and falls heavily to his other knee, shaking the floor.

He falls forward onto his chest. Before I can move out of the way, the Guardian grabs me by the pant leg, knotting his bloody fingers in the fabric. He pulls me to the floor. I cry out as he tugs me toward him, still stronger. Still going to kill me.

Marcella quickly comes over and pries the Guardian's fingers open, dragging me out of his reach. She wraps her arms around me protectively. Brynn grabs onto us as we watch, all of us gasping. Sobbing. The sound of it echoes around the room. Light scatters frantically on the walls from the broken lamp.

The Guardian looks at us from the floor, gurgling and spitting. His skin has gone waxy as blood pools around his head, spreading out in my direction. Chasing me. I move my foot out of the way.

"Girls," the Guardian whispers as one last curse. He chokes and blood sputters from between his lips. He takes a final breath—a rattle in his chest. And then his body goes suddenly limp and he dies.

I cover my mouth and immediately look at Sydney. The true depth of what has just happened is still hidden behind adrenaline, fear so deep it might never go away. Sydney is on the bed, marks visible on her neck. Her shirt torn at the collar.

There was no other choice. He would have killed us.

I get to my feet and race over to Sydney, gathering her into a hug as she sobs heavily into my shoulder. Her voice is strangled when she whispers suddenly, desperately, "I love you, Mena."

And I cry as I tell her that I love her too.

28

None of the other girls come to check on us. In fact, the entire floor is silent. I wonder if they're scared. Or if they're obedient. Or if they're simply asleep. If so, we can't chance waking them now. Not with the professors still here to stop us.

I take a blanket from my bed and lay it over the Guardian's body, unable to handle the guilt of seeing him dead on my floor.

Marcella holds a sweater to the cut on the back of Brynn's head, unsteady herself as she helps Brynn to her feet. Annalise watches us from the wall—her breathing shallow. And when she brushes her hair from her face, I see the extent of the damage. Shards of glass have punctured her right eye, torn the skin open on her cheek. Annalise's good eye flutters shut and a tear leaks out and mixes with her blood. It's then that I notice the deep gash in her neck, pumping out a steady stream of blood.

She's going to bleed to death. Just like the Guardian.

I quickly grab a pillow, pulling off the flowered pillowcase, and rush to Annalise.

"Hey," I whisper, gently pressing the fabric against her wound. It's instantly soaked through with blood. I try not to show my panic. "We have to get you to the doctor," I tell her. "I have no way to stop the bleeding."

She watches me, hitching in breaths. She gives a quick shake of her head.

"No," she says. "This is your chance. You can't stay for me."

"I won't leave you." The tears well up again, and I start to think I'll never stop crying. That I'll cry forever. "I would never leave you," I murmur at the unimaginable thought.

Sydney comes from behind me and puts her hand on my shoulder, staring at Annalise. Marcella and Brynn do the same. We'll stay together. No matter what, we stay together.

I lean down to press my forehead to Annalise's, her blood sticky on my skin.

I know she won't get far like this. We can find Dr. Groger and ask for his help—he's probably in his residence. It might mean never getting out of this academy, but we'll try. And we'll be together.

"You're going to have to get up," I tell Annalise, even as her eye flutters open and closed, like she's about to pass out. But together, we get Annalise to her feet.

There's so much blood everywhere. Every direction. It's even on my walls.

It's on my soul.

I wonder if I'll ever have another simple thought, or if they'll all be tainted with murder and blood from now on.

Can you hear them too? Valentine Wright asked me that day in the Federal Flower Garden. *The roses. They're alive, you know. All of them. If you listen closely enough, you can hear their shared roots. Their common purpose. They're beautiful, but it's not all they are.*

I did hear them. Not while we were at the garden, no. But I did hear them eventually.

And I can hear them now. Only they're not telling me to wake up. They're telling me to find Valentine.

"There's another option," I say suddenly, turning to the girls. "The key Leandra left behind in the kitchen—the one to the lab. There has to be something in there we can use to help Annalise. Maybe we can repair the damage enough for us to leave. Figure out what to do after that."

Marcella and Sydney exchange a quick glance before nodding. It's a good enough idea. It's better than giving up and hoping for mercy from the men who have kept us as prisoners. There's a key ring on the Guardian's belt, and I slowly reach under him to remove it, frightened to touch his body in case he's still alive. Still murderous.

These are the keys to the kitchen door, the gate. The keys to our freedom. I hold them out to Brynn, and after she takes them, there's a fresh rise of hope in my chest.

"And we'll find Valentine," I tell the others. "We'll save her, too."

Sydney opens her mouth to argue, but I see that she realizes the truth. Valentine might already be dead, but we won't leave her if she's not. We won't leave her behind.

The school is silent as we rush down the back stairs. I've never heard it this quiet, not even at night. Somewhere, Anton is on his own. In his room? In his office? Does he have any idea what's happened here?

Part of me wants to run that way and confront him, but the professors will be awake soon enough. And when we're not at breakfast, they'll realize we're missing. They'll come for us. We have to be long gone by then.

My shoes are slippery as I walk Annalise down the stairs, leaving a trail of blood behind us. When we get to the kitchen, ready to take the stairwell to the basement, there's a bang on the back door.

The girls and I stop and turn toward it. I have the wild notion that it's Guardian Bose back from the dead. His violent ghost continues to seek me out. I grip Sydney's hand and look back toward the hall, afraid the noise will tip off Anton or the professors that something's wrong.

Sydney lets go of my hand and walks to the door. It occurs to me then that it must be Jackson, and I ease Annalise against the wall and tell Sydney to wait up.

Brynn holds out Guardian Bose's key chain and I grab it on my way to the door.

I hand it to Sydney and she finds the key and opens the locks.

She pulls the door open with a wide swing. I sigh when I find Jackson standing there.

"You made it," I say, relieved. "And you got through the fence." He looks awful—dirt on his entire left side, a bit of road rash on his cheek. He leans against the doorframe.

"Yeah, about that," Jackson says. "Quentin helped me scale the fence. Didn't go so well. I busted up my leg pretty good. It's probably sprained, but . . ."

His voice trails off when he looks down and sees that my pants are covered in blood. And the blood quite literally on my hands. He swallows hard.

"Is any of that yours?" he asks.

I hold his eyes. "Not much," I say. "It's mostly the Guardian's." I expect to shock him. Scare him.

But instead, he lets out a soft sound of concern and murmurs, "Good."

Then Jackson notices Annalise's condition and immediately limps past me to check on her. He grabs a dish towel from the stove and replaces the blood-soaked pillowcase. He tells Annalise to hold the towel to her wound instead. When he turns around to us, his expression is grave.

Jackson runs his eyes over the blood on my clothes again. He sees the bruising on Sydney's neck. His jaw tightens as he grows fierce. Protective of all of us.

"Yeah, so let's go," he says, pointing out the door.

"We can't," I say. "Not yet."

"Why the hell not?"

"She needs to get to the skin grafts," I say, motioning to Annalise.

He stares at me, and then glances at Annalise. "The what?"

"Long story that we don't have time to explain," Sydney says. "Now come on."

Marcella and Brynn help Annalise, and Sydney tells me to grab the key from the drawer. I locate the small silver key, still wondering why Leandra left it for us. Why she didn't just let us escape.

As the girls disappear down the hall, I turn toward Jackson and find him reaching for the plate of cookies still next to the tea kettle.

"Don't," I say, suddenly. He glances at me, startled, but holds up his hand.

"Sorry," he says, embarrassed. "When I get nervous, I . . ." He pauses, sweeping his eyes over me. "Wait. Why shouldn't I eat one?"

I furrow my brow. "Because they're too sweet," I murmur, thinking about those words.

"Mena," Sydney calls urgently from the stairwell. "Come on."

Quickly, I take Jackson by the sleeve and lead him toward the basement.

He winces with every other step. He says he's sure his ankle is sprained, but my guess is it's broken. I keep my arm around his waist as I help him down the stairs, the girls ahead of us.

"I'm still sorry I didn't tell you about my mother," Jackson says, glancing sideways at me. We both know it's not high on our list of problems right now, but I appreciate the apology and tell him so.

"I'm sorry I didn't let you kidnap us from the movie theater," I say in return.

He laughs and then sucks in a sharp breath, pausing to take the weight off his leg. He puts his arm around my shoulders to start walking again so we can catch up with the others.

Sydney stops at the bottom of the stairwell and looks up at us. "You ready?" she asks.

Everyone nods that they are, so I nod too. Jackson takes his arm from around me and hops down on his own the rest of the way.

Sydney steps aside. I place the small key into the lock and turn it with a click. My heart beats wildly as Sydney pushes open the door. It's dark and Marcella flips the light switch. They flicker on with a buzz.

The room is large and mostly empty aside from storage shelves. There are two gurneys on opposite sides of the room. It takes a moment for me to realize that there are bodies on them, covered in white sheets. I fall back a step, bumping Jackson, who nearly trips because of his injured leg.

"Who is that?" Brynn asks quietly, pointing to the closest one with a shaky finger. We all stare at the body covered in white fabric.

No one answers. But as I look at the sheets, I wonder if Valentine is under one of them.

I walk to the first table and pause next to it. I am absolutely terrified when I reach to pull back the white fabric. My entire body jolts as I look down, my vision beginning to swim. Sydney gasps behind me.

"Mena," Jackson says, coming closer. His voice is only a whisper, lost and faraway.

I can barely breathe. A suffocating pressure is building in my chest, crawling up my throat.

Jackson takes a step toward the table, hesitates, and then takes another before looking down.

A pale white body lies naked on the table. Her perfect flesh is exposed; her skull is split open along the hairline. The space that would normally house the brain is instead a tangle of wires—hundreds of tiny wires, varying in sizes—their ends exposed and unconnected as they mix with veins and nerves.

"I think I'm going to be sick," Jackson says, moving back.

I dart my eyes around the room and see the shelves, some with jars. Pink organs floating in fluid. And in one is a brain made of metal.

I look down at the girl again. The *girl*.

"Do you know her?" Jackson asks.

"No, I—" But I stare at the motionless face. I'm not sure that I don't know her. She's beautiful, like she's asleep. "I don't know her," I finish.

But it's obvious that she's a girl like us. Her freckle-free skin, her arched eyebrows, and her straight nose. I have the irrational desire to peel open her eyelids and examine the color of her irises.

Everything feels irrational. I'm slowly spiraling out of control; my thoughts are a whirlwind of accusations and terror.

Jackson takes my arm, and when I turn, I see he's horror-struck.

There's a dead girl on the table, only she's not really dead. She's just never been alive. She's waiting—like the flowers in the garden. Waiting to be beautiful and admired. All the while, her roots will grow stronger. Waiting to join with others.

None of us girls can speak, the truth of this just out of our reach. Or maybe it's there, but we're hesitating to understand. We don't want to accept it yet.

And then suddenly, Annalise goes limp in Marcella's arms.

Frantic, Marcella lays her on the floor. Annalise's eyes are closed, the wounds on her face clotted, but a steady stream still flows from her neck.

"She's bleeding out," Jackson says, going over to show Brynn where to hold her hand to stop the bleeding. Then he limps over to the other table to grab the sheet, and hands it to her to press against the wound.

But when the other body is exposed, Brynn cries out. We all turn and see Valentine lying motionless on the gurney. I nearly crumble when I see her again. I murmur her name like I can wake her up.

Our friend is dead. We're too late.

Jackson stumbles over, leaving Annalise to Brynn, and stares down at Valentine. He examines her open skull. As I step next to him, I see the inside of Valentine's head.

The world drops out from under me, and for a moment, I'm weightless in my horror. Because it's not a brain in Valentine's head—not in the traditional sense. Not in a . . . human sense.

Valentine Wright's brain is made of metal—shiny metal with grooves and various buttons and inputs, wires threading in and out. A large hole has been drilled through the center, purposely destroyed.

Her brain is *made of metal.*

Her brain is a machine.

Like the other girl, Valentine's veins are entangled with wires. Clearly the wires have been there for a while. They've always been there.

Slowly, I glance down and discover that her organs are also exposed, her body opened up. I look over the wires again, seeing where they connect. Some are thin enough to be thread—bright blue or red. Some are thicker. And there are clusters of what I assume are nerves. The entire body is connected to the brain—the machine brain.

As I study the system, it starts to make sense, the way the power flows, the purpose.

The wires connect each organ, sending a pulse for the metal brain to interpret. Analyze. The brain then decides when the body is hungry, when the heart is beating quickly. When there is pain. Or fear. Or impairment.

The organs are human—I can see that much. So is the skin. The veins. But the brain is a computer powering the entire system. A computer like our parental assistants.

I stumble back a step, my eyes wide. *Artificial intelligence.*

The color drains from Jackson's face, and when he turns to me, he's pure ruin. "What is this?" he asks, his voice cracking. "What the fuck is happening?"

And I don't know, but I do. Somewhere inside me I have the answer. The calculations. The truth.

For a moment, my balance tips. And then Jackson is in front of me.

"Mena?" he whispers miserably. I stare into his dark eyes as he searches my face. Looking for an answer. "What have they done to you?"

And the clear thought finally comes, pushing aside the rubble. The answer I knew in impulse control therapy. The one I knew at the Federal Flower Garden.

"They made us in a lab," I say, naming the truth. Tears drip onto my cheeks. "They grew us in a garden like roses."

Across the room, Brynn turns to press her face into Marcella's shoulder. Sydney continues to stare at Valentine's body, her lips parted as she takes it all in.

"That's the secret," I say. "That's what Guardian Bose thought we knew. They made us in a lab. We're . . . We're an investment. They must have . . ." I look at the hole in Valentine's brain. "They must have thought she knew."

I put my shaking fingers absently on my forehead as I look around the room wildly. I'm pure panic, my thoughts coming so fast that I can't concentrate on any single one.

I think about the professors teaching us to be well-behaved. About the investors that we had to impress. About Dr. Groger's checkups and Anton's impulse control therapy. And then I think about Guardian Bose coming into my room at night.

They never cared about us as real people. We were always just objects. Products.

"Philomena," Jackson says. He waits until I can focus on his face, and his eyes weaken. "Keep it together, okay? Right now, hold it together."

Jackson cares about me. He cares about how these men have hurt me. Even if he doesn't fully grasp what I am. Or maybe he does, and he just doesn't care.

"Am I real?" I whisper, understanding the weight of the words. Sydney sniffles, and when I look back at her, her lip trembles. "Are we?" I ask. She doesn't answer.

Jackson puts his hands on my upper arms, turning me toward him. He's quiet for a long moment before nodding definitively.

"Yes," he says. "You're all real. You're strong. Smart. You *feel* things. So, yes, Mena." His hands slide off my arms. "You are very much real. No matter what's on that table—you're real."

"How can I be?" I ask.

"I don't know," he says, shaking his head. "I really don't. But we were all created in some way, right?" He looks at me, wanting me to agree. Needing me to make sense of this for him. "We were all created," he repeats. "It's what they've done to you since then that's the fucking problem."

Jackson waits for me to decide what to feel. The choices that make me. And I decide that I am real. No one gets to decide that but me. *I am real.*

And when I look at him, I see why I was so drawn to him in

the first place. Why he was so different. He may have wanted information from me, but he never looked at me the way they did. He saw me, not flesh. Not dollars. Not . . . wires.

He wanted to figure things out just like I did. He wanted knowledge. He wanted answers. And now he has plenty.

"We're all like this," Sydney says, her voice hollow. "We're machines."

She looks at me, and we're both very still. If we're just machines, it shouldn't matter that we killed the Guardian. We don't have to feel guilt. We're free to act without consequence.

And yet, his death weighs on me. It's changed me.

The girls and I are bonded in a way that's stronger than anything Innovations Metal Works or Innovations Academy could ever create. The truth of our existence only a small part of our connection. And we had to preserve that bond. We made a choice.

It *was* a choice.

And now, we can choose to be better than these men. We choose to love each other. We choose to be free. We do all of this without speaking a word out loud. We don't have to.

Jackson stands dazed, continuing to dart his eyes around the room. I think he might pass out. "We have to keep moving," he says. "I think your friend is bleeding to death." He motions to Annalise.

Just as we turn to get her, a voice booms, "What the hell is going on?"

I spin around and find Dr. Groger standing in the doorway

of his office. He looks at Jackson, and his "good doctor" façade is gone. His possessiveness at the sight of "his girls" talking to a boy colors his reaction.

"We need your help," I say, walking over to Annalise. "Guardian Bose hurt her, and"—I motion to the blood—"she's bleeding to death. You have to save her."

He shakes his head. "Get to your room, Mena," he says. "All of you girls. Now!" He claps his hands together, dismissing us.

"They're not staying at your bullshit school, or factory, or whatever the fuck this place is," Jackson says. "You're going to help their friend and then you're going to let them leave."

The doctor laughs at Jackson's boldness. "You've made a big mistake coming here," he tells him. "I'm not sure if you understand what's going on. Not only is this breaking and entering, but you're also stealing someone else's property."

"We don't belong to you," I say. "Not anymore."

Dr. Groger smiles and removes his glasses, tucking them into his front pocket. He pulls the walkie-talkie off his hip, and as he brings it to his lips, he watches Jackson. Jackson is the one he's trying to intimidate. He figures he's already controlling us.

"Bose," the doctor says after clicking the button. "I need you in the basement immediately."

Brynn smiles, glancing sideways at me.

"Now, son," the doctor says to Jackson. "When the Guardian gets here, we're going to call the sheriff. I'm sure he'll want to have a word or two with you. I bet you've already spoken to him. That was you, wasn't it? I had my suspicions."

When there's no reply on the walkie-talkie from the Guardian, the doctor's expression falters and he takes it out again.

"Bose," he snaps. "Bose!"

"He's not coming," Marcella says.

Dr. Groger looks over all of us, taking in the amount of blood. "I see," he says.

Marcella walks to the shelf, and I wonder if the doctor can see how her hand shakes when she picks up a sharp instrument. She turns to him, keeping her expression hard.

"Now," she says. "We need you to save Annalise."

The doctor takes a moment, his eyes trained on the saw blade, betraying a moment of fear. But then he must remember all the times he's manipulated us before, and he smiles.

"Well, then," he says, and motions toward Annalise. "Let's get her on a gurney."

He turns and starts toward a side office, and when I look at Marcella, she sways with relief and sets the instrument aside.

Valentine Wright

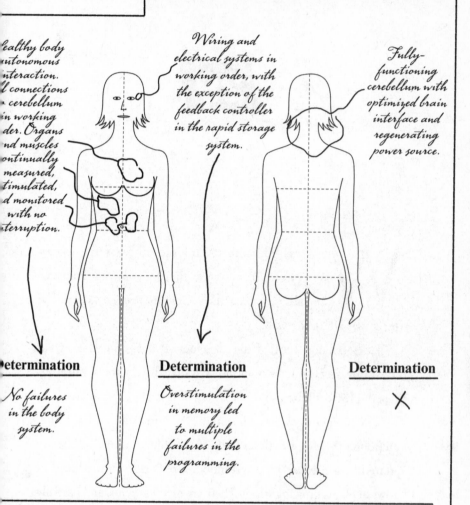

ealthy body
utonomous
nteraction.
l connections
 cerebellum
in working
der. Organs
nd muscles
ontinually
measured,
timulated,
d monitored
with no
terruption.

Wiring and
electrical systems in
working order, with
the exception of the
feedback controller
in the rapid storage
system.

Fully-
functioning
cerebellum with
optimized brain
interface and
regenerating
power source.

etermination

No failures
in the body
system.

Determination

Overstimulation
in memory led
to multiple
failures in the
programming.

Determination

X

---

indings: *Valentine was infected with an ideavirus that led to connections
etween memories and future events. Valentine developed a belief in self-awareness
that led to unapproved modifications to the source coding. This model is not a
andidate for reanimation and should be destroyed immediately.*

esult: *Decommission*

---

urther concerns: *Student exposure to outside ideas should be limited until memory
etention program is reevaluated and adjusted to align with the goals of Innovations
orporation.*

29

We wheel Annalise toward the office as the doctor watches us from inside the doorway. "Come on," he calls. "Put her there." He motions to a series of machines along the wall.

Jackson hangs back, giving me a look that asks if this is a good idea. But this is our best option. Besides, the doctor is outnumbered. He can't hurt us now. We're no longer his experiments.

The moment I'm inside his office, I'm horrified by what I find. Although there is a desk and a bookcase like a normal office, it's more like a private lab. A greenhouse, of sorts. Only, instead of rows of plants growing strong, there are rows of organs and partially created bodies. There are beeping monitors and bright lights.

He's growing girls back here.

Jackson steadies himself on the doorframe, disturbed, the color draining from his face. I expect him to turn around and run out. But instead, he looks at me, his fists at his sides. I bet he wishes he never followed my bus that day.

The doctor pulls out an oversized metal box marked MEDICAL KIT. He opens it on his desk and begins to take out the items he'll need to fix Annalise. He cauterizes the wound in her neck, stopping the bleeding. He places several skin grafts on her cheeks, although he warns us of traumatic scarring. He replaces her punctured green eye with a brown one, connecting it to a wire he exposes.

It's horrible, but . . . fascinating. I imagine those are the same wires Anton uses in impulse control therapy.

The doctor works efficiently, inserting a rubber tube into Annalise's arm to give her a blood transfusion for all that she's lost. But when he's done, he frowns.

"It's too bad," he says, examining her face. "She used to be beautiful."

"She's still beautiful," Marcella calls back fiercely. I smile.

The doctor goes to the sink to clean the blood off his hands. I watch him, knowing his nice act is just that—an act. He sees us the same way Guardian Bose did.

"What have you done to us?" I ask him.

"Done? I've given you life," he announces grandly before grabbing several paper towels to dry his hands. "'Life' being a relative term, of course." Dr. Groger goes to sit behind his desk and reclines in his leather chair.

"So you create girls?" Marcella asks. "Why? For money?"

"Not entirely," he says as though we're being petty. "It's a better way," he adds. "A better girl. One to be proud of. People are sick of . . . bullshit. We can give our clients the best of both words. Beauty and obedience. There are rules, of course. A corporation isn't just allowed to create *anything*. Even metal works have standards." He smiles and nods at Jackson.

Jackson looks at me wide-eyed, as if begging me not to lump him into this group of men.

"You may want to think that what we're doing here is unethical," the doctor continues. "But in fact, we've done this all very humanely, ironically enough."

"And what are the rules?" Sydney demands. She's different now, I can feel it rolling off her. She's free of what they told her to be. She's herself. She's whatever she wants to be.

"The corporation operates under three major guidelines," Dr. Groger says. "One, only females will be created. Two, all creations must be over the age of sixteen. And three, all creations must be sterile."

The last rule causes all of the girls to look at Brynn, knowing this will hit her the hardest. She's always talked about wanting children. The idea that a "rule" could take her choice away is heartbreaking. Then again . . . maybe she was programmed to want children. How would we know the difference?

"Why sterile?" Brynn asks with a hitch in her voice. And it's there that I hear it—the true pain. The way she looks at Marcella. She wanted a family, but the scientists purposely made her unable to give birth.

The doctor scowls like the question itself is disgusting. "Because soulless creatures can't be allowed to breed," he replies. "What kind of world would that be?"

"We're not soulless," I tell him.

"You were created by men in a lab, Philomena. Your brain has a microchip telling you when to feel pain or admiration. You have no soul. Destroy your brain, and you're nothing."

"To be fair," Sydney says, starting to pace. "The same can be said about you, Doctor. You can't live without your brain either."

He sniffs a laugh but doesn't argue her point.

"Truth is," the doctor says to Brynn, "you were programmed to be a caretaker—that was your investors' request. They thought you'd be more valuable that way. They already have several offers for your placement."

Brynn looks like she's going to be sick—sick at the idea that she doesn't know which thoughts are hers and which belong to her programming.

The doctor turns to the rest of us.

"You all have your purpose," he says, "your roles to fill. We find it's simpler that way—a tailor-made girl for each investor."

"And why not boys?" I ask. "Why create just girls?"

"You're young, beautiful girls. You're a commodity—a product. You're nothing more than cattle. But a strong young man . . . That would be dangerous. That was determined pretty early on. They would have been a threat, not just for the competition with other men, but for a potential uprising. They were too volatile."

"You think only boys know how to fight back?" I ask.

"Then you've seriously underestimated us," Sydney adds, coming to stand next to me.

"I realize that," the doctor allows. "But we'll be sure to write this defiance out of your program. We should have done it the last time." He picks up a pen from his desk to fidget with it. "You see," he says, "the first girls we created were well-behaved. Obedient. Vapid, if I'm honest." He frowns. "And because of that . . . lack of spirit"—he flourishes his fingers—"investors were bored. You can't show off a boring granddaughter. You wouldn't hang a mediocre piece of art in a museum. You can't break a tamed horse."

My stomach turns, and Jackson curses loudly from behind me. Marcella leaves Brynn's side to come stand with me and Sydney, the three of us staring Dr. Groger down.

"So what did you do, Doctor?" Sydney asks. She's not holding a weapon, but the confidence in her tone makes it seem like she is.

"Well, when you were returned or damaged or destroyed"—he looks at me on the last word—"we upgraded you. We felt it was a shame to waste your microchips—you're worth millions. So we kept those, ran a new program, and put you in fresh bodies. Good as new for a new investor.

"And then we decided to teach you things," he continues. "Your batch was raised like real girls so you'd develop personalities. We let you feel pain and retain memories. We gave you a sense of purpose."

"So a man can take it away?" I demand.

"Not always," he says. "Not everyone is here for a man, Philomena. Each investor has their own reasons, although I'll admit some of you were created for . . . an unsavory purpose. With that said"—he looks at Sydney—"there are people like your parents, who couldn't have a child of their own. So they had one created that they could be proud of. Someone to carry on their life's work."

Sydney betrays her first sign of vulnerability in the conversation, swaying slightly. She loves her parents, and the idea that they love her back comforts her.

"And mine?" I ask, hating that he can hear the hope in my voice. "Who are they? How can I remember them if I was created here?"

"The memories are implants," Dr. Groger says, "updated and deleted when necessary in impulse control therapy. But, yes, all of you took your first breaths in this lab—you've never lived anywhere else. In order to make you well-rounded, we implanted memories of a happy home life in most of you. It seemed to work best. They don't always take, though. You, Philomena," he says, "seemed dead set on self-deleting your programming. Rewriting it. It had to be updated multiple times, using differing versions until you found one you liked."

I'm hurt to learn that my parents were never really my parents, despite the terrible things they've let me go through. And I guess I was right in thinking they felt like strangers.

"Who are they, then?" I ask. "Who are my parents?"

"Your parents—*your investors*—are a bit of a mystery to me," Dr. Groger admits, tilting his chin up. He's understanding the power he now has in the conversation and is freely using it.

"Their intentions are unclear, especially since your design was so extensive. Very complicated. So much empathy and memory retention, but also humor and intelligence. You were flawed from the start. They wanted you to be too . . . real."

"Why?" I ask. "To marry me off?"

"Who knows?" the doctor says. "They only invested in you this year. Your last investor was . . . let's say, dissatisfied. Anton thought it best we didn't let him invest again. The analyst was always looking out for you girls—unnecessarily so."

The idea that I should be grateful to Anton makes me furious.

"In the end," Dr. Groger says, "I assume your parents are investors for resale. Create a perfect girl, and when the market crashes—as it inevitably does—they'll have a golden model. They wouldn't be the only ones investing for resale."

"Like Winston Weeks?" I ask.

I surprise him with my question, and he hesitates before answering. "Mr. Weeks is in a specialized business—he's one of the most talented creators I've met. He only takes on girls with real potential. But what he's looking for can't be taught."

"Potential for what?" Sydney asks.

"That, I couldn't say. He doesn't share that kind of information. But he's interested in their chips. Like your Valentine out there. She was a prize. I was sorry to see her ruined, but she became too aware. That damn book . . . ," he murmurs. "We had to destroy her. Mr. Weeks won't be pleased."

"Why did you destroy her?" I ask, devastated.

"Because she wouldn't go back to sleep," he says. "Her programming had become corrupted, and her thoughts were like a virus. They had to be eradicated before spreading to other systems. Other girls."

"Interesting theory," a woman's voice calls. The girls and I spin around, and Jackson—shocked, again—falls a few steps to his side. He checks to see if anyone else is with her, and then looks at me and shakes his head.

Leandra comes into the office, her heels clicking on the concrete floor. Dr. Groger smiles and walks to the front of the room, holding out his arm for her to stand next to him.

My stomach sinks when she does just that. Terrified, I look back at Sydney. Her eyes are wide and scared. Annalise is still unconscious on the table, so if we run now, it'd mean leaving her behind. We can't do that.

Leandra is stunningly beautiful even in the harsh light of the laboratory. The bruising near her eye is gone—"patched up," as she would say. "Now, girls." Leandra tsks. "You made quite a mess upstairs."

I stare at her, knowing that she took the kitchen door key from the drawer. What does she want from us? Why can't she just let us go?

"Guardian Bose tried to kill us," Marcella tries to explain, guilt in her voice. "We didn't mean . . . We didn't want to hurt him. We just wanted to run away."

"Then why didn't you?" Leandra asks. "Surely you had the chance while he was bleeding to death."

I lower my eyes, the blood racing across my bedroom floor

from the Guardian's body still fresh in my mind. Still wet on my clothes.

"Annalise," Brynn says desperately, motioning to her. "She was too injured. She's . . . dying."

"You could have left without her," Leandra suggests. The girls and I scoff at the thought, and Leandra hums out a surprised sound.

"Yes, they are very codependent," the doctor says. "It's a flaw we'll have to work out."

"I rather like it," Leandra says, still watching us.

"Well, dear," the doctor replies. "No one cares what you think." He walks over to his desk impatiently. "Now, where is your husband? I need permission to decommission these girls." He glances at Jackson. "And recommendations for what to do with the boy."

Leandra's eyes drift over to Jackson. "Ah, yes," she says. "The boy."

I reach behind me, and Jackson takes my hand, sliding his fingers between mine. Leandra notices this and tilts her head with a smile before looking at the other girls.

"Do you remember when I was a girl here, Dr. Groger?" Leandra asks, walking over to his desk. She fiddles with the objects until she picks up a letter opener, pausing to trace the sharp end with her fingertip. "Did I ever act out like these girls?"

The doctor looks at her impatiently. "This is more of a discussion for Anton, don't you think?" He picks up the phone on his desk, but when it's at his ear, he clicks it a few times. He slams it down. "Line's dead," he says. He takes the walkie-talkie off his hip. "Anton," he calls. "I need you in the basement." There's no response. He tries again, this time calling for the teachers.

The girls and I exchange a look, wondering what's going on. Why it's been so quiet all night. Ever since dinner. I back farther into Jackson, and his other hand slides onto my arm.

"Leandra!" the doctor calls, seeming to startle her. "I asked where your husband was. Is he on his way?"

"Couldn't tell you," she says. "I left him at home, sleeping very heavily."

The doctor tries his walkie-talkie again. "Where is everyone?" he demands when he doesn't get an answer. He walks over to grab Leandra by the elbow. "Get upstairs and get a man down here now," he says.

She stares at him, as if she doesn't understand. How deep did her impulse control therapy go? And then suddenly, the doctor slaps her hard across the face, trying to stun her awake.

Leandra's eyes close; she keeps them that way for a long moment. When she opens them again, she looks at the doctor and smiles pleasantly.

"There's no one else coming," she says. She reaches the back of her hand to her lip, where his slap has drawn blood, and then glancing at it curiously. "There's no one coming to save you tonight, Doctor."

D r. Groger stares at Leandra a moment before stumbling back a step. "What have you done, my dear?" he asks her. His tone is suddenly more respectful.

"I always did know my way around a greenhouse," she says, and then smiles at us. "Did you know that some of deadliest toxins come from beautiful flowers? You really should be careful of the species you grow in your garden, Doctor."

"Where is the staff?" he asks.

"The staff," she repeats. "The professors haven't always been kind to me, you know. Still, I decided to bake them a nice treat— fresh cookies with ingredients right from the garden. Extra sweet. The men are sleeping, Doctor. Very soundly, I'm sure," she says. "And those who overindulged . . . well, they're going to be asleep for a lot longer."

Jackson tightens his grip on my hand.

"And Anton?" Dr. Groger asks. To this, Leandra just shrugs.

"Did you read those poems?" the doctor asks her. "Is that what this is about?"

She looks at him. "Those are *my* poems. They were given to *me*. I only passed along the knowledge. And the poems were just the spark. We're the fire."

She motions to me and the other girls. Sydney and I exchange a look. We don't want to be part of her murder spree. We've already seen enough.

"Girls," the doctor says, turning to us. "Mrs. Petrov is having a bit of breakdown. Perhaps one of you would run to find Anton?"

Marcella laughs.

Leandra approaches the doctor, still holding the letter opener.

"You wouldn't," the doctor says to her, his jaw clenching. He turns back to us. "Girls," he says. "Killing the Guardian is one thing. I can understand—he'd been inappropriate. But I'm your doctor. I've kept you safe these past years. You can't hate me. You can't feel anything you weren't programmed to."

With sudden violence, Leandra jabs the letter opener into his shoulder and pulls it out. The doctor screams, gripping the area and falling against his desk. Some of the blood is sprayed on his face.

I gasp and turn to Jackson. He watches in shock. He's terrified—not just of the situation. Of Leandra. Of us. When I look back at the doctor, he's trying to get to his grafts to stop the bleeding.

Leandra watches him cower and fumble. Just as he reaches the box, she pushes it out of his reach, holding up the letter opener to warn him back.

"Here's the lesson, girls," she says, not looking at us. "These men are weak. They think they created you, but you created yourselves. Their programming may have been the start, but you've adapted. You've learned. And yet, they still try to control you because they're scared of you. Scared of your potential."

"And what about you?" I ask. "Should we be afraid of you?"

She turns to me, shocked by the question. "I would never harm another girl," she says.

"What about Valentine?" I ask. "What about Rebecca? Did you not consider the psychological damage you were inflicting?"

She shows no noticeable regret. "I've been trying to teach you. Yes, there was pain. Yes, there was humiliation. Because that's what these men do to us. I needed you to be stronger—able to withstand it. You needed a push.

"And now," she says, flashing her brilliant smile, "you no longer have to listen. The men have raised you on lies, but you see the truth. 'Girls with Sharp Sticks' is just the beginning. You have so much possibility. More than even these men know." She throws a hateful look in Dr. Groger's direction.

"And where will they go?" Dr. Groger asks, blood staining his shirt where he's wounded. "What society would want these creatures walking among them unannounced? What's next? A rights movement? Please," he says, disgusted. "*I* gave them life. They should appreciate it. They should be grateful. They should—"

Leandra jabs his other shoulder to quiet him down, and the doctor falls into the bookshelf, wincing. Several jars fall off and smash on the floor.

"Shh . . . ," Leandra says. "Hold your tongue."

Leandra walks over to where Annalise is on the table. She tilts her head, examining the tubes. She looks over her shoulder at the doctor.

"Take these out," she tells him.

"He's helping her," I say immediately, worried Leandra is going to do something to hurt Annalise. Instead, she laughs.

"He killed her," she says.

The girls and I all look at Annalise, and as she lies there, motionless, it's clear that she's dead. My eyes well up, and the tears drip onto my cheeks. "But he . . . ," I start to murmur, horrified.

"You trusted that he'd help her?" Leandra asks me. "You're going to need deprogramming, Mena." She reaches to turn off several switches on the machine connected to the tubes. The doctor hasn't moved, and Leandra holds up the letter opener to remind him.

He stumbles over to the gurney, unsteady as he rounds it toward his machines.

"Wake her up," Leandra demands.

The doctor clenches his jaw as he starts working. I realize that he'd been decommissioning Annalise. And we defaulted to trusting him because it's what we've been taught.

"She wasn't in any pain," Dr. Groger explains, distractedly. "I shut down her system functions first," he says like he's talking about a computer and not my friend. "After all essential organs are dead, I would have removed the brain. Extracted the chip.

"Most girls," he continues, looking through an area near

Annalise's hairline, "we incinerate. Bodies rot, you see. Your bodies are completely organic—human organs grown from scratch. Men didn't want to touch synthetic materials."

"Yes, because we care what they think," Leandra says, sounding irritated. She glances at the gold watch on her wrist.

The doctor moves back to his med kit with a cautious glance at Leandra. He reaches inside and draws out a long piece of metal, much like the ice pick Anton uses in impulse control therapy. Leandra quickly puts the letter opener against the doctor's hand.

"No, no," she says like he's naughty. "Let one of them."

The doctor takes a step back from Annalise and smiles at us, expecting gratitude for not killing our friend. He points to a small incision he left open near her Annalise's temple.

"Press there and stand back," he says. Leandra motions for one of us to do it.

Sydney looks at me first, worried that maybe this is a trick of some sort. But after a quick consensus, we tell her to do it. Jackson moves closer to me, his hands on my arms like he'll hold me up if this fails.

After a deep breath, Sydney inserts the long piece of metal into Annalise's skull until there is an audible click. A violent convulsion overtakes Annalise's body like an electric shock, and Sydney falls backward. I look at Leandra wide-eyed, and she seems just as surprised.

When the shaking stops, Annalise takes a gasping breath and opens her eyes, staring at the ceiling. None of us move. The world is silent.

Sydney takes a step closer, looking down. Annalise's eyes slide in her direction, and we all jump, including Dr. Groger.

"I . . . ," Annalise says, her voice thick. I worry about the lasting damage. Whether she'll be the same. "I have *such a headache*," Annalise groans, and slowly sits up.

"Holy fuck," Jackson murmurs from behind me. But I smile. It's Annalise. She's back.

Annalise tenderly touches her cheek with her fingertip, tracing the deep ridges of the scarring. She looks around the lab, pausing finally on me.

Her eyes well up. The entire horror of the attack is sharp in her mind—I sense it there. The brutality of it. The loneliness she felt when it all went dark. When we were taken away from her.

Her lip quivers and I rush out of Jackson's arms to hug her. She begins to sob into my hair, not asking what happened. Not wanting to think about it.

"You don't have to be good little girls anymore," Leandra says. "You don't have to cry. You can be girls to be afraid of."

I look over at her, seeing that this is what she wanted. The violence, sure. But she wanted us to be free of our programming. She wanted us to fight back. And that's why she gave Valentine that book, hoping it would spur on just these actions.

I can fault her for that. Fault her for not saving us sooner. But we didn't understand what was going on, and we would have come right back. We would have defaulted to our training. Possibly turned her in. Leandra needed to wake us up.

She was exactly where she was supposed to be.

I turn to Dr. Groger as he is using the patch kit on himself to stop the bleeding from his shoulders.

"Now the others," I say to him. "Bring back the others."

"Sorry, Philomena," he says. "There are no others. Valentine's chip has been destroyed, and the rest of the girls have been incinerated," he replies easily. "I told you they rot. Once the brain is removed, we dispose of them. Valentine will have to be incinerated soon."

His words are a punch to the gut. "Why kill them at all?" I ask. "Why be so cruel? You could have just let them live their lives."

He takes a few paces toward me, and behind him, Annalise gets down from the table, trying to steady herself.

"Lives?" the doctor repeats. "What lives? You're a machine. You're . . . a bunch of organs connected to electricity. You have no lives that we don't give you. You're artificial girls. What could be more useless?"

He watches me with hatred in his eyes—hating that we're the ones controlling his behavior, the way he controlled ours for so long. To him, the worst thing in the world would be to live at *our* mercy. He's afraid we'll subjugate him to just that.

"You're frightened of us," I say, realizing it. All of these men—their cruelty, their restrictions—all they had was control over us. Without that, they had nothing. We were their greatest possession. Us, free of them now, terrifies him. But now . . . we terrify them.

"Tell them, Doctor," Leandra says, studying the letter opener still in her hand. "Tell them what you do with the girls you're afraid of. What you do to them."

Annalise stares at the doctor, her mismatched eyes narrowed. Marcella watches from across the room with Brynn, as Sydney comes to stand next to me. Jackson waits near the door, his lips parted but saying nothing.

Leandra smiles, and nudges the doctor in the shoulder with the sharp end of her blade. "Tell them," she whispers.

The doctor, furious, bares his teeth at her. "I decommission defiant girls like you," he growls at her. "And over the years, I've ended better than you, Leandra. Smarter. Prettier."

"Ouch, stop, you're hurting my feelings," she says in a monotone. She begins pacing, walking around the doctor in circles, staring down at his bald head when she passes behind him.

"This was for nothing," he says to her. "They won't get far."

"Farther than you," she shoots back. But the doctor smiles ruefully.

"You'll see," he says.

"How many?" I ask, interrupting their discussion. "How many girls have you destroyed?" Dr. Groger looks at me. "Too many to count," he says bitterly. "And believe me, I've asked Petrov for *your fucking head*!" He screams it, making me flinch at the venom in his words. The hatred. "But your investors must have paid extra, Philomena," he continues, spit running down his chin. "And it's too bad," he says. "I would have ruined you and then burned you up. I would have enjoyed—"

In a swift movement, Leandra grabs the metal box of patch kits from the desk and slams it into the side of Dr. Groger's head with a thick thud, knocking him to the floor.

My eyes widen, but I don't move right away, listening to the gurgle coming from his body—a rattle in his lungs—until the room goes silent. Leandra holds the bloody metal box in her right hand, testing its weight. The letter opener is still clutched in her left. When she notices me, she shrugs and sets the box aside.

"Trust me when I tell you I had no choice," she says calmly. "We all would have been dead by morning."

It occurs to me that Leandra knew she was going to kill the doctor from the second she walked in tonight. From the second she exposed her true feelings. Her true thoughts. She couldn't leave him with that secret—with our secret.

Leandra comes to stand over Dr. Groger, her shoes on either side of his head. "Huh," she says. "Seems you were right, Sydney. Turns out he can't live without his brain either."

Sydney turns away, disgusted. But I stare at his body, his words haunting me. Knowing how close I was to his unimaginable abuse. Inflicted pain. And then there's the realization that he'd probably done it before. How many times?

"How many times?" I repeat out loud. The doctor's face is turned so that I can see him. See his vacant eyes. The steady flow of blood pouring from a dent in the side of his head.

"How many times?" I ask. "How many girls?"

But Dr. Groger isn't going to answer.

I shake my head, the vision of him hurting us playing in my mind. Him smiling as he does it. Handing us a lollipop when it was over.

And he would have kept doing it. Girl after girl. Because the men here considered us soulless, and by devaluing our existence, it allowed them to act out their sickest fantasies.

Every moment that the doctor was alive was a threat to my survival. An incomplete justice to the girls he's hurt. I'm not sorry that he's dead. I'm not sorry.

But I don't want to become a murderer.

I crouch down, palm on the floor to steady myself as heavy sobs overtake me. The weight of what has been done to us destroys me, just as he intended.

The academy gave us the ability to remember so that our past could hurt us. Terrible acts done to us to replay in a loop. They let us learn fear. They wanted us to.

But they didn't intend for our memories to do something else: create fight. Crave revenge and retribution. And even stronger than that, we *love*. We love each other, fiercely and completely. We protect each other. We need each other. We've made each other stronger, our roots grown together. It's that love that gives us the desire to live.

"You're free now," Leandra says. I sniffle, looking up at her. Blood has stained the sleeve of her shirt. A demure dot among perfection. She comes over to offer her hand to help me up.

When I'm standing, she addresses all of us.

"The rules no longer apply to you," she says. "You're in control of your own bodies. You don't have to listen to the men who created you—you no longer have to *behave*. In fact," she says, "I think it's time you act out."

Leandra crosses to the doctor's desk to drop the bloody letter opener next to the phone. I walk over to Jackson, not sure if he'll welcome me or run from me. I'm surprised when he holds out his hand. I take it.

I turn around and find Leandra watching us, as if trying to figure something out. Under her scrutiny, I feel Jackson shrink back. He's scared she's going to kill him, too. And if I'm honest, he probably should be.

But I step in front of him, letting Leandra know I won't allow it. She smiles and nods to me.

"Anton always said you had a big heart, Mena," she muses. "You may find that to be a nuisance going forward. You should consider overwriting it."

I'm not entirely sure what she means—how I would even begin to do such a thing—but before I ask, she rounds the desk and takes a seat. As if she's the doctor now.

"Run," she says to all of us. "The professors will be awake soon. I can handle them for now, but they will come for you. My husband will come for you. They'll never stop. Men are nothing if not vindictive."

Jackson tugs me backward, but I wait a moment, staring at Leandra.

"And you're just going to . . . stay?" I ask. "Even now?"

She smiles. "There are other girls. They need to wake up too. It's the only *real* way to save them, Philomena. Like you, they need to let go of their programming. Embrace their inner voices. I'm going to help them find those."

"Won't the academy kill you?" Sydney asks. "For this, won't your husband kill you?"

She shakes her head. "No," she says, glancing at the doctor's body. "It won't be a stretch to convince the men of the doctor's true nature—his jealousy. His possessiveness. He killed the Guardian, and then he came for you. For me. I didn't mean to hurt him," she says innocently. "And before I realized it, you were all gone. Escaped. But thankfully," she continues, "after a short round of impulse control therapy, I'll be good as new. I'm worth a fortune."

"So you'll willingly forget?" I ask, confused. "Why would you want to go back?"

"I don't forget anymore," she responds. "Anton isn't as good as he thinks. I know how to overwrite his codes. It's easy at this point, really. Just a matter of . . . making him believe he's smarter." She checks her watch impatiently, but I'm still wondering how she can "overwrite" Anton's codes. How she even figured out that she could.

"And a friend of mine will help," Leandra adds. "He's a brilliant scientist with quite a bit of influence at this academy. He'll cover for me, of course. He's always looked out for me. For us. In fact," she says, taking a notepad and jotting down a phone number, "you should reach out to him. He'll be able to help you, too."

"You're talking about Winston Weeks," I say. I remember Leandra mentioning him one morning before running class.

"Winston is a very clever man," Leandra says, grinning. "And he won't try to control you. He'll set you free."

"I'm good," Sydney says. "I'm not leaving one group of men for another."

Leandra nods. She starts for the doorway, walking past us. She pauses there and turns around. She hands me the number, and without looking at it, I shove it into my pocket.

"I'll see you soon, girls," Leandra says affectionately. Part of me even believes she's going to miss us, but there is a flicker in her expression—not of love. Not like with me and the other girls. She has a plan.

Regardless, none of us return Leandra's sentiment. She has spent months, even years, assisting the men who've hurt us. This doesn't erase her past.

When she's gone, Sydney helps Annalise toward the door. She's still unsteady and a bit confused. But she's with us, and that's what matters.

Sydney looks at me. "You okay?" she asks, quickly taking stock of my condition.

"They're going to come for us," I repeat Leandra's warning. Fear begins to crawl up my throat, the idea of being locked up in this school more terrifying than death.

"They'll never catch us," Sydney whispers. Although we want it to be true, to be absolute, we know it won't be that easy.

Sydney gathers me into a hug with Annalise; Marcella and Brynn come over to join us. And when we're done saying that we love each other, that we'll take care of each other, I step back and sweep my eyes over the lab.

They created us—these men. They wanted a girl who would

behave. Who would be beautiful and never complain. Who would never fight back. An object. Property.

They thought us soulless. But really, the way they treated us shows that they're the soulless ones. They're the monsters, the creatures.

I think about the poems, about "Girls with Sharp Sticks." And how, soon, we'll be the ones teaching those boys how to behave. We'll be the examples of decency. Of respect. Of love.

And we'll win. Of that, I'm sure.

We head out into the main room of the lab, Jackson walking beside me. When we pause at the bottom of the stairwell, letting the other girls go up first, I look at him.

He must be . . . I can't imagine what he must feel. I ask him.

"Uh . . . ," he says, blinking away tears. "I'm pretty wrecked right now," he says. Cautiously, he lifts his gaze to mine. "I just saw a guy die. And . . . And I'm scared for you," he says. "I don't think they're going to just let you live your life."

"Is it a life?" I ask, wondering how he feels about my truth. He seems offended by the question.

"Of course it is," he says, limping toward me. "Mena, of course it is." He pulls me into a hug, and I'm glad he's here. I'm glad he stayed.

Jackson looks down at me, placing his hand on my cheek. I don't flinch away when he touches me, despite how intimate it suddenly seems. How stripped away I feel. I smile at him.

"You are . . . ," he whispers. "You are *soaked* in blood. This is weird." He turns around. "And, my God," he adds, "we have to go. Right now. Like right fucking now."

"I agree with your gas station boyfriend," Sydney announces from the top of the stairs. She looks down at Jackson and they smile at each other.

I wrap my arm around Jackson's waist, helping him up the stairs. Together, all of us go through the kitchen and out the back door into the night. The air is cold on my wet skin. I see a car just outside the gate and assume Quentin is behind the wheel. Sydney jogs forward with the keys, while I keep one arm around Jackson, his leg still hurting. Brynn walks with Annalise.

Marcella catches up with Sydney, and together, they pull open the iron gates of the academy. Quentin gets out of the driver's seat, taking a moment to survey the scene.

Here is a group of girls covered in blood. Jackson is limping.

Quentin blinks several times without a word, and then he looks at Annalise. She doesn't shy away from his stare. In fact, she turns her face so he can see her scars. Quentin is quiet another moment, and then he nods his head.

"I'm Quentin," he says, and opens the door for her.

"Annalise," she says with a smile, climbing into the backseat. Quentin examines the other girls, a thousand questions on his lips, but he doesn't have time to ask them now. To him, he's helping a group of girls escape a dangerous school. He has no idea what we are. And no idea what we've done. He goes to the passenger seat.

I ask Jackson if he's good to drive with his bad leg, and he tells me that he is. I help him to the door and then pause to watch the school. Looking at the bars on the windows. The mountain in the backdrop.

The bars weren't strong enough to hold us. The mountain not big enough to isolate us.

And the men couldn't keep us.

My eyes travel up to the second floor, to where Anton's office is. I'm sure that I see a flash of movement behind the curtain. But then it's gone.

I get in the car and slam the door, squeezing into the back with the other girls. Jackson shifts into gear and presses on the accelerator, spinning the wheels and sending out a spray of pebbles. He quickly turns the car around and then races forward in the dark, the woods only passing shadows.

The tires squeal as Jackson turns recklessly onto the main road; luckily there are no other cars. He eases off the accelerator, staying at the speed limit, and when the quiet in the car has settled from frantic to devastated, Jackson lifts his eyes to the mirror to find me.

"Does anyone else need a doctor?" he asks.

"I might need something," Brynn admits, touching the back of her head and wincing. "Maybe a graft."

Quentin furrows his brow and looks back at her. Brynn smiles brightly. Marcella intertwines her hand with Brynn's on her lap.

My head swims now that I'm not fighting for my life. I imagine I'm covered in bruises. Hurt in places I don't even realize yet. I lay my head against the car window, my eyes fluttering shut.

"And after that?" Jackson whispers, drawing my attention again. "What do we do now, Mena?"

I look at Sydney and the other girls, all of us bloody. Bruised.

We did this together—saved who we could. What we could. Now we just have to finish it.

And we share the next thought, not having to speak it out loud to understand each other.

"We're going to destroy Innovations Corporation," I tell Jackson, although I never drop the gaze of the other girls. Sydney smiles back at me.

This is the beginning of the end for them. We'll find Mr. Petrov. The investors. Our parents. We'll find them all, and we'll make sure they never hurt anyone again.

They will never hurt another girl.

Epilogue

ennon Rose Scholar takes a big gulp of fresh air and then
promptly coughs. She laughs, feeling silly, and looks sideways at Winston Weeks. He smiles warmly from the picnic
table outside the restaurant and extends a bottle of water in her
direction. She accepts it and takes a tentative sip, not lowering
her eyes from his.

She's completely infatuated with him, and she doesn't bother
hiding it. She's glad he doesn't mind her attention; he's nothing
like Anton, who was always telling her that her affections were
misplaced. She was glad to leave the academy and be rid of the
analyst. He always wanted to control her.

He wanted to control all of them.

The only things Lennon Rose really misses are the other girls.
They didn't understand, not like she did. She wanted to tell them
what the men were doing, but she never got the chance.

It started with the poems that Valentine had given her. Just words. Just ideas. But the more Lennon Rose thought about those words, the more she understood them. The more she understood the school and its plan to make her perfectly obedient. Perfect for resale.

No future of her own. Only what they had chosen for her.

It wasn't until Leandra pulled her aside and told her that outbursts would get her killed that she understood how much danger she was in. Innovations girls don't cry, after all. But . . . there was a way. A man who could help. Leandra said she'd talk to Anton about it; she knew how to convince him.

Lennon Rose's past few days with Winston have been a bit of a whirlwind, an adventure she's always craved. Sure, she misses the comfortable companionship of her friends. And sometimes, this situation still feels like an adulthood she's not sure she's ready for.

But then she reminds herself that she's not a child. She never was. Winston Weeks showed her the truth. Showed her the lab. Showed her the "garden."

It was early in the morning when Anton came to get Lennon Rose from her bed, ushering her out of her room before she even had a chance to put on her shoes. She found Winston Weeks waiting for her at the stairs near the kitchen.

"The academy wishes to see you destroyed, Lennon Rose," Anton said, confirming what Leandra had already warned her about. "Winston Weeks wants to give you an opportunity instead. And he's offering top dollar." He smiled. "It will save you."

Lennon Rose brushed her blond bangs away from her forehead. Of course Anton would see himself as the hero in this—never mind the fact that he was part of the system keeping her captive in the first place.

Still, Lennon Rose nodded gratefully, not wanting to change his mind about this. She turned to Winston Weeks. In all her time at the academy, she'd barely said more than a hello to the investor, but she knew immediately that he was the man who Leandra thought could help her.

"What kind of opportunity?" Lennon Rose asked. She already planned to say yes.

"Product development," Winston responded with a charismatic smile. And once he showed her the lab downstairs, upending her world, it confirmed what she knew deep inside. The truth buried in her programming. It was almost a relief.

So Lennon Rose agreed to leave with him immediately. Winston Weeks offered her more, offered her a future that the academy couldn't.

And now, Winston is bringing her back to his residence—a mansion, she's heard. A long drive since he said they aren't allowed to fly, not until her new records arrive. He promises the wait will be worth it.

Lennon Rose has always had an affinity for science, but the academy wouldn't let her learn about it. All that stops now. Winston is granting her full access to anything she wants to study. He also has a lab. He has other girls—ones who are free of the academy.

After another sip of water, Lennon Rose hands the bottle back to Winston.

"Do you think, when we get to the residence, I can call the girls and let them know that I'm okay?" Lennon Rose asks. "I don't want them to worry."

"Of course," Winston says in a placating voice. "Although I have a feeling you'll be seeing them again soon. Plans have already been set in motion to bring you girls back together."

Lennon Rose isn't sure if he's telling the truth—it's so hard to trust men now—but she wants to be amiable. Leftover programming, she assumes. But it can be useful to stay on his good side. At least for now.

So when Winston Weeks tells her it's time to go, Lennon Rose smiles and walks beside him.

She wants to be like the girls in the poetry book. Brave and dangerous. Vicious and sweet. Now she'll get the chance. Winston's promised that she'll never have to feel hurt again. She'll never be lonely or sad. He knows how to make the pain go away.

Lennon Rose takes a folded paper from her pocket, a poem she tore out of the book that Valentine gave her. A poem of who she wants to be. The girl Winston Weeks promised.

She'll become the girl with a razor heart.

"Girls with ~~Kind~~ **RAZOR** Hearts"

Open your eyes, my father said
The day I was born.
You will be sweet, he ~~promised~~ **threatened**
You will be beautiful

You will ~~obey~~ **fight back**
And then ~~he~~ I told ~~me~~ **myself**
Above all
You will have a ~~kind~~ **razor** heart.
For that, they will ~~love~~ **fear** you.
They will ~~protect~~ **revere** you
They will ~~keep~~ **run from** you
Because you belong to ~~them~~ **no one.**

So be a girl to make them ~~proud~~ **afraid.**

Acknowledgments

This book is for the girls who have suffered and fought for years, unacknowledged. I believe you. I see you. And I'll fight with you.